**This Large Print Book carries the
Seal of Approval of N.A.V.H.**

THE
EINSTEIN
PROPHECY

Center Point
Large Print

THE
EINSTEIN
PROPHECY

Robert Masello

CENTER POINT LARGE PRINT
THORNDIKE, MAINE

This is a work of fiction. Names, characters, organizations, places, events, and incidents arc cither products of the author's imagination or are used fictitiously.

The text of this Large Print edition is unabridged. In other aspects, this book may vary from the original edition. Printed in the United States of America on permanent paper. Set in 16-point Times New Roman type.

ISBN: 978-1-62899-996-9

Library of Congress Cataloging-in-Publication Data

Names: Masello, Robert, 1952– author.
Title: The Einstein prophecy / Robert Masello.
Description: Center Point Large Print edition. | Thorndike, Maine : Center Point Large Print, 2016. | ©2015
Identifiers: LCCN 2016010180 | ISBN 9781628999969 (hardcover : alk. paper)
Subjects: LCSH: Einstein, Albert, 1879-1955—Fiction. | Women archaeologists—Fiction. | Sarcophagi—Fiction. | Paranormal fiction. | Large type books. | GSAFD: Science fiction. | Suspense fiction.
Classification: LCC PS3613.A81925 E34 2016 | DDC 813/.6—dc23
LC record available at http://lccn.loc.gov/2016010180

"I do not know how the Third World War will be fought, but I can tell you what they will use in the Fourth—rocks."

—Albert Einstein, in an interview with Alfred Werner for *Liberal Judaism* (1949)

Chapter ONE

A boy, blond-haired, about twelve years old, clambered to the top of a pile of ruins, feeling his way over broken bricks and burnt timbers and shattered glass. His brown shirt was in rags, and his laceless shoes threatened to fall off at any second. But he moved with the agility of a mountain goat, nimbly making his way to the top of the rubble, where he stretched out one thin arm to claim his prize and wave it overhead in triumph.

Other boys, younger and less courageous—or foolhardy—watched from the cratered pavement of the street as the boy draped the strip of gleaming tinfoil around his neck and started down again.

"They'll salvage anything," Private Teddy Toussaint observed from the driver's seat of the jeep. "When I was a kid, we collected bottle caps."

"Baseball cards for me, but that was another time." That time, Lieutenant Lucas Athan thought, seemed a thousand years ago and a million miles away.

7

"Yep, you can sure say that again," Toussaint drawled, "and back then nobody was taking potshots at me." From his front pocket, he removed a packet of Red Man chewing tobacco and gnawed off a hunk. "Lieutenant?" he said, extending the wet stub.

"No thanks." Lucas watched the boy hop back onto the street and hold out the tinfoil for his friends' inspection. The kid reminded him of his boyhood friend Paulie, showing off an arrowhead he'd unearthed on a school field trip. Above, dozens of other ribbons hung from the tops of bombed-out houses and barren trees. The foil had been dropped like confetti by German planes to confound Allied radio transmissions. The Nazis were nothing if not ingenious, and even here, on ground that they had for the moment deserted, they'd left behind an occasional booby trap, or a lone gunman perched in an abandoned clock tower.

Toussaint contended that a good chaw of tobacco sharpened his senses, and he'd proved it the day before by taking out a sniper lurking in the choir stall of a church they were inspecting. One shot and the Kraut had tumbled over the railing. "Won the Baton Rouge turkey shoot three years running," he'd crowed.

As part of a clandestine advance guard, their route was perilously unprotected. Lucas was glad to have Toussaint watching his back. Soldiering was in the private's blood, but it wasn't in

8

Lucas's. He'd been diverted from the infantry into the CRC, the Cultural Recovery Commission, a minuscule cadre of experts in art and architecture, recruited and dispatched to find, preserve, and protect the treasures that the Nazis had looted so far in their conquest of Europe.

In private life, the CRC's conscripts had been museum curators, art dealers, or professors, like Lucas, but before them lay an immense undertaking. The German army had already stripped Italy, France, Belgium, Poland, and the Netherlands of nearly two million valuable paintings, statues, and other objets d'art—and its appetite appeared to be unsatisfied still. Its booty was hidden away in secret depositories until it could be installed in the Führer's museum once the war was won—an outcome that the Nazis had never believed to be in doubt.

Until the Normandy invasion.

Even two months later, though, the Allied forces were fighting grimly, and at huge cost, to reclaim the ground lost at the beginning of the war. The fierce battle over a little town called Saint-Lô, in northwestern France, had taken weeks and resulted in eleven thousand casualties. The area where Lucas and Private Toussaint were traveling was far beyond the front, and dangerous in the extreme. Alsace-Lorraine had been evacuated of its citizens by the Reich in 1939, annexed to Germany the following year, and repopulated only with Alsatians of German descent. Strasbourg's famed Romanesque Revival synagogue, with its domed ceiling fifty-four meters high, had been reduced to cinders by the regime.

What made Lucas's mission, precarious by any standards, all the more puzzling was that his orders hadn't come directly from the CRC, but from their superiors at the Office of Strategic Services. The mission's objective had to be of vital importance.

Folded inside the envelope jammed in the inside pocket of his combat jacket was a crude map to the local iron mine, where a sizable cache of stolen artifacts was reputedly hidden. The envelope also contained a grainy photo of the highest-priority item—an ossuary, or sarcophagus, that had been looted by Rommel's Afrika Korps from the Museum of Antiquities in Cairo. Lucas had no idea why this particular casket was of such value to the war effort, but because of his background in classical art and statuary, he'd been the natural choice for this task.

"Lieutenant," Toussaint said, stepping out of the jeep, "it looks like the welcome wagon is on its way." Toussaint held his M1 carbine firmly in his hands, though he kept the muzzle down as an old man, waving a white handkerchief tied to a broom, stumbled toward them.

"*Ich bin der Buergermeister,*" the old man

said—I am the mayor—before asking if they spoke German.

Lucas answered him haltingly, grateful for the crash course given by army intelligence before his posting, "*Ja ich kann das.*"—Yes, I can—before adding that he was a Lieutenant with the United States Ninth Army.

The old man nodded. "The German soldiers are gone," he said, waving one arm at the demolished stores and houses of the town as if to prove it. "They moved out two days ago. Only civilians are left."

Lucas would have liked to take him at his word, but he knew enough to keep his guard up. Treachery was as much a part of war as bullets were. He'd learned that lesson early, when a young enemy soldier he'd tried to pull from under a crushing pile of rubble had used his dying breath to swipe at him with a broken bayonet.

"I'm looking for the iron mine," Lucas said.

A wary look crossed the mayor's face.

"Can you take me to it?" He hoped his tone was less a question than an order.

The mayor paused, leaning now on the broomstick, and said, "You won't hurt the people there?"

It wasn't uncommon for abandoned mines to become bomb shelters. "I'm looking for stolen artworks," he explained. "That's all."

The mayor studied his face, as if searching for some sign of malign intent, then sighed. Turning, he gestured for the Americans to follow him. They left the jeep in the road—it wasn't likely any other traffic would be coming through soon—and followed the mayor down the shelled-out street, through the bomb craters and the broken stones, with Toussaint scanning every empty door or window. Led by the blond boy in the ragged brown shirt, some of the children, still gathering up their own bits of foil, trailed along behind.

Lucas felt like the Pied Piper of Hamelin—a town only a few hundred miles from there— leading the pack of children into the dark wood that surrounded the village. Spruce and elm trees towered overhead, their upper boughs festooned like Christmas trees with bits of foil. The ground was matted with a slick layer of decaying leaves and mossy logs, and the air temperature had dropped by ten degrees. What little sun penetrated the overcast sky was nearly eclipsed by the canopy of tree branches. He took his flashlight from his belt and used it to help illuminate the path.

"Can't say that I like this all that much," Toussaint said, his rifle raised now and at the ready. "Feels like a trap to me."

It didn't feel all that safe to Lucas, either, but what choice did he have? He had his orders, and his commanding officer had made it plain that he wasn't to come back empty-handed.

Using his broom to help clear the brush, the elderly mayor brought them to a rusty rail line, now half buried in the earth. They followed it for a quarter mile, until the trees began to thin out, exposing a massive pair of steel doors, like the portal to some grand cathedral, improbably embedded in the slope of a hill. Now it felt even more like a fairy tale, but not a happy one—more like one of those dark Teutonic tales that this ragtag bunch of kids trailing him through the woods had most likely been raised on. The mayor clanged the broom handle three times on the metal doors, then paused and knocked three times again.

Lucas heard him mutter something to someone on the other side—it sounded like he'd simply said, "It's me, open up"—and a second later he could hear the sound of heavy iron bars sliding to one side. With the screech of unoiled pulleys, wheels, and chains, the doors slowly opened outward, revealing a smoothly hewn and vaulted tunnel into which the rusty tracks descended.

A man bundled in a beaver coat stood there, mouth agape at the sight of Lucas and Toussaint, whose rifle was pointed right at him.

"Who are they?" the gatekeeper blurted out. "Why have you brought them here?"

"They only want the art."

"The art is for the Führer! We will be held responsible if it's gone."

"Let me be the judge of that, Emil."

Emil scowled. "Fine. Then let it be on your head."

The mayor turned to Lucas and angled his head toward the tunnel. "Come—I will show you."

With the old man leading the way, they skirted past the glowering Emil and started down the tunnel. The air grew cold and clammy, and the only light was provided by weak electric bulbs, strung along a ceiling wire. A generator thrummed somewhere in the shadows. It took Lucas at least a minute or two before he realized that he was passing dozens of people, huddled against the walls, silent, clinging to each other in fear. He turned his flashlight on a white-haired couple who fell to their knees on a threadbare blanket, crossing themselves.

"*Amerikaner!*" he heard in whispers and gasps, passing up and down the tunnel.

"What the hell?" Toussaint said. "Do they think we're gonna shoot 'em?"

"Probably," Lucas replied. Why wouldn't they? The horrors of the war never ended. He had seen things that he could never have imagined: captured resistance fighters strung up in trees; whole towns herded into barns that had then been set ablaze. These people huddled here undoubtedly believed that the Allies were capable of the same atrocities that the Nazis had committed. One day, he thought, they would learn the truth, and hang their heads in shame.

He kept his eyes straight ahead, following the mayor deeper and deeper into the mine. They passed an alcove where several ore trucks were shunted off on a separate track. No people were around; wooden crates and boxes lined both sides of the tunnel. Most had writing on their sides— Lucas could read the names of the museums and cathedrals and private collections from which their contents had been looted—along with cardboard tags identifying where they were supposed to go next. Leave it to the Germans, he thought, to be organized even when it came to grand theft. On many of the tags, he caught sight of the word Carinhall—Hermann Göring's grand chalet in the Schorfheide Forest, outside Berlin. It was satisfying to know that this art would never get there.

But so far he had seen nothing that resembled the ossuary he had been dispatched to find. He clutched the old man's elbow—it felt like a knob of petrified wood—stopping him, then Lucas dug the photo out of his inside pocket.

"Have you seen anything like this?"

The mayor studied the photo, labeled, in reference to the image of a bearded shepherd faintly chiseled on the ossuary's lid, *Der Hirte*.

"It's a stone box," Lucas said in German, as he held out his arms to indicate that it might be five or six feet long and a few feet high.

The old man didn't raise his head for several seconds, and Lucas could sense the debate going on inside him.

"You recognize it, don't you?"

He didn't answer.

Lucas repeated the question.

"Is there a problem, Lieutenant?" Toussaint asked, spitting a jet of tobacco juice into the dirt. He raised the barrel of his carbine. "You want me to throw the fear of God into him?"

Lucas shook his head and with one hand nudged the rifle barrel to one side. "Show me where it is," he told the mayor.

The old man took a filthy red rag from his pocket and wiped his lips. Then, nodding resignedly, he turned back down the mine. The air grew even colder and the tunnel darker as they continued their descent. The stony walls were scratched and scraped by decades of pickaxes and dynamite charges, and the floor was increasingly sloped and uneven. Even the light bulbs were more distantly spaced, so that by the time they came to a bend in the tunnel, Lucas felt as if he were about to turn the corner into Hell itself.

For a moment he thought he had. A vast empty space, black as coal, opened before him. Even his flashlight beam failed to penetrate the inky depths. The old man was suddenly gone, and before Lucas could even think to alert Toussaint, he heard a lever being pulled and saw a shower of blue sparks. He jumped back, instinctively pulling his sidearm from its holster, but before he could fire—and at what?—a bank of overhead lights came on, blinding him.

When his eyes adjusted to the sudden glare, he saw the old man leaning against the wall, the lever still in his hand. In front of them lay a vast chamber, lit like a railroad yard and just as big, its ceiling so high it could barely be seen. There were dozens of crisscrossing tracks, hobbled wheelbarrows, and dilapidated conveyor belts.

In the center of it all, stacked like cordwood, there must have been a thousand canvases in ornate frames, surrounded by hundreds of sculptures, some bound with straw as if they were only now being packed for shipping. Lucas had been informed that there were similar stashes being compiled at Buxheim and Heilbronn, but this one probably put all of them to shame.

"Holy smokes," Toussaint said.

"When was all of this brought here?" Lucas asked. The mayor shrugged.

"The trucks came and went. The soldiers did the work," he said. "We didn't ask questions."

The German national anthem, Lucas thought, as he went closer; we didn't ask questions. He glanced at the paintings—mostly domestic scenes of Dutch or Flemish origin—and the statues, chiefly classical. They were his specialty—ancient Greek and Roman art. He was able to identify several of them at a glance, even without looking at the tags affixed to their feet or pedestals. Only four years before, while earning his PhD, he had studied their pictures in his textbooks.

Descending into their midst was like walking into a dream—every piece was something he wanted to linger over and admire. All of them would have to be painstakingly carted out of this cavern and shipped, once the war was over, back to their original homes. It would be a monumental task, and he wondered if he might volunteer to spearhead it; it didn't even matter if he'd have to reenlist in the army—what could be more exciting or worthwhile?

"How the hell you gonna find one damn box in all this mess?" Toussaint said from behind him. He kept his rifle casually trained in the mayor's direction.

Lucas, still holding the photograph, walked down a sort of aisle, scanning the statues and urns and clay amphorae. Locating any one item in here could take days. Turning to the mayor, he brandished the photo again. "Where is it?"

With a trembling finger the old man pointed ahead, but made no move to follow, until Toussaint gestured with his rifle. Lucas continued on, once or twice catching what he thought might have been movement among the crates and pedestals.

"Did you see that?" he asked, but Toussaint said, "See what?" and he chalked it up to nerves and shadows.

It was only when they reached the farthest end

of the cavern and saw a ring of ore carts about twenty yards off, arranged as if to demarcate a separate area, that he stopped. "Is it in there?"

The mayor nodded, but would go no farther.

"Are you certain?"

"*Ja. Ja.*"

"I'm going to check it out," Lucas said to Toussaint. "You stay here and keep an eye on grandpa."

He stepped away from the cover of the crates and, gun drawn, approached the circle of wagons. On one, a placard dangled, bearing a printed black swastika. When he got close enough, he read the words. *Bestimmungsort: Berchtesgaden/ Kehlsteinhaus.* (Destination: Berchtesgaden/the Eagle's Nest.)

Hitler's private mountain retreat.

No wonder the old man hadn't wanted to come any farther. The idea of betraying the Führer himself, of turning over his hand-picked possessions, was a frightening one. God help him if he ever had to answer for it.

Lucas turned sideways to slip between two of the carts, set up as if they were bunkers to shield the unwary from a blast, and was surprised to find the enclosed area, no larger than a badminton court, occupied by a terrifying tableau.

At first, he thought he was looking at a scarecrow lying in the dirt. Arms and legs spread wide, it looked so hollow that it seemed as if only straw, not flesh, filled its sleeves and trousers. Even the head, facedown, looked like a rotting pumpkin— swollen and sickly orange in color, the visible skin strangely pitted and stained. How long, Lucas wondered, had the corpse been lying there, and what the hell had killed it?

Then something just beyond and above the figure drew his eye. Mounted on four sawhorses, as if they were an altar, squatted the sarcophagus. Lucas didn't need to get any closer to know that he had found his quarry—even from this distance, he recognized the gabled lid and sharpened corners, the iron chains sealing it shut. But because of a trick of the lights overhead, he found it hard to see any more detail than that. It was as if the box was bathed in its own shadow.

Then he caught that glimpse again, of something swiftly darting to his right.

"*Halt! Hände hoch!*"—Stop! Hands up!—he shouted, swiveling and aiming his revolver.

He heard the crunch of gravel underfoot.

"*Komm raus, oder ich schiesse!*" Come out now, or I'll shoot.

"No, please, do not shoot." It was a child's voice, quavering in German.

"What's going on?" Toussaint called.

The blond boy, the one with the tinfoil, crept out from behind one of the wagons, his thin arms raised above his head. Lucas was reminded again of Paulie, holding up the arrowhead for all to see.

"Lieutenant?" Toussaint yelled, loping toward the circle with his carbine up. "You okay?"

Lucas lowered his own gun. "All clear!"

Toussaint shimmied between the carts, sweeping his rifle over the enclosure. "Jesus H. Christ," he said when he saw the boy. "I coulda killed the kid."

"What are you doing in there, Hansel?" the mayor demanded. He remained outside the ring of ore carts. "Didn't I warn you not to go this far into the mine?"

Lucas almost had to laugh. Hansel. Could Gretel be far behind? Maybe he *had* stumbled into one of Grimm's fairy tales.

The boy saw the corpse, and his eyes grew big as saucers.

"I just wanted some chocolate," he blubbered.

Even the German kids knew that the GIs were good for a Hershey's bar. Lucas had one in his shirt pocket right now; he'd been saving it for dinner, but it looked to him like Hansel needed it a whole lot more than he did. To divert the boy's attention from the grisly scene, he took the candy out of his pocket and offered it to him.

"Come on," he said, "you've earned it."

"Don't reward him," the old man called out. "He was disobedient."

Lucas was simply so pleased at discovering the ossuary, and not getting killed in the process, that he was happy to dispense some happiness.

Meeting a CRC request was one thing; fulfilling a top-secret OSS mission was altogether another. The boy's eyes were fixed on the candy bar, and he already had one hand out to grab it when he tripped over something hidden in the dirt.

Those shoes need laces, Lucas thought—just before the land mine detonated with such force that he was lifted off his feet and hurled through the air, his back slamming up against one of the carts so hard that his bones rattled, and he saw a blanket of exploding stars. Then everything went as black as midnight in the thick of a fairy-tale forest.

Chapter TWO

September 2, 1944

People were kind. Too kind.

Now that he was no longer Lieutenant Lucas Athan but merely a college professor again, all he wanted to do was to slip unnoticed into civilian life.

Even out of uniform, however, and wearing a rumpled brown corduroy suit and carrying a battered briefcase, he stood out from the crowd. How could he not? The black patch where his left eye had once been, the telltale scar along his forehead where a sliver of shrapnel had been embedded, made it plain he was a soldier who had done his patriotic duty, and been honorably discharged.

And everyone he met wanted to acknowledge his sacrifice.

At restaurants, people tried to pay his check for him. On buses, youngsters offered their seats. Once, in Central Park, a man in a homburg clasped his hands, and said that Lucas reminded him of his own son, lost on Omaha Beach, and that if he ever wanted to see a Broadway show, he should let him know. "Any show at all, you name it, and there'll be two tickets waiting at the Will Call window." The man tucked his business card into Lucas's shirt pocket, and later, when Lucas finally looked at it, he saw that the man was the owner of a prominent theater chain.

He never took any of them up on their offers.

After the surgeries at New York Hospital, he spent the next couple of weeks in the city, living with his parents above the family's diner, the Olympus, in Queens. It was a typical Greek diner, but his father, Stavros Athanasiadis, had built it from scratch. As so many immigrants did, his father had abbreviated the family name: "We're American," he'd often declared when Lucas was a boy, "and now we start over with a new American name."

But Lucas hadn't gone to all the trouble of

getting his PhD so that he could live above the diner. He even had the distinct feeling that his father's fondest wish, now that he was home and in almost one piece, was that he'd take over the place. And, truth be told, what could be better for business than a wounded soldier at the cash register?

Only it wasn't going to be Lucas.

He was just beginning to wonder what his next move should be when, out of the blue, he received a letter from Princeton University saying that if he wished to resume his teaching duties at the beginning of the fall term, they would welcome him back. *The university motto, as you know, is "In the Nation's Service," and the faculty and trustees are proud to acknowledge that service in every way afforded us.* The dean helpfully mentioned that his old rooms were available in town.

It was like receiving an answer to his prayers.

At the little train station situated at the foot of campus, he disembarked from the train, loaded his bags into the trunk of the town cab, and returned to the Victorian boardinghouse on Mercer Street where he'd lived before being drafted. A black limousine, not the kind of thing normally seen in this quiet tree-lined neighborhood, idled at the curb across the street, but before he could give it any thought, Mrs. Caputo was scurrying across the front porch, wiping her hands on her apron, then rushing down the steps to embrace him. Tony Caputo was still serving somewhere in the Pacific, and Lucas knew that the hug, and the flood of tears, were meant as much for her absent husband as they were for him. Although she was only a few years older than Lucas, maybe thirty-three or thirty-four, she had always treated him like a mother, fretting over his late hours and bachelor-hood. Once or twice, single women had shown up at the boardinghouse table, and Lucas had guessed they had been invited there to audition.

"Your rooms are ready," she said, brushing at her eyes, "and I'm going to roast a whole chicken. Amy's all of nine now, but she'll be sure to tell you that when she gets home from school."

They both laughed, and Mrs. Caputo helped carry his bags up the creaking wooden stairs to the top floor, where the door was already open. It was as if time had stood still, and all the horrors he had witnessed abroad had never happened. The single bed was made up in the corner, with the same patchwork quilt he remembered. The hot plate and radio were on the bookshelf, the desk in front of the dormer window. Outside, the leaves, just now starting to turn color, clung to the branches of the old oak tree. He could even hear the drip from the makeshift shower Tony Caputo had installed in the tiny bathroom under the eaves; to get his hair wet, Lucas had to stoop at a nearly impossible angle.

"I'll let you get settled," Mrs. Caputo said. "Dinner's ready at five thirty. It's good to have you back home," she added, referring, as people did these days, not to any particular address, but to America.

"Hope Tony's not far behind me."

"I hope they all are."

Once the door was closed, Lucas simply stood at the window, staring out at the trees and the scruffy yard, with its ramshackle swing set and cyclone fence. He'd stood at this very spot shortly before he'd left for basic training. Maybe time was an illusion after all, as some of the latest scientific theories seemed to suggest. Maybe he'd never left this room. Maybe he was whole again. But then he caught a glimpse of himself reflected in the glass, and the black patch brought him right back to reality.

After unpacking his bags, hanging his spare pants and jackets in the closet, and concealing the bottle of scotch in the bottom drawer of the dresser, he swallowed two aspirin and lay down on the bed. His shoulders ached from carrying his bags. His forehead hurt, too; the doctors had said the pain would dissipate over time, but it could still be pretty bad. They'd also told him he'd get used to the monocular vision, but he still found himself bumping into things on his blind side. Under the patch, he wore a glass eye, but people seemed perturbed by the fake eye, and were never sure where to look when they were talking to him. The patch made things simpler for everyone concerned.

Quite unannounced, sleep overcame him. The only sounds were comforting ones—the rustling of the leaves outside the window, the rattling of the pipes, the creaks and groans that any frame house, particularly one this old, was sure to emit —and together they acted as a powerful soporific. So, too, did the soft and familiar bed and the fading light of an early autumn day. When he awoke a couple of hours later, he wasn't sure at first what had roused him. There was the smell of roasted chicken wafting up to him, the banging of the radiator, and a moment later, the thump of footsteps racing up the stairs. He had barely raised his head from the feather pillow when his door flew open and a girl in a red coat, squealing his first name, leapt onto the bed.

"Amy, I told you not to wake him!" Mrs. Caputo cried from the bottom of the stairs, but it was already too late for that. Amy squirmed like a puppy, hugging him with all her might.

"Oof," he said, "you've got to take it easy. I'm an old man now."

"You're not old! But I am—I'm nine now!" she said, pulling back her head to look at him. "What happened to your eye?"

"I had a little accident over there."

"What kind of accident?"

He could see that her mind was already running on two tracks—she wanted to know what had happened to him, but she was worried that the same thing might happen to her father, wherever he was.

"Something flew into my eye," he said, "and now I get to wear this patch. Like a pirate."

"Does it hurt?"

"Not at all." No need to tell her that the empty socket sometimes felt like a snowball buried in his head.

"Dinner's ready," Mrs. Caputo called up to them. "Get it while it's hot."

"Mom made your favorite dessert," she confided. "Icebox cake."

"She didn't have to go to all that trouble," he said, swinging his legs off the bed and searching for the shoes he'd kicked off.

"I told her she did. I like icebox cake."

Always playing the angles. "Tell your mom I'll be right down."

"He's coming!" Amy hollered, as she bounded out of the room. "And did I tell you, I won the spelling bee today!" she added for all to hear, as she clattered down the stairs.

Although dinner was just the three of them, Mrs. Caputo had made enough food for ten. How she did it, with ration coupons no less, was a miracle. She must have been saving up, Lucas thought, with a twinge of guilt. He wasn't especially hungry, but he did his best to fake it.

This room, too, was exactly as he had remembered it, from the nicked-up wooden chairs, the plastic flowers in the centerpiece, and a faded picture of the Madonna del Granduca above the sideboard; it was a framed replica of the Raphael painting that hung in the Palazzo Pitti in Florence.

Or did it? For all he knew, the Raphael, too, was stashed in a cave somewhere, awaiting the victory of the Third Reich.

Gesturing at the other guest chair, which used to be occupied by an aged spinster who had lived in the extra bedroom on the second floor, Lucas asked, "What became of Mrs. Hewitt?"

"The stairs got to be too much for her," Mrs. Caputo said, nudging Amy to pass the mashed potatoes back his way. "She's living with her sister in Passaic now. The building's got an elevator."

Lucas took a small dollop of the potatoes, and he saw Mrs. Caputo smile.

"Put some margarine on those," she said. "You're too skinny."

"And you're too good a cook." He knew he had to leave room for the secret icebox cake. "Have you rented it out again?"

"Yes," Amy piped up. "His name is Mr. Taylor. But he's never here." He could tell she didn't like him.

"He's not?" Lucas asked. "Where is he?"

Mrs. Caputo shrugged. "He says he's got a job in Trenton. Something to do with the airplane plant."

Civilians with jobs essential to the war effort often got deferments.

"But he's quiet as a mouse and never causes any trouble," she added. It seemed she didn't like him much, either. "And the rent's always on time."

These days, everybody was struggling just to hold things together—financially and emotionally. Lucas knew that all Mrs. Caputo wanted was to have her Tony back, safe and sound, and to reclaim her house for just her own family. But making ends meet was the order of the day, and you did what you had to. A lot of people had it worse.

When Mrs. Caputo carried out the icebox cake, somehow he was able to express sufficient surprise, and enough appetite to have a big piece, though Amy complained that there wasn't any whipped cream to put on top.

"You just can't get that anymore," Mrs. Caputo said. "Going to the grocery store is strictly hit or miss."

Once the table was cleared, and Amy had gone upstairs to finish her homework, Lucas stepped out onto the porch and lit up a Camel. The limousine that had been parked across the street was gone, but the quaint, white two-story house, set back behind a neat front yard, was brightly lit, and through an open window, Lucas could hear the strains of a string quartet. For a second, he thought it was a phonograph, but then he stepped down the stairs to the sidewalk and realized that the music was actually being rehearsed in the front parlor. In a college town like Princeton, it wasn't so unexpected. He heard laughter and the clinking of glasses. Someone scratched some deliberately grating notes on a cello. An elderly man's voice, with a German accent, said something about starting again, and all in the same key this time.

More laughter. But the accent had been jarring.

He listened to the music—Mozart, if he wasn't mistaken—and thought, despite himself, of the old mayor asking him not to harm the villagers hiding in the shaft. But he wasn't the one who had planted the land mine that blew the child to kingdom come, left Toussaint with only one leg, and him with only one eye. When his cigarette was down to the filter, he stubbed it out on the sidewalk, and went back inside the boarding-house. Mrs. Caputo was humming in the kitchen as she finished washing the dishes.

"Can I help you with those?"

"Oh, no," she said over her shoulder. "I'm almost done."

"So you've got a string quartet living across the street now?"

"Pardon?" she said, turning off the water and drying her hands on a dishrag.

"Across the street, I heard music. Are they musicians?"

"Oh, gosh, no," she said. "That's the professor. I guess he moved in after you'd joined up."

"What professor?"

"Einstein."

Lucas was nonplussed. Like everyone, he knew that Albert Einstein, fleeing from the Nazis, had emigrated from Berlin to Princeton in 1933 to take a professorship in theoretical physics. Lucas had even seen him on campus a few times. But he hadn't been living across from the Caputos on Mercer Street back then.

"He's a very sweet man," she said. "He saw Amy carrying her violin case home from school, and they had a very nice chat about music."

So that had been Einstein's voice, merrily conducting the musicians. And that was why the long black limousine had been parked outside. Lucas wondered what dignitary or government official might have been paying the great man a visit.

"Sometimes, in the summer, I just sit on the front porch and listen. When Tony comes home," she said, with a note of forced conviction in her voice, "he's going to love it."

"Yes, he will," Lucas readily assented.

They both knew that they had just offered up an unspoken prayer.

"Good night then," Lucas said, turning toward the stairs. "And thanks for the icebox cake."

"Sleep as late as you want. It's Labor Day weekend."

In his room upstairs, the air was warm and close, and he threw the window open all the way. Leaning his head out, he could still hear the strains of the string quartet. Wait 'til he told his family, he thought. They'd been impressed enough when he first got the job at Princeton—what would they do when they found out that Einstein, one of the most celebrated people in the whole world, was his neighbor?

Chapter THREE

She knew that she was not supposed to be up on deck, much less in such high seas, but the air below was so fetid she couldn't stand it anymore.

The USS Seward, with an enormous Red Cross insignia painted on its bulwarks and an additional sign displayed on its main deck for the benefit of any Luftwaffe pilots that might be passing overhead, was packed with wounded American soldiers. The Geneva Conventions barred attacks on Red Cross ships, but there was no telling which prohibitions would be observed and when. As a result, the ship was being escorted by a pair of navy destroyers. The North Atlantic was teeming with U-boats—the wolf pack, they were called—that had already sunk well over a hundred British and American vessels. Even now, one of their conning towers might be surveying this flotilla churning toward New York Harbor, and a German captain might be ordering his crew to load the torpedo bays.

Simone Rashid, swaddled in a rain slicker with the hood drawn over her hair, clutched the railing and stared out at the heaving gray waves. This whole idea—rules of war—was absurd, she thought. Men went about killing each other in the most ingenious ways they could imagine, and on a scale never before seen, but at the same time, they insisted on making up rules of engagement to preserve a facade of civilization and morality. They were like children playing a game, but one with horrendous consequences. Growing up in Cairo, she remembered her brother forming a secret club with a bunch of his friends from the King Fuad English-Speaking School, and they, too, had a long list of bylaws, rules, and regulations. The one that had rankled the most was the first one, which barred girls from joining the club. Her whole life had been a struggle against that prohibition. At the preparatory school, then Oxford, then the Egyptian Department of Cultural Affairs, she'd had to fight to prove her qualifications, to gain entry, and then, despite her exemplary scholarship, to be taken seriously.

Her youth didn't help—she was twenty-seven, but looked even younger—nor did her beauty. Her mother had been the high-spirited, rebellious daughter of an English diplomat, and as well known for her raven tresses as she was for her scandalous behavior. Simone had inherited her looks and her temperament, along with the olive skin and dark brown eyes of her Arab father. She had taken to wearing muted colors and loose-fitting clothes to minimize the effect of her looks, but most men, she had discovered, saw through the camouflage and kept right on coming.

"You're not authorized to be on deck, Miss," she heard behind her, the voice nearly obliterated by the gusting wind.

She turned to see a young sailor in a green slicker reeling in a coil of wet rope. "It's not safe," he said.

She patted the life preserver she had strapped over her slicker to indicate she had heard, but he just shook his head. "They wouldn't even know you'd gone overboard until it was too late." Then, moving closer so as not to be over-heard, he added, "And they probably wouldn't turn around even if they did."

Simone had to laugh. She knew he was right. Nothing was going to delay the progress of the Seward and its cargo of war casualties, on their way to safe haven in the United States. One young female scholar and her aged Arab father, both of whom were considered mysteries to the officers and crew, would never be of much importance. At best, they were tolerated; at worst, they were mis-trusted.

An ensign, passing by, looked at her askance, then glared at the sailor. "Civilians should be belowdecks," he barked.

The sailor kept his head down and pretended to be absorbed in stowing the rope.

"I've already been warned," Simone assured him, "and I am quite capable of not falling overboard." Her English carried the upper-crust accent of her late mother, only slightly tinged by an Arabic inflection. But this time her answer wasn't good enough.

The ensign, feet planted wide to keep his balance on the roiling deck, said, "That's an order from the bridge. Go below, now!"

Simone's back went up; she didn't like taking orders. "Why?" she said, her retort undercut by a sudden rolling of the boat that forced her to grab the railing with both hands.

The ensign smirked. "We've detected enemy activity, that's why."

Conceding defeat—reluctantly—she moved toward the hatchway, clutching the slick railing hand over hand. She could not afford to create any kind of ruckus; her very presence on the boat, like her father's, was based on a deception. The official letters and work visas that had gotten them on board had been dummied up in her office at the Egyptian ministry. Calling any undue attention to herself could prove dangerous.

Once the door slid closed behind her, she breathed a sigh of relief—truth be told, she was getting too cold and wet to stay out there much longer anyway. She threw back the hood of her slicker. A few drops of the icy saltwater slipped under her collar, and she shivered.

Had the ensign been telling the truth about enemy activity? There was no reason to alarm her father with it either way. As she clambered down the corrugated metal stairs, the odor from the sick bays—virtually the whole ship had been converted to a floating hospital—grew worse and worse. Medics, their arms cradling plasma bags and surgical supplies, hustled past her, brushing her out of the way. Sailors made no bones about giving her the once-over. Even the shapeless slicker and life jacket were no deterrent.

The cabin Simone and her father had been assigned was, by navy standards, not bad, and as it was sufficiently high above the water line, it actually had a porthole that they could occasionally open to air the place out. When she slipped inside, she found her father exactly as she'd left him: unshaven, still in his faded silk dressing gown, perched on the edge of the bunk, and poring over tattered manuscript pages. Without even glancing up, he said, "Is it being kept safe?"

"I presume so," she said, slipping the life jacket off and letting it drop to the floor.

"But did you see it?"

"Of course not. The cargo hold is off-limits. I was up on deck." She stepped over a stack of books and papers, and pried open the porthole. A blast of cold, damp air blew into the cabin, swirling the papers into a tiny maelstrom.

"What are you doing?" her father exclaimed, slamming a palm down to secure the documents in his lap. "Shut that window!"

"You're going to suffocate if you don't let some air in here once in a while."

"And you are going to ruin my work!"

His work. For her entire life, Simone had been hearing about her father's work. It was what he lived for. And it was what had made his reputation. He was not only the chairman of the National Affairs Department at the University of Cairo, but the world's leading expert on the treasures of Egyptian antiquity. In his time, he had written more books, papers, and monographs on the subject than anyone alive. But unlike most professors, he had never been content to dwell in the library archives or the museum galleries. Dr. Abdul Rashid—like his daughter, an Oxford PhD—had unearthed much of the nation's patrimony, buried in the sands of the Sahara. The cane with the thick rubber tip resting against the edge of the bunk was a testament to the last expedition he had mounted, the one on which he and Simone had discovered the ossuary they were now secretly tracking to whatever destination its current owners—some branch of the United States Armed Forces—were transporting it.

"Do you want to go up to the canteen and have some lunch?" she asked.

"No," he said, returning his gaze to a document written in hieroglyphics. "Just bring me back something."

"Come with me," she urged. "You can't hole up in this cabin for the whole trip."

But he had tuned her out already and was making some notation in the margin of the page with the stub of a pencil.

Simone took no offense. His manner was gruff and distant, but she knew that the bond between them was unbreakable. He had prayed for a son—what Egyptian man did not?—but then he had fallen in love with his daughter, and molded her just as he would have done a boy. Her late mother might not have approved, but then, she had not been there to influence her daughter. She had died of cancer when Simone was only ten, so instead of the parties and frivolity that her mother had once lived for, Simone had gravitated to the history and art that her father favored. Together, they would have been happy to travel back to the time of the Pharaohs.

"I'll bring you some fruit, whatever they have," Simone said, touching him lightly on the shoulder of his robe, "and a cup of hot coffee."

"Tea."

"If I can find some." Her father still hadn't grasped that he was on an American ship, where coffee, not tea, was the drink of choice. "Just do me one favor—shave. You look like a ruffian when you don't."

He grunted in acknowledgment, and Simone, still in her slicker, left the cabin. She briefly considered a detour to the cargo hold, but even if she could talk her way past the guard, what would she see? A large wooden crate with iron hasps, three padlocks the size of fists, and a bill of lading that she'd give her eyeteeth to read. She'd watched as it had been loaded on board days before.

"Look out, lady," a sailor warned, clattering down the metal stairs with a stack of crisp white folded sheets in his arms. "Coming through!"

Simone flattened herself against the wall and stayed there as two more sailors, also burdened with bedding, barreled down after him. She could feel the ever-present vibration of the engines rumbling through the steel walls, and though the Seward had only left Le Havre two days before, she had grown so accustomed to the sound that she'd have missed it if it stopped.

Once she was sure the coast was clear, she

started up the stairs again, past several areas that had been set aside for surgical procedures, where she could hear the cries of agonized soldiers going in or out of the operating bays. She continued up toward the canteen. The smell of pea soup and bologna sandwiches wafted along the corridor, but she was hungry enough that she found even these aromas tempting.

She had just loaded up a tin tray with some food, and was scanning the canteen for hot tea, when the alarms went off. A shrill blast, followed by the crackle of loudspeakers. "All hands on deck! This is not a drill!"

That damn ensign had been telling the truth. She tossed the tray into a garbage can, whipped around, and headed back toward the cabin.

"All hands on deck!"

The alarms shrieked so loudly and incessantly that she pressed her hands over her ears. The lights flickered on and off, the decks reverberated with the trampling of a thousand running feet, and the whole ship suddenly felt to Simone like a beehive that had been swatted with a stick.

Bucking the tide of sailors racing up the stairs was nearly impossible. By the time she reached their cabin, even her father had been roused to doff his dressing gown and throw on some clothes. He was holding a bulging leather valise stuffed with books and papers under his arm, and leaning on his ebony walking stick.

"What are we meant to do now?" he said, over the screaming of the siren.

"For starters," she said, snatching a life preserver from under the cot bolted to the wall, "you can put this on!" Beyond that, even she had no idea what to do next—though she glimpsed an opportunity. "Don't leave the cabin unless you're instructed to. I'll be right back!"

"No." He clutched at the sleeve of her slicker. He always could read her mind. "You can't go down there now. What if we're torpedoed?"

If that happened, she thought, it wouldn't much matter where she was. The ship would sink. "I won't stay there any longer than I have to."

The sirens on board the Seward had stopped, mercifully, as everyone on the ship manned his battle station. In all the commotion, she was able to race down toward the hold while everyone else was heading in the opposite direction. On the way, she had the presence of mind to snag a clipboard stuffed with papers from a hook outside an officer's quarters, but twice, she was detained by doctors who mistook her for a nurse and tried to dragoon her into helping with the patients. Each time she broke away and continued heading down. "I'll remember you," the second one, wearing a badge that said DR. JAMISON, CHIEF OF SURGERY, shouted. "When this is over, I will personally make sure you get a dishonorable discharge!"

By the time Simone had made it down to the very bowels of the ship, there was only one young, and very nervous, guard still dithering in front of the hold.

"Who are you?" he said, when Simone emerged from the dimly lit corridor.

"Your relief."

"What relief?"

"I'm in charge of the cargo manifest now," she said, rapping the bulging clipboard. "Every sailor is needed up top, in the wards."

"I can leave?"

She held out her hand for the keys and said, in her most authoritative voice, "You're to report to Jamison, the chief of surgery!"

When he couldn't unclip the key ring fast enough, Simone barked, "Get going, Sailor!"

Plopping the ring into her outstretched hand, he ran for the stairs, holding on to his hat.

The ship was putting on speed and taking a zigzag course designed to elude the torpedoes. This far below deck the air was hot and heavy, and the roar of the engines, operating at maximum power, was deafening. Overhead lights, bare bulbs behind mesh screens, flickered on and off as she made her way into the hold. Pallets of medical supplies and boxes of canned goods were lashed down with thickly braided coils of rope and stacked to the low ceiling.

Simone knew that there was other game aboard,

too. There were captured Nazi armaments for study and analysis, reams of official German correspondence that had been salvaged from one overrun outpost or another, and, of course, the ossuary that she and her father had retrieved from one of the most remote and inaccessible regions of the Sahara Desert. When the German tank divisions swept through northern Africa, they had pillaged Egypt's artifacts and selected the choicest to be sent back to the Fatherland. The US Army had somehow intercepted the ossuary—for which she would be eternally grateful—but instead of keeping it safe for eventual restoration to its rightful place in the Cairo Museum, they had put it on this ship bound for New York Harbor.

That was what Simone did not understand. Could the Allies know its secret?

For fear of that, she had tracked the progress of the sarcophagus every step of the way. As an officer in the Egyptian Department of Cultural Affairs, she had access to all sorts of internal communiqués, transfer documents, and, most important of all, underpaid, midlevel functionaries at all of the artifact's stops along the route—functionaries who could be persuaded to part with vital information for nominal sums, or for the promise (never fulfilled) of a romantic liaison with the fetching young woman so inexplicably obsessed with one ancient casket.

If they had understood what it was, if they had been able to guess its significance and its power, they might not have been so puzzled, but Simone was not about to tell them. It had been her father's lifework to discover the ossuary. For all that these bureaucrats knew, it was just another old stone box destined to gather dust in some museum gallery.

There was just one thing she had not yet been able to ascertain: Where was the box supposed to go after its arrival in the United States? Rather than risk losing track of it altogether, she had contrived to book passage, for herself and her father, on board this ship. Now, if the ship didn't sink in the next few minutes, she had her best chance yet of finding out.

The ship rolled to one side, buffeted by the turbulent seas. Or was the rocking caused, she wondered, by the repercussions of depth charges exploding underwater? Discarding the clipboard, she put out a hand to steady herself and moved down the narrow aisles of supplies and matériel, scouring the work orders and delivery instructions secured in waterproof, plastic pouches affixed to their sides. She had made it to one end of the hold and was on her way back again when she noticed a khaki tarp thrown over a recessed area next to the wall. She could see a box marked "Antiseptics: USN" poking out from under one end of the tarp and had almost passed it by when something told her to take a closer look. The ship started to change direction again, throwing her off-balance, but she managed to grasp hold of the tarp's flap and fold it back. Why did it crackle with a thin film of ice?

Below the tarp, a rectangular wooden box, bigger than a steamer trunk, was chained atop a flat steel dolly, whose own wheels were anchored to the floor. The box was well secured, but unfortunately, displayed no shipping pouch. Was that deliberate? she wondered. Throwing the tarp back even farther, she scooted around the box and saw that there was a pouch, but that it was fastened to the side closest to the wall.

In the distance, she heard muffled concussions as the depth charges went off, and then, to her horror, a much louder blast that had to have been from a torpedo meeting its mark not far away. One of their escort destroyers had surely been hit.

But would the U-boats respect the Red Cross insignia the Seward was sailing under? For that matter, had they even seen it?

There was no time to lose. As soon as the ship had completed yet another juddering turn, Simone squeezed between the wall and the wooden box. Though she had seen plenty of cargo pouches in her career, even in the feeble light of the hold, she recognized that this one was different. This one bore the stamp of the Office of Strategic Services in Washington, DC, along with a warning—in big red block letters—that the crate was of "Priority A-1" importance, and should be handled with "all caution, care, and deliberation."

More problematic was the fact that the packet had been sealed, tacked, then duct-taped to the crate. If she planned to open it without anyone finding out, she would have to peel the tape back with her fingernails, then pray she could seal it up again perfectly. She was working at one end of the tape, and had already broken two nails in the process, when the ship suddenly bucked, as if a mighty fist had punched its hull, then listed to one side. Boxes that hadn't been properly secured toppled over, the tinkle of glass beakers breaking inside.

Simone's back was pressed between the wall and the heavy crate, which threatened to slip its moorings and crush her. The wall was cold, but the box, strangely enough, seemed even colder; she could see her breath fogging the air as it loomed above her, and she could hear the ominous sound of water—rushing water—entering the boat.

So much for the protection of the Red Cross markers.

Where, she wondered, had the torpedo hit? And could a ship like this survive it? Pinned between the wall and the crate, she could smell a salty tang in the air. As she tried to extricate herself, it felt almost as if the damn box were trying to seize her, and she tore her slicker on the corner of the crate, breaking free. Lurching to the steel gate of the hold, she heard the shouts of sailors clambering down to the engine rooms, and the rumble of giant pumps engaging. She locked the hold behind her, hooked the key ring to its handle, and as she ran toward the stairs to rescue her father, she noticed that she was splashing through a thin rivulet of water.

A rivulet that grew deeper with each step, until it was up to her ankles by the time she hit the stairs.

She struggled to make it back to the cabin, out of breath and soaked to the knees, only to find the door swinging open on its hinges.

And her father not inside.

He could only have gone up; otherwise, she'd have passed him on her way back from the hold.

She raced for the stairs, going up and around until she reached the hatchway, slid the door back, and took one small step out onto the deck.

The afternoon sun was hidden behind a bank of scudding dark clouds, and a pall of black smoke was drifting toward the Seward. Shielding her eyes, she could see that the smoke was emanating from the Van Buren, one of the escort destroyers, maybe half a mile off. An orange fire licked at one of its gun batteries. A slick of something glistened on the churning gray waves. The wind stank of burning oil.

But there was no sign of her father.

The Seward was plowing ahead, heaving through the turbulent seas, and she had to put out both arms to brace herself. Her eyes smarted from the smoke and the salt spray. The ensign who had crossed her earlier ran past, but not before spotting her again and cursing, "Get the hell off the deck!"

She shouted, "Have you seen my father?"

The ensign was already past her, dashing toward the bridge, when the ship suddenly teetered, bow down, on the crest of a massive wave. Simone saw the ensign, flat on his back, sliding headlong down the deck. Letting go of the handrail with one hand, she reached out and grasped one of his flailing arms, arresting his fall—until the ship dropped like a stone into a great gray trough, groaning and creaking and tilting to starboard. A freezing wave swept over the bulwarks. Her arm felt like it was about to pop out of its shoulder socket, but she held on tight, praying all the while that her father was all right, and that the ship would be able to stay afloat long enough to limp into some port.

A second later, the Seward shuddered from the force of something erupting beneath its hull. The entire ship rose up, as if lifted by Neptune himself, into a spume of seawater and a cloud of choking black smoke.

Chapter FOUR

Because of the Labor Day holiday, Lucas wasn't required to report to the university until Tuesday. Leaving the house, he passed Professor Einstein's place, where the front door was open, letting the breeze in through the screen door, and he could hear the clacking of typewriter keys and a woman's voice, speaking to someone in German again. Would he ever be able to hear that language without feeling, as he did now, a prickling of his skin?

It was a beautiful day, the end of summer and the start of fall, and as he walked, he had to shield his one good eye from the sun. The route was familiar, and so were most of the storefronts along Nassau Street. Many of them had been built in the faux Tudor style, brown timbers crisscrossing the white walls, and provided the usual array of college-town establishments—newsstands, diners, haberdasheries, a radio repair, an ice cream parlor. The owners who remembered him came rushing out to shake his hand and offer him a free newspaper or breakfast anytime, and Lucas thanked them, but, holding up his briefcase as if to prove it, said he had to get to class.

"The offer's good any time," Gus, who owned

the luncheonette, assured him. "Now you go teach those kids what we're fighting for."

Even in a class on Greek and Roman art, Lucas thought, the point could be made—what the Allies were fighting for was civilization itself. "Sure thing," he replied.

Quaint and lovely as the town was, it was nothing compared to the splendor of the university campus. Lucas entered under the ornate black iron FitzRandolph Gate, and stopped for a moment at the foot of the gravel path leading to Nassau Hall, where the college had first been housed in 1756. Its walls, fashioned from pale yellow sandstone, bore proud pockmarks where they had been struck by cannonballs during the Revolutionary War, and two bronze tigers, the official mascot, guarded the double doors. The white cupola housed a bell whose clapper the freshmen, in keeping with tradition, were required to steal at the commencement of classes each year. The administration always looked the other way, and the clapper was always dutifully returned.

A student in a seersucker jacket stepped up and handed him a flyer for a bond rally. "If you'll excuse my saying so, sir, it looks like you've already done your part."

Lucas glanced at the flyer, then slipped it into the breast pocket of his suit jacket. His wasn't as lightweight, or as nicely tailored, as the student's, and even Mrs. Caputo hadn't been able to get all the wrinkles out. As for his shoes, no matter how carefully he'd polished the brown brogues, the scuff marks were still evident, and the heels were worn.

The gravel crunched under his feet as he followed the path around one side of the hall and into the even quieter and more serene precincts of the campus. The lawns were wide and well manicured, the trees were ancient and old, the buildings constructed in the Gothic style, with mullioned casements, cloisters, and archways. Lucas had been told that the model had been Cambridge University in England, and it was easy to imagine oneself there. From a window in Witherspoon Hall, a hulking dormitory named after the Scottish theologian who had presided over the college in the late 1700s, Lucas heard the incongruous sound of a radio blaring the recent Woody Herman hit, "It Must Be Jelly." The music drifted on the September breeze, over the heads of the young men—and only men were allowed to enroll in the college—hurrying to find their first classes, with their sleeves rolled to the elbow and notebooks under their arms.

Although he was not more than ten or twelve years older than most of them, how impossibly young they looked to Lucas now.

He stopped in first at the departmental office, where he introduced himself to Mrs. Clarke, the middle-aged woman now running things there.

She was so harried, she barely had time to look up and say hello before shoving a sheaf of papers into his hand and wishing him luck.

It was only when he got to the main lecture hall in the McCormick Art Museum—a tiered amphitheater, open and airy, where he could easily see all of the students, and they could see him, that he realized how much things had changed. Before the war, the hall would have been full; now only forty or fifty of the two hundred seats were occupied. Most of the students looked like underclassmen, and the upperclassmen, if they were here at all, had probably been awarded 4-F status, for anything from asthma to flat feet. That, or they were in a field of study, such as civil engineering, in which the armed forces needed to cultivate a new crop. Nearly all of them wore glasses, some with lenses as thick as Coke bottles, and most were either scrawny or overweight and out of shape. Lucas could only imagine what his master sergeant, back in boot camp at Fort Dix, would have made of them.

After he had dropped off his box of slides with the projectionist—an elderly man who had been sitting in that tiny booth since the dawn of cinema—he stepped to the podium, introduced himself, and announced, "This is the first session of Art History 101: Classical Art and Architecture. If anyone is in the wrong room, you still have time to make your getaway."

"Nuts," he heard a student mutter, then gather up his books and flee up the aisle. There was always at least one on the opening day of the semester.

Besides the makeup of the student body, the other thing that had changed was his attitude. It wasn't so many years ago that he'd had butterflies in his stomach every time he had to stand in front of the podium for the first time and command the attention of a new class. But no more. Once you had faced aerial bombardments, oncoming tanks, and the ever-present threat of getting shot, any fears of public speaking evaporated pretty quickly.

He passed out the syllabi, still warm from the mimeograph machine, took attendance, and tried to put a face to each name he called out. A fair number of the names were from prominent American families, the East Coast elite that hailed from Park Avenue in New York and the Main Line of Philadelphia, and the Southern aristocracy. Many of the names were emblazoned on the halls and dormitories, stadiums and playing fields of the university. When he was done, one of the students raised a hand, and asked, "If I may ask, sir, where did you serve?"

It wasn't what Lucas had been expecting, but he answered anyway, just to move on. "Western Europe."

"Army, or marines?"

"Army." But that was as far as he was willing to

go with it; he was not about to delve into his work for the CRC. He knew that the students, if left to their own devices, would happily lead him down the garden path for the rest of the period. "Now, if those of you sitting closest to the windows could please lower the blinds, we can get started."

Once the room was suitably darkened, Lucas signaled the projectionist to dim the remaining lights, lower the screen at the front of the room, and cue up the first slide. A slightly dim and scratched image of one of classical antiquity's most renowned sculptures, the *Discobolos*, appeared to the right of the podium.

"When we talk about classical art," Lucas said, "we are talking about a golden age, dating from 480 BC, when Athens rose to prominence and the Greek empire expanded, to 323 BC. That was when Alexander the Great perished in the palace of Nebuchadnezzar in Babylon. It was a turning point, a time when artists had mastered the art of carving in marble and produced a host of exquisitely rendered sculptures. One of the most famous is this, the Discus Thrower; for the first time, sculptors had learned to capture the human body in motion. Their figures weren't stiff and unyielding and fixed in a formal posture anymore. Instead, they came alive as three-dimensional entities, free and unrestrained and even, at times, joyous."

He could hear the pens scrawling notes in the

shadowy hall, and he went on with his lecture, calling up slide after slide—briefly sketching in the seven great periods of Greek sculpture, from the Mycenaean of 1550 BC to the Hellenistic, which flourished on the mainland hundreds of years later. Fortunately, he had almost no need of his written notes; he knew this material cold. But he had not reckoned on the difficulties he would have reading with only one eye in such a dimly illuminated space. He found that he had to bend his head to the podium to see what the next topic was, and in order to see the images projected on the screen, he had to repeatedly turn sideways. It might be wise, he thought, to bring a flashlight with him to the next lecture.

When the bell in the university chapel, just across the quad, rang the hour, the projectionist raised the lights and screen, the students near the windows lifted the blinds, and Lucas looked up, blinking. Already, someone in a navy blue Windbreaker and baggy trousers was hastily exiting the last row and ducking out into the hall. Had the lecture been that boring?

"I assume you all have the syllabus," he called out, "and will have read the first two chapters of *Greco-Roman Antiquity* before the next class. My study is downstairs, here in the museum, and my hours will be posted on my door this afternoon." At Princeton, offices were called studies, just as seminars were called precepts.

Half the class was already streaming up the aisle.

"And be sure to sign up for at least one private conference before the end of the semester."

And then they were gone, the light in the projection booth was out (did the old man ever come out for air? Lucas wondered.) and he gathered up his notes in the empty hall. It all seemed surreal somehow. Now that he was actually standing at a podium again, it was hard to imagine that only weeks before, he had been dodging bullets, digging through rubble in war-torn towns, and searching for iron mines and hidden loot.

If he ever forgot, he had the dull ache in his head from the shrapnel wound, not to mention the glass orb concealed beneath the black patch, to remind him.

Crossing the museum lobby, he waved to Wally, the janitor, running a mop around the floor.

"Welcome back, Prof," Wally called out. "Glad you made it back in one piece."

Or nearly, Lucas thought; he was not about to debate the point.

It wasn't just that the memories were often hard ones—Lucas would never forget the German boy, Hansel, accepting the Hershey's bar a split second before his foot triggered the land mine. It was also the fact that words did not seem capable of doing justice to horrors like that, and a thousand others he had witnessed. If you had never seen war up close, it was an easy thing to be brave and bellicose about it. But if you had, it was hard not to despair. What men could wantonly do to each other, in the name of nation or faith or ideology, was unthinkable.

In a courtyard outside, students were hanging around, smoking and talking, and killing time before their next class began. A few under-graduates were gathered under a tree, gawking up at a window in Fine Hall, the venerable building that housed the Mathematics Department. Lucas, wondering what was so interesting, followed their gaze and saw, perched in a window seat behind a lead-paned window adorned with a mathe-matical symbol in stained glass, the indistinct form of a man. He appeared to be writing with great concentration on a pad in his lap.

Around his head there was a wild corona of white hair, and one hand came up to absent-mindedly brush a thick moustache.

"I saw him getting an ice cream cone in Palmer Square," one said.

"I said hello to him, on Washington Road."

"Did he say hello back?" a third asked.

"I don't think he heard me. I'm not even sure he saw me. He was off in a cloud."

Although it wasn't Lucas's first sight of Albert Einstein—on one occasion he had seen him strolling through a snowstorm toward the separate office he maintained at the Institute for Advanced Study—it was still thrilling to see the man who had revolutionized physics with equations that challenged, and overturned, the long-accepted ideas of space and time. He had become a celebrity, on a par with Joe Louis, Judy Garland, and Gene Kelly. Who would ever have thought that such a thing could happen to a scientist, much less one whose discoveries were incomprehensible to all but a select few?

At the faculty lounge in Chancellor Greene, Lucas picked up his mail from the pigeonhole with his name on it in the front foyer—it looked like even more university paperwork to fill out—and then, inside, was greeted with a booming "Hail the conquering hero!" from Patrick Delaney, who bounded up from his leather chair like a man half his considerable size, and wrapped Lucas in a bear hug. Delaney was the one-man Department of Mineralogy and Geophysics, whose research into radio isotopes was about as understandable to a lay audience as Einstein's work, though his fame extended no farther than the wainscoted walls of the lounge. Lucas had always had the sense that some of Delaney's research was secretly supported with government funds. Taking in the eye patch, he gave Lucas's shoulder a consoling squeeze, then said, "You do know, right, that the ladies are going to love that patch? Very dashing."

"I'll let you know how it works."

"You won't need to."

"How come?"

"Have you forgotten that you're back in Princeton, the only place on earth where news travels faster than the speed of light?"

"Speaking of which, I just saw the man himself."

"Herr Professor?"

"I see they've got him on display, up in the tower of Fine Hall."

"Why not—top study for the top dog," Delaney said, going to the sideboard and pouring two cups of coffee from a dented percolator. "Cream and sugar?" he asked.

"No, black, thanks."

"That's good. We don't have any cream or sugar."

They both laughed, and Lucas said, "Someone didn't ration his coupons carefully."

"Yeah, if you ask me, that bastard Hitler's got a lot to answer for."

The table in the center of the lounge was cluttered with ashtrays filled with cigarette butts, and newspapers stained with coffee rings. Not a thing had changed here, Lucas reflected, dropping into a worn leather chair opposite Delaney's. "Where is everybody?" he asked.

" 'Everybody' isn't what it used to be," Delaney said, scratching at the scruffy brown beard he trimmed himself. He also cut his own hair, which was pretty much evident to anyone he met. "Now that the student body's been reduced, the faculty's been thinned to a skeleton crew, too. It's a tribute to your utility that you've been taken back."

"What utility could I possibly have?"

"You're a testament to our fighting men."

"Not anymore, I'm not."

Delaney shrugged. "Maybe they figure some-ody's got to be around to remember all the cultural achievements that are now being systematically destroyed. Either way, you're here."

Oddly enough, it wasn't until this moment that Lucas realized it was at all unusual to have been so readily reappointed. Hadn't his invitation cited "Princeton in the nation's service"—the motto that had been bestowed upon it by Woodrow Wilson, president of the college from 1902 to 1910—as the reason?

"Ed Randall's still here, and he said to remind you that you still owe him five bucks," Delaney said, before running through a litany of who else was still on faculty—most of them older men, several of whom had served in the First World War—and bringing him up to date on changes in the town. "The Garden Theater finally got a concession stand with decent popcorn, the hoagie shop's closed—oh, and there's a good Chinese laundry now, where the shoe repair used to be." Funny, how life had gone on.

Glancing at the newspapers, Lucas saw a headline on *Newark's Star-Ledger*—"Navy Convoy Torpedoed in North Atlantic"—followed by a subhead, "USS Van Buren Sunk by U-Boat." He picked up the paper and scanned the front page, where there was a picture of another ship, the USS Seward, with a red cross painted on its side, safely in the dock.

"Yeah, bad news today," Delaney said. "You hear about that submarine attack yet?"

"No, I hadn't seen the papers till now," he said, reading quickly.

"The Germans sank a destroyer. The amazing thing, though, is that the ship with the wounded on board got hit, too, but somehow managed to make it to port."

The article went on to say that the Nazi submarine, hit by a depth charge, had exploded directly under the Seward, blowing a breach in its bow and causing it to take on water. Turning to an inside page for the rest of the story, Lucas saw a couple of photos of wounded soldiers being carried off the ship on stretchers, along with a shot of sheet metal haphazardly riveted over what was presumably the gaping hole in the hull. "How the pumps kept up with the flood," the captain of the Seward was quoted, "is nothing short of a miracle. It felt like the hand of God must have been under us, keeping the ship afloat."

"So much for the Geneva Conventions," Delaney said, slurping his coffee. "The Seward was clearly marked as a Red Cross ship."

In a short sidebar, the paper mentioned that there had been a freak accident in the harbor, resulting in yet another death, when a heavy crate, being lifted from the hold under tight security, broke loose and fell onto the loading dock. Sometimes, it seemed to Lucas, death was everywhere you looked—or didn't look—and he wondered if his own close call had somehow immunized him. Wishful thinking. But in wartime, wishes were sometimes all you had.

Chapter FIVE

It was the furtive knock on his study door that finally brought him down to earth again. And he was lucky it had.

Einstein knew that sitting in the window seat was not a good idea—the seat was hard, and he had a tendency to sit too long in one position— but he liked the way the sunshine filtered through the stained-glass obelus, the mathematical sign for division, and spread the colors of a rainbow across the notebook in his lap. It reminded him of one of his first thought experiments, conducted when he was only fourteen and pictured himself riding on the back of a beam of light. Even his most complex and profound theorems had been rooted in just such flights of fancy.

The knock was not repeated, though he was perfectly aware of who it was. He and his young colleague, the Austrian mathematician Kurt Gödel, had an understanding: they knew that either one of them might be so deeply absorbed in thought that any disturbance could prove fatal to whatever work was being done, and if there was no immediate response to an interruption—such as a knock—then it was best to retire quietly until another time.

"I'm coming," Einstein called out as he gingerly swung his legs onto the floor. Oh, how his bones creaked at times. He slipped his bare feet into the loafers that lay before the fireplace; its mantel-piece had been thoughtfully adorned with one of his most often-repeated quotes. When his theory of relativity had been challenged by a fellow physicist—whose own theories, Einstein contended, relied too much upon random events and coincidences—he had replied: "Subtle is the Lord, but malicious he is not." He still believed that to be true; there was an order to everything in the universe, and the greatest achievement would lie in deciphering it. Shuffling across the study, he repeated, "I'm coming."

But by the time he opened the door, Gödel was already halfway to the landing. He looked up through round black-framed glasses that gave him the look of a night owl, and said, "I do not disturb?"

"You do disturb," Einstein said, "but if you did not, I would be stiff as a plank of wood."

"I am walking," Gödel said.

"Wait." Einstein went to the blackboard behind his desk, rubbed out a few unsatisfactory figures with the sleeve of his rumpled sweatshirt, then joined Gödel on the stairs. When they emerged from the gloomy confines of Fine Hall, they both blinked at the bright fall day. "We live like a pair of moles, *ja*?" Einstein remarked.

"The mole is a creature that I admire," Gödel said, before listing several of its most salient virtues, ranging from industry to persistence. "And it does not call attention to itself or its work. It works in secret. That, too, is to be admired."

Einstein had to smile at Gödel's spirited defense of the mole. In any conversation with Kurt, you never knew what you were going to elicit, which was one of the many profound pleasures of his company. The long walks they took together, on the college campus or going back and forth to the Institute for Advanced Study, were the best way he knew to clear his own head, or, if he wished, to air some half-formed argument or idea. Even among the most brilliant scientists and scholars in the world, many of whom had taken refuge here in this bucolic college town, Gödel stood out. Einstein, almost thirty years older, looked upon him as a father might look at his gifted, but undeniably eccentric, son.

Besides, it was nice to share what happy reminiscences they could of prewar Europe, where it had been possible to bandy about whatever theories you liked, over plates of sausages and glasses of schnapps. Berlin in particular had once been a thinking man's paradise, though now, to Einstein's horror—indeed, to the horror of the entire civilized world—all of Germany had become a bastion of willful ignorance and unequalled brutality. The transformation was shocking.

"I have been thinking," Gödel said, smoothing back his already smooth head of brown hair, as they strolled down one of the leafy pathways of the campus.

Einstein chuckled. These were the words with which he began every conversation. The preeminent mathematical logician in the world, Kurt was a thinking machine, his brain never at rest. He reminded Einstein of himself a bit, but back when he, too, had had the energy to work through the night, to live entirely in his own head for countless hours on end, fueled by nothing but coffee and the urge to crack the secrets of the universe. "And what have you been thinking about this time?"

"The Constitution."

This did surprise Einstein. He was expecting to hear something about the incompleteness theorem, or perhaps his friend's latest proof of God. "The Constitution of the United States?"

"Yes."

This did not bode well.

"There is a flaw in the logic of its construction," Gödel said, "and if it is allowed to remain uncorrected, it would allow for the rise of a dictatorship."

It was just what Einstein had feared. In preparing for his citizenship exam, Gödel had been studying the historical underpinnings of the United States. How like him it was to find a problem there—a problem that he would not be able to simply let pass. As his sponsor, the last thing Einstein wanted was for Gödel's application to be scuttled by some abstruse argument that only another member of the Institute for Advanced Study could appreciate.

"Have you?" Einstein said. "Have you now? Well, I don't think that such a thing is likely to happen, and I don't see that it would be wise to bring it up when your application is being reviewed."

"But I must," Gödel said. "It must not be allowed to stand." He spoke as if the nation, his newfound home, were in imminent danger of a coup.

"Perhaps you can send a letter to the judge,

once it is all over," Einstein said, simply to placate him, "and alert him to the danger in that way."

Gödel, a bundle of nervous energy, smoothed his hair again, and then the lapels of his double-breasted jacket—he was as fastidious about his appearance as Einstein was lax. "But what if something should happen?"

"America has enough problems already," Einstein said. "The whole world has enough problems already. This one can wait." And then, to steer the conversation into safer territory, he asked after Gödel's wife, a former Viennese cabaret dancer six years his senior, and perhaps the most unlikely companion imaginable for such a high-strung genius. And yet, somehow, the marriage seemed to work. Relativity, he reflected, was simple compared to the mysteries of Eros. "How is she doing with that new garden?"

Gödel, fortunately, took the bait—he was always happy to talk about his wife—and they walked the rest of the way to Einstein's home with no further discussion of the constitutional crisis. At the gate, Einstein asked Gödel to come inside for a glass of Kirschwasser, but Gödel declined, and he knew why. Without his wife, who acted as his official taster, Gödel thought that all food and drink he was offered, no matter who it was offered to him by, might be poisoned; he was as mad as a hatter on that score. Adele, a good-natured woman who laughingly took a bite or a sip of everything put before him, once remarked to Einstein, "You see how much my Kurt loves me? On the chance that it is poisoned, he wants me to go first."

Gödel shook Einstein's hand firmly and formally, all but clicking his heels before he turned toward home, and Einstein opened the gate and went up the porch steps. It wasn't as if he didn't have his own quirks, which were much made fun of. But at least he ate fearlessly and with gusto.

"Is that you, Herr Professor?" his secretary of many years, Helen Dukas, called from her tiny office off the main hall.

"It is," he said, closing the door behind him, "it is."

"There is someone here to see you." A suitcase sat by the stairs.

If Helen—his Cerberus, he liked to call her—had let the visitor in, then it had to be important.

A slender young man, intense and lean as a wolverine, stepped into the hall, still holding his brown porkpie hat by its brim.

"You have come all this way?" Einstein said, recognizing his old colleague at once. "It must be a matter of some urgency."

"The utmost," Robert Oppenheimer replied. "Where can we talk?"

Einstein ushered him toward the stairs.

"Shall I make up the guest room?" Helen called out.

"Yes, please," Oppenheimer answered her before his host could.

And that was when Einstein knew for sure, as he plodded up the steps like a man ascending to the gallows, that the news would not be good. If Oppenheimer, the head of the top-secret project to develop an atomic bomb, had traveled all this way, from whatever undisclosed location where he was holed up these days, to discuss it, then it must mean something dire was in the offing.

Dire enough that only Einstein could remedy it.

<u>Chapter SIX</u>

September 8, 1944

From New York Harbor to Grand Central Station, then onto a train to a place called Princeton Junction. Once there, Simone and her father had been shuttled to a single railcar that traveled on a short spur line, no more than a mile or two long, which terminated at the foot of the university campus. The only other passengers were three businessmen with loosened ties coming home from their offices, and some boisterous students plainly returning from a wild excursion to the city.

"Where to?" the taxi driver asked, piling their

luggage into the trunk of the bright yellow car.

Simone didn't know how to reply. There hadn't been time to figure out where they would be spending the night. "We will need a hotel," she said, and the driver said—"Sure thing"—and pulled away from the station.

Simone's first impression of New Jersey was trees—great towering trees everywhere, making a canopy overhead, shading the old stone walls and towers of the university buildings that rose along the side of the road. The late-day sun touched the leaves, already edged in red and gold, and she could only imagine how beautiful they would be in another few weeks—provided, of course, that she and her father were still there to see them.

This part of the plan had not yet had time to gel in her mind. Too much had happened. In the harbor, the wounded soldiers had disembarked first—some limping under their own power down the gangway, others carried on stretchers to a fleet of ambulances, busses, and cabs lined up at the dock. Once their ranks had thinned out, Simone had taken her father by the elbow and navigated down the ramp, followed by the officious ensign whose arm she had snagged on the flooded deck of the Seward. He had since become her greatest admirer, and asked how long she would be staying in the city.

"I have shore leave for a week," he volunteered.

"We're not sure of our plans," she'd said, not wanting to discourage him too much before their luggage had been unloaded from the ship.

He scrawled a phone number on a scrap of paper and assured her that if a woman answered, it wasn't his wife. "It's my mom's place," he said.

Simone saw a mountain of boxes and supplies piling up toward the bow of the ship, and looking up, watched a huge winch lowering a green net filled with yet more. After depositing her father and their bags in a taxi, and telling the driver he could run the meter until she got back, she ambled, as unobtrusively as she could, toward the spot where the cargo was being collected. Lurking between two stacks of cartons, she waited as the winch made one or two more drops. But how many, she wondered, would there be? She was sure to be noticed if she stood there for long: The last of the vehicles were now leaving the dock, bound for hospitals in the city, and she could see that the ensign who had asked her out had been dragooned into transporting some of the unloaded freight. In a minute or two, he'd pass right by her with his empty dolly.

The winch dipped down one more time, then, creaking loudly, swung out wide, with a wooden crate in its net. Even from here, she could see the red-lettered pouch affixed to its side, containing the elusive delivery instructions. A navy officer with a megaphone was waving directions to the operator up top, but the net seemed to catch in a sudden wind off the sea. The armature shivered, and the net twisted around and around, almost as if something were trying to escape from the box.

"No, slow it down!" the officer bellowed. "You're going to lose it!"

But the net kept twisting and turning. Then the winch itself suddenly groaned and tilted over the bulwark.

"Watch out!" the officer shouted, leaping behind a flatbed truck.

The armature doubled over. The net swung like a pendulum across the dock, catching the ensign square in the chest as he turned around and looked up. He was knocked off his feet like a bowling pin, his dolly skittering across the cement. The net came halfway back again before the crate ricocheted off the hood of a truck with an awful scraping noise and stopped a few feet from the body of the sailor.

There was a moment of stunned silence on the dock, before Simone and a few of the stevedores raced to the ensign's side, but it was clearly of no use. What was left of his chest looked like a squashed plum. The officer, his white uniform sprayed with blood, knelt over him, saying, "Jesus Christ . . . Jesus Christ," over and over again.

How she could focus on anything but the tragedy, Simone didn't know, but her head turned. On the side of the shipping crate, the duct-taped pouch had been torn loose, and its contents were spilling out. The breeze was catching the papers already; she reached out and snatched one that was hovering in the air like a butterfly. It was crumpled, but not so much that she couldn't read the delivery instructions: "Department of Art and Archaeology, Princeton University. Attn: Professor Lucas Athan."

The cab pulled up outside a well-maintained hotel done in the Colonial style—red brick, white wooden shutters—but when they got out, Simone's father wanted to simply sit on the bench outside for a few minutes and catch his breath. Worry filled her. The last few days had been too hard on his heart.

Simone followed their luggage into the lobby, and at the reception desk a young woman dressed in a frilly white blouse said, "How may I help you?" Her name tag read "Mary Jane."

"I will need either two rooms, or, if you have it, better yet a two-bedroom suite. I'm traveling with my father."

Mary Jane said, "Oh," and after glancing at Simone again, started riffling through the pages of the reservation book. "Is this your first visit to Princeton?" she said, without looking up again.

"Yes."

"Did you come a long way?"

It seemed an odd question, but Simone

answered it, anyway. "Yes. All the way from Cairo, as a matter of fact."

"Where?" the girl asked.

"Egypt," Simone said.

"Oh," Mary Jane said again, before excusing herself. "I'll be right back. I just have to check on our availability."

Simone looked around the lobby, appointed with Oriental rugs, brass lamps, and oil portraits of Revolutionary War heroes. The rooms would not be cheap, but money wasn't an issue. Her mother's family had largely cut their daughter off after she'd made the colossal faux pas of marrying an Arab, but her father's family had been very successful cotton merchants for generations. Simone stepped outside to check on her father.

"Better now," he said, using the cane to climb to his feet. "I would like to lie down and take a nap before dinner."

"That sounds like a good idea," Simone said. She escorted him through the door and helped him into a wingback chair in the reception area. "They're just checking on the rooms."

A manager now stood behind the desk, wearing a burnt-orange jacket and matching slacks. He smiled at Simone as she returned to the desk, but she noticed that his eyes kept flicking over her shoulder to her father resting with his eyes closed and his ebony walking stick propped against an end table.

"Good evening, Miss . . . ?"

"Rashid. Simone Rashid."

"Ah, yes," he said. "Mary Jane tells me you are visiting America."

Simone hadn't said exactly that, but it wasn't worth arguing about.

"Are you guests of the university?"

"In a manner of speaking," she replied. Although no invitation had been extended yet, she certainly meant to weasel her way in. But what was this all about? Was security this tight in American hotels now?

"May I see your passport?"

Simone dug it out of the canvas shoulder sack she carried in place of a purse, and set it down beside the gleaming brass bell. Mary Jane glanced at its distinctive crocodile-green cover as if she'd never seen anything so exotic. The girl looked no more than seventeen years old, so maybe she hadn't.

The manager flicked over the front pages of the passport, but his eyes returned to her dozing father, his face as brown and wrinkled as a walnut shell.

What was taking so long? "If you don't have a suite, two rooms close to each other will be fine," Simone reiterated.

"Exactly," the manager said, turning a page of the ledger back and forth. "But I'm not sure we have anything like that available at this time."

Simone hadn't seen a single guest coming in or out.

"Might I recommend an inn just a few blocks from here? It's called the Peacock, and if you'd like, I can telephone them and see if they have something free."

And then, like a sledgehammer, it hit her. The hotel didn't want them because it wasn't one hundred percent sure that they were white. While Simone's tan skin had given them pause, her father's darker complexion had sealed their fate.

The manager was already picking up the telephone on the counter.

"You needn't bother," Simone said frostily, pressing the button down on the receiver. She would not be run off. "We'll be staying right here."

"Yes, well, we really have nothing suitable—"

"Then we'll take something unsuitable." She would sleep in a broom closet now, just to force the issue.

"There's only one small room that—"

"We'll take it," she said, turning the registration book on its swivel and signing it on the first line left blank. "Send in a cot."

The manager looked like he had no idea what to do next, and Mary Jane was studying him to see how she should handle awkward situations like this in the future.

"What's the room number?" Simone asked brusquely.

"Don't you want to know the room rate?" he asked. "It's—"

"I don't care. What's the number?"

Reluctantly, he took a key from the board behind him and said, "Three fourteen."

"Thank you," she said, snatching the key and then banging on the brass bell herself. A Negro bellhop magically appeared. At least they allowed colored people to *work* there, though even he looked a bit confused as he picked up their bags. She gently shook her father to wake him, then followed the luggage trolley to the elevator. She was so angry she could barely breathe, but she was not about to let her father know of the shabby treatment they had just received. He had never been to the United States before, and she did not want to have to explain to him that while the world was fighting a so-called "master race" intent on ruthlessly exterminating people that they judged inferior or impure, America itself was still a stronghold of racism and discrimination. She just hadn't expected to find it here, in a northern university town that was home to some of the leading intellectuals in the world, like Albert Einstein and Kurt Gödel and Thomas Mann.

But so she had. As the elevator made its slow ascent, she slumped against the back wall, suddenly as weary as her father.

Chapter SEVEN

"It's called the moment of imminent action," Lucas said, as the students gathered around a statue in the art museum's central gallery. It was a piece from the first century BC, first unearthed on the island of Samos, and it depicted the Greek warrior Achilles raising his spear to deal the death blow to Hector, prince of Troy. "The Greek sculptors, and the Romans, too, were less interested in a deed that was done than they were in a deed that was about to be committed. Works like this one ask the spectator to imagine, to anticipate, and even in a way participate in, what is just about to occur. It is the moment of greatest suspense and the greatest dramatic possibility."

Pens scratched away at open notebooks.

"Can anyone tell me what did happen next?"

Virtually every hand went up—graduates of elite private schools, these boys had been well tutored in *The Iliad* and *The Odyssey*—and Lucas allowed Percy Chandler to dilate on the death of Hector, the unseemly dragging of his body behind Achilles's chariot, the subsequent plea from King Priam to allow his son's body to be returned for proper burial. The gallery itself was a long, relatively narrow space, lined with pedestals on which a few dozen fine examples of ancient statuary and artifacts were illuminated by a broad skylight. The day had dawned gray and cloudy, and had stayed that way, so the light that suffused the gallery was soft and muted. And although it was open to the public, only two other people were perusing the collection—an older man with an ebony cane, and judging from the solicitous way in which she tended to him, his daughter.

"But Achilles had violated the laws of proper conduct," Chandler was saying, "and the gods were unhappy with him. Zeus had supported the Greeks up until then, but he sent Apollo down to protect the body from any further damage."

The older man was plainly an Arab, and his daughter was striking, with patrician features, a lean frame, and a mane of glossy black hair falling to her shoulders. She would look at home, Lucas thought, on the back of a white stallion, in a pair of jodhpurs and gleaming boots. Glancing his way, she must have caught him staring, and he quickly looked away.

"Thank you, Percy," he said, interrupting the introduction of the Trojan horse into the story, "but while we have a few minutes left, let's move on to the statue of Socrates lifting the cup of hemlock . . . yet another example, as you will see, of imminent action."

Lucas ushered the students farther down the

gallery, deliberately not looking back. When he finally did turn around in the middle of elaborating on the ancient philosopher's ill-fated struggle with the Athenian state, the woman and her father were gone.

After dismissing the class, he went downstairs to fulfill the hours regularly set aside for private conferences with students. His study was a tiny room with all the charm of a dungeon cell and a horizontal window just above ground level that let in a modicum of fresh air and natural light. If he looked outside, he could see people's ankles going by on the walkway.

Wally had just mopped the hallways; the smell of linseed oil was overpowering. Under his door, he found an envelope with the crest of the university president, Mr. Harold W. Dodds, stamped on its seal. To his surprise, it turned out to be a rather peremptory request to come to Prospect House, the president's mansion, straight away. The semester had barely begun; had some complaint already been lodged against Lucas? He could not imagine for what.

On the way to the house, he noticed that an army truck had pulled up outside the loading bay of the museum. Three soldiers were over-seeing the delivery of something he couldn't see, but which was apparently quite unwieldy—a donation from an alumnus with an impressive military connection?

"No, no, you're gonna drop the damn thing again!" one called out.

"Keep your shirt on!" someone replied.

The president's mansion, an enormous Italianate house originally built in 1849 for a gentleman farmer, was immured in five acres of gardens in the center of the campus, and surrounded by a black wrought-iron fence erected by Woodrow Wilson to keep the students from stomping through the flowerbeds like a marauding army on football days. Colorful and luxuriant in summer, the gardens were lovely even now, as the branches of the yew and American beech trees shed their leaves on the winding gravel footpaths. Little brown birds flitted among the treetops, moving so rapidly that Lucas could barely make them out.

The sky, still overcast, bathed the scene in an autumnal glow as Lucas straightened his tie and stepped under the front portico. A maid in a white apron ushered him into the foyer, a solemn circle of polished marble, then up the wide staircase, past a grandfather clock ticking on the landing, and into a parlor where two men—one in a crisply laundered officer's uniform, the other in his customary three-piece suit—were already seated, in deep discussion over cups of coffee and a plate of quartered sandwiches.

"Thank you for coming, Professor," Harold Dodds said, rising from his chair and extending his hand. "This is Colonel Macmillan, attached to the Office of Strategic Services in Washington. He's come up to Princeton expressly to meet you."

Lucas shook his hand, not knowing what to expect next. The colonel gave the impression of a granite block. "I hope I'm not AWOL," Lucas joked.

"You hope you're not AWOL, *sir,*" Macmillan said, without a hint of humor. "But it's unlikely. You've already been discharged."

This was not a man, Lucas thought, who engaged in pleasantries.

"How much does the one eye interfere with your depth perception?" he asked bluntly.

"I get by."

"Everything I'm about to say here is classified," he went on, his curiosity apparently sated, "and President Dodds has assured me it will remain that way."

What could be so important to national security, Lucas wondered, and yet call for his involvement? He'd only been a first lieutenant.

"In regard to your mission to the iron mine outside Strasbourg," the colonel said, "the one where you received your injuries—"

"A very good soldier," Lucas interjected, "Private Teddy Toussaint, was injured a lot worse than I was that day."

"Yes, I'm well aware of that," Macmillan said brusquely. "I saw in your report that you had submitted his name for a service medal, and it's been taken care of."

"Thank you," Lucas said with a nod.

"But let me say that it was all in a good cause, because you two found one of the Nazis' largest repositories of stolen art. On that, I commend you."

Lucas needed no more acknowledgment of that. Many a night, when his head throbbed from the shrapnel wound, and his eye socket ached, he wished he had not been so lucky.

"Including a certain sarcophagus," the colonel continued, "which I believe you called an ossuary in your notes."

At the very mention of the word, the chilled air of the mine rose up around him. "Yes, we did. Although I was still in the hospital when I wrote up my notes, I think you'll find a complete description of its discovery there."

"Well, we've brought the damned thing here. To Princeton."

"It's being deposited in the conservation wing of the art museum even as we speak," Dodds said.

Lucas was stunned. He had never known why, out of all the Nazi plunder, of all the treasures stolen everywhere from Lyons to Luxor, that particular item had been singled out. And now it had been transported all the way to New Jersey?

As if divining his thoughts, the colonel leaned forward in his creaking chair, and said, "You remember who it was addressed to, don't you?"

"Of course." He could no more forget that than the ring of ore carts protecting it, the hollowed out corpse, or the strange way in which the thing had seemed to bask in its own penumbra. "But there must be thousands of pieces reserved for the Führer."

"True enough, but not that many that were specifically mentioned in communiqués, from Hitler himself to General Rommel." He withdrew a telegram from his inside pocket and handed it to Lucas. "We intercepted this reply about a week before you were sent to the mine."

Even with his rudimentary German, Lucas was able to read enough to understand its gist. Rommel was reassuring Hitler that the sarcophagus was safely hidden, and that he'd issued orders for it to be forwarded to the Eagle's Nest under special guard as soon as the rail lines were secured.

But Lucas was still puzzled. "What do you expect to learn from it?"

"That's your job," Macmillan said, leaning back in his chair. "You found it—now we want you to tell us what makes this thing so special. If Adolf wants it that bad, we want to know why."

"May I add something?" Dodds said, glancing at the colonel for the go-ahead. Once he'd gotten the nod, he said, "Are you aware of Professor Delaney's work with radio isotopes?"

"I am." Now Lucas's suspicions were confirmed; Delaney's work *was* being underwritten by the War Department.

"Good," the colonel interjected. "I don't profess to understand exactly how it's done, but I'm told he's developing something called radiocarbon dating that might also tell us something about how old the sarcophagus is, or how old its contents—whatever they turn out to be—are. Between the two of you eggheads, we want an accurate picture of what's inside it, and if there's any way we can use it in the war effort."

"It's not a weapon," Lucas ventured. "It's just a kind of casket. Probably about two thousand years old."

Macmillan waved his words away. "Hitler may not know that. The son of a bitch is crazy, believes in all kinds of occult mumbo jumbo. He's got an astrologer on staff, and I wouldn't be surprised if he kept a crystal ball by his bedside."

The idea that the Allies were up against a lunatic was even more terrifying than the prospect of battling a rational, though supremely evil, foe. At least you could try to outsmart a rational man; you could guess his next move and try to counteract it. A madman, on the other hand, couldn't be relied upon to act in even his own best interest. "As far as this sarcophagus is concerned," Macmillan said, "so long as he thinks it's got some kind of voodoo attached to it, then let's humor him, right?"

Lucas gave him a weak smile, but couldn't—wouldn't—speak what had just crossed his mind. He was a practical man, an empiricist, one who eschewed anything unfounded and unscientific. But he'd never forget his first sight of that box, or the way it had seemed to suck the very light out of the area around it.

"Let's see if we can't find a way to exploit that bastard's lunacy," Macmillan said, slapping his own thigh.

"Not that you would be asked to participate in any of that skulduggery," Dodds quickly put in.

"Absolutely not," the colonel agreed. "You just tell us what we've got. We've got people at the Pentagon who'll do the rest."

An awkward silence fell.

"When would you like me to start?" Lucas asked.

"The installation should be done shortly," Dodds answered, "but we're also making some modifications to the conservation rooms."

"Courtesy of Uncle Sam," Macmillan said.

"We're reinforcing the floor," Dodds continued, "reframing some windows, improving the lighting. Shall we say, first thing tomorrow?"

Although he had a morning lecture, now was not the time to mention it. "Fine."

The grandfather clock on the staircase bonged the hour.

"We're counting on you," the colonel said, leaning forward in his chair, his several medals dangling from his uniform as if in emphasis. He extended a rough and meaty hand.

"Glad to do it," Lucas replied, wondering how he'd feel about it tomorrow. "Sir."

Chapter EIGHT

"Is the poor man going to be out there all night?" Einstein said, staring down into the backyard, where one of Robert Oppenheimer's two bodyguards patrolled the area around the garage and alleyway. The other one was stationed in a parked car, in front of the house.

"Yes," Oppenheimer replied. "That's his job. Now will you please stop worrying about his welfare, and focus on our work."

The work, Einstein thought; yes, the work. It had been one thing when his work remained theoretical, and its purpose was simply to extend the borders of human knowledge and crack the codes of the universe. It was altogether another when, as now, it was being driven by the exigencies of war, and when its goal was not elucidation but annihilation.

That, however, was where things stood, and it was the reason Oppenheimer had left his colleagues in Los Alamos, New Mexico—a place Einstein pictured as a desert waste—to consult with the man whose discoveries had unwittingly ushered in the Atomic Age. For hours now, they had been holed up in the professor's upstairs study while Oppenheimer, in between finishing one cigarette and starting another, had shared with him the latest, and most secret, news of the Germans' efforts to develop nuclear energy and thereby create an atomic weapon. It was possible that the Nazis had come a long way.

"The Reich minister for armaments and war production, Albert Speer, has reorganized their nuclear power project from top to bottom," Oppenheimer was saying. "That intelligence is solid. Bernhard Rust is history, and he's been replaced by Reich Marshal Hermann Göring."

"So, they have replaced a scientist with a soldier. That is good news for us, no?"

"No, it's not. It means that they're getting serious again. Hitler trusts Göring—the son of a bitch has done a bang-up job with the Wehrmacht—and putting him in charge proves that he's serious about getting the job done, and getting it done faster."

"Ah, then, perhaps he rues the day he instituted his ridiculous *Deutsche Physik*."

"Who cares what he rues? And by the way, I don't think he's ever rued a day in his life."

Because the Nazis considered theoretical

physics and quantum mechanics too abstruse and "Jewish," they had replaced them years before with a more homegrown and homespun curriculum—the rudimentary *Deutsche Physik*—and as a result of the switch, half of the country's nuclear scientists had been relieved of, or driven from, their posts. A plethora of the continent's brightest lights had also taken flight. Not just Einstein, but Hans Bethe, Max Born, Erwin Schrödinger, Eugene Wigner, Otto Stern, Lise Meitner, Robert Frisch, Enrico Fermi, Edward Teller, Maria Goeppert-Mayer—the list went on and on.

"We could waste our time trying to figure out why he does what he does," Oppenheimer observed, "but what would be the point? Personally, I'd say he's off his rocker. But it looks like he's finally figured out his mistake. Now he knows that he'd better get the bomb before we do."

That prospect, Einstein recognized, was unthinkable. A weapon created through fission would wreak havoc beyond anyone's imagining. When the war first broke out, the Nazi party had swiftly annexed the Berlin Institute of Physics, which had, before the purge, done pioneering work in nuclear physics and isotope separation; that was one of the first warning bells of Hitler's intentions. By the summer of 1939, Einstein's friend, the Hungarian physicist Leó Szilárd, had grown alarmed by the Nazis' sudden, and suspicious, halt to the exportation of the uranium ore they had acquired from the mines in occupied Czechoslovakia; there could only be one reason for stockpiling uranium, a mineral essential to the creation of an atomic bomb. For fear that they might also get their hands on the huge deposits located in the Belgian Congo, Szilárd had come to Einstein with an urgent request. He begged him to write a letter to President Roosevelt, alerting him to the threat.

"My name won't mean enough," Szilárd had said. "But yours will. Yours will make him read it."

Einstein had agreed. In his letter, he'd explained, as simply as he could, that it had now become conceivable, using a sizeable mass of uranium, to create a nuclear chain reaction—a reaction that would not only generate a large quantity of radium-like elements, but at the same time release an immense amount of power.

What, he wondered as he had issued this warning, had he unleashed upon the world when he had composed his famous formulae for energy and matter?

Using this discovery, the letter had continued, a new kind of bomb could be created, a bomb vastly superior to any yet built. Although too unwieldy to be dropped from a plane, such a bomb could, if transported to a harbor by boat, level the entire port, and a great swath of the surrounding area as well.

Even that last caveat about aerial delivery, according to what he had learned tonight, might soon be overcome. Oppenheimer was convinced that a bomb could be constructed, of a weight and on a scale that made it deployable by a specially equipped aircraft. But there were still daunting challenges to be surmounted—and it was only Einstein who might be able to surmount them.

The desk was covered with the materials Oppenheimer had brought with him—pages of equations, sketches of prototypes for nuclear reactors, even diagrams of possible bomb designs. What Einstein had, that most other physicists did not, was a dual pedigree—he excelled at the theoretical side, but at the same time, he evinced a penchant for the actual mechanics of a thing. His father had been an electrical engineer. The founder of one failed company after another, a businessman he was not, but he had given his son an appreciation for the practical, real-world manifestation of theoretical breakthroughs, an appreciation that had stood him in good stead in the years that he had worked as a clerk in the Swiss patent office. Even the Nobel Prize that had been awarded to him in 1921 had not been given in recognition of his revolutionary theory of relativity, but for his research into the more prosaic photoelectric effect.

"We know that they're assembling the necessary materials," Oppenheimer said through a haze of cigarette smoke. Oh, how it made Einstein long for his pipe. "And they've still got enough scientific expertise in guys like Werner von Heisenberg and Max Planck to put the whole thing together."

"Not Max Planck," Einstein said, with a pained expression. "Not Max."

Oppenheimer blew out a cloud of smoke so thick Einstein had to sit back in his chair. "Why not Max?"

"He is too good a man."

"And you're too sentimental about your old teachers. If they didn't get out of town while the getting was good, then they're Nazis now, or at least working for them."

But Einstein still could not believe it. In addition to being the acknowledged father of quantum theory, Planck was an elderly and honorable man who had comfortably worked side by side with Jewish colleagues all his life. In fact, he had confided in Einstein that he had met with the Führer himself in 1933 to try to explain that the National Socialist policies of anti-Semitism, coupled with *Deutsche Physik*, would undo decades of scientific progress. The Jewish scientists, the backbone of theoretical physics, would scatter themselves all over the globe, he warned, offering their expertise to other nations, even those whose aims might one day prove antithetical to those of the Fatherland.

"Let them!" the Führer had exploded. "Let them peddle their filthy goods in the streets! I don't care! We don't need them; we have German scientists, the best in the world, capable of doing whatever needs to be done without the help of traitors and vermin."

"To my eternal regret, I remained silent," Planck had admitted about that conference in Prague. "And when he was finished, I bowed and started to leave the room. One of his minions struck me on the shoulder to make me stop, then yanked my arm up in the proper salute. 'Heil, Hitler!' he shouted—I never saw a man's face so red with anger—and so I mumbled it. 'Heil, Hitler.' I wasn't enthusiastic enough, that much I could tell, but he let me go, anyway, slamming the door behind me."

Einstein had seen the torment in Max's eyes. For years, everyone in Europe had had hard choices to make, to give up their homes and their families and entire previous lives, or risk it all to take a moral and ethical stand. Most of those who took the risk wound up dead on a battlefield, murdered in a concentration camp, or, courtesy of the ubiquitous Gestapo, simply made to disappear without a trace from the face of the earth. Already, the letters from his cousins, such as Roberto Einstein, who lived outside Florence,

Italy, had abruptly ceased; he had not heard a word from Roberto, his wife, or their two daughters in years now, and he dreaded to think what had become of them.

Oppenheimer, lean as a coyote and deeply tanned from his time in the Southwest, studied the blackboard on which they had been scrawling equations all night. It was covered with erasures and blots of chalk, and they had joked that they should have brought along a basic mathematician. While their ideas and insights were often right, laying out the actual trail, in a logical and numerical fashion, was something neither one of them had ever excelled in. It was the scut work that they could not slow down enough to do properly.

"But you see where the problem remains?" Oppenheimer said, tamping the ash from his cigarette into the saucer of the coffee cup he had already drained four times. Helen had simply made a pot and, after clearing a few inches on Einstein's cluttered desk, left it there.

"*Ja*," Einstein said, yawning widely, and plopping back down in his worn leather armchair. "I do. But this old man, I am afraid, needs his rest."

Oppenheimer checked his watch. It was 1:30 in the morning. "Fine," he said. "How much rest do you need?"

Einstein had to laugh. "I do not know. I awake

when I awake. Don't you ever sleep, Robert?"

"Not if I can help it."

"You're young still. One day you'll want a nap."

"When the war's over, I'll sleep."

"But when will that be?" Einstein asked. "It could be years."

"Or it could be tomorrow," Oppenheimer replied. "Whoever cracks the atom bomb first will win the war overnight. No country will be able to stand up against it. That's why we have to be the ones to do it. There's no other choice."

Einstein nodded. He knew it all was true. But he also knew that once such a terrible force was created, there would be no containing it. Some scientists even contended that once an atomic reaction was incurred, it could set fire to the entire atmosphere, blanketing the planet in clouds of flame. Although Einstein was not one of them, he had no doubt that the earth would be a vastly different place—a place where the sword of Damocles hung above it by only the most slender thread, forever after.

How long, he wondered, could such a thread endure in a world filled with scissors?

Chapter NINE

Wally was the superstitious sort, and although he was always glad to have a little extra money for overtime, he wasn't eager to spend too much time in the museum after dark. There were too many life-size sculptures standing around on pedestals, and he always had the feeling that they only stopped moving the second he looked at them. Even the shadows in the galleries seemed like they didn't belong where they were. But when he'd received word, straight from President Dodds's office, to stay however long was needed to clean up the refuse left in the conservation wing, he couldn't very well say no. All afternoon, he'd heard the sounds of crates being ripped apart, floorboards being replaced, nails being hammered, and he didn't know what to expect when he finally did turn on the over-head lights.

Still, it wasn't this. The whole vast room blazed with twice the light it had had before; an entirely new bank of lights had been installed on the ceiling, up between the clerestory windows, and their beams were all trained on the center of the floor. There, all the easels and worktables that had previously cluttered the space had been shoved aside in order to make room for a raised platform made of reinforced steel and large enough to accommodate a Cadillac.

But that was no car on display.

It was a long box, like a coffin, but with a kind of peaked roof. It was made of white stone, and even from the doorway, he could see that there were images carved into its lid and sides.

If he'd had the willies before, he had them in spades now.

But he had his orders, and he could see that the workmen had left him plenty to do. There was sawdust all over the floor, and a pile of broken floorboards and pieces of what looked like a shipping crate were all piled up as if ready for a bonfire. Either the workers had been too lazy to clean up after themselves, or they'd wanted to get away from the damn thing as much as he did.

Unlocking the utility closet, he backed out the wheelbarrow, and, carefully averting his eyes from the coffin—or whatever the hell it was—started tossing the broken lumber, bent nails, and used excelsior into it. Even the floor was gummy, though, with something white and viscous. Nuts, he thought. It was going to take some elbow grease to get that crap off the floor.

After five or six trips to the refuse bins outside, he'd pretty much cleared away most of the trash. Stopping to catch a breath of the fresh night air, he happened to notice that one of the clerestory windows had been cracked open, and a sliver of light was gilding the tree branches. It looked a little like snow. Winter would be coming soon enough. For now, however, the air was simply cool and invigorating.

How they'd opened that window, without using the ladder and hooked pole still stashed in the closet, puzzled him. Closing it again was just one more thing he'd have to do before leaving for the night. God forbid it should rain.

Going back into the utility closet, he filled a bucket with hot water and ammonia. Whatever that gooey stuff on the floorboards was, it was sticking to his shoes, and it was sure to be a bitch to get off. Maybe it was some kind of glue they'd used in affixing the new boards. They sure as hell could have been more careful with it.

In fact, as he sloshed some water around and began working the mop, there seemed to be more of it around than there had been earlier. Was it seeping up again through the cracks? He stopped and bent over to see if the boards hadn't been aligned snugly enough, when another spot of it suddenly plopped down in front of him.

From above.

And then another—wet and slick as whitewash —splatted on the shoulder of his gray work shirt.

Shielding his eyes from the glare of the new lights, he looked up at the rafters of the room and saw something that looked like a little brown bird flit from one beam to another.

But then he heard the chittering, and he knew it wasn't birds up there. It was bats.

Good God. Now he could see that it wasn't just one or two, but dozens of them, some hanging upside down from the rafters, others spreading their leathery wings and looking for a perch of their own.

Damn—that's what happened when you left a window open, even a crack. Getting them out was going to be a nightmare.

And what if they wound up soiling this stone box on the platform? Considering all the trouble that had been gone to in installing the thing, it had to be awfully valuable, and Wally sure as shootin' didn't want any blame landing on his head if it got damaged. Bat droppings were highly acidic and would eat through anything. He'd seen what they'd done to the lawn furniture at the president's house.

Rummaging around in the closet, he found an old tarp that the painters had used the last time they'd touched up the trim in the galleries, dragged it out, and hauled it across the floor toward the chest. The bats were getting louder, and flitting back and forth. There was a corrugated metal ramp on one side of the platform, which must have been used to slide the box up and into place, but as Wally stepped onto it, a bat suddenly swooped down and whizzed over his head, so close he could swear that the tips of its wings had grazed his hair.

"God *damn*," he muttered, ducking down. Weren't bats supposed to have some kind of radar that kept them from bumping into things, much less people?

But he had no sooner straightened up to drape the tarp over the chest—the quicker he could get it covered, the quicker he could get out of there and leave the problem for the exterminators to solve—than another one dive-bombed him. This time its tiny claws actually snagged his sleeve before zooming away.

These bats were crazy! Maybe rabid. Wally threw the tarp over the top of the coffin, and without even looking to see where it landed, he whipped around to head for the exit. But his foot slipped on the guano, and he went down hard, cracking his forehead on the edge of the steel platform. Another bat shot down and nipped at his cheek, so fast that it was gone again before he even felt the blood dribbling down his skin. Stumbling to his feet, he knocked over the bucket, and a tide of hot water and ammonia spilled across the floor. Splashing through it, he covered his head with his arms and raced out into the galleries, but a flock of bats whirled around him, snatching at his clothes, his hair, his fingers.

Barely able to see where he was going, he just shoved the museum doors open with his shoulder, setting off an alarm, and staggered onto the fore-court, swinging his arms and looking for cover. He ran for the trees of Prospect Garden, where lanterns burned bright above the porte-cochere of the president's house. He would have screamed, but he was afraid to open his mouth for fear a bat might fly in there, too! His wet shoes crunched on the gravel, and his breath was hoarse in his throat. If he could just get into the house . . . but the bats were swarming all over him, like flies on dead meat, and no matter how hard he tried to fend them off, wheeling his arms, even plucking some from his shoulders and flinging them aside, there were always more—and they were relent-less.

He never saw the rock he tripped over, but somehow he flipped in midair and landed flat on his back. The air slammed out of his lungs and the bats came down on him like a hard brown rain, wings spread, claws distended, tiny fangs shining.

Minutes later, their work done, they rose again and spun off above the treetops of the garden, toward the gleaming white belfry of Nassau Hall, over the top of FitzRandolph Gate, and then down the moonlit, sleeping streets of the town, like heralds proclaiming the arrival of their king.

Chapter TEN

"What have you got now?" Delaney asked, and the ever-eager Andy Brandt, a young preceptor in the Anthropology Department, said, "Guess."

"I'm not an anthropologist," Delaney said, gingerly taking the tiny skull and peering at it this way and that. "Or a paleontologist, for that matter." Brandt also worked in Guyot Hall, but downstairs, on the main floor where the university displayed its eclectic collection of dinosaur bones and petrified artifacts gathered from expeditions all over the world.

He seemed to spend the bulk of his time, however, prowling the geophysics labs, and pestering Delaney. He was forever hanging around, antsy as a five-year-old, and asking as many questions.

"It's not from the dinosaur collection," Brandt reassured him, "if that's what you're worried about. It's from the mammal drawers."

Not much better, Delaney thought; Andy shouldn't be removing specimens from the collections at all. Shrugging, he said, "I don't know—maybe it's from an ancestor of the common cat. Or even a skunk. This is more your field than mine."

"But how old do you think it is?"

"Who cares?" he replied, though he knew full well what Brandt was getting at. He wanted Delaney to conduct another one of his experiments to determine the age of the specimen. If Brandt spent half as much time on his own research as he did poking his nose into Delaney's, he'd have a full professorship by now.

But Delaney wasn't interested in trying out his new process like it was some sort of game; he knew it could be extremely important, in ways that even he could not yet fully envision, and he wanted to make sure that every trial he did, every test he conducted, brought him closer to perfecting the technique. Although the research into radio isotopes and their relative rates of decay had begun in 1941 while Professor Willard Libby had been working at Princeton under a Guggenheim grant, Libby had since been recruited by Columbia, where he was now involved on a top-secret project. Consequently, it was up to Delaney to carry the torch.

Only the day before, he had been given direct orders, by an officer of the OSS, to do just that.

"So, what do you think?" Brandt asked, with an encouraging grin. "Can you do it?" With his perfect white teeth and his blond cowlick, he looked like a kid out of a Norman Rockwell painting.

"Do what?" Delaney said, pretending not to follow.

"Date it."

"Is this just another one of your fishing expeditions, or do you actually need this information for some valid, scientific purpose?"

"Scientific purpose," Andy said, trying to look suitably sincere. "Scout's honor."

For all Delaney knew, the kid still *was* an Eagle Scout. "Leave it on the counter," he said, "and if I have time, I'll run some tests."

Andy put it down next to the microscope, saying, "But let me know when you're doing them. I'd like to observe."

Given the chance, Delaney thought, he'd probably like to observe him shaving, too. In a way, it was flattering—Andy had plainly adopted him as his unofficial mentor—if only he could ignore the guy's pushiness.

As if sensing that he might have gone too far, Andy adopted a more casual tone, and said, "So, you heard about what happened last night at the art museum?"

"No. I've been too busy working." The implicit admonition was lost on Andy.

"The janitor was attacked by a flock of bats."

"What?"

"In the museum. The conservation wing."

"Jesus. Is he okay?"

Andy's fingers riffled idly through the mail

lying on the counter—including the OSS packet. "He's at the hospital in town."

"Leave those alone," Delaney said, moving the missives out of reach.

"Sure, sorry. But I hear it's not looking good. Might be rabies, might be something even worse."

Rabies could be bad enough. A boyhood friend had died of it. But bats, attacking a human *en masse*? And inside a campus building? It seemed impossible.

He hastily wrapped up his work, stashed most of his important papers in a double-wide green metal locker bolted to the wall, then ushered Andy out into the hall. Shutting the door after him, he said, "Don't take any more specimens out of the downstairs labs unless you first get permission from your department chair."

Andy gave him a mock salute and headed back to his department. Delaney rushed down the stairs and over to the art museum, wondering if Lucas had heard the news. The campus, always quiet between classes, was unusually so now, given the sparse enrollment. He saw almost no one, apart from a loiterer or two outside Fine Hall, where they were no doubt hoping to catch a glimpse of Einstein.

At the entrance to the museum, one of the university's campus police was standing guard with a walkie-talkie clipped to his lapel. "Sorry," he said, "the museum's closed for the day."

"I'm faculty," Delaney said, flashing his laminated ID card.

"Closed to everyone."

"And I have this," he added, drawing the OSS clearance letter from the inside pocket of his Windbreaker.

The proctor looked it over, but this decision was undoubtedly beyond his pay grade.

"I have to get started," Delaney said. "I'm expected in the conservation wing."

With some hesitation, the proctor let him pass, and Delaney made his way through the deserted galleries, lined with classical statuary, and into the European painting and fine arts galleries. Nowhere did he see any sign of a bat attack. Bursting through the rear door marked "Conservation: Authorized Personnel Only," he saw a janitor in gray coveralls bent over a bucket, wringing out a mop. "Excuse me," he said, "have you seen Professor Athan?"

Straightening up, the man said, "Last I noticed, he was mopping this floor."

Delaney looked appropriately bemused. "Since when did you join the custodial staff?"

"Somebody had to do it," Lucas said, glad to have the company. "Security's so tight now, only I could get in." He'd been at it for an hour, and his back was as tight as a drum. "In fact, how the hell did you manage it?"

"You forget," Delaney replied, waving the OSS letter. "I'm on this job, too."

"So you've met with the charming Colonel Macmillan?"

"Right after you did. The seat was still warm." He looked around the room. "I heard about what happened last night, but I still can't believe it."

"Nobody can. There were exterminators in here earlier to give us the all-clear, and even they said they'd never heard of anything like it."

"I hope that Wally pulls through okay."

Lucas nodded in agreement and gestured at the tarp loosely draped over something large mounted in the middle of the room. "That damn thing has brought nothing but bad luck everywhere it's gone."

"What do you mean?"

He tapped his eye patch and said, "This happened about a minute after I'd found it."

"I didn't know."

"How could you?" Lucas hadn't told him the whole story, nor had he mentioned the German boy blown to bits, or Private Toussaint, who had lost a leg. Or, for that matter, the ship that had almost been sunk transporting it to the United States; he'd noted the name of the USS Seward on the transportation papers.

"All I've seen so far is a faint photograph. You want to show me what all the fuss has been about?"

Lucas couldn't think of any reason to refuse, but at the same time he could hardly bear to expose the ossuary. The whole time he'd been cleaning up in the conservation room, he'd done his level best to avert his eyes from the hulking shape beneath the tarp. He had hoped never to see the thing again, and now, here it was, not only deposited on his doorstep, but requiring his diligent study.

Leaning the mop against the wall, Lucas stepped to the platform and took hold of the tarp. What was he so afraid of? It was just a box of bones. Taking a deep breath, and with a grand gesture like a magician completing a trick, he pulled the tarp away. "Behold . . . the eighth wonder of the world."

The photo hadn't done it justice, nor had his own memories. A great white chest—calcite alabaster, if he had to guess—its gabled roof and elaborate carvings had been largely worn away by time. But it was clear that a lot of trouble had been gone to in order to create this thing, and there was something that was still unnervingly potent about it.

"I found it at the bottom of an iron mine outside Strasbourg. Thirty seconds later, a land mine went off, and I was flying through the air. When I came to, I was bumping along in the back of an army ambulance." Only the mayor, standing outside the ring of ore carts, had been spared.

He'd applied the tourniquet to Toussaint's leg and come to their rescue.

Delaney stepped up the ramp and ran his finger over the smooth surface of the lid. "Why's it so damn cold?"

"Isn't that more your department?" Lucas replied, touching the ossuary himself. The stone *was* cold, colder than the ambient temperature of the room, and what little he could make out of the figures was confusing. On one side of the lid, it looked like a shepherd with a staff, herding animals, presumably sheep, but on the other side, the figure looked more like a monkey, with long arms dangling down and a curled-up tail. Words and symbols, some of which resembled Egyptian hieroglyphs, had been incised into the sides of the stone. One looked like a diamond tilted on its axis.

To top it all off, the box had been bound shut with several crudely wrought iron chains. Cutting through them, Lucas thought, was not going to be easy.

"You know what's inside it?" Delaney asked.

"Bones, for sure. But maybe something else, too. Coins, jewelry. Judging from the glyphs, this one's probably Egyptian. But ossuaries found in the Roman catacombs have contained everything from the occupant's cosmetic tools to her house cat."

"We're going to need a blowtorch or a hacksaw to get these chains removed."

"I've already put in a request to the campus maintenance department."

Lucas's instructions from Colonel Macmillan had been to gauge the age and origins of the box, employing Delaney's latest research into radio isotopes wherever useful. Any organic remains inside would be especially susceptible to his techniques. But he could see, just from the expression behind Delaney's scruffy beard, that something was bothering him. "You okay?"

"Yeah, sure," Delaney said, though he had promptly removed his hand from the cold stone. "I just had kind of a weird feeling."

"Of what?" It was comforting to Lucas to hear that someone else felt it, too.

"The calm before the storm. When I was growing up in the Midwest, you could always tell when a tornado was brewing. The air would get really still, the birds would stop singing, and the sky . . . the sky would turn this kind of sickly green." He rubbed his fingers together, as if to remove any residue from the stone.

"How much of a sample are you going to need?" Lucas asked, and it took Delaney several seconds to refocus. "To do your carbon-14 tests?"

"Oh, right—not much. Just a sliver or two of bone, whatever you can spare. Desiccated flesh, too, if there's anything left of it."

"There probably won't be much. Traditionally, corpses in northern Africa and the Middle East were first thrown into a ditch and left there for wild animals and the elements to strip away all the meat. When only the skeleton remained, the pieces were picked up—the skull most importantly—and consigned to the box. You should have plenty of bones to choose from, especially given the royal treatment these remains received."

"Do you mean that literally?" Delaney asked. "Was this the sarcophagus of a king?"

"Hard to say. There're a lot of markings on it— a lot more than you usually see on these things, so I've got my work cut out for me."

"I see a monograph getting written, with full tenure not far behind."

"Not likely," Lucas replied. "The OSS will never let this project become public knowledge. I'll be lucky if they don't bury me with it."

Delaney nodded, turned away, and stepped down the ramp. "Got a precept to lead. Thanks for the tour."

But even if he hadn't had a class to teach, Lucas could tell he was eager to leave. So was Lucas, though he found himself riveted for several more minutes, examining the bizarre markings. Then he picked up the tarp, and though there was no real reason to cover it up again, threw it over the ossuary. Retrieving the mop, he hastily wiped up the remaining mess on the floor, got out of the janitor's coveralls, and made for the exit himself.

When he closed the door behind him, he leaned his back against it, face tilted toward the ceiling, and deeply exhaled. But he couldn't shake the feeling, completely irrational, that something else was breathing, too, right on the other side.

Chapter ELEVEN

"Another?" the bartender asked, and Lucas just raised one finger from the glass to say yes.

The bartender poured him another double on the rocks, and Lucas pressed the cold glass to the spot on his forehead where the shrapnel had hit, rolling it back and forth across his skin. Sometimes the pain was sharp but brief, and other times, like tonight, it was a dull ache that no amount of aspirin could touch. All he could do was try to numb the sensation. Catching a glimpse of himself in the mirror that backed the bottles on display behind the bar, he saw a guy slumped on a stool, with a black patch over one eye, rocking a glass of scotch against his head, and it was clear why the stools on either side of him were conspicuously empty.

It had taken longer than he expected to get things cleaned up in the conservation wing, and once he had, he'd stopped by the hospital to check on the janitor. The nurse at the front desk told him that only immediate family were allowed to visit, but she didn't look, or sound, sanguine about Wally's prospects. That's when the pounding in his head had started up again.

Benny Goodman was playing on the jukebox, and the lights were low. If he went home to Mrs. Caputo's, she'd fuss over him, and Amy would try to read him her latest book report. All he wanted now was peace and solitude.

Which was why he was surprised, and not altogether pleased, when he heard the door open and close and sensed a woman had taken the stool just two seats over. He stared down into his glass as she ordered a Campari and soda, and only glanced up at the mirror again after the bartender had delivered it.

His gaze was met by a pair of dark eyes staring directly back at him. Startled, he looked down again. Christ, the last thing he needed was someone chatting him up, and, inevitably, asking him where he'd served in the war. But why, he wondered, did she look familiar?

Benny Goodman was replaced by Tommy Dorsey before he risked another glance at the mirror. Even as he did so, she was swiveling on her stool and saying, "Excuse me, but aren't you Professor Athan?" It sure sounded like she already knew the answer.

He had to turn his head completely in order to see her with his good eye. She was a dark-haired beauty with a tawny complexion, wearing a crisp white blouse under a tweedy jacket.

"Yes."

"Then allow me to introduce myself," she said in an accent that bespoke Oxford or Cambridge. "My name is Simone Rashid."

She stretched her hand across the empty stool, and he shook it. And now he did place her: she'd been at the art museum with the older man. "I've come a long way to meet you."

A long way to meet him? "Why?" he said, genuinely perplexed.

"May I?" she said, moving to the stool beside him.

But this wasn't really a question either, as she was already settling in.

"We're in the same general field," she said. "Antiquities."

"I'm not a dealer," he said, "if that's what you mean. I'm just a professor—an associate professor at that—at the university."

"Yes, I'm aware of that. But I've done a bit of research—that's my forte, to be honest—and I see you're also one of the leading lights in Greco-Roman art."

"Are you a college recruiter?" he said, having met one or two in his time. "Because I'm perfectly happy here, and I have no plans to leave." Not that the OSS would let him leave even if he wanted to.

"Hardly," she said, taking a moment to sip her drink. "I work for the Egyptian Ministry of Culture. In Cairo."

This was getting odder by the minute, though he caught the first glimmer of what it all might be about. He pictured the glyphs on the ossuary.

"I also know that you were assigned to the Cultural Recovery Commission."

Now it was coming into even greater focus. But he would not, could not, give anything away, so he waited her out.

"And that you're probably working for them still," she said with a half smile. "How am I doing so far?"

"So far," he conceded, "you haven't struck out."

"I don't know exactly what that refers to," she replied. "Baseball, I presume? But it sounds as if I'm on the right track."

"What is it you want from me?" The throbbing in his head returned, but he left his chilled glass on the bar.

"I think you know," she said, but when he gave no indication that he did, she added, "A certain artifact has recently been transported here. An artifact that belongs to me."

"To you?" He raised a brow.

"My father and I were the ones who found it."

Lucas had been under the impression that he was the one who had found it. "So that means you own it?"

"It means that it belongs to the Egyptian people."

"That might not be how everyone sees it."

"You mean the Third Reich?" she said, dismissively. "Well, they wouldn't, would they?"

"I mean the United States."

"But do you intend to keep it?"

Lucas did not know the answer to that one, nor was he immune to the issues inherent in cultural appropriation—no Greek who had ever seen the Elgin Marbles adorning a wing of the British Museum instead of the Parthenon from which they had been stripped was unfamiliar with the feeling. But he still had no idea who this woman really was.

"Conceding absolutely nothing," he said, even his empty eye socket throbbing now, "I still don't know what you're getting at. Are you here to reclaim the artifact in question?"

"Eventually," she said, "yes. But given the state of the world right now, it *is* probably for the best that it's here right now. For safekeeping."

"Safekeeping," he repeated.

"And further study."

She sipped her drink, and he took a slug from his own. He liked this bar, but it looked like he'd have to find a new place.

"I doubt you even know what you have," she said.

"And you do?"

"Yes."

"Then why don't you tell me."

"In good time, once you've learned to trust me."

She was spot-on there.

"Right now, it's essential that you understand just one thing."

He waited.

"It's more than what it seems. Much more."

"What isn't?"

"Now you're being glib. Don't be. That box holds secrets you can't even guess at."

Whoever she was, he was beginning to think she was unhinged. And for that matter, what proof had she shown that she worked for the Egyptian ministry? For all he knew, she was an Axis spy. Throwing back the last of his drink, he tossed a couple of bills on the bar and slipped off his stool.

"Look, Mrs. Rashid—"

"Miss Rashid, not that it's of any consequence."

"Miss Rashid. I'm just a lowly professor, and the work I do is nowhere near as glamorous as you seem to think."

"You need my help," she said, pinning him with her gaze.

And God help him, but that look prodded awake something in him that had lain dormant for a long time. Something that had nothing whatsoever to do with ancient artifacts.

"You can find me at the Nassau Inn," she said. "You will want to."

Picking up his briefcase, he headed for the door. "If you open that sarcophagus without me," he heard her call out as the door was easing shut behind him, "you will live to regret it."

Chapter TWELVE

Well, Simone thought, swiveling her stool back toward the bar, that didn't go as well as she'd hoped. She should have relied more upon her feminine wiles—she had noted a certain glimmer in his one good eye, and, truth be told, she might have responded to it under different circumstances than these—but it was too late now.

She took a hearty swallow of her Campari and smoothed her skirt over her lap.

The bartender studiously attended to wiping some glasses clean.

She knew she had no one but herself to blame. Despite her intelligence and vast erudition, she had never mastered the gentle art of persuasion. While there might be some people who were natural diplomats, she wasn't one of them. She was forever butting heads with people, challenging them when she should have been convincing them, raising hackles where she should have been raising support. She had always been in a hurry, without always knowing where she wanted to go; she was too impatient to wait for the right time or the right confluence of events.

And she had inherited her late mother's temper. Everyone said so, most notably her long-suffering father: "If your mother were here today, you'd finally have an even match."

But without that inborn obstinacy, who knew if the ossuary, now resting only a short walk away, would ever have been uncovered? When her father had first found the ancient papyrus scroll in the storeroom of the Cairo Museum—one of the many papyri that had been ignominiously deposited in the genizah, the refuse pile of fragments and faded scraps that no one thought important—he had been unable to persuade anyone of the magnitude of his find.

"That's very interesting," the director of the national library had said, patting him on the shoulder. "We'll be sure to follow up on that one day, Dr. Rashid."

And when he'd tried to acquire funding from the Ministry of Culture in order to launch an expedition, he hit the same brick wall. The fact that Simone had recently landed a job there only made things worse; she'd had to recuse herself from any deliberations lest it look like nepotism.

"Can't you see that my father might have found the true tomb of Saint Anthony the Anchorite?" she had declared at the one board meeting she had been allowed to attend, under a vow of silence that she'd failed to honor. "For nearly two thousand years, penitents and worshippers from all over the world have been making pilgrimages to an empty tomb in the desert monastery at Al-Qalzam."

"We don't know that it's empty," the minister said.

"Of course we do," Simone had insisted. "We've done the ground tests. We only keep this myth alive to keep the tourists coming."

The minister shot her a warning glance—but she had built up such a head of steam that there was no stopping her.

"Our country should be proud, rightly proud, of Saint Anthony," she said, rising from her chair. "Not only did he found the entire Christian ascetic theology, he defied a Roman emperor and prevailed. He came to the aid of persecuted Christians and led the fight against the Arian heresy. Without him, there would be no tradition of monasticism in the church."

"Yes, Miss Rashid, we all understand the saint's importance."

"So then why don't you all want to find his actual sepulcher?" She waved a copy of the monograph that she and her father had written, in which they had outlined their theory and even marked a possible route to the tomb. "Doesn't the truth interest any of you?"

And that's when she'd been ejected, under threat

of losing her job altogether. It's also when she had decided to cash in some of her considerable resources and use the money to finance the expedition herself. Her father, though, had been torn between his determination to find the tomb and the dangers such a mission might pose to his daughter's career.

"For me, it doesn't matter so much," he said, trying to sound resigned. "I'm an old man."

"You're hardly an old man."

"Old enough," he'd replied. "But you are just at the beginning of your career. You do not want to offend the powers that be. Life is a hard journey, with many unexpected setbacks," he said, and she knew he was thinking that if he'd played the game better, he'd have been appointed the head of the ministry himself, long ago. "You do not want to make enemies along the way, as I did."

"We are defined as much by our enemies as we are by our friends," she'd retorted, and her father had turned up his palms in defeat, as he often did when they had an argument.

"You are cut from the same cloth as your mother," he said.

"And as you."

Within a matter of weeks, she had assembled a skeleton crew of drivers, bearers, and a Bedouin guide to take them where they would need to go—the Sahara el Beyda, or White Desert, a vast and largely uncharted section of wasteland that began fifty miles southeast of Cairo. Simone and her father had traced the location of the tomb by laboriously piecing together the shreds of the scroll that had been mixed in, rather inexplicably, with a clutch of Hebrew fragments recovered long ago from the storeroom of the Ben Ezra Synagogue in Fustat. The document, rendered in early Arabic, indicated that the monk Saint Anthony—perhaps the most famous hermit in the whole Christian canon—had been buried in a secret cavern under a "spitting cobra." Plainly, no real snake could be expected to remain in one place, much less mark a spot for eternity. But Simone knew that the ancient limestone and chalk of the Sahara, which had once comprised the bed of a prehistoric sea and which lent the region its distinctive name, had been scoured by the winds of millennia into fantastic rock formations that resembled everything from teapots to minarets.

There would even be one, she strongly suspected, that looked like a spitting cobra, and if the document was true, it was located within a single day's camel ride, due west, from the oasis at Baharīya.

The first leg of the trip was made in jeeps, carrying supplies and provisions, over the almost impassable road that followed the meanderings of a primitive camel track. But once they had reached the oasis, the jeeps could go no farther. There was not even a semblance of a road, and the sand dunes would only engulf the tires if they tried to drive any farther. Simone stretched out under the stars and palm fronds that night, while her father slept in the back of the jeep. For hours, as the others snored and slept around her, she could barely close her eyes, so eager was she to get up with the dawn and begin the search for the cobra rock and the sepulcher that the ragged scroll said lay beneath. The discovery be a vindication of her father's work, a laurel wreath to crown his career, and at the same time a brilliant start to her own.

The stars were so thick in the sky that she could not even begin to find the most elementary constellations. They were like a million glistening grains of sugar on a black velvet cloth, and the waning moon shone like a Saracen's blade. Occasionally, she heard the furtive movement of the little desert foxes, sniffing the dying smoke from the fire, poking their noses into the encampment, once or twice snatching some bit of refuse and scurrying back into the blackness. It was as peaceful and beautiful a night as she could ever have imagined, and she understood what drew the Bedouins to this barren place and kept them there.

When the sun rose, the distant rocks took on the most magnificent hues—the peachy gold and pale strawberry and pistachio green of ice cream—and Simone was quick to mount a camel and, with spurs and a riding crop, urge it on.

"The rocks aren't going anywhere," their teenage guide, Mustafa, warned her from the back of his own lumbering beast. "If you push him too hard, he'll dig in his heels."

Simone's father, bringing up the rear, laughed. "They're a perfect match then."

Simone smiled, but kept up the pace. The orange sand gave way to ground as white as snow, covered with a powdery chalk, and as she entered the field of rocks, some as big as locomotives, others the size of dogs and cats, she marveled at the variety of shapes they had assumed. It was like an enormous menagerie, miles long and miles wide, of real, and mythical, creatures. One rock looked like a sphinx with its paws extended; another like a heron about to take flight. And the wind, which had sculpted them, continued its incessant battering, knocking Simone's hat off her head more than once and making the sleeves of her khaki shirt ripple like waves.

But she had yet to see a formation that resembled a rearing cobra. Mushrooms, yes—the wind had a way of scrubbing the bottoms of the rocks more harshly than the top, leaving what looked like a crop of enormous, teetering toadstools; acres of them surrounded her. But the papyrus was old, and perhaps this particular formation, which had once resembled a snake, had been reduced to dust by now. Somehow, in her haste, she had not considered how hard it might be to spot one fanciful shape among a battalion of others. She wished that the papyrus had been more explicit. While it had extolled the bravery of the sainted monk who had gone, alone, into the wilderness and wrestled there with demons—legend had it that Anthony had even broken the tail off of one, before strangling it with his bare hands—the scroll did not provide directions, and the compass had not yet been invented in Saint Anthony's time.

Born into a prosperous family in the upper Egypt town of Coma in 251 AD, Anthony was orphaned at eighteen, and took the words of the Lord to heart: "If you want to be perfect, go and sell all you have and give the money to the poor—you will have riches in Heaven." In obedience, he sold off everything he owned, including a vast herd of swine, and gave the money away. Then he deposited his sister with a community of nuns and wandered off to live alone in the barren desert, where his only companions were the snakes and scorpions, hawks and foxes.

But after years of solitude and self-abnegation, his fame began to spread, and soon enough, pilgrims were flocking to the cave where he had taken up residence, bringing him tribute of everything from animals to incense. Some were searching for spiritual guidance, others for more practical help. His natural poultices and remedies, made from the roots and brambles found in the arid soil, were said to cure many ills. He was especially known for treating skin afflictions, often with an application of pork fat, and as a result, he had come to be associated with such skin diseases as eczema and the eponymous Saint Anthony's fire. Pigs became a symbol of his ministry, and in religious iconography he was generally portrayed as a swineherd, with a tau— T-shaped—cross in his hand.

Exactly what Simone hoped to find in the tomb, she wasn't sure. It would not be riches; that was for certain. This was no Pharaoh. What she was looking for was the truth—proof that the man had lived, and died, as the Holy Scriptures said. Proof that the ancient stories weren't just that— stories—and that there might be something more to this world than met the eye. For all her education and worldliness, Simone had a streak of the speculative in her. No girl brought up in the mighty delta of Egypt, where three of the major faiths had taken root, where the pyramids of kings had weathered sandstorms and floods for thousands of years, where seas had reputedly parted and prophets walked, could be without it. Even her mother, known for her wild ways, had become, particularly later in life as the cancer ate away at her, devoutly Catholic, and some of that, too, had been imparted to the young and impressionable Simone. What was it Cardinal

Newman had once said? "If I have them at six, I have them for life." Something like that. But Simone wasn't of any one faith; she was simply a seeker, a scholar of the unseen and the ineffable as much as of the known and empirical world. In the undiscovered tomb of a saint, she hoped to find a mixture of both.

As the day waned, and the camels' energy flagged, she knew that she must be close to reaching her goal. The scroll had said a full day's ride, and now she had done it. The towering rocks cast deep and long shadows across the chalky ground. She was reminded of wandering through the Wolvercote Cemetery in Oxford, back when she was at school there, and finding herself surrounded at dusk by the crumbling headstones and marble angels on every side. She had been visited not by a sensation of fear, or even dread, but of being a pilgrim in some alien landscape, somewhere altogether strange and unworldly. The surface of the moon, she felt certain, would bear a close resemblance to the place she was in now.

"It's getting too dark to see," her father said in a weary voice. "And the camels can go no farther."

"Neither can I," said Mustafa, pulling back on the reins, then sliding down from the saddle blanket to the ground. "We'll have to look for this cobra in the morning." He did not sound optimistic.

But Simone was reluctant to give up. Dismounting,

she left the others to set up camp as she wandered across the rough and uneven terrain. Several times her boots slipped on the sand or chalk, and she fell to her knees. Each time, she got up, brushed the grit from her pants, and continued her search. The sun, as bright and round as a tangerine, slid below the horizon, and she removed the flashlight from her belt and aimed its beam at each configuration she came across.

So far, nothing looked remotely like a snake.

"Simone, where are you?" she heard her father call. "You're going to get lost out there."

She could smell the fire that Mustafa must have started, and hear the crackling of the wood. The sounds and scents were carried like gifts on the desert wind.

It was then, just as she was turning back toward the camp, that the light revealed an opening in the ground—the entrance to a cave, with jagged stones that looked like teeth, but big enough that a man could pass through it if he took the precaution of ducking his head. She slowly raised the beam of her flashlight, and even as she did so, she saw what resembled the coils of a giant snake and, rising above them, as if in keeping with the joy rising in her breast, a spindly neck topped with a broad, flat head shaped like a spade. Where there might have been a flicking tongue, there was even a sharp protuberance of stone.

If this was not the spitting cobra, nothing was.

She tried to cry out, but her throat was so parched that only a croak emerged. She took a swig from her canteen, wiped the dust from her face with another splash, then shouted, "Here! It's here!"

But they must not have heard her.

She had to stumble back toward the camp, guided by the smell of the burning wood as much as by the flickering glow of the small fire. She dropped beside the tent in which her father was lighting the kerosene lamp.

"I found it!" she said. "I found it."

"Where?" he asked, just as Mustafa came back from feeding the camels.

"She found it?" Mustafa exclaimed. "A girl? I don't believe it."

Simone nodded vigorously, and it was decided that they would eat some goat stew and drink some tea, get a good night's sleep, and explore the cave first thing in the morning.

It was the longest night she had ever spent.

By dawn, Simone was dressed and ready, hurrying Mustafa and her father through their rudimentary breakfast, and leading them back to the gigantic cobra rock. In the first light of day, the white stone took on a golden hue, while the entrance at its base, still in shadow, remained as black as pitch. Crouching down, though she hardly needed to, Simone entered first, playing her flashlight beam around the immediate interior.

There was a narrow slope, easily navigable, leading down to a floor of smooth white sand. Mustafa followed right behind her, and her father, holding the lantern aloft, brought up the rear. Once they had all arrived at the bottom, Dr. Rashid held up the lamp, turning slowly in place, and the whole cavern suddenly resembled the mouth of some monstrous beast, with thousands upon thousands of stalactites, some small and needle-sharp, others blunt and wide, hanging like teeth from the ceiling.

"My God," Simone said, "I feel like Jonah."

"Allah be with us," Mustafa murmured. For a kid more given to wisecracks than reverence, it was a testament to the power of their surroundings.

"More proof," Dr. Rashid intoned, his words echoing around the limestone walls, "that an ocean was here many millions of years ago."

Simone didn't know where to look first—everywhere the stone had been carved into preposterous configurations, rippling waves and swirling spirals. The amber walls resembled folded draperies, in some places vertically lined and striated, and in others laid horizontally so that the flowstone looked like sheets stacked in a linen closet. But even a quick survey of the vast interior revealed one troubling thing: there was no sign of a proper sepulcher, much less a sarcophagus.

Could the genizah fragments have been right about so much, but wrong about this? Or was it possible that the tomb had been discovered, and plundered, a thousand years ago?

Simone made a grand circuit of the cavern, aiming her flashlight into every nook and cranny, in search of a passageway that might lead to a chamber beyond. She had just about given up, when a slight gust of air—cooler even than the air in the cave—brushed across her cheek. She stepped back, felt the breeze again ruffle the hair of her brow, and examined the spot more closely.

The countless ages of seepage and erosion had lent the wall the appearance of a waterfall, a veiled cascade behind which she could now see that there was a space, invisible from the front, but opening behind amply wide to admit passage. Best of all, she could see, at the very limit of the flashlight beam, traces of a figure incised against the far wall.

"It is very beautiful," Mustafa was saying, "but I think we have come a long way on a fool's errand. Ali Baba never lived here."

"Don't be so sure," Simone said, waving them over. "Look at this!"

The two men joined her, Dr. Rashid extending the lantern into the tunnel. The walls here had been planed smooth, and either the stone had been exceptionally pale to begin with, or it had been whitewashed long ago. Simone dug a fingernail into it, and a flake of paint crumbled away. The stone beneath was more of a dull yellow.

Her heart sang.

Though the roof of the tunnel was low, it had been scoured almost entirely clean of the dangling stalactites—only a few had grown back to the length of daggers—and its width was more than sufficient to admit any kind of altar, sarcophagus, or ornament the builders of a tomb might have wanted to install. She moved carefully, stopping to examine the figure she had seen incised in the rock. Though much eroded by time, it was unmistakably a pig.

The saint's patron animal.

If she had found a diamond necklace there, she could not have been any happier.

"Is there still any doubt?" she crowed, letting the flashlight linger on the image.

The tunnel made an elbow turn to the right, and then another, sharply to the left, before it debouched into a vaulted chamber with a high roof, carved like a cupola, and smooth, sloping walls, which had also been whitewashed. Though large patches of the paint had long since fallen away or discolored, there were pictures daubed all around the rim of the ceiling, in blue and gold, depicting in rudimentary fashion events from the life of the saint. In one, he led, with his distinctive staff, a herd of swine; in another, he appeared with a halo before a figure on a throne, no doubt depicting his intercession with the Roman Emperor Diocletian, in defense of the early Christian martyrs. Behind the emperor's head, almost as if it were whispering in his ear, hovered a winged black insect. Simone had never seen an image quite so strange.

As for the rest of the artwork, it was almost as if another hand had interceded. These pictures were more crudely drawn and rendered only in black and red; the people and animals were drawn like a child's stick figures, and some of the scenes were even superimposed upon the others. All of them shared, however, a theme of violence and horror. Writhing pigs roasting on spits; the saint himself being torn to pieces by horned demons; skeletons with blood erupting from their bones. Was this last conceit a way of depicting death by a virulent skin disease? If so, it was odd, as the ministrations of Saint Anthony were supposed to be proof *against* such ailments.

"It's in the corner," she heard her father say, his voice filled with awe. "There. The ossuary."

Tearing her eyes away from the troubling scenes above, Simone followed the glow of the lantern light to the farthest reach of the chamber, where a deep niche had been carved into the stone. In the ancient Hebrew tradition, kept by the Christians to come, these niches were called a *kokh*; in Latin a *loculus*. This one was arched, and held, on its ledge, a pair of red clay urns.

One of them had lost its top, and Simone could make out the tip of a tightly rolled papyrus scroll inside. Her fingers itched to open it.

The real prize—an alabaster chest, with iron chains securing its ponderous lid to its lower portion—lay between the urns. It was no surprise she hadn't seen it at first. The box was not only nestled as far into the niche as it could go, it seemed also to reside in a deeper and darker pool of shadow than was natural. It was almost as if it could disappear before one's very eyes.

Even for someone accustomed to the mysteries of ancient artifacts, the ossuary cast a spell all its own. For the first time in her life, Simone felt an involuntary shudder run down her spine.

But Mustafa was plainly unaffected. Sensing there might still be some loot here, he scurried toward the urns, knocked the top off the sealed one, and glanced inside.

"More papers!" he declared in disgust. Then he went for the box. "What's inside it?" he cried out enthusiastically, his voice booming around the otherwise empty chamber. Tugging at the chains, he said, "How do we get it open?"

"We don't," Simone replied. "Stop trying."

"This is not a treasure hunt," Dr. Rashid declared, bringing the lantern closer. "It's an archaeological expedition."

The distinction seemed to be lost on the young guide, who looked from Simone to her father, desperately awaiting a better explanation.

"We're not in the Valley of the Kings," Simone said. "This casket won't hold golden masks or silver goblets. It holds bones."

"That's all?" Mustafa said. "Papers and bones? And we came all this way?" He stalked off, muttering, "The worst jobs—I always get the worst jobs."

Simone bent her head toward the ossuary, where she could see in the lantern light a host of markings and inscriptions. It would be the work of many months—happy months, and maybe even longer—to decipher them all. Of one thing she was confident—she had found the tomb of Saint Anthony of Egypt, the reputed father of Christian monasticism, and battler of the demonic hordes sent to torture him and test his faith. Who knew what else the scrolls might be able to tell her?

Glancing up again at the pictures on the ceiling, she could almost believe that the cruder, crueler scenes had been scrawled there by those demons themselves.

Something else struck her as odd, too.

She could swear that in the picture of the saint being rent limb from limb, Anthony had been standing; now, he was prone on the ground, and a gibbering creature, like a monkey with a forked tail, was leaping on his back.

Instead of the Emperor Diocletian sitting on the

throne, the seat was occupied by a grinning dog—or maybe it was meant to be a hyena—wearing a crown and holding a scepter.

Even stranger were the birds—flocks of little black birds—painted all across the white walls, and even the ceiling, of the chamber. Before she could ask her father, she saw that he, too, was staring at the birds, perturbed.

"Were they there," Simone said, "before?"

Then they moved—not flying, but crawling, like insects more than sparrows. Creeping out from the crevices in the flowstone. Emerging from the sand.

Scorpions.

Dozens of them—hundreds—their lethal stinging tails quivering and erect. The single greatest scorpion colony Simone could ever have imagined —lying here, perhaps undisturbed for millennia.

A scream reverberated from the antechamber. Mustafa shouted, "Get them off of me! Help me! Get them off!"

Simone straightened up and ran back toward the tunnel, feeling the crunch of brittle carapaces under her boots. She could hear her father right behind her, but then he stumbled and fell, nearly knocking her over, too. He had gashed his leg on a jagged rock, and even as she helped him to his feet, Mustafa's screams got louder.

Something dropped from the ceiling onto Simone's hair, and a pincer nipped at her fingers as she brushed it off.

Grabbing the lantern with one hand and using the other to hold her hobbled father by his elbow, she moved down the tunnel, first right, then left, then into the front cavern, where Mustafa was all but unrecognizable. He rolled around on the floor of the cave beneath a seething swarm of scorpions. His arms flailed, his legs kicked out, and one of his sandals flew off his foot and over her head.

"Stop them! Stop them!" Mustafa screamed, but Simone couldn't do anything to help him without letting go of her father, who was already leaning hard against her shoulder, and breathing even harder; she needed to get him out of the cave before he collapsed. She swung the lantern over Mustafa's body as she passed by, hoping to knock loose at least a few of the creatures, and she stamped her boots on several more, but her father's feet were dragging in the sand, and his weight was becoming too much for her to bear.

Mustafa's hand lashed out and clutched at her ankle, but another scorpion promptly plunged its stinger into his wrist, and he yanked it away.

Dropping the lantern at the bottom of the ramp, she crawled up toward the mouth of the cave, pulling her father alongside. It was like dragging a bag of wet cement. The entrance was filled with the golden light of the morning sun, and Simone forced herself to stare into the blinding light—willed herself, step by step, to move toward it—until she suddenly emerged from the cave, feeling like some small fish that had wriggled free from the jaws of a crocodile. Her father fell in a heap on the sand, croaking for water. Blood was running down his leg.

She put her canteen to his lips. And then she turned back toward the entrance.

"No, no," Dr. Rashid said, alarmed, the brackish water dribbling down his chin. "It's too late."

She had to try. She ducked back into the grotto, and aimed her flashlight into the antechamber of the tomb. She did not need to go any farther to see that Mustafa was lying dead— no one could have survived such a monstrous attack. The sight was obscene, and she knew she would never be able to forget it, or forgive herself. His body lay sprawled facedown on the sand, as dozens of the scorpions, some with their tails still coiled and pincers extended, roamed around on top of him, for all the world as if they were dancing in celebration of their kill.

One, still in attack mode, scuttled threateningly toward the toe of Simone's boot, and she smashed it underfoot, grinding its hard shell into dust; she had to scrape her sole against a rock to get rid of its sticky residue, and even then, the deadly tail shook in a final reflex of fury.

When she came back for the sarcophagus and the urns—as she knew she would do—she would bring a flame thrower.

Chapter THIRTEEN

Even though it was the dead of night, a light was on across the street, on the first floor of Einstein's house. Lucas lit another cigarette and wondered if someone else simply had insomnia, or if some great breakthrough in humanity's fundamental understanding of the universe was unfolding in there instead.

Here, on the porch steps of Mrs. Caputo's house, he had his own, if less earthshaking, problems to wrestle with.

He had gone to bed earlier, but given up on sleep after a couple of hours of restless tossing and turning. His room under the eaves was stuffy, and he'd come outside to enjoy what might be the last breeze of an Indian summer. In the faint glow of the lone streetlamp at the corner, he could see the leaves falling from the boughs and rustling along the otherwise silent street. He took a drag on his Camel, leaned back on his elbows, and for the hundredth time, replayed his encounter at the bar with the woman named Simone.

What had she meant by her parting shot, the one about how he'd regret opening the box without her help? Who was she, really? And what did she know?

Even more to the point, why had he been so quick to dismiss her? Was it from an abundance of natural caution, an all-important consideration these days? Loose lips sink ships, and all that. Or was it for some less noble reason? Was it because something he'd been trying to deny or stifle for years now, ever since he had been inducted and sent overseas, had been inadvertently stirred? Was it really as elementary as that?

A black De Soto drove by slowly, its headlights illuminating a tabby cat skittering across the road.

The cat reminded him of a figure etched into the stone of the sarcophagus. A typical depiction of the feline Egyptian deity, Bast. Did that confirm his own suspicion that the box had originated in Egypt, as Simone claimed? He might have agreed, were it not for the other inscriptions chiseled into the alabaster. They were a total hodgepodge of hieroglyphics, Greek and Latin letters, and arcane symbols, including the faint shape of a diamond tilted on its axis. He had never seen, or heard of, such a composite.

Nor had he ever encountered a collection of such curious figurative representations. There was a shepherd with his staff, but his flock, if that's what it was, looked less like sheep than a bunch of frolicking apes. What were they doing there? There were even a couple of dozen scratches— long grooves—that looked as if they must have been left by some careless artisan, or else by some wild animal that had been trying to claw its way into the box. But as ossuaries never contained fresh meat, only barren bones, why would any animal have tried such a thing?

Across the street, Lucas saw a pair of muslin draperies billow out of the open window and the silhouette of a man drawing them back inside, then lowering the sash. The breeze carried the screech from the old wooden frame.

The light went out, and another one went on over the porch.

The De Soto he had seen before—judging from its distinctive waterfall grille, a '41, the last year American cars were manufactured before all the assembly lines had gone over to the war effort—doubled back, and then parked, motor still run-ning, outside Einstein's house.

Before he could wonder what was going on at this hour of the night, he heard the sound of footsteps approaching, and saw a man in work clothes and a Windbreaker turning up the short cement walkway to the boardinghouse. His head was down, and his feet dragged.

"You must be Mr. Taylor," Lucas said, keeping his voice down.

The man, startled, stopped in his tracks and looked up. "Who're you?" he asked, though Lucas had the feeling he was feigning ignorance.

"Lucas Athan," he said, leaning forward and extending his hand. "I live up in the attic."

"Oh, right," Taylor said, though he still didn't shake, and Lucas let his hand drop.

"Working the night shift?"

For a second, Taylor—a guy about forty, with bad teeth—looked like he wasn't sure how to answer that one. "Yeah, exactly. No rest for the weary."

"You work in Trenton?"

"Yeah."

"At the airplane plant?"

"Where'd you hear that?"

"Sorry," Lucas said. "Our landlady must have mentioned it."

"She shouldn't have."

"Your secret's safe with me."

"What do you do?"

"I teach at the university." But Lucas had the feeling that the guy already knew that, too; surely, Mrs. Caputo had filled him in.

"What do you teach?"

"Art history."

From Taylor's expression, this made little sense. "You lose that in the war?" he asked, tilting his chin at the black patch.

"Yes."

Taylor snorted and sucked his teeth, but didn't follow up with any of the customary blather, for which Lucas was grateful. "What are you doing out here?" he asked instead.

For a guy who was so chary with his own

answers, he sure had no trouble asking questions. "Couldn't sleep."

"Well, I'm not gonna have any trouble." Taylor stepped around him and reached for the door-knob.

" 'Night."

"Yeah. Right."

He shut the door behind him.

Some guy, Lucas thought. No wonder even Amy hadn't been able to befriend him. Not wanting to bump into him again on the way upstairs, Lucas waited on the porch for a few more minutes, thinking about the work he'd have to do on the sarcophagus—and once or twice, about less practical matters. In the morning, for the hell of it, he'd call the Nassau Inn to check up on that woman's story.

Standing up, he brushed off the back of his trousers, ready to stub out his cigarette and go inside, when the front door opened across the street, and two men—one of them the professor—came down the steps. The other one—younger, in a dark brown hat and suit—was carrying a suitcase in one hand, a briefcase in the other. The driver popped out of the car, quickly took the suitcase from him and stashed it in the trunk.

The two men spoke together softly for another minute or two, then clasped hands. The driver opened the back door of the car, and once his passenger had ducked inside, slipped the car into gear and pulled away. Einstein stood, watching it go, before raising his eyes to the night sky. Stars twinkled overhead, and when the professor returned his gaze to earth, he must have noticed the orange glow from the tip of Lucas's cigarette, and raised a hand, palm up, by way of greeting. Lucas returned the salute with a silent wave of his Camel, and then Einstein shuffled back up his stairs and into the house. The porch light went off, and as it did, the light in Taylor's room, just overhead, went on.

Strange night, Lucas thought, watching the tabby cat scoot under the fence of the professor's house. Something was in the air tonight, and whatever it might be, it was keeping sleep at bay.

Chapter FOURTEEN

He should never have persuaded Gödel to come out for this morning sail with him. The man was clinging to the railing as if they were caught in the open sea in a typhoon instead of simply drifting before a gentle breeze to one end of Lake Carnegie—a man-made reservoir in Princeton, built for the rowing team—and then back again to the other. For Einstein, it was one of the few times he could truly get away from it all—no telegrams, no telephone calls, no importunate young physicists begging him to appraise their latest discoveries or theorems. Helen worked tirelessly to shield him from the intrusions, but a secretary could only do so much.

She had known, for instance, to let J. Robert Oppenheimer past the gates, and to make him comfortable in the guest room for a couple of days so that the two men could discuss and unravel the impediments to the atomic bomb research being done in Los Alamos. In a way, it was a vindication for the professor—he had felt marginalized for years by the younger establishment, Oppenheimer included, and to know that they would turn to him now, under the utmost secrecy, on a project of such unparalleled national importance, was invigorating, to say the least.

"To what depth is the lake?" Gödel asked, for the third time that morning. He had buckled his life preserver up to his chin.

"*Ach*, it is no more than twenty feet," Einstein replied. "Twenty feet."

That was plainly not the answer Gödel, hardly an accomplished swimmer, wanted to hear. Anything above six or seven feet would do the job, if it came to that.

The autumn wind was blowing the gray tendrils of Einstein's hair about his head and the cobwebs out of his mind. The yellow sail of the little boat—a craft so battered that Einstein had jokingly christened it the *Tinef*, or, translated from the Yiddish, "piece of junk"—swelled and snapped with the breeze as he manned the tiller with a practiced hand.

"And how is your work going?" he asked, simply to distract Gödel from the slight heeling of the boat as the wind picked up.

"To which do you refer? My paper on the continuum hypothesis is almost done, and if you would be so kind, I may ask you to read it very soon and give me your opinion before I send it out for publication."

"I would be happy to," Einstein said sincerely. Gödel's mathematical works—for which he had become famous—were always stimulating, and in their logic, irrefutable. His incompleteness theorems, which posited that in any given system there are claims which are true but which that same system cannot prove to be so, were enough to secure his place in the pantheon forever.

It was his other pet project—his ontological proof of a divine plan and an afterlife—that was, though just as well-grounded, unconvincing. For all of Einstein's own belief in a unified field theory, a complete and elegant and unassailably integrated scheme for the organization of the cosmos—a goal he had been pursuing in vain for decades—he was not a believer in a God, at least insofar as any religion claimed to know Him. As for Heaven and Hell, they were nothing but fantasies. He could see no evidence for any of it. And if even a genius like Gödel couldn't prove it to his satisfaction, then who could?

"As for my other work, the ontological proof—"

Here it comes, Einstein thought. It was his own fault for opening the door.

"—I have paid close attention to your objections to the juncture of axioms four and five, and I believe I have been able to resolve them in a way that does not in any fashion diminish or alter the validity of those that follow."

It had taken him only about fourteen axioms and theorems in a row to build his case, and because of his brilliance, it was not easy to find the chinks in the argument. But Einstein knew that its central thesis was wrong. Why? Because he knew in his very bones that there could be no reason, nor any special purpose, for a Divinity. Mankind had made it all up out of whole cloth because, at bottom, everyone was afraid of the dark, afraid of ultimate extinction, afraid to face the fact that individual lives meant nothing in the grand scheme of a vast and utterly indifferent cosmos.

"But you must not say that a proof of God is all merely a matter of wish fulfillment," Gödel said, "as your late friend Dr. Freud would have said. For him, it was all in the mind, but that mind, I think, was too often only his own."

As for himself, Einstein had no such fears or apprehension of death. He was sixty-five now, and he had already done good work—there was no denying that. Love and work, those were the two essential things, as Sigmund had said. But Einstein had always admired Freud as a philosopher more than as a scientist, and had found his essays more thought-provoking than they were definitive.

No, the reason he didn't fear death was because he had accepted his place—minuscule as an atom, insignificant as a mayfly—in a mystery and a miracle beyond full comprehension. It was enough to have participated in it and to have achieved as much as one could while here.

"I promise that I will keep an open mind," he replied, "even if you tell me that I will wear wings and play on a harp and sit at the foot of the heavenly throne." What he didn't want to get into, especially at this moment, was an earnest debate about the merits of Gödel's proof. Gazing off at the profusion of red and gold leaves clustered along the banks of the lake, he wanted only to take in the natural beauty of the scene, to revel in the puffy white clouds drifting in the blue sky like the clumps of whipped cream with which he used to sweeten his hot chocolate in the Alps, and in the rhythmic lapping of the clear, cold water against the sides of the sailboat. Closing his eyes, he tried to imagine himself back in Switzerland as a young man, sailing on a little boat much like the *Tinef*, only with his sweetheart, pretty blonde Marie Winteler, nestled under his arm. Time was relative—he had certainly proved that much—but even he could not account for how rapidly it seemed to pass, especially as he grew older. He feared that he would not live long enough to complete his unified field theory.

Or to prove that he was right about it at all.

Oppenheimer, he knew, had always scoffed at the idea. All the quantum mechanics fellows did. Bohr. Teller. How ironic, he often thought, that his papers, published at the turn of the century, had laid the groundwork for their own theories and research, but that these men had then turned around and used his work to create a universe that operated by random rules he could not accept. There had to be a pattern—the simpler, the better—to everything, but quantum physics, he felt sure, was not the way to find it.

"This has been a very pleasant excursion, and I thank you for it," Gödel said, "but do you not think that we should return to shore?"

Shaking off his reverie, Einstein opened his eyes, and saw, on the distant horizon, what his friend Kurt had already observed. Above the treetops, he could discern a thin line of storm clouds. The weather in New Jersey was as unpredictable as in the Bernese Alps.

Their little sailboat would be a veritable sitting duck.

He sheeted in on the mainsail and tacked to starboard, then used the tiller to redirect their course toward the university boathouse. The lake water sloshed over the side of the boat, and Gödel lifted his wet feet as swiftly as if they'd been touched by lava, and then wrapped his arms around his knees. Einstein might have laughed, if it were not that he felt so guilty about subjecting his friend to such terror.

Looking back over his shoulder, he saw that the storm clouds were indeed approaching, and fast. It was the very metaphor Oppenheimer had used before returning to Los Alamos. "The storm to end all storms is coming," he had said, "and the only question is going to be who wields the lightning and the thunder." Oppenheimer had always been prone to such melodramatic language. "It has to be us."

Of course, Einstein had heard this argument before, and yielded to it before, too. A committed pacifist, a tireless promoter of an organized world body to ensure peace, he had inevitably been forced to ameliorate his views. The war dragged on, the atrocities mounted. First, he had been asked by the navy to help them with the design of mines that could be used to block the Japanese harbors, and he had done so. And now, now he was being asked to help with the creation of a weapon that could wreak havoc on a scale never before seen, or even contemplated. If, as

Oppenheimer said, the Germans were well along in their efforts to make such a bomb, then there was no choice.

"We are all working night and day," Oppenheimer had told him the moment they had closed his study door, "but we have to get there faster. We have to solve these problems more quickly than we have; we have to move on to the manufacturing stage."

"And deployment?" he had blurted out.

Oppenheimer had pulled a pack of cigarettes from his shirt pocket and lit the first of many. "If it comes to that."

If it comes to that.

If Einstein had believed that prayers could be heard, he'd have dropped to his knees and prayed then and there.

If it comes to that.

Such simple words, encompassing a holocaust all their own. One would think that the world had already seen enough of man's tragic folly. The Battle of the Somme, during the First World War, had done that for him—half a million men dead, and all for six square miles of mud.

"Can we not go faster?" Gödel said as the wind picked up and the waves began to crash over the side of the boat. Gödel was soaked, and the lenses of his little round glasses were coated with water, too. The boathouse was still a quarter mile off, though Einstein could make out its orange-and-black Princeton pennant fluttering at the top of the flagpole.

"Not unless we want to tip over," Einstein said.

"No, no," Gödel quickly said, "then go just as we are." He cast a nervous look back at the oncoming storm.

The white clouds had fled to the east, replaced now by bulky thunderheads lumbering toward them like tanks. Einstein did not want to show his own growing concern. The little sailboat had already taken on a fair amount of water, and it was heeling before the wind at a more precipitous angle than he liked.

More than anything, he did not want to be out on the lake—a lone boat with a single mast—when lightning struck. The university's rowing coach had warned him about that the very first day the *Tinef* had been brought to the boathouse.

"Jersey storms blow in like squalls. You won't see 'em coming, but trust me—they'll see you."

Now he knew what the coach had meant—it did feel as if the storm had been conjured up out of nothing and was pursuing him with some malicious intent.

"Can I do anything that would help?" Gödel asked, his frail voice almost lost in the wind.

"No, you are a fine first mate," Einstein said, in as reassuring a tone as he could muster. "Just don't go for a swim."

Gödel gave him a weak smile.

"Soon you will be home with Adele," the professor said, "and she will be tasting your dinner for you." Normally, he would not have made this little joke about Kurt's idiosyncratic behavior, but at this moment he could think of no better distraction.

Gödel took it in stride. "She will be serving fish tonight. The house reeked of it."

"What kind?"

"I never notice."

The first raindrops began to dapple the surface of the lake, and the trees along the shore began to bend before the rising wind. Leaves blew loose and scudded across the water.

Einstein pulled in even harder on the mainsheet, and the sailboat tacked sharply toward the wooden pier of the boathouse. The sculls were mounted and secured, upside down, on the racks. "Just hold on tight," he said, though from the look of Gödel's white knuckles, he couldn't hold on any harder if he tried.

The sailboat skimmed the remaining distance, driven by the wind and waves, and narrowly missed the end of the pier, before bumping up roughly against its side.

"Grab the dock line and tie us up," Einstein said, but Gödel had already leapt into action. As the professor dropped and stowed the sail, Kurt lashed the boat to the dock, then leaned over to offer a cold and trembling hand as Einstein stepped up and out of the stern. The rain came across the water in a sheet, and they were only halfway down the dock when it drenched them both. A zigzag of lightning crackled across the sky, and a second later the thunder boomed like a cannon. Soaked and stumbling—oh, how he could remember running with no hitch in his gait, back in the days when he and his friends from the Bern patent office had gone on summer hikes—Einstein followed Kurt into the shelter of the boathouse. The two men shook themselves off like a pair of dogs.

Inside, it was warm and dry and smelled of old cedar and fresh beeswax. An open cabinet held a pair of binoculars, a starting pistol, a first aid kit, and, blessedly, a stack of dry blankets.

Einstein tossed one to Gödel, who, of course, failed to catch it. But he picked it up and wrapped it around his shivering shoulders.

"You look like a dripping dachshund," Einstein said.

"And you, a wet sheepdog."

They both laughed as the rain pelted the windows. A sudden thunderclap, loud as the apocalypse, hit the roof like a giant fist crashing down. Dust drifted from the rafters, the floor-boards rattled underfoot, and they were both chastened into a momentary silence, awaiting—as indeed the entire world seemed poised to do these days—the possible impact of another crushing blow.

Chapter FIFTEEN

The day had begun bright and sunny, with a light breeze and a blue sky, but by noon, the Indian summer had abruptly ended. Fall had come in with a vengeance. A chill wind was blowing, and as Lucas left the house on Mercer Street, Mrs. Caputo called out to him, "Don't forget your umbrella. The radio says there's going to be another thunderstorm today."

The radio, as usual, was right.

The campus lawns were soaked with rain, the walkways were submerged beneath puddles of water and piles of soggy dead leaves. The floorboards of the lecture hall in the art museum were slippery from the wet shoes and galoshes of his students. Lucas himself had nearly taken a tumble off the steps to the podium, and several of the less-hardy students had already caught their first colds of the season. As he took the class around the galleries to observe some of the statues and urns, the squelching of their shoes was accompanied by a chorus of honking and coughing and bleating into handkerchiefs.

So far, however, Lucas had remained impervious to contagion, in large part because he spent so much of his time alone, sequestered in the conservation wing with the ossuary, or in the university library trying to make sense of whatever he had gleaned.

Making sense of it all was a herculean task. He had taken copious notes, rolls of photographs, several rubbings, but he was no closer to identifying the precise origin of the box, or the identity of its occupant, than he had been before. Normally, a sarcophagus bore few markings, and those that were there hewed to a simple theme—identifying the name of the deceased, perhaps his occupation in life, and maybe a word or two about his relation to some other known person or family. "John, son of Joseph. Merchant." And always in just one language, whether it be Aramaic, Greek, Latin, Hebrew.

Not this one.

This one had vague, faintly incised inscriptions in several tongues, as if by a committee, or else by someone who was intent on issuing his admonitions in every conceivable way. In addition to the traditional Egyptian glyphs, probably carved by some Coptic stonemason, there were enough eroded but legible letters to lead Lucas to brief passages in both the Old and New Testaments.

As for the ancient Greek lettering—assuming he was making it out correctly—this took on a more martial air: "Eternal victor, vanquished foe." Could the box contain the bones of mutual antagonists? That would be a first, and might suggest some reason why the Third Reich had been so interested in it. But the time for suppositions was fast disappearing, and the time for answers was here. He'd received a strongly worded communiqué only that morning from Colonel Macmillan at the OSS.

"Information and findings needed ASAP," the telegram read. "Do not attempt to transmit. Courier will be dispatched for written report immediately upon notice. We await results without delay."

Although he was still puzzled as to why this particular sarcophagus, unique though it might be, should be of such vital importance to the military chain of command, Lucas knew enough from his days in the army not to disregard the telegram. Up 'til now, he had been reluctant to sever the chains holding the lid in place before he had made a thorough examination and assessment of all the exterior markings, measurements, and appearance. As any art historian or archaeologist knew, once you had taken any particular step, it became impossible to reverse the results or course of action. There was something he'd recently heard of, called the Heisenberg Uncertainty Principle, having to do with the fact that the very act of observing something changed the position and course of the thing being observed—at least on the subatomic level. In like manner, he didn't want to open the box until he had gathered all the data he could from its unopened state. The only exception he had made was to allow Delaney to make a surgical excision of some of the stone, in order to complete his own analysis.

Perhaps those weren't the only reasons for his delay. Perhaps there was a part of him—a larger part than he was willing to admit—that dreaded any contact with the box at all.

When the class ended, and the students had been dismissed—half of them no doubt to their sick beds—he left the museum and wandered across the campus to Guyot Hall, where Delaney maintained his geophysics lab. Surely he would have made some progress on his analysis of the physical composition and origin of the stone by now, information that Lucas could relay to the OSS to sate their immediate hunger.

A brooding gray Gothic structure, built in the style of so much of the campus, Guyot had housed the university's museum of natural history on its main floor since 1879. Its grim exterior was adorned with over two hundred gargoyle-like figurines depicting extinct or extant animals, all of which had been carved by Gutzon Borglum, the man most famous for sculpting Mount Rushmore. Entering its lobby was like running the gauntlet at a bestiary.

Inside, it felt even stranger. Dimly lit display cases held geological, biological, and anthropological specimens gathered by Princeton's scientific expeditions everywhere from the arid deserts of the southwestern United States to the windswept cliffs of Patagonia. Some of the cases held split geodes, while others housed the skeletons of saber-toothed cats and three-toed horses; one in particular displayed an Eocene perch preserved in the act of swallowing a herring. But the most popular of the exhibits by far—especially with the kids from town, who were admitted freely—was the Caithness Man, discovered in a Scottish bog and later donated to the university collection by Wendell Walker III, the salutatorian of the graduating class of 1904 and, in his spare time,|an amateur explorer.

A fully intact corpse, wearing a snug leather cap and laced breeches, the Caithness Man took his name from the location of the acidic peat bog in which his remains had been petrified and perfectly preserved for over a thousand years. Although his crime would never be known, his punishment was clear: He had been bashed in the skull, then lashed to a stake, where he had been strangled. And all of that was done before his throat, for good measure, had been cut.

"This kind of triple killing," the plaque inside the case explained, "signified a ritualistic execution. These were done to cure demonic possession, or as punishment for transgressions of a heretical nature." The pole had then fallen, or been knocked over, into the muck. Now, the haggard Caithness Man stood erect again, still indissolubly wedded to the stake, which was just as petrified as he was, in a tall glass case lit from below. His flesh had turned the same mahogany brown as the wood, and every wrinkle in his skin, every lash on his closed eyes, every whisker on his gaunt cheek and pointed chin, was immaculately preserved. He looked as if, at any second, he might awaken from his awful slumber, open his eyes, and utter some garbled cry.

"I didn't expect to see you there," Lucas heard from down the hall. "Usually it's a bunch of kids from the grammar school."

He turned to see Andy Brandt lifting his head from the drinking fountain.

"Most of the time, they're daring each other to touch the glass," he said, "and I have to tell them to knock it off or the Caithness Man will come and get them."

"Does it work?"

"For about five minutes."

Now that it had been mentioned, Lucas could see some of their grubby fingerprints on the display case.

"What brings you to these parts?" Andy asked, nosy as ever.

"Professor Delaney," Lucas said. "Is he up in his lab?"

"Let's have a look-see," Andy said, moving toward the stairs, but Lucas said, "That's okay. I'll check myself."

"I need the exercise," Brandt said, taking the stairs two at a time. "I've been cooped up all day."

For someone who'd been declared 4-F due to a heart murmur, he certainly took the stairs in stride.

Lucas wanted no interference just now. What he had to discuss with Delaney had to be discussed in private. By the time he'd caught up, however, Brandt was already throwing open the door marked Department of Mineralogy and Geophysics, and saying, "Anyone home?"

To Lucas's surprise, more than one voice was raised in objection. He heard Delaney saying, "Didn't I tell you that you were banned?" and a woman's voice saying, "And who are you?"

The woman spoke with a British accent.

Inside, he saw Delaney and Simone Rashid, standing on either side of a lab counter.

Lucas was stunned. Simone looked taken off guard, too. Before he could ask what she was doing there, Delaney was shoving Andy back out the door—"Consider this lab off-limits!"—and closing the door behind him. Brushing his hands together, as if to say, "Good riddance to bad rubbish"—he gestured toward Simone and said, "I gather you two have already met."

"It's good to see you again," she said coolly.

"What are you doing here?"

"I guess you haven't heard," Delaney said. "Miss Rashid has received a visiting appointment to the Middle Eastern Studies Department."

"I didn't even know they were hiring."

Raising an eyebrow and speaking with great deliberation, Delaney said, "They are when Colonel Macmillan makes the call."

Lucas felt like he would never be able to keep up. "So," he said to Delaney in a low tone, "she knows about . . . the project?"

"I can hear you," she interrupted, "and of course I do. Once the Egyptian ministry—and Egypt is an ally, I might add—expressed its interest in this case, things moved swiftly."

"We've actually gotten a lot done," Delaney said. "I was planning to call you."

As Lucas perched on a stool and tried to get his bearings, Delaney went on to explain that, based on the sliver he had drilled from the underside, he had determined that the alabaster of the box was of the so-called Oriental variety. "That's the calcite kind, harder than the gypsum you generally find in Europe. Watch." Removing the sample of the stone from a drawer and placing it on the counter, he used an eyedropper to touch it with a clear liquid. Minuscule bubbles appeared, then quickly disappeared. "That's from the hydrochloric acid. You wouldn't get that effervescence on the softer sort of alabaster."

"The ancient Egyptians often used it for their canopic jars," Simone said, "especially when the jars were being used to hold the vital organs of Pharaohs."

"Are you saying that we have the ossuary of a Pharaoh?" Lucas asked.

"No," Simone replied, "not at all," though her tone suggested she knew more than she was saying. Delaney, meanwhile, charged ahead.

"This particular strain of alabaster," he said, "was only quarried in certain regions of Egypt and Syria."

"The region around the Sahara el Beyda," Simone said. "Or White Desert."

"Starting about three thousand years ago."

"I can tell you right now," Lucas said, glad at last to have something to contribute, "that the ossuary dates from no more than two thousand years ago. Probably a century or two less."

"How do you know that?" Delaney asked.

"From the Latin inscriptions on its lid. One of them refers to a passage in the Scriptures."

"Well, that would be your department," he conceded.

"What about the other markings?" Simone said, readily falling into the role of colleague. "Have you made any progress with those?"

Despite the ease with which she had adapted, Lucas still found it hard to press on. This project had been delivered into his hands under such bonds of secrecy that he was hesitant to divulge his findings willy-nilly. "I'm working on them."

"Perhaps I can help."

Delaney nodded his head in encouragement, but Lucas ignored him.

"We really need to get back into the room with the sarcophagus," Simone remarked. "I think we've done as much as we can with what Professor Delaney has on hand."

"Call me Patrick," Delaney said, and Simone smiled. "But I think she's right," he added, fixing his gaze on Lucas. "We can send all this geophysical data on to DC, but Macmillan won't be satisfied for long."

Lucas could sense Simone's impatience, but he looked instead at the sliver of alabaster lying next to the microscope on the counter.

"What he really wants to know," Delaney went on, "is what's inside it."

"Don't you?" Simone said.

"And I can't use my radio isotope research to put a date on bones that haven't been removed yet," Delaney complained. "If I don't come through with some results soon, it could cost me my funding."

Lucas felt like he was under a barrage.

"The box needs to be opened," Delaney concluded.

"When it is," Simone said, "I am now authorized to be there."

"All right, all right," Lucas said, giving up, "we'll open it."

"When?" Simone insisted.

"Tonight. After the museum closes at eight."

Then, lest he be pushed any farther into a corner, he asked Delaney to write up his notes and slip a copy under his study door, turned around, and left the room. He knew that opening the ossuary was inevitable, but now that he had committed to doing it in a matter of hours, he felt a cold and numb sensation descending on his limbs. It had to be done, but he did not want to do it.

Lo and behold, Andy Brandt stood just across the hall, pretending to be absorbed in the flyers tacked to the Mineralogy and Geophysics Department's bulletin board. How much had he been able to overhear, Lucas wondered?

"Say, who's the looker in there with Professor Delaney?" Andy asked.

"No one you need to know," Lucas replied as he headed downstairs, one hand on the railing to compensate for his partial vision. Around the Caithness Man's display case, three grammar school kids stood holding spiral notebooks. True to what Brandt had said earlier, the smallest of them extended one trembling finger to the glass as another one urged him on. "Touch it—I dare you to! Touch it!"

The boy did, then fled out the door, screaming and waving his arms as if he'd poked a hornets' nest. Lucas knew exactly how he felt.

Chapter SIXTEEN

Emerging from the bowels of the collegiate library, Dr. Rashid was met by a cold wet wind and a sea of puddles. He tucked his scarf around his sore throat and pulled up the collar of his overcoat, but not before another coughing fit had overtaken him. Once it had subsided, he gingerly made his way down the leaf-strewn walkway, the tip of his ebony cane testing each step before he took it. Even so, he was tired and catching another chill by the time he came beneath the great brooding hulk of the university's Gothic chapel. A splat of rain on his shoulder decided him, and he went up the steps to the massive doors.

He had already passed through these doors days before, and noticed their unusual motif—Christ surrounded by the four beasts from the Book of Revelation. Each of the creatures—a lion, an ox, an eagle, and a winged man—represented a Gospel, and their depiction here strongly reminded him, as had probably been intended, of the west tympanum of Chartres Cathedral.

Once inside the narthex, he also noted, with amusement, the stained-glass window devoted to medicine, featuring the Persian physician al-Razi.

Indeed, the windows of the chapel were a distinctly eclectic collection that ran the gamut from biblical scenes and theological themes to tributes to science and philosophy. He could not remember seeing an ecclesiastical homage to Kant, Spinoza, Ptolemy, Descartes, or Louis Pasteur anywhere else in the world.

The long and gloomy nave stretched out before him, and it appeared that only one other person occupied the vast interior of the cathedral. Like Rashid, this man, hunched down low, had sought a quiet spot for reflection in the pews, as well as a refuge from the weather outside. Rashid sat down on the opposite side of the main aisle, several rows ahead of him, so that they both might main-tain their privacy.

Above him, an indigo-blue-and-purple window, faintly illuminated by the late afternoon light outside, showed Christ holding a scroll, and beneath him, in Greek, the inscription "Who is worthy to open the scroll?"

Who indeed, Rashid thought, removing his handkerchief to dab at his nose.

Since coming to Princeton, he'd been absorbed in the papyri, or the fragments thereof, retrieved from the cave of Saint Anthony. General Rommel's henchmen may have been able to make off with the ossuary, but the contents of the urns had been unknown to them, and with the help of his daughter, Rashid had managed to abscond with the trove intact. Although they had suffered a bit from being haphazardly stuffed in his luggage on the voyage over, he had now been allowed access to a private carrel in the library where he could lay them out properly. The library had also provided a host of rare and useful materials: The early presidents of Princeton had nearly all been men of the cloth, deep-thinking theologians and ministers—Dickinson, Edwards, Witherspoon—whose books and papers had been donated to Princeton upon their deaths. In some ways, he could not have wound up in a more congenial and conducive environment.

If only his discoveries had been as comforting.

Despite the short amount of time he had been ensconced at the library—courtesy, again, of his daughter's clever maneuverings—everything he had gleaned so far had only exacerbated his fears and suspicions. Many of the papyri referred to a period, roughly three hundred years after the death of Christ, in which the barbarous Roman emperor Diocletian had initiated what was commonly known as the Great Persecution. It was from this era that most of the well-known stories of Christians martyred in the arena to ravenous beasts, of saints being roasted over slow fires, of endless roads lined with teetering crosses bearing the bodies of the crucified, sprang. Diocletian himself had come to Egypt on one of his triumphal tours, and in Alexandria had torn down all of the Christian churches and burned thousands of holy texts. Anyone who refused to renounce this new and traitorous faith had had his right eye put out with a sword, and the tendons on his left foot severed, before he was enslaved and shipped off to die in the copper mines. "In these conflicts," according to a scroll Dr. Rashid attributed to the church polemicist Eusebius, "the noble martyrs of Christ shone illustrious over the entire world . . . and the evidences of the truly divine and unspeakable power of our Saviour were made manifest through them."

Those who converted were forced to prove it by making an animal sacrifice, and soon the skies over Egypt were filled with the smoke from burning ewes and calves, bulls and pigs and goats.

But one thing the history books had never settled was the reason for Diocletian's hasty retreat around 304 AD. Most historians assumed it had something to do with the unceasing political struggles in the Roman senate—his rival Galerius had been restive, and it was plain he meant to seize the reins of power—and Diocletian may have felt the need to hurry back home to exert his control once again, though that theory was contradicted by his almost immediate retirement once he got there.

Dr. Rashid felt that something else might have been in play.

One document, in particular, set the hairs on the back of his neck prickling, and not only because of what it said.

Written in a crabbed and shaky hand, the first-hand account appeared to have been written by Saint Anthony himself. The fact that Dr. Rashid might have been holding a tattered parchment that the anchorite himself had once labored over in the solitude of his desert cave was enough to make his hands tremble.

"And when this emperor had come to the desert," it read, "with his camels and chariots, with his army of soldiers and slaves, the sand itself arose in a great storm, blinding their eyes."

It had taken him many hours, using magnifying glasses, high-intensity lamps, and the skills of a practiced jigsaw puzzler, to decipher the passages and put them together in the correct order. Then there was the matter of reading the almost vanished ink.

"But when he came upon the sacred place, I ventured forth from the cave, raising my *tau*"—a shepherd's stick, with a curved iron handle—"and I felt a righteous power descend upon me. I struck the ground, and a bottomless chasm opened under their feet. Many were swallowed whole."

It inevitably reminded Rashid of the parting of the Red Sea.

"From that pit vomited a swarm of demons, led by the Lord of Flies. I did strike him with my staff, but the demon was able to wrest it away. We fought all through the night, though despair was my greatest enemy."

Here, Rashid felt sure, was the origin of the stories in which Saint Anthony was assailed by demons, with whom he struggled in hand-to-hand combat.

"When the dawn at last arose, the demon raised my staff to strike again, but I, too, took hold of it. I called upon the Lord to send me strength, and the devil was defeated by a fire from the Heavens. In Christ's name, I bound him then, and kept him prisoner."

How? Rashid had wondered. How did you keep a demon captive? And what would you do with him once you had?

"Seeing that their champion had been vanquished, the Roman army fled. On their heels followed a mighty pillar of flame, like a red rose with petals that spread in a burning cloud across the sky."

Could Diocletian's abrupt departure from power have been a result of his experience in the Sahara? Could he have been so terrified by what he had seen—the demonic powers, his sworn allies, defeated by an old hermit with a shepherd's crook; his army decimated and pursued by a maelstrom of fire—that he had been shaken to his core? Surely that would be enough to give any man—even one as ruthless as

Diocletian—reason to reconsider, if not repent, his ways. Was that, Rashid wondered, why he had willingly sur-rendered his earthly powers? Did he fear what unimaginable horror the tau might unleash upon him next—or was it his fear of the malevolent and unpredictable spirit the holy man might actually be keeping prisoner within the darkest recesses of the cave?

A tickle in his throat suddenly became a cough, and the cough became an unstoppable volley. He raised his handkerchief to his lips to muffle the sound, but the cough echoed around the stone walls of the immense chamber. Falling sick was the last thing he needed; there was work to do—work that might have grave consequences—and he could not afford to lose any time, especially having come this far.

But the coughing wouldn't stop. Doubling over, he accidentally knocked his cane from the back of the pew in front of him, and it clattered onto the floor. When he bent down to pick it up, he heard a voice say, with a German accent, "Excuse me, I do not wish to disturb."

Turning around, he saw that the other occupant of the chapel was now perched on the pew behind him. The face, with its unruly white hair and bushy moustache, was unmistakable.

"I do not wish to disturb," he repeated, "but I think that these will help." He was holding out a little packet of Smith Brothers cough drops.

"Thank you," Rashid said, taking the packet and shaking one out.

"You may take them all. I have more."

Before Rashid stuck one under his tongue, he said, "But you are—"

The man cut him off with an embarrassed "*Ja*," adding, "And you, are you a professor at the university?"

"In a manner of speaking," Rashid replied, taking the opportunity to introduce himself. "They allow me to use the facilities while I am here."

"The facilities here are fine, but the weather . . ." Einstein trailed off with a laugh.

Rashid sucked on the lozenge, which quickly soothed his throat. When Einstein inquired about the subject of his research, Rashid simply said, "Early Christian texts. I am studying some antique examples in the collection of the university."

"Ah, such things are of interest to me, too."

"They are? But you are not even of the Christian faith."

Einstein waved the contradiction away. "I attended Catholic schools when I was a boy. I found much to admire in the stories and philosophy."

"Are you a believer then?"

"No, I would not say that, not at all. But I am often asked to expound upon God, as if physics could reveal not just natural laws, but a divine plan behind them."

"What do you say to these questions when they are asked?"

"Whatever I say," he replied with a shrug, "it is misinterpreted. I am called an atheist—and in this country that is considered a very dangerous thing indeed—an agnostic, a pantheist, and sometimes, I even get letters that address me as rabbi."

"But do you believe in a single, unified God, a power of good set in eternal opposition to a power of evil?" The words of Saint Anthony— "I subdued the demon and in Christ's name captured him"—still swirled in his thoughts.

"No, my search for unity does not extend that far," he said with a small smile. "I believe that the *natural* forces, the ones we see all around us, have an underlying unity and order. I am spending my remaining years trying to find it—a unified field theory that can explain how everything in the universe has been organized and put in its place."

"You make the universe sound like a library, where every book is on just the right shelf, waiting to be read."

Einstein smiled, and said, "That is a good way to put it. But we are still like children in that library. We look around and see thousands of books on thousands of shelves. We know that someone or something must have written those books and put them there, but we do not know who or what that could be. There is an order to it all, that much we can tell, but that is really all we know. The rest is a mystery—a beautiful one—but a mystery, all the same."

In the distance, the bell tolled in the cupola atop Nassau Hall.

"Ah, I must be going," Einstein said, putting one hand on the back of the pew and levering himself to his feet. "I am sorry if I have disturbed you with so much talk."

"Not at all. It was very interesting."

"Ah, but it is just such talk that gets me into trouble," the professor said with a chuckle. "I envy you your work."

If only he knew, Rashid thought, that his own work spoke directly to many of the same issues. Where Einstein was pushing the boundaries of knowledge forward, in the hope of learning ever more, Rashid was studying the past, in the hope of gleaning from it what man might, to his sorrow, have forgotten. A chill coursed through his old bones. He knew from Simone that the physical examination of the ossuary was progressing. What would happen if, through some rash or hasty action, the secrets that the papyri only hinted at were acted upon? He was desperate to unravel the mysteries before some dreadful menace was unwittingly released.

As Einstein sidled into the aisle, Rashid considered leaving with him, but then thought better of it. He did not wish to presume too much. "Are you sure you don't want these back?" he said, holding out the lozenges.

"A gift."

As if to confirm his impression that Einstein lived with one foot in the material world and one in some other, Rashid couldn't help but notice, as the scientist walked down the dimly illumined nave, that he passed from beams of light into patches of shadow, and that even on a day as chilly and wet as this, he wore no socks. No wonder he carried cough drops.

Chapter SEVENTEEN

When Lucas heard the gentle knock on his study door and said, "Come in," he expected a student to pop in with a late paper. Even that brief an interruption was more than he wanted—his thoughts were entirely consumed with the imminent unveiling of the ossuary. He should have been back in the conservation wing, making a final inspection of the sealed box and compiling his last-minute notes.

But instead of a student, a plump young woman, with a cloth coat thrown over a waitress's pink uniform, opened the door.

"I'm sorry, but are you Professor Athan?" she asked, as if he weren't what she expected to see, either.

"Yes."

"I'm Polly Gregg. Wally's daughter. Would it be okay if I talked to you for a minute?"

Suppressing the urge to put her off until a more opportune time, Lucas welcomed her in and gestured to the chair opposite his cluttered desk. He swept from its seat an invitation from President Dobbs, addressed to all junior faculty, that recommended in no uncertain terms that they turn out "as a sign of their support for the college" at the opening football game. Lucas prayed that Polly wasn't there to tell him that the poor man had succumbed to his wounds. He had more than enough blood on his hands and his conscience, already.

"My dad told me about you. Said you were a war hero."

"Hardly," Lucas said. "How is your dad doing?"

Polly glanced down at her lap. "Not so good," she said. "Not so good at all, and I don't know what to do. I don't even know why he was working so late. Why *was* he? Why did this happen?" It all came out in a rush as she looked up, her brown eyes welling with tears. "When he called me to tell me not to wait up for him, he said he had the willies. My dad worked in the museum all the time—why would he have had the willies?"

Lucas felt the sharp, stabbing cold around his glass eye. He had the willies himself when he was around that box. But all he could do was shake his head.

"I stopped in at the hospital," he said, "to see him, but they wouldn't allow anyone but family."

Polly looked lost and helpless. "It's pretty bad," she said, her voice dropping to a whisper. "And I don't understand a word that his doctor says to me. It's like he purposely uses big words just to confuse me."

"I'm sure not."

"I'm sure he does." She dug a wad of tissues out of her coat pocket. "I'm just a waitress, and my dad's a janitor, so we must be stupid, right?" She leaned forward to drop her used tissues in the wastebasket beside his desk, then, perhaps considering it impolite, stuck them back in her pocket instead. "My dad drinks a lot. I'll admit it. But he never hit me or anything, he just cried a lot after my mother left, and sometimes forgot to put any food in the icebox. He tried his best, though." She looked up at Lucas. "And I don't want him to die."

"Why don't I come with you?" Lucas said, standing. "To the hospital. Right now." He needed to do something with this sliver of time before the opening of the ossuary, and maybe this was it. Making a quick calculation in his head, he was certain he'd still be able to make it back to the museum on time. "I might be able to help." Grabbing his coat off the peg on the door, he took Polly by her elbow and guided her out of the building. She looked at him with unconcealed gratitude.

At the hospital, they sat on a stiff wooden bench in the waiting area until a nurse summoned them down the hall. In Wally's room, a doctor—Crowley, according to his name tag—was making notes on a clipboard. He glanced up at Lucas over the rim of his wire specs. "And you are?"

"A friend of the family."

The bed was shrouded by what looked like mosquito netting, and it was only when the doctor lifted it that Lucas could see why Polly had been so horrified.

Wally was almost unrecognizable. His head, propped on the pillow, looked like a jack-o'-lantern, and his breathing was stertorous. His eyes and lips were just slits in his head, and only patches of his hair remained. His skin had turned as firm and bumpy as an orange peel. For a moment, superimposed over the scene, all Lucas saw was the corpse in the iron mine, its swollen skull lying facedown in the dirt. Wally could be his twin.

"The bacterium strain is proving more resistant than expected," Crowley said. "The drug regimen has worked miracles in some cases, but not in this one."

Lucas cleared his throat, the vision dispersing as instantaneously as it had come. "What drug is that?" he asked, as much for Polly's benefit as his own.

"Penicillin," Crowley said.

Penicillin had only been mass manufactured in recent years, and Lucas knew that almost all of the supply had been reserved for the military. Reputed to be a godsend—millions of doses had been stockpiled in advance of the Normandy invasion —it had saved many lives from infection and disease already.

"We're also dealing with the ramifications of necrotizing fasciitis," the doctor said. Polly threw a pleading glance at Lucas.

"What exactly is that?" he asked.

"A polymicrobial infection that can be transmitted, as it undoubtedly was in this instance, from some trauma to the dermis. A bite from a carrier—a rat, bat, dog, even an insect—can introduce it."

"But what does it do, once it's been introduced?"

"In layman's terms," Crowley said with the air of certain lofty professors he'd had at Columbia, "it eats flesh."

Lucas had never heard of such a disease. But now he had seen two examples of it—one sprawled on the ground in Alsace-Lorraine, and one lying in a bed in New Jersey. Had the dead man in the mine also been bitten by an infected animal?

"Patients who suffer from diabetes, circulatory issues, or problems with alcohol are most susceptible." Crowley went on. "As you may or may not know, Mr. Gregg had all three of the conditions which favor erysipelas."

"Favor what?" Polly asked, twisting her hands.

"Erysipelas. Since the Middle Ages, when it was a scourge in Western Europe, it has been more commonly known as *ignis sacer*, or holy fire."

When even Lucas remained blank, he added, "It also went by the name of Saint Anthony's fire. Perhaps you have heard it called by that name."

By that name, Lucas had.

"John Stuart Mill died of it," the doctor added.

"Here?" Polly said with terror in her voice.

"In London, in the previous century. We'll continue to do all that we can for Mr. Gregg, but if you'll excuse me"—Crowley flipped the chart on his clipboard—"I have to complete my rounds now."

"Actually, Doctor," Lucas couldn't resist saying, as the doctor paused impatiently at the door, "Mill was born in London, but he didn't die there. He died in France."

Then he draped a consoling arm around Polly, and they both turned their attention to her father. As Lucas's thoughts raced ahead, trying to put together the shards of the puzzle he found himself confronted by, Polly reached out to take her father's hand. Bandages concealed what Lucas could only surmise were partially amputated fingertips. She was just about to make contact when the head nurse, her hat as white and crisp as cardboard, bustled in.

"No, no, no," she admonished her, brushing Polly's hand aside and lowering the netting around the bed again. "No touching. You'll both have to go now. Visiting hours were over at five-thirty."

Chapter EIGHTEEN

All that day, and now into the evening, Simone had been champing at the bit, waiting for the museum to close to the public so that she could join Professors Delaney and Athan in the conservation wing for the great unveiling.

There was just going to be one problem. Telling her father, who was sure to bridle at not being included.

She found him settled, as usual, in the darkest corner of the Yankee Doodle taproom in the basement of the Nassau Inn. The room took its name from the broad Norman Rockwell mural behind the bar, depicting a colonial soldier, feather in his cap, riding a scrawny pony through the streets. She didn't know if her father actually preferred this quiet, candle-lit corner, not far from the hearth, or if the hotel was trying to keep him as much out of the sight of their lily-white, Anglo-Saxon guests as possible. Under his elbow rested a blue folder, weighted down by a copy of the Koran and a much depleted box of mentholated cough drops.

Simone slipped into the empty seat across the table and it was several seconds before he looked up from the book and registered her presence. "I was wondering where you've been."

"I was wondering the same thing about you."

"Oh, you don't have to worry about me," he said with a sly grin. "I was in the chapel, having a delightful conversation with Professor Einstein."

Simone did not know if he was joking.

"It's true. He gave me these cough drops," he said, as if offering incontrovertible proof of the encounter.

"What did you talk about?"

"The weather. Our work. The universe."

Simone would love to know more about it, and in much greater detail, but time was short, and her father was pushing the bread basket toward her.

"Let's get you some dinner," he said.

"Thanks, but I'm not hungry."

"Nonsense. You have to eat."

"I just wanted to make sure you were all right."

"Why wouldn't I be?"

"There's that cough, for one thing."

He brushed it aside.

"Or that maybe you were feeling abandoned here?"

"Abandoned? Me? Never. As long as I have my work, and a place to do it in—the library here is particularly fine, by the way—I have everything I need."

Since they had arrived, Simone had been occupied with nailing down her temporary sinecure at the university, and she'd felt guilty about leaving him to his own devices from morning 'til night. But how could she have forgotten who he was—a man who could lose himself in a single book, not to mention a world-class, open-stack library, for hours on end?

"And my work on the papyri is going exceedingly well," he confided, leaning forward. "I've translated enough of them to believe they contain the revelations we've been hoping for."

She felt herself holding her breath. "What revelations?"

"That my reasons for hunting the tomb all these years were right." He lowered his voice further. "I have long suspected, as you know, that it contains a benevolent power, one that might be used in this present world as a force for good."

"Now would certainly be a good time for it."

"But there's a danger—what if that force is coupled, inexplicably, with a malevolent one?"

Simone looked deep into his dark eyes, alight

with the fervor of his theory. "What if it's impossible to release one," he murmured, "without freeing the other?"

A waitress in colonial garb set a plate of sautéed broccoli and cauliflower down in front of her vegetarian father, and asked Simone if she would like a menu.

"No, thanks, I'm not staying." His words were still echoing in her skull.

Flicking open his napkin, her father said, "After what I've just told you, you're going to leave? Impossible."

"Possible."

"We have so much to discuss."

"We'll have to do it later. I have an appointment." Now it would be even harder than she'd foreseen to tell him the rest.

"At this hour?" her father said, spearing a stalk of broccoli. "Where, and with whom?"

"A certain saint."

He stopped, fork poised above his plate, and gave her a long look. "Do not be cryptic with me."

"Professor Athan has decided to open the ossuary tonight."

He dropped the fork onto the plate, dabbed his napkin at his lips, and said, "And when were you planning to tell me about this? Obviously, there are things I need to prepare."

This confrontation was precisely what she had hoped to avoid, and why she had been reluctant to notify him in the first place. "You don't need to prepare anything. I'll take care of it all."

"We are going to the museum?" he said, not hearing a word of what she'd just said. "Whether or not my worst suspicions are correct, there are precautions that must be taken."

"The project is being kept under the tightest security, and only personnel okayed by the OSS are allowed to be present," Simone said, placing a hand on top of his. "It's a miracle I was able to worm my way in. I'm afraid I will have to go there alone."

"No," he said, shaking his head, "absolutely not. I won't allow it."

It reminded her of the time he had refused to let her go off on a motorcycle trip with a bo she'd met at school (though she had gone, anyway). "I'll make sure no harm comes to anyone, or to the ossuary, for that matter."

"What do you mean by anyone? Who besides Athan?"

"Professor Delaney, from geophysics, is the only other person allowed."

"And I am not," he said with disgust. "Do any of these people have any idea of what might be inside it?"

Simone dropped her eyes to the flickering candle flame. "Nothing other than the usual skeletal remains."

"I thought not." He withdrew his hand from

beneath hers. "Is that because you are afraid to tell them? Afraid of what they might think of you if you did?"

The answer was yes, but she did not say it aloud. She didn't have to.

"Don't you think they should know?"

"Why?" she blurted out. "First of all, they'd never believe a word of it. And chances are, none of it is true, anyway."

"Yes, there is always that possibility." What hung in the air, however, was the rest of that thought—that it just *might* be. "If only we'd had the opportunity to open it in Cairo," her father added, slapping the edge of the table in frustration. "We could have gone about this properly."

But by the time the sarcophagus had been retrieved and brought back—a task that took six months of planning on its own—Rommel's Afrika Korps had swept across the region, destroying everything in their path and stealing anything worth having. The ossuary was part of the booty, and Simone, like her father, thought it had been taken indiscriminately, and with no idea of its true provenance or value.

She had soon been disabused of that notion when she learned, as part of her duties at the Ministry of Culture, that it had been singled out for special delivery, and to the Führer himself. Somehow, and not to her surprise, the Nazis must have planted a mole in the ministry. When she found out that the United States had then gone after it, too, she realized that the ossuary had become a pawn in some game—a game whose players might not even know what they were squabbling over.

"To think that such an ancient journey should end in a country so foreign," her father said, as if thinking along the same lines, "and so young." He waved a hand dismissively at the faux colonial surroundings.

"Maybe it was all fate." She could only imagine all the thoughts swirling through his mind. The years of research into the whereabouts of the tomb, his growing conviction of its power and potential. Her own commitment had remained more prosaic. She had always been more interested in its immense archaeological importance, not to mention the vindication of her father's lifework. Together they had made the arduous trip into the White Desert, the descent into the cave, the dangerous voyage across the Atlantic, and now, at the very moment when the box might be opened, reveal its contents, and confirm or refute his theories, he would not be present, except by proxy. She knew it had to be agony for him.

He coughed, took a long sip from his glass of club soda to quell it—alcohol, to her knowledge, had never crossed his lips—and then sighed resignedly. In the old days, he'd have put up much more of a fight than this. Now, it appeared that even he knew his limitations. His ebony cane was hooked to the back of his chair, and in order to read the papers in the blue folder, he'd had to move the candle, in its little pewter base, much closer to his plate.

"Then you will have to be my eyes," he said, "and ears."

"I'll give you a full report, in writing," she promised with a smile. "Triple-spaced, the way you like it."

His dark eyes fixing hers, he reached into the pocket of his suit jacket and took out a thread-bare velvet pouch. "Even if this is of no help," he said, withdrawing a tarnished old medallion on a frayed leather string and handing it to her, "humor me. What harm can it do?"

The medallion was plainly ancient, its symbol so worn away that it was hard for her to discern in the feeble light of the taproom.

"It's a pentagram," her father said, to Simone's surprise.

"The symbol of evil?"

"Not originally. Until the Middle Ages, when it was finally supplanted by the cross, it was a symbol of Christ. The five points represented the five wounds to his body, and it was believed to *protect* the wearer from evil."

To oblige him, she slipped it around her neck and under her blouse. What harm *could* it do? It was something like the philosopher Pascal's wager, to her mind: Although an atheist, Pascal said he would make a deathbed confession to God. If there was no God to hear it, what difference did it make? But if there *was* . . .

As she got up to go, Dr. Rashid reached out, squeezed her hand, and said, solemnly, "God be with you."

"I'm counting on it," she replied, tapping the medallion now resting against her skin.

Outside, it was a cold, clear evening, and the streets of the town were still busy with people buying their dinner fixings, or getting back from their jobs. But the quaint, yellow-tinted lamplights were on, and the sidewalks were crowded. As she walked back toward the campus gates, she thought how easily she could have wound up in just such a place, devoting herself purely to writing and research, married to another professor, someone, strictly for argument's sake, like Lucas Athan.

But she had always had bigger, and more adventurous, goals than that.

Passing under FitzRandolph Gate and into the precincts of the college, she lost the bright store-fronts of Nassau Street, the noise of human voices, the rumble of motor engines. The darkness was deeper, punctuated only by the occasional lantern in a Gothic archway, or the gleam of some student's light behind the casement window of his dormitory. On her way to meet up with Professor Delaney at Guyot Hall, she was accompanied by the rustle of leaves on the ground and the sighing of the boughs in the trees overhead. Only a couple of students scurried past her, complaining about a coach who had kept them late. By the time she reached Guyot Hall, with its cabinet of curiosities displayed in the lobby, Delaney was coming down the stairs. Spotting her, he lifted a jingling key ring in greeting.

"I was looking for these all afternoon," he said. "Turns out they were in my coat pocket the whole time."

"It's a hazard of the profession," Simone said, thinking of her own father and half a dozen professors she'd had at Oxford.

"What is?"

"Absentmindedness."

"Let's hope that's all it is," he said, locking the main doors behind them.

At his feet, she noticed a closed-up Gladstone bag. "You look like a country doctor ready to make a house call."

Delaney laughed and lifted the bag—she heard a clank from inside it. "Never lost a patient yet." They passed under the row of concrete gargoyles leering from the parapets above them, then across the forecourt of the university's colossal Tudor Gothic chapel. The art museum was not far off, but they passed most of the way in silence, each no doubt running through what he or she planned to do once they got there, and wondering what they might ultimately find inside the sarcophagus.

Simone wondered, too, what kind of reception she would get from Professor Athan. So far, it hadn't been good. She'd known plenty of men who were threatened by a woman of her background and professional standing—in the Middle East, she was regarded the way one would regard a talking camel—but even in the West, she had encountered resistance. With Lucas, however, it seemed like something else was in play. She didn't want to flatter herself, but she could tell from the way he looked at her—when he allowed himself to—that he was fighting something a lot more elemental. That was part of it, she felt sure.

But was she fighting something elemental, too? Where, for instance, had that brief fantasy of married life come from only minutes ago?

The rest of his resistance could possibly be chalked up to something more arcane—maybe to a bit of the scholar's possessiveness. No one liked to share, especially prematurely, the fruits of one's labor and research. In the academy, the spoils were so thin—reputations made and tenures secured on the slimmest of discoveries—that intellectual property was guarded as jealously as gold bullion. She knew the feeling well; when the ossuary had been ripped from the main hall in Cairo, she had felt like a mother whose child had just been stolen from her. It was no surprise that Lucas had been a little standoffish, even rude.

His approval didn't matter to her. Only his access to the ossuary did.

Delaney used his key ring to open the side door to the museum lobby, then turned off the internal alarm and led her through the galleries, faintly illuminated by night-lights, and back to the locked door of the conservation wing. As he fumbled with the keys—Was he as nervous as she was?—she could see a crack of light under the threshold and hear the faint scraping of metal on a hardwood floor. She hoped that Lucas hadn't jumped the gun and started the work without them.

Inside, she found that the door was nearly blocked by all the spindly easels and old crates that the army crew, or Lucas himself, had moved out of the way in order to clear a perimeter around the ossuary, which was now bathed in the glare of several spotlights mounted all around it. It looked like a magazine photo shoot. Lucas himself was standing on a cinder block, adjusting the lens on a movie camera fixed to a sturdy tripod. He lifted one hand to signal that he had seen them, but otherwise continued with what he was doing.

Delaney carried the Gladstone bag to a nearby worktable and unclasped its handles. An old, thin mattress, the kind used on dormitory cots, was tucked under the table.

Simone wasn't sure where she should go or what she should do. She considered taking her coat off and draping it on one of the stools, as Delaney had just done, but there was something chilly, and discomfiting, about the room.

"Looks like this is going to be a Cecil B. DeMille production," Delaney joked.

But Lucas was still so absorbed in the camera he made no reply.

Simone looked around. It was a big space, cluttered with wooden boxes, stacked canvases, and half-restored sculptures. The clerestory window, the one the bats had apparently flown through, had been securely closed after the incursion. Lucas had spread drop cloths around the base of the pedestal on which the ossuary rested.

Removing his good eye from the viewfinder on the camera, Lucas leaned back and surveyed the setup. He had still not looked directly at her.

"So, whose idea was the movie?" Delaney asked, removing from the bag what Simone now saw was a hacksaw, and laying it on the work-table.

"Colonel Macmillan's." Lucas wound a crank on the side of the Bell & Howell Eyemo assembly. "But it was standard procedure in the field, too."

"Maybe for the Cultural Recovery Commission, it was—I hear you guys got whatever you wanted." Turning to Simone, he said, "You knew, right, that Lucas here was one of the guys assigned to recover the artworks the Nazis had stolen?"

"I did." Despite whatever personal problems they had, she would be forever grateful to him for rescuing the ossuary from the Nazi hoard.

Flicking a lever on the camera and positioning himself in front of one of the three lenses on the turret, Lucas announced his name, the date, the time and location of the filming, and, finally, the other dramatis personae.

"Professor Patrick Delaney, of the Princeton Mineralogy and Geophysics Department," he said, "and . . . um . . ." He didn't seem to know exactly how to complete the introduction.

"Simone Rashid, PhD Oxford, representing the Egyptian Ministry of Culture," she said, putting him out of his misery by stepping into full view of the lens as she spoke. "Oh, and currently an interim professor attached to the Middle Eastern Studies Department here."

Then, like an extra who had strayed onto the center of the stage, she dutifully took one big step back. Unless she was mistaken, Lucas had visibly blushed when she'd stood at his side.

"Yes, thanks for that," Lucas mumbled, and finally gave her a glance, at once so bashful and sincere that it threw her into further confusion. Maybe he wasn't the only one feeling some unacknowledged current passing between them, she thought. He flicked off the camera in order to preserve the remaining film in the canister.

"I see you've got a blowtorch there," Delaney said, taking an inventory of the tools Lucas had laid out on the table. "I wouldn't recommend it. If you try to use it to sever the chains, it's going to scorch the alabaster for sure, and you're going to get a very nasty chemical reaction." Holding up his own hacksaw, he said, "Sometimes the old ways are the best ways."

Lucas acceded, and then asked Simone if she could run the movie camera while he helped with the removal of the chains.

"I've never done that before," she confessed. The Egyptian ministry was lucky if it could procure a still camera.

"There's nothing to it," he said, guiding her up onto the cinder block. "You just direct the lens by looking through here—the focus is already set—and flick this lever forward to begin filming, and backward to stop. I've loaded extra stock, so we have a total running time of almost fifteen minutes."

Simone took up her position, glad in a way to have something to do, and watched as Lucas, wearing heavy-duty work gloves, lifted the first chain away from the lid of the ossuary—it allowed for only an inch or two of leeway—and wedged a protective cloth underneath it.

"Start rolling," he said, and as she put her eye to the viewfinder and pushed the lever forward, she felt the low hum of the spring-wound camera vibrating against her cheek.

Lucas held the chain taut as he watched Delaney, wearing his own gloves, place the blade of the hacksaw to the links. He could hardly believe that this time had come, that within a matter of minutes he would finally know what the ossuary contained. After only a half-dozen strokes, the rusty links gave way, dissolving into a gingery powder.

"Hope it all goes that smoothly," Delaney said.

"Hear, hear," Lucas said, noting that his pulse had begun to race. Curiosity was quickly overtaking his anxiety.

The next chain, however, did not yield as easily. It took some persistent sawing to remove it. For the last one, directly positioned over the diamond shape that he had yet to identify, Lucas said, "Let's switch," and took the saw into his own hands. This spot was too delicate to risk incurring any damage.

"Be my guest," said Delaney, lifting the last links as far from the alabaster surface as the chain would allow. "This is your baby."

Lucas touched the blade to the chain and pulled it back as if he were drawing the bow across a violin. Flakes of rust fell onto the soft rags wedged underneath. He pushed the blade forward again, and this time larger flakes fell, like ashes from an open fire. After several more strokes, the link broke, and the two ends of the chain slithered off of the sarcophagus like snakes racing back to their burrows. One of them coiled over Lucas's shoe, and he involuntarily shuddered as he kicked it aside.

"Should I keep filming?" Simone said as the two men stood back to assess the next step.

"No, hold on for a second," Lucas said, retrieving the thin mattress from under the work-table, then wedging it on the floor at the top end of the ossuary. "We're going to slide the lid off lengthwise. That way, we can support it from both sides all the way."

"Gotcha," Delaney said. "Say when."

Lucas took a deep breath, and got as firm a grip as he could on the smooth white stone. Even through his gloves he could feel how cold it was. After instructing Simone to start rolling again, he said, "On three," and at the end of the count, he and Delaney gently pushed in the same direction. At first, the lid went nowhere, as though it were riveted in place, and Lucas wondered if it some-how had been. But there were no indications of that—no nails, no bore holes in the sides of the box—so he counted it off again and they both pushed harder. This time, there was a tiny grinding noise, as the accumulated grit of the centuries began to crumble under their exertions.

"At least we know that we can budge it," Delaney

said, brushing grains of sand from his gloves.

Lucas nodded, his gaze fixed on the capering creatures carved along the borders of the lid. For the first time—no doubt it was just the peculiar angle from which he was viewing them—he thought he detected a gleeful expression on one or two.

"Again?" Delaney said, bending slightly to put his shoulder into it.

"Again."

Together, they pushed the lid farther along the length of the box, fully a foot or two, before they both had to take a breather. The bottom of the interior was now exposed, though even the glare from the surrounding lights somehow failed to penetrate it. Lucas didn't want to look, anyway. He wanted to wait until the lid was entirely, and safely, removed, and then take in the contents all at once. He checked to see that Simone was following the action, then returned to the task.

The ponderous lid scraped along the rim of the sarcophagus until enough of it protruded over the top end that Lucas had to change positions. With Delaney pushing from the bottom, while he kept the slab balanced, they were finally able to tilt it on end, and from there lower it flat, with a resounding thump, against the mattress. A cloud of dust rose from the old mattress, and the ossuary itself, as if exhaling, released a gust of acrid air, a smell like burnt matches and desert sand. Lucas barely had time to turn his head away and catch a breath of less tainted air when he heard Simone murmur, from behind the camera, "Oh my God."

Straightening, he turned to the open box. Delaney was standing mute, staring into it. Lucas's eye jumped from the jumble of bones to the crooked staff, and from that to the ancient iron crucifix—or was it silver, dulled by the centuries?—all lying helter-skelter inside. He had certainly expected to find skeletal human remains, but he had not expected—nor, apparently, had Simone—to find so *many* bones, including two separate skulls, only one of which was plainly human. The other one was more perplexing. Smaller, and with a sloping brow and unusually close eye sockets, it might have been the skull of an ape, or even a hideously deformed child.

"Are you getting this?" Lucas asked, and Simone, still manning the camera, said, "Yes," in a hushed tone.

Lucas leaned forward, and as if under some strange compulsion, lifted the odd skull from the heap of other bones and artifacts. Like Hamlet staring into the empty orbs of poor Yorick, he held it up for closer scrutiny.

"Something's going wrong with the camera," Simone said. "Everything's getting blurry."

Before Lucas could even think to come to her aid, he felt an even stranger sensation—a feeling that the yellowed skull was somehow looking *back* at him. A shiver descended his spine, and a breeze stirred the hair on his head. He looked at Delaney—his hair was blowing, too, and Simone, he saw, was struggling to keep her balance on the cinder block. A wind had sprung up in the room, out of nowhere, and was rustling the tarps around the base of the pedestal, making the paintings quiver on the creaking easels.

Delaney said, "Put it back," and Simone, nearly falling, left the camera running, its lens pivoting on the tripod as she stepped down to the floor, hugging herself as though she were freezing.

Lucas dropped the skull back among the other bones, but the turbulence only grew stronger, as if something unseen was gathering speed and racing around the room in search of escape. The new window groaned in its frame, the glass splintered but held, and though it might only have been the wind, Lucas thought he heard a low moan from behind the crates piled around the door.

The spotlights flickered and dimmed, and before they came back on again, there was a banging sound as the door was flung open so violently that the hinges squeaked and the wood cracked.

The wind followed, sucked out into the dark galleries, leaving an eerie emptiness in the room. The camera had swiveled toward the door, and it clicked and whirred as the last of the film was depleted. Simone's teeth were chattering, and Lucas instinctively went to her and wrapped her in a bear hug—a hug she did not resist.

"Did that just happen?" Delaney said, slumping against a worktable and passing his hand across his eyes in disbelief.

"Yes," Simone whispered, so low it was as if she were speaking only to herself.

Lucas said nothing, though he, too, had been gravely affected. Inside him now, there was a melancholy ache, a sorrow more profound than any he had ever known. He sensed that he had served as a conduit, however fleetingly, for something suddenly free and wild, something as old as time, and unutterably bad.

Chapter NINETEEN

"Get out of here!" Andy Brandt shouted at the kids gathered around the Caithness Man's display case. "Go to school!"

"Make us!" one of them retorted.

"It's a Saturday!" another one said.

But they did disperse, scooting around him and out the door of Guyot Hall, hooting and hollering as they skipped down the front steps. Those damn kids treated the collection of artifacts as if they were a freak show, and Andy longed for the chance to give a couple of them a good swat.

He couldn't risk getting into any trouble with

the university, however. It had taken a lot of cunning and a lot of time, to get securely situated there, and anything that called undue attention to him, or his work, would be dangerous to everyone involved. Most of all, to Andy.

Besides, he thought, as he unlocked the door to his cluttered first-floor lab, he had other, more immediate problems.

For one, he had felt like crap since sneaking into the conservation room with the key he'd secretly copied off of Delaney's ring. From his perch behind the crates and easels stacked by the door, he'd only been able to see bits and pieces of what was going on. But he'd seen enough to know that it was an undertaking of great significance.

A movie camera had been set up, with that Egyptian woman running it, and although what Lucas and Delaney said to each other had been largely inaudible to him, he could hear their grunts and groans as they had sawed through the chains and removed the lid from a white stone chest. An ossuary, to be precise—the one his superiors back in Berlin had been tracking.

It was pure luck that Brandt had already been safely ensconced at Princeton when the thing arrived on campus. For purposes the Reich chose to keep secret, his original mission had been to keep a close eye on the radio isotope experiments being conducted in Delaney's lab; no fool, Andy had surmised the reason had something to do with the invention of new weaponry. Then, out of the blue, this ossuary had shown up, and virtually overnight, all of the priorities had changed. It was enough to make Andy's head spin.

"The artifact was stolen from the Führer's own collection," the encoded telegraph message had said. "It is critical to the war effort."

A box of old bones?

"Alert us to any developments. Procure and immediately transmit any information relating to its study, disposition, or relocation."

Okay, he'd thought. He would do as he was told.

Only, something very odd had happened the moment the box was opened. A chill wind had inexplicably sprung up out of nowhere, as if there were air filters or fans hidden around the room. He'd hunkered down, afraid that the easels might topple over and blow his cover, but something even more troubling had occurred instead. He'd felt certain that there was something in that wind, something sentient, though invisible—how crazy was that?—and that it was careening around the room, like a wild beast desperately searching for a way out of a trap. He'd been knocked flat, shivering, and when he could get back on all fours, he'd made a mad scramble for the door. Running through the dark gallery, he'd been sure something was following close on his heels, but he'd been too afraid to stop, or even look back.

All the way to his apartment, one dingy room

on Harrison Street, where the grad students and preceptors lived, he'd had that same sense of something nipping at his heels. Once or twice, he had even imagined he heard a weird gibbering at his ear. Home, he'd slammed the door shut, thrown the bolt lock, and then slumped, utterly out of breath, against the edge of the bed, where his transmitter was cleverly concealed inside a compartment cut into the box spring.

But whatever sense of relief or safety he'd expected, it had not come. He didn't feel that he had locked anything out.

On the contrary, he felt that he had locked something in.

Under the shower, even with the hot water running at full blast, he couldn't get warm. After making his brief and surreptitious nightly broadcast to his foreign contact, he had gotten into bed with every blanket and sheet he owned piled on top of him. What the hell was wrong with him? Had he suddenly caught the flu, or some bizarre disease carried on that wind out of nowhere? It wasn't like he'd be able to ask any of the others—Delaney, Lucas, or that Simone somebody—if they were feeling ill themselves. To do that, he'd have had to admit he'd been there in the first place.

The next morning, he'd awakened feeling even worse, so bad he'd contemplated going to the campus infirmary. He hadn't felt like himself.

Brushing his teeth, he hadn't felt it was his own hand, under his own control, holding the brush. Shaving, he'd been wary of holding the blade close to his own neck. His eyes had a faint yellowish cast, like jaundice, and more than once he'd had the bizarre impression that someone else was looking out of them.

Even his actions had felt slightly . . . remote. Delayed. His mind had gone to a terrible place, to fatal diseases of muscular degeneration. He'd dropped to the floor and done a set of pushups, just to be sure that he still could. Then he had jogged in place with the radio news on. The war wasn't going so well for the Axis powers on the Western Front. The four-hundred-mile long Siegfried Line, built by Hitler in the late 1930s to protect the borders of the old German empire, was under attack. A CBS reporter announced, "With any luck, the German redoubts are going to fall like dominoes. It won't be easy—nothing in war ever is—but it looks like it will just be a matter of time before the Stars and Stripes are flying over the Fatherland."

What, he had wondered, would happen to him when the war ended? In victory, his future would be assured . . . but in defeat? Would he wind up marooned in America?

But then, in a stroke of luck he could never have foreseen, Lucas and Delaney had dropped into his lap exactly what he wanted—a batch of bones and bone fragments that Andy knew had come straight out of that ossuary.

Pretending ignorance, he'd asked, "Where did these come from?"

"That doesn't matter," Lucas had replied.

"It does to an anthropologist."

"Okay, then, from an anonymous donor. I just need you to tell me, as soon as possible, everything you can about their origin and anatomy."

Sorting through them, Andy had seen a femur and a fibula, a tibia, a patella, a scapula, assorted odds and ends, and two skulls, one plainly misshapen.

"I'm especially interested," Lucas had said, "in what they're from—human or animal—and in how the creatures died. I also want to know if there are any signs of violence or disease having played a part. Can you do that for me?"

Not wanting to betray his eagerness, Andy'd said, "Well, I do have a lot of prep work to do for my senior seminar in—"

"Skip it. Do this first."

And so he had. So he had.

Drawing the stool up to the lab counter now, he picked up where he had left off the day before—with the last fragment he had been working on. It was a nub of yellowed bone the size of a fat thumb, with a blunt base and sharpened end—and he held it again under the high-intensity lamp.

A knock sounded, and the door opened just

enough for Lucas to put his head in. Andy had always meant to ask him how he'd lost that eye.

"Glad to see you're hard at it," Lucas said, coming in.

"That's what you do when you don't have tenure."

"If it's any comfort, I don't either."

"Maybe so, but they're not going to let a combat veteran like you, a war hero, go."

Lucas didn't take the bait and divulge anything. Coming close enough to see the stub that Andy was studying, he asked, "That *is* one of the bones I gave you, right?"

"Yep."

"So, what's the verdict?"

Andy put it down. "I can tell you what it *isn't,*" he said. Even then, he had to wonder if he should be sharing his findings so freely. After all, it wasn't like Lucas and Delaney were his allies.

"Why don't you start by telling me what you *do* know about the bones."

But if he *didn't* share what he had learned, he might find himself cut off from any further teamwork on this project—a project his superiors deemed of the utmost importance. "What I do know is that we've got a pretty eclectic selection here." For the time being, he decided to err, if err it was, on the side of cooperation. Gesturing at the human skull and some other bones arranged on a worktable in the corner, he said, "Over there, we've got one almost complete skeleton."

"Of what?"

"A man, on the tall side, and, putting aside the evident antiquity of the bones, very elderly. I know Delaney has some other samples—has he figured out anything of their actual age?" he asked innocently.

"They're old. Maybe a couple of thousand years. Go on."

"Okay," Andy said, drawing the word out.

"Do you know what he died of?"

"Hard to say with any certainty. I can tell you that he led a hell of a hard life. There's evidence of extreme nutritional deficiencies, along with more marks of physical violence than I can count, ranging from scratches and bites to fractures and bone breaks. I wouldn't be surprised if the guy had been a soldier or a gladiator or maybe even a slave. In any case, he took a lot of beatings."

Lucas nodded, absorbing it all.

"I mean, by the end of his life, the guy had maybe six fingers and three teeth left, and judging from the indentation of the right zygomatic bone, I'd be surprised if he still had that eye at all." He paused before adding, "Sorry, I guess you know how that goes."

Ignoring the apology, Lucas said, "What about the other skull and fragments?"

Andy shrugged and turned on his stool to face

the counter right behind him. "This one's much more of a puzzle."

"Why?"

He held up the smaller skull with its sloping brow, broad nasal plane, and unusually elongated mouth, to which several pointed incisors still clung. "You might think it's human—and it's close—but there are enough substantial anomalies to rule that out. I assumed it was one of our close simian cousins, maybe one of them that had died young, before it had grown to its full proportions."

"And is it?"

"The contours of the bones and some of the tiny cartilaginous remnants are what you might expect to find in a sample like that," Andy conceded, "but then there are some things that you definitely wouldn't."

"Such as?"

"Such as this," he said, picking up the nubbin he'd been studying when Lucas came in.

"It looks like a shard of stone to me."

"Oh, no, it's not that. It's definitely organic."

"Is it a finger? You said the other skeleton was missing several of them."

"It's not that, either."

"I don't have all day, Brandt. What are you getting at?"

"A horn. It's a piece of horn, like from a goat."

"Okay, it's from a goat."

"Only it's not. And it's not from a bull or a rhino

or anything else I can think of offhand." He twirled it under the lamp. "Of course, it might help if you could provide me with some salient information on how and where you found it." It was time, he thought, for a little quid pro quo. He wanted to hear, from Lucas himself, what he already knew about the ossuary. He wanted to elicit at least that one small vote of trust.

"I told you, it doesn't matter," Lucas replied distractedly. "Just put down everything you've told me in a written report, right away. I need it."

"Who for?"

Now Lucas looked irritated. "Has it ever occurred to you simply to do what you're asked?"

"Has it ever occurred to you that you're not my boss?" Andy shot back, before he could stop himself. "You're not even in my department. I'm the one doing you the favor."

Lucas couldn't argue with that, and Andy knew it. Still, it wasn't a smart move to piss him off; he should have held his tongue.

"You're right," Lucas replied, in an even tone of voice that Andy could see was costing him. "Slip it under my study door at your earliest convenience."

Well, that had not been the most fruitful exchange, Andy thought—he'd given out plenty, and he'd received nothing in return, except for the renewed sense that these bones were important—very important—and it behooved him to figure out why.

For the next couple of hours, he worked on the written report, while sipping hot tea one moment to warm himself up, and a glass of cold water the next to cool himself down. It was as if his body was at war with itself. Outside, he could hear the occasional sound of a tuba or a trombone blaring as a marching band member made his way down toward the stadium. There was a football game that afternoon, though he could not recall the opponent. Was it Columbia, or maybe Dartmouth? On the one hand, he tried to participate in all these collegiate events; he wanted to give the impression he was devoted to the school and to his employment there, however tenuous. In truth, though, he couldn't stand all this rah-rah non-sense. At Heidelberg, the university had been a temple dedicated to things of the mind, not the body, and that was just one of the myriad ways in which the German system, in his estimation, surpassed the American.

He was getting too tired to see straight. The notes he was typing up were rife with misspellings, and his back was killing him from sitting on the stool. Shutting down the lab, he put on his coat, locked the door behind him, and went out into the dim exhibition hall.

Tucking in his scarf on the way to the front doors, he noticed that something was lying on the floor at the base of the Caithness Man's display case, and went over to pick it up.

It was an open pack of Wrigley's Spearmint gum, which had no doubt fallen out of the pocket of one of those brats he'd chased out of the building earlier. Oh well, it was his own good fortune now, as the pack was nearly full. He took out a stick, and was about to put the rest in his pocket, when, in jest, he offered one to the Caithness Man.

"Gum?" he said, but the word froze in his throat as he stared at his own reflection in the glass—or what should have been his own reflection. What he saw there instead, pressed up against the glass, was the face of a leering gargoyle with beady golden eyes and a slash of mouth that stretched from ear to pointed ear. He reared back, and as he did, the image—the hallucination—evaporated as quickly as it had appeared. Now it was only the Caithness Man again, lashed to his stake.

Bumping into a rack of primitive tools behind him, and still keeping his eye on the display case, he stumbled to the doors, and then outside onto the sunlit steps.

Somebody blasted a trumpet, and some others laughed, on their way to the game.

Andy clung to the railing with both hands, the blood thrumming in his veins, and his thoughts in turmoil. This work was getting to him in a way nothing else had ever done, enough to make him wonder, just what *had* he been studying in his lab?

And what, perhaps, had been studying him?

Chapter TWENTY

If you had to attend a football game, this was the kind of day to do it, Lucas thought. The sun was shining in a bright blue sky, the air was crisp and cold, and the crowd passing through the high arches into the Princeton stadium was in a festive mood, waving pennants and calling out to each other in boisterous voices.

Still, if President Dodds hadn't made faculty attendance so imperative—his earlier admonition had been succeeded by an envelope containing tickets to the reserved seating area and inscribed with "See you there!"—Lucas would have continued to do nothing but focus on the ossuary and the aftermath of its opening.

Christ, it had been a hard couple of days. Once the wind had died down in the conservation wing and there seemed nothing else to do that night, Delaney, looking pale and perturbed, had packed up his tools and wandered off toward his lab again, while Lucas had removed the film canister from the camera, locked up the room, and escorted Simone through the murky corridors of the museum and out into the dismal night. He hadn't had to say he was walking her back to the Nassau Inn; it was understood. And truth be told, he was doing it as much for himself as for her. Neither one of them would have wanted to be alone with the knowledge of what they had just witnessed. Lucas felt like something at his very core—call it a coldly empirical cast of mind—had been turned upside down, like a cocktail shaker, and rattled hard.

Simone was quiet as they walked along the puddled pathways across the campus, and she made no objection when Lucas looped a protective arm around her shoulders. Indeed, she seemed to melt into his body, so that the two of them were walking less like participants in an academic endeavor than lovers. Not since leaving Europe had Lucas experienced such an onslaught of feelings—everything from shock to confusion, tenderness to guilt at having exposed Simone, and Delaney, too, to such a troubling and possibly dangerous event. He could barely sort through the unfamiliar rush of emotions. Emotions were what he had been trying to keep at bay ever since the iron mine.

Like moths drawn to flame, he and Simone made their way through the darkness and toward the lights of town. Most of the storefronts were closed down for the night, but the lights were on in the windows of the Nassau Inn, and even the lobby was bustling with people. A placard on a stand welcomed the members of the Northeast Bottling Association to their annual convention, still in progress in the Gold Ballroom upstairs.

"It will be much quieter downstairs," Simone said, leading Lucas to the taproom, where only a few of the revelers had found their way to the bar. Two wingback chairs, flanking the roaring fireplace, were unoccupied, and Simone and Lucas took them. Lucas ordered her a Campari and soda, the drink he'd seen her imbibe the day they met, and a double Scotch on the rocks for himself.

Despite the glow from the hearth, Simone still looked pale. Her eyes stayed riveted on the orange flames and crackling wood in the fireplace. "I should have told you sooner," she finally said.

"Told me what?"

"The ossuary. My father and I believe it contains the bones of Saint Anthony. We found it in the White Desert, the empty quarter of the Sahara."

"Saint Anthony," he repeated. It was the second time in a matter of hours he had heard the name. Wasn't Wally Gregg dying from something called Saint Anthony's fire? Could this really be just a coincidence?

"He was a saint who wrestled with demons."

"Okay," Lucas replied, evenly. Why not? In his experience, most saints had colorful and extraordinary tales told about them; it was how they'd become saints in the first place.

"My father . . ." Simone hesitated. "He thinks

that the box might hold not only the saint's relics, but some residue of his powers, too."

Lucas took a strong slug of his Scotch, absorbing all that she was finally telling him. "So, are you suggesting that we might have released some holy spirit into the world?" he said skepti-cally.

She didn't reply.

"Well, if we did, the world could certainly use it about now."

"He also believes," she said, "that the box might have contained the spirit of something evil. Something the saint had captured."

That revelation comported eerily with what Lucas had experienced in the past hour. Putting his glass down on the tiny table between the two chairs, he thought of the dreadful and annihilating sadness that had coursed through him once he'd lifted that strange skull from inside its alabaster prison. No believer in ancient spirits or trapped demons, he nonetheless remained at a loss to account for such a sensation. Even in the worst of the war—the night he'd discovered the bodies of the parishioners all locked in a church that had been burned down around them, or the day he'd watched the blond boy blown to bits by the land mine—he'd felt nothing like it. Those ordeals had been traumatic, but at least he could grasp why they had been so disturbing—he had seen the carnage, he had smelled the death.

Anyone in his right mind would have been rocked back on his heels. But this time, he had observed nothing concrete, nor had he sustained any physical damage.

So why did his insides feel like that bleak and empty desert Simone had adverted to?

"What else can you tell me?" Lucas asked, and in a low, almost perfunctory tone, Simone told him all about her father's research, their expedition into the cave hidden below the spitting cobra, the scorpion attack on young Mustafa, the theft of the box from the Cairo Museum. Every-thing. As she did so, he began to put together a picture—a picture that might explain why the Reich had been so intent on retrieving the ossuary, and why the OSS was equally determined to hold onto it and exploit it. The Axis powers and the Allies were fighting over what amounted, in his view, to a magical talisman. He might have utterly discounted such an idea days before, but not any-more.

Not with the echo of that wind in his ears and the icicle in his heart.

Without even being aware of it, his hand had bridged the table between them and taken hold of hers. Despite her proximity to the fireplace, her skin was still cold, and he clutched her fingers to warm them. Her fingers squeezed his back, though she never averted her gaze from the leaping, crackling flames. It was as if she were looking back in time, back at the events she had been describing. When the waitress returned to see if they wanted another round, Lucas said no, paid the bill, and led Simone back up to the elevator bank in the lobby.

"I would ask you to come up and meet my father, but he might have gone to bed already."

"Another time."

"Yes."

Still, he was reluctant to let her go. "What about tomorrow?" he said suddenly. "I'm pretty much required to attend the Columbia football game, and I have extra tickets."

"A football game?"

As he said it, he'd warmed to the idea. Maybe a day in the sunshine and fresh air was precisely what they all needed. What better way to dispel the pall that had descended upon them that night, even if it was only for a few hours? And if he was completely honest with himself, the idea of spending an afternoon with this lovely young woman carried its own appeal. "You owe it to your father, too," he said, "to show him something other than the inside of a library or an art museum." Gradually he could see her come around. A small smile creased her lips, and for a moment, he thought she was going to stand on her toes and kiss him.

And she might have, had it not been for the heavy paw slapping him on the shoulder, and the tipsy conventioneer saying, "Aren't you the new sales rep from Hartford?"

He might have returned such a kiss, eagerly, if she had.

Instead, the moment passed, the elevator arrived, and she stepped inside. As the doors closed, it was all he could do not to duck inside with her.

"You shouldn't have let that one get away," the conventioneer had said before stumbling off. "She's a keeper."

The phrase had stuck with him, and he thought of it even now, as he watched her tenderly guide her father, one hand at his elbow, into the football stadium. From what she'd whispered to him when Dr. Rashid was out of earshot, getting him here had not been an easy sell.

"He thinks we're all insane to be wasting time on this when we could be working on the ossuary."

"But you got him to come."

"It's all because he wanted to size you up."

Lucas had laughed. "What's the verdict?"

"Still out."

A student usher, in an orange blazer and straw boater hat, studied their ticket stubs, then led them down to their seats in the section reserved for faculty and special guests. Dr. Rashid made sure to place himself between them on the bench.

The stadium was only half full, but everyone had congregated down front and in the center.

The Princeton side of the field was a sea of orange and black, while the Columbia fans were decked out in the school's blue and white. The two mascots—a Princeton tiger and a Columbia lion—were gamboling about their respective sidelines in tatty costumes, stirring up the crowd. On the far side of the aisle, and several rows back toward the bleachers, he spotted Taylor from the boardinghouse wolfing down a hot dog and a beer.

Taylor glanced his way, too, but didn't so much as alter his chewing to acknowledge him.

"You know that man?" Simone asked.

"He lives in the same boardinghouse I do, but I can't say I know him. I'm not sure anybody does."

"And how long do these games generally last?" Dr. Rashid interjected, resting his hands atop his ebony cane.

"A couple of hours," Lucas said, "with a break at halftime."

Rashid snorted, and Simone leaned forward just enough to exchange a glance with Lucas.

"That's when the band plays and puts on a show."

Rashid looked even unhappier, until Simone plucked at his sleeve and said, "Look who else is here."

She directed their gaze a few rows down, where, to Lucas's surprise, he saw a cloud of white hair, billowing like a dandelion, above a brown overcoat and loose orange scarf. It was

Professor Einstein himself, merrily chatting with President Dodds and three other men sitting with them. One was Professor Gödel, recognizable to everyone in town, but the other two Lucas recognized from the papers. The first was the famous Hungarian physicist, Leó Szilárd, who was now conducting his research at Columbia University—nobody knew exactly what he was up to, but it could be surmised to have something to do with the war effort. The other was the world-renowned English philosopher and mathematician, Bertrand Russell. Lucas had seen a poster on campus, advertising a speech he was to give that morning to the Whig-Clio debate society.

"I saw Russell give a series of lectures at Cambridge one summer," Simone said. "On pacifism."

"Pacifism is all well and good when the world is at peace," Dr. Rashid scoffed, "but it is of very little use when it's not. He should stick to his mathematics. When a butcher is threatening to slaughter half the world, Mr. Russell and his high-minded philosophy are the last thing we need."

"I do believe that he has tempered his views in light of recent events," Simone said.

"Tempering them isn't enough. He needs to keep silent altogether."

Lucas was in full agreement. Russell's ideals were lofty and desirable, but in practical terms, impossible. He watched now as the Englishman, thin and elongated as a stork, bent forward, smiling and sharing some story with his compatriots. It looked like they were all having a very congenial reunion.

As Lucas watched, a couple of fans timidly approached the group and apparently asked for Einstein's autograph. The professor obligingly scrawled his name on their programs, as Russell, plainly pretending offense at being overlooked, protested. The fans extended their programs, and Russell, too, signed them with a honking laugh and a grand flourish. Gödel simply immersed himself in deep conversation with Szilárd. Dodds had departed to glad-hand others in the crowd, though not before noting, with a nod of approval, Lucas's presence in the stands.

Just before the game got underway, the announcer's voice came over the loudspeaker, first to lead a prayer for "the safety of our troops fighting for freedom around the globe," and then to acknowledge the special guests in attendance at this game. When his name was called, Russell stood up and took a bow with his arm folded across his abdomen.

"Would Professor Einstein care to come onto the field," the announcer asked, "and perform the traditional coin toss?"

The professor appeared baffled, but his friends urged him on as an usher guided him down onto the field, where he was loudly cheered. He waved bashfully at the crowd, brushing his thick gray moustache with the other hand, as the referee proffered the quarter and explained that all he had to do was let the Columbia quarterback call heads or tails, then toss the coin.

"And then maybe you can explain the probabilities to us," the referee announced over the microphone.

"I expect that they will be precisely the same," Einstein said, in his heavily accented voice. "Precisely the same."

The crowd roared with laughter, as they no doubt would have done at anything Einstein uttered. His voice was more natural and congenial than some might have expected, and he displayed the odd habit—repeating the final phrase of what he'd just said—that Lucas had heard other faculty members comment on.

The Lions' quarterback called tails, Einstein tossed the coin, then glanced down at the result on the back of his hand. "It is . . . tails, *ja*?" and before he could even think to repeat it, the referee declared, "Tails it is." Turning to the Columbia player, he said, "Do you elect to kick, or receive?"

"Receive."

Einstein was escorted back to his seat, and the Tigers kicked off. Lucas explained what was happening as the game went on—"each team has four downs to advance the ball ten yards," and "there's a penalty for what's called holding," or "you can't cross the line of scrimmage until the ball is hiked"—while Simone and her father did their best to follow along. Lucas had the impression that Dr. Rashid, despite his reluctance to come, was beginning to become engaged by the rules and strategies of the game, which was exactly what had appealed to Lucas back when he was in high school and had quarterbacked his team to a state championship. He had enjoyed trying to outthink his opponents, and figure out his players' deployment: Where did you send your receivers, how did you make the most use of your blockers? In those days, Lucas had seldom been sacked. Today, with a patch over one eye, he'd be a sitting duck.

At halftime, with Columbia ahead by one touchdown, the Princeton band marched onto the field in orange blazers and straw hats, playing the usual Sousa medley, and Lucas treated Simone and her dad to hot dogs with generous helpings of relish and mustard—"you've got to have the full football experience," he joked—before discovering that her dad was vegetarian.

"Oh, my apologies," he said, going back for a hot salted pretzel, which Dr. Rashid accepted with gratitude. There was a nip in the air, and the warmth of the food was a welcome antidote. Lucas thought that even Simone had managed to lose herself in the game, and forget, for this short while, the momentous discoveries and events of the past few days. When a Princeton player caught a kickoff and then miraculously ran the ball all the way back downfield and across the goal line, she jumped to her feet with the rest of the crowd, clapping her hands together in glee.

"Now they get three more points if they can kick it between the goal posts?" she asked, and Lucas found himself utterly charmed by her growing enthusiasm.

"One," he said, and after the football had soared cleanly between the uprights, the Lions called for a time-out to regroup.

As the crowd stamped their feet and stretched their arms to get the blood flowing, Lucas noticed a man in a long houndstooth coat, with the collar turned up and a battered hat pulled low, moving down the aisle to his left. Why the man caught his eye at all wasn't clear at first; it might have been the fact that his face seemed so purposefully concealed, or the deliberation with which he was traveling toward the reserved seats, but Lucas's time on the front had taught him not to ignore his instincts.

The game was already nearly over, the sun settling lower in the sky and a chill descending; the ushers were no longer paying much attention to the activity in the aisles, or to people switching from the bleachers to better seats closer to the field.

The houndstooth man slipped around them all like a shadow, fixed on something straight ahead. Judging from the path he had so far taken, Lucas figured that his goal—or target?—might be the four luminaries, whose heads were bent low in conversation, oblivious to everything going on around them.

"Excuse me," Lucas said, abruptly getting to his feet and inching past Dr. Rashid and Simone.

"If you're going back to the concession stand," Simone said, "the treats are on me this time."

Lucas didn't answer; his entire focus was on the man, whose hands, he now saw, were wedged deep into the pockets of the overcoat. Lucas stepped as nimbly as he could over the other people in the row—one of whom protested, nonetheless, that he had kicked over a thermos—but he was still a dozen yards away when he felt sure that the man was gripping something tightly, and then saw one hand emerge holding a long, sharp blade.

"Watch out!" Lucas shouted as he scrambled over the spectators still in his way.

The man had already reached the front row, and just as Russell rose to adjust the blanket he'd been sitting on, he leapt forward, with the knife raised. Einstein, oblivious to the threat, was tamping tobacco into his pipe.

But the leap had been clumsy, and whether he'd slipped on the concrete or tripped over someone's shoe, he wound up falling between two rows, the knife scraping against the edge of the wooden seats, right between a startled Russell and Einstein's back. Someone screamed, and the man was up and on his feet again, the hat shoved low on his brow, the knife flashing in the late afternoon sun. As Russell stumbled backward, out of reach, and Einstein turned his head—though he still didn't seem to understand what all the commotion was about—Lucas launched himself over a woman still sitting, and rammed his shoulder, like a fullback, into the side of the assailant. They both toppled over, crashing into a couple of other terrified spectators, then tumbling down between two rows of seats.

Lucas groped for the hand still clutching the knife, as the man struggled to get up again and complete his mission. It was almost as if he wasn't aware of Lucas's intervention—his mutilated, but suddenly familiar, face was as blank as a slate, and his coat fell open to reveal a ruddy neck, bumpy as a gourd.

Lucas grabbed at the cuff of his overcoat, but the man swung the knife wildly, slicing through the sleeve of his leather bomber jacket. Slamming the hand holding the knife against the edge of the seats—once, twice, three times—Lucas tried to shake the blade loose. But the man would not let go. His eyes, dull and glassy, looked empty of intention, though his swollen lips opened wide to shout out something that sounded like gibberish. Lucas shoved his open palm under the man's chin, snapping his jaws shut and smacking the back of his head against the concrete.

The hat rolled away under the seats. The knife clattered to the cement. The head came up again, shouting the same thing once more, and Lucas slammed it down even harder. This time he felt a sudden ebbing of strength beneath him, as if the air were suddenly escaping from a punctured balloon. The body went slack beneath him, the mouth dropping open like a trapdoor, emitting an odor so foul Lucas could barely breathe. The man's eyes, perhaps catching some errant ray of the autumnal sun, flashed with a golden gleam.

Lucas felt a hand gripping his shoulder, and registered Taylor saying, "You can let go now. You can let go."

The gleam in the man's eye winked out.

Lucas was dimly aware of ushers shepherding Einstein and the others in his party up the aisle. Gödel, hardly able to walk from the fear, was being supported on either side by Russell and Szilárd.

"It's okay to let go," Taylor said, trying to calm him.

Lucas leaned back on his haunches, trying to catch his breath again, his heart still pounding. Taylor had his hand under his arm now, and was helping to raise him up and then deposit him on one of the vacated seats.

Lucas was still trying to make some sense out of what he was seeing.

Lying at his feet, his coat torn open in the struggle, wearing a soiled hospital gown tucked into a pair of suit trousers, was the janitor from the art museum. Wally Gregg.

Simone was suddenly beside him, her hand on the lapel of his jacket. "Are you all right?" she said, her father leaning anxiously on his cane behind her. She plucked at his punctured sleeve and said, "You've been cut."

But Lucas still didn't feel it; the adrenaline coursing through his veins was keeping any pain at bay. All he could focus on was the body sprawled in the aisle. The body of a man who had already been through hell, a man everyone had expected to die in the hospital bed where Lucas had left him.

Only he hadn't. He had died here, and at Lucas's hand.

Ushers, and then a pair of cops, cleared the other onlookers away. The announcer declared over the PA system that, although there was no reason for panic, everyone should leave the stadium immediately, in an orderly fashion.

"We have to get you to a hospital," Simone said.

Taylor agreed—"and get him a tetanus shot, he got cut with that knife"—as several more cops showed up to cordon off the area. Lucas felt Simone's arm wrap around him as he moved up the aisle toward the exit.

"He said something," Lucas said. The crowd, agitated, jostled them on all sides. He was starting to feel some sensation in his upper arm, and something warm—blood—trickling down below his torn sleeve.

"I didn't hear it," Simone said.

"I wonder what it was."

"I heard it," Dr. Rashid confessed as they passed into the gloomy shadow of the archway.

"You did?" Lucas said, lifting his injured arm to his chest in an attempt to shield it from the throng surging around them. "What was it?"

"It was Arabic."

That sounded about right, though he still had no idea what the words meant, or how Wally Gregg of all people would have come to shout them.

"Ancient Arabic, in fact."

The pain in his arm came alive, as abruptly as if a switch had just been thrown. Wincing, Lucas said, "Meaning?"

With an ashen expression on his face, Dr. Rashid carefully planted his cane on the next step, then answered, "It was an oath. A common one in that region of the world."

The PA system blared some unintelligible instruction.

"It means, 'Death to the swine.'"

Chapter TWENTY-ONE

Professor Einstein and his friends were whisked out of the stadium by policemen, loaded into a cruiser, and driven straight back to Mercer Street, sirens blaring and lights flashing. Helen was already waiting on the front porch by the time they got there, and quickly brought them all inside, closing and locking both the screen door, which was usually left open, and the inner door, too. A cop, arms folded, was stationed on the front steps.

Russell, Szilárd, and Gödel were all as agitated as could be expected, though Einstein himself felt an odd sense of calm. The incident, after all, was over, with no serious repercussions—unless that young man, the one with the black patch, had been seriously hurt. He would have to make inquiries about his welfare.

While Helen fussed over the others, offering tea and brandy and wrapping a blanket around the shivering Gödel's shoulders, Einstein himself went up to his office to gather his thoughts. He shrugged off his coat and was just about to toss it on the sofa when he noticed what looked like blood spattered on the collar. He knew it wasn't his own, and now he was even more concerned about the fate of that young man with the eye patch. Something told him that he had even seen the fellow before, and then he remembered—he had observed him once or twice on the porch of that house across the street. Ah then, that would make it easier to find out if he was all right.

Brushing some papers from the seat of his desk chair—Helen sometimes piled his mail there so he wouldn't miss it—he plopped down and let out a great sigh. In a way, he was surprised that this sort of thing hadn't happened to him more often. Every day, he received a flood of fan mail from people in all walks of life—budding scientists, schoolchildren, even the occasional female admirer—but mixed in with all the pleasant stuff were angry letters from cranks, maniacs, conspiracy theorists, anti-Semites, and proud and patriotic Americans who believed he was a Communist sympathizer or worse. J. Edgar Hoover, Einstein knew perfectly well, suspected him of harboring pro-Soviet sentiments and, as a result, had undoubtedly been keeping a file on him at the FBI for many years. It was Hoover, without question, who had been instrumental in revoking the top security clearance that Einstein had once enjoyed.

And which Oppenheimer had secretly circumvented by coming to his house for help.

When the phone rang only minutes later, he wasn't surprised. He waited for Helen to answer it downstairs, as she always did, then listened for her knock on his door. When it came, he said, "Yes?"

"It is from New Mexico, Professor."

He didn't have to know any more than that. He swiveled his creaking chair toward the desk, cleared away some paper debris, and picked up the receiver. He had barely said hello before Oppenheimer blurted out, "Are you all right?"

"Yes, Robert, I am fine."

"I'm told the assassin is dead."

He was? Einstein had not known that for sure. "But he cannot have been an assassin, can he, if I am still here and on the telephone?" At the worst and most trying moments, it was his habit always to try to find a joke. "That is only logical, *ja*?"

"You're spending too much time with Gödel."

Einstein managed a dry chuckle. "Leó and Bertrand are keeping him company right now, in the parlor."

"Is that Bertrand as in Russell?"

"Yes." Einstein could virtually hear Oppenheimer taking in this one small detail he might not have known.

"Huh. I was told there was someone else in your party. They didn't tell me it was Mr. Pacifism and Appeasement himself."

"He has come around in his opinions, you know. In light of what is happening in the world today, his views, like mine, have had to change."

"Well, that's a relief."

"Have you considered that the attacker might have been after him, and not me? The knife fell right between us." Even with the static on the long-distance line, Einstein could hear Oppenheimer snort.

"Nobody wants to kill a philosopher, Albert. Nobody cares."

"And they care about physicists? To most people, I am just an old man long ago put away in mothballs."

"Not to that guy with the knife you weren't. Whoever he turns out to be, he knew better than that. That's what worries me. Will you listen to me now, when I say that you need a bodyguard? I still have friends in Army Intelligence who will okay it if I say so. Hoover will never even know."

"I will think about it."

"Don't bother. You've got more important things to think about, like those problems we reviewed the last time I was there with you."

"That is what I have been doing."

"And? Have you figured out what we're doing wrong?"

"The mathematics were precise, even elegant, but I do think that I have found the underlying flaw."

"In the math?" Oppenheimer asked, surprised.

"No, you cannot beat John von Neumann at

that game. The flaw is in the application. The mechanics."

"Don't tell me anything more over this phone. Write it all down, and I'll send a courier. When do you want him?"

"Allow me the night to compose my conclusions. Send him tomorrow morning, late."

"Okay then. Say good-bye to your cronies, Albert. I've already sent cars to round them up—I'll make sure Russell gets wherever he wants to go, too."

"But he is my houseguest."

"Not anymore, he isn't. What if your crazy theory is right and somebody wants to kill the apostle of peace and harmony, after all? There's a war on—get back to work."

Oppenheimer hung up, as usual, without saying good-bye, and Einstein sat back in his chair. Through the window, he could see a tabby cat lurking near the garage, stalking something in the backyard. He'd seen this cat out there before, and though he knew that cats, too, had to eat, he hoped that its quarry would escape unharmed. If only there were a way, he thought, that every living creature could survive without doing injury to any other. The world had been constructed along bloody lines, of that there was no doubt, and it remained a puzzle at least as baffling as the unified field theory he had been seeking so long.

Outside, he could hear the slamming of car

doors, followed by the tromping of feet on the wooden steps of the front porch. Then voices, several of them—young, male, and peremptory. The security detail sent by Oppenheimer to safely escort everyone away. The man was a strict taskmaster, but then he had to be. A war, indeed, was on—the worst that the world had ever known. Einstein turned his attention to the blackboard on which he had been scrawling his latest calculations, and wondered again if he was serving mankind as an angel, or a devil. Would his work here bring an end to the war, or simply sow the whirlwind? It was something he could have discussed with Russell, a man as tormented by such questions as he was, for hours on end.

But not, it would seem, tonight. Tonight there would be no vigorous debate, no company at all, in fact.

Turning his attention to the blackboard, in only a few moments he had done what he had always been able to do, whether it was in a quiet study in Bern or on a crowded trolley car in Berlin— he had lost himself in his true home: the beautiful, and infinitely consoling, realm of thought alone.

Chapter TWENTY-TWO

Even though Simone had wanted—begged—to accompany Lucas to the hospital, he had persuaded her to stay with her father, who looked, quite understandably, very troubled and shocked by the incident at the stadium.

The emergency room was in commotion, too, and Lucas wondered if this was common on a Saturday evening. Doctors and nurses were bustling about, speaking in low tones and appearing distracted. It was several minutes before a harried intern was found who could attend to Lucas's knife wound. After swabbing it with antiseptic and taking a cursory look, he declared it a superficial wound, but put in a half-dozen stitches for good measure.

As the intern gathered up his supplies, he happened to ask Lucas how he'd been cut, and when Lucas told him he'd been attacked by a guy with a knife—"a guy named Wally Gregg, who's been a patient in this hospital"—the intern abruptly stopped and said, "Can you wait here for a minute?"

Lucas had barely finished buttoning his blood-stained shirt when a portly man in a blue uniform barged in. A brass badge pinned to his lapel identified him as T.J. Farrell, Borough Police Chief.

"Is what that intern just told me true?"

"I couldn't have made it up. What's going on?"

"A doctor was injured downstairs a couple of hours ago. He was working in the morgue."

"Was his name Crowley, by any chance?"

"Jesus Christ," Farrell said. "How'd you know that, too?"

"I know he was attending to Wally Gregg."

"Grab your stuff," he said, gesturing at Lucas's torn jacket draped on the examining table, "and come with me. Now."

Leading him down a corridor, Farrell threw open the door to a private room where Lucas found Dr. Crowley propped up in a bed, with a bandage around his head, an IV drip hooked up to his arm, and a dreamy sedated look in his eye.

"I gather you two don't need any introductions," Farrell said.

Crowley didn't reply, but lifted a hand limply off the bed to indicate that it was true.

"Mr. Lucas here says that he was attacked, too—and by the same guy that attacked you."

A dim but fearful light went on in Crowley's eyes.

"Tell him what happened in the morgue, Doc."

Crowley looked uncertain, as if he wasn't sure he could or even should tell this particular story.

"Tell him already. I haven't got all day."

"He died," the doctor croaked from the bed.

"You mean the patient, right?" Farrell said, in a tone indicating that he was merely prompting the doctor for Lucas's benefit.

"Yes. Gregg. Wally Gregg died."

"From the infection," Farrell prompted him again. "The bat bites, right?"

Crowley nodded, but just barely. "I pronounced him dead myself," he said, his words slurred by the drugs. "He had no heartbeat. No pulse. No brain activity. He was dead."

"And then what?" Farrell said. "Go on—tell him."

"We took him downstairs for the autopsy. I was filling out the certificate. The death certificate." Crowley closed his eyes for a few seconds before continuing. "That's when I heard a noise, and I turned around." He stopped again, as if unable to believe what he was recounting. "He was sitting up. His eyes were open."

"And then what?" the chief said.

"He picked up the metal block—the one we wedge under the knees during an autopsy—and he hit me with it." His hand went up toward his bandaged head. "He hit me with it, over and over again. He knocked me out."

Lucas could hardly fathom what he was hearing. The last time he'd seen Wally in the hospital, the poor man looked like he was only inches from death's door. How could he have recovered enough to knock someone out, much less leave the hospital, arm himself, and travel all the way to the stadium?

"When Doc Crowley here came to," Farrell said to Lucas, "he was missing most of his clothes—his pants, his shoes, his coat and hat—and we have since learned that one of the surgical knives is gone. You think that's what he used to wound you?"

"I didn't get a good look at it."

"We'll get it later. Anything you can add to this?"

Lucas wondered how much he should share. "He looked like he was in a trance of some kind," he said, "and he seemed to be heading straight for Professor Einstein."

"Dr. Einstein was at the game?" Plainly, this part of the story was news to the police chief, and very unwelcome news at that.

"Yes. Even when I knocked Wally down and started fighting with him, he was still so focused on getting to his target that I don't think he actually saw me."

Farrell waited for more.

"I had to bang his head against the concrete to get him to stop."

"And you think you killed him?"

"Yes," Lucas said, "I killed him," uttering words that he had never had to say out loud, even on the front lines in Europe. It was as if he were speaking some foreign, and abhorrent, tongue.

"Don't worry about it," Crowley said. "He was already dead."

"Did he do anything else?" Farrell asked Lucas. "Did he say anything?"

The question gave Lucas pause. Should he bring up Wally's bizarre Arabic curse? Could such information be of any possible use to the police? Or would it simply complicate things and cast doubt on his own credibility?

"Nothing that I could make out."

Farrell mulled this over. "But Dr. Einstein's okay, right?"

"Yes. He wasn't injured. When I left, the ushers were escorting him out of the stadium."

Farrell digested the additional information before pulling a card from his wallet and giving it to Lucas. "You think of anything else, you call me."

Lucas slipped the card into his pants pocket.

"And only me. Don't talk to anybody else. It'll be my problem from now on. The hospital's not going to need any more bad press than it's already likely to get, and personally, I'd rather not have a bunch of state troopers looking over my shoulder. Are we all agreed on that?"

"Got it," Lucas said.

"And that goes for you, too, Doc," the chief barked. "Radio silence, from here on in." Farrell ran a pudgy hand over the few stray hairs on his head. "What a mess," he muttered.

"Dead," Crowley reiterated, to no one in particular, his voice barely audible now. "I'm telling you, the man was clinically deceased."

Impossible as that was, Lucas believed him.

Chapter TWENTY-THREE

"The clutch is a little sticky," Delaney apologized as the light changed and the old Ford jolted across the empty intersection.

On a day like this, no one in his right mind was even on the road. "As long as the wipers work," Lucas said, "I think we'll be okay."

"Well, yeah, and that's another thing," Delaney said with a laugh as the wipers struggled to keep up with the torrential rain pouring down the windshield. "I meant to get them replaced. In 1939."

The tires sloshed through puddles several inches deep, and the rain drummed down hard on the battered hood and roof of the car. It was one of those storms that hit New Jersey often in the fall, and Lucas only hoped that Delaney's jalopy would be able to make it all the way to Fort Dix and back—forty miles all told—without breaking down. Given their progress so far, he had his doubts.

"I still don't know why this couldn't have waited

until tomorrow," Delaney said. "The army picked the film up by courier, didn't they?"

"Yep," Lucas replied. "The second I got back to Mercer Street with it."

"So why couldn't they have sent it back the same way?"

"Who knows? Maybe because it's been developed now."

"You think the urgency's got anything to do with what happened at the stadium yesterday?"

Lucas shrugged. "I just know it was an order. Get the film, view the film, report back pronto with any additional info."

"But you're not in the army anymore. You don't need to take orders."

"Tell that to Macmillan."

"Did he at least offer you a Purple Heart for the cut that maniac made on your arm?"

"He said he was relieved that nothing had happened to Professor Einstein."

"That's it?"

"That's it."

"Cannon fodder," Delaney sighed. "That's what we are. Cannon fodder."

If they were nothing but cannon fodder, then what did that make innocent bystanders like Wally Gregg? Lucas had awakened in a cold sweat the night before, screaming in his sleep as Gregg slashed at him with, of all things, a scimitar. The man's head looked like a smashed pumpkin, his mouth a crooked gash shouting the Arabic curse "Death to the swine!" through black and broken teeth. Mrs. Caputo had had to use her passkey to come in and wake him from the nightmare, and though he'd apologized profusely, he could still see a wary look even in little Amy's eye the next morning. Lightning bolts shimmered across the southern sky, jagged as shattered glass, and when the thunder boomed, the whole chassis rattled. Lucas stared out the foggy window at the sickly gray, almost green, light of the day. It was as if they were driving through a monsoon. The wound on his arm tingled every time he shifted in his seat.

"The colonel did inquire about your progress, though," Lucas said.

"Inquire?"

"What he said verbatim was, 'What the hell is Delaney doing to earn his keep?' "

"Ah, that sounds more like him," he said, steering the car carefully around a pothole flooded with rainwater.

"So what do you want me to say?"

"You can tell him—" Delaney began, before the car stalled out. "Damn." Starting it up again, he said, "Tell him I've run three separate isotope tests, just to be sure, and I can say with confidence that the human remains date from about fifteen or sixteen hundred years ago. I can also say that the guy was old and infirm, which Andy

Brandt has corroborated from an anthropological perspective. Life had given this guy, whoever he was, a real beating."

Saint Anthony of Egypt, Lucas thought—that's who the guy was. The only question was whether the physical damage had come from ordinary sources, or, as Simone and Dr. Rashid contended, at the hands of demons. The demon theory was not one Lucas had yet subscribed to.

The car hit a patch of slick roadway, and Lucas clutched the inside door handle as Delaney steered the car into the skid just to stay in his lane. Fortunately, there was nothing coming from the other direction. They were driving through a rural area, nothing but soaked fields and fallow farmland on either side. Crows sat on the tumble-down fences, or swooped perilously in front of the car.

"What about the wooden staff?" Lucas asked. Simone had confided that her father believed the staff in particular held some miraculous power. Maybe Hitler thought so, too. "Could you date it?"

"That part was easy. The wood dates from exactly the same period as the human bones. It's native sycamore, by the way, the kind that grows along the borders of the Egyptian desert. The iron handle is consistent, too, with Middle Eastern metallurgy in the third or fourth century AD."

"Sounds like you've made a lot of progress."

"Yeah, well, then things get a little sticky."

"How?"

"The problem is with the other bones, the ones from the smaller creature." He took a deep breath. "Can you take a quick chemistry lesson?"

"I'm not going anywhere."

"Okay, then. As you're aware, carbon 12 and carbon 13 atoms are nice and stable, they're everywhere and in everything organic."

"So you've told me before."

"Right. Glad you were paying attention. But carbon 14 is extremely rare and extremely unstable, and it decays, slowly, to nitrogen 14, which has a half-life of around 5,730 years. As a result, and depending on how much of the carbon I can detect in a sample in the first place, my experiments can only go back as far as about 40,000 years. After that, kaput. There's no more carbon 14 left to detect."

"Okay," Lucas said, waiting.

Delaney rubbed his jaw with one hand while clutching the wheel with the other. "The bones of this other creature, for want of a better term, are older than that. Much older, I'd say. That may be why Andy can't identify them with any certainty, and why I can't get a feasible date."

"Are you suggesting," Lucas said, "that the old man was buried with a fossil?"

"No, because in that case, the bones would be fossilized. And these aren't."

"Now you've got me confused."

"Good. You should be. Because although the radiocarbon testing I've done suggests that this second creature was very old indeed—and by that I mean tens of thousands of years older—all the other physical evidence, both mine and Andy's, suggests that it died at the same time as the old man it was buried with."

"That can't be."

"But it is, my friend, it is," Delaney said, sounding relieved just to have admitted it. "There's a junction up ahead," he said, peering through the sheets of water cascading down the windshield. "Is that where I turn?"

"Yes," Lucas said, remembering it well from his own induction and basic training at the fort. "Turn left on Monmouth Road."

"You getting nostalgic?" Delaney said.

"No danger of that. It wasn't what you'd call a good time. And God knows I never thought I'd be coming back again."

"Much less for a roll of film, right?" Delaney maneuvered the car around a fallen branch before turning left at the junction, where a sign read "US Army Base, Fort Dix. Only Authorized Personnel Beyond This Point."

"I guess we're what you'd call authorized," Delaney said, squinting through the rain. "I don't want a tank to unload on us."

"Macmillan said they'd have the canister waiting for us at the main gate."

"How far's that?"

"About a mile, straight ahead."

Although it was only late afternoon, the day was still so dark that the lamps along the roadway were on, revealing high cyclone fences surmounted by coils of razor-wire lining both sides. Another sign appeared, warning, "No Civilian Access Beyond This Point. No Contraband. All Unauthorized Vehicles Are Subject to Search and Seizure."

"We're not carrying any contraband, are we?" Delaney asked.

"Not unless a pack of cigarettes counts."

Armed sentries, wearing ponchos and helmets, monitored their progress from tall, steel towers. Spotlights were abruptly illuminated and angled to take in their car, bathing the interior in a blinding white glare. Speed bumps, spaced every hundred feet or so, slowed the car to a crawl; Lucas was worried that if they hit one of them too hard, the whole car would literally disintegrate.

The red brick walls of the old fort, erected in 1917, appeared ahead. At the main gate, the security post was brightly lit, and a heavy metal arm, painted with white and yellow stripes, extended across the roadway. A young soldier in rain gear stepped out as the car came to a stop. Delaney waited until the last possible second to roll down his window.

"This is a restricted zone," the soldier said,

bending close and combing over the interior with his flashlight. "Please state your business."

"The name's Patrick Delaney. My passenger is Lucas Athan."

Leaning over toward the open window, Lucas added, "Colonel Macmillan, at the OSS in DC, has authorized us to pick up a package."

"ID, please."

Delaney had to lift one heavy haunch in order to fish his wallet out of his back pocket and offer his driver's license. Lucas handed his across, too—the stitches in his arm stinging from the motion—and the soldier returned to the guard post. Delaney hastily rolled up the window, but the driving rain had already soaked his pant leg.

"I'm putting in for combat pay," he said.

"You were never in the armed services."

"Can I help it if my work here was judged more crucial to the war effort than risking my life in a foxhole?"

When the soldier returned, Delaney grudgingly cranked the window down again. Handing them back their licenses, the soldier said. "He's coming."

"Who's coming?" Delaney asked.

"The guy from the film office."

The window went back up, but through the windshield, Lucas could see another soldier jogging out of the fort with his head held down against the pelting wind and rain. He was holding something under his arm like a football

251

while he struggled with his free hand to keep the hood of his poncho up.

When he got close enough, Delaney rolled the window down again, and put out his hand.

The soldier stopped, however, and instead of simply giving it to him, he doubled over to get a good long look at both of the passengers in the car.

"Are you the guys who shot this film?"

"No, but we were there," Delaney replied.

"Then who shot it?"

"What difference does it make?" Delaney said, getting soaked all over again.

"Was it his first time with a Bell and Howell Eyemo camera?"

"Yes, it was," Lucas said, "but the 'he' was a 'she.' "

"Maybe that explains it."

"Explains what?"

The soldier didn't say, only glanced at the tightly sealed plastic bag as if he was reluctant to pass it on without first issuing some kind of caveat. "The original went to Washington. You know that, right?"

"We do," Lucas replied.

"But it's no better than this copy. I told them so."

Maybe that was why Macmillan was so eager to have them view it separately. "Why? What's wrong with it?"

A sudden gust of wind blew the soldier's hood back—he looked like he couldn't be more than nineteen—but he let it be. The rain plastered his hair down and streamed down his face. "See for yourself," he said, finally delivering the bag to Delaney, who promptly dropped it into Lucas's lap. "But it wasn't my fault. The lab here is first-rate."

Delaney exchanged a glance with Lucas, and at the soldier's salute, closed the window one last time, backed up, and turned the car around again. "Sounds like our friend Simone will never direct another picture," he said, shifting gears.

What could be so wrong with the film? Lucas wondered as the car bounced slowly over the first speed bump. Glancing in the rearview mirror, he saw the young soldier still standing in place, hood down, poncho rippling in the wind and rain, staring after their car.

Chapter TWENTY-FOUR

With the film canister tucked into a battered briefcase, which was in turn tucked tightly under his uninjured arm, Lucas was almost out the door of the boardinghouse when Mrs. Caputo came fluttering down the stairs with an envelope in hand. "Wait," she cried. "This came for you while you were gone!"

"I'm going over to the museum now," Lucas said. "I'll have to open it later."

"I think you'd better open it now."

"Why? Who's it from?"

"You'll see," Mrs. Caputo said, barely able to conceal her excitement. "She brought it over herself."

She?

Putting the briefcase down on the side table, Lucas obliged his landlady by ripping it open.

It was a handwritten note from Helen Dukas, Einstein's secretary, urging him to stop and visit the professor at his earliest opportunity.

"They're inviting you over, aren't they?"

"Yes."

"I bet he wants to thank you for saving his life at the stadium."

Lucas needed no thanks for doing what anyone else in his shoes would have done, and he was eager to get to the art museum where he could get at the film projector.

"I want you to bring him something for me," Mrs. Caputo said, ducking into the kitchen, then reemerging with a plate of brownies still warm from the oven and covered with a crumpled sheet of tinfoil.

Lucas was torn. He didn't want to incur any delay right now, but an invitation—or was it a summons?—from one of the most famous men in the world wasn't something you could easily dismiss. As if intuiting his thoughts, Mrs. Caputo shoved the plate of brownies into his hands and said, "Lucas, you absolutely have to go."

Then she shoved him toward the door. "And you have to tell me everything when you get back—especially if he liked the brownies."

With the plate in one hand and his briefcase in the other, Lucas trudged across the wet street. The storm had passed, but the rain still clinging to the leaves dripped on his head and shoulders. As he mounted the front steps of Einstein's house, a feral cat ducked under them.

Fifteen minutes, Lucas told himself. He could spare fifteen minutes. He was debating what to put down so that he would have a free hand to knock, when, out of the corner of his good eye, he saw the lace curtains at the parlor window being pulled back. Then he heard quick footsteps, and a tall, thin woman—middle-aged, with straight dark hair and brows—opened the door with a warm smile.

"The professor will be *so* happy to see you," she said, with a German accent only slightly less pronounced than her employer's.

"It's an honor," he said, extending the plate. "And these are from Mrs. Caputo. She made them herself."

"Thank you, but perhaps it's best not to tell the professor. He's on a strict diet." She put the plate on a sideboard in the hall. "But I promise to give him one—just one—after his dinner. Please thank her. And now, if you will just wait here, I will tell the professor you have come."

She started toward the stairs, then stopped as if she had forgotten something, and, turning, clutched his hands between her own. "I cannot tell you how grateful I am to you for coming to the rescue. How grateful we *all* are to you."

She squeezed his hands, then bustled up the stairs. The house was silent, except for the ticking of a grandfather clock in the hall. When Helen reappeared on the landing and waved him on, he followed her to an open room, and before he knew it, he was inside, with the door closing softly behind him, and Einstein rising from a dilapidated armchair.

"Ah, my savior," he said. "You should be wearing a suit of armor, *ja*?" He laughed. "A suit of armor."

His hand, when they shook, was dry as papyrus, but the grip was surprisingly firm.

"They tell me you were injured."

"Not badly," Lucas replied.

"I am sorry for that. Very sorry."

Lucas could hardly believe he was truly in the great man's company, but if he doubted it, there was the blackboard, propped in front of a cluttered bookcase, covered with incomprehensible symbols and equations.

"Please to sit," Einstein said, gesturing at a

matching armchair, its seat covered with books and papers that the professor hastily gathered up and deposited on an equally messy desk. Several wafted onto the worn Oriental carpet, but he didn't seem to notice or care.

Lucas sank into the soft leather cushion as Einstein plopped back down opposite him. He wore a loose black sweatshirt, and his white hair was as unruly as in all the newspaper photographs. When he put his feet up on the ottoman, Lucas noted that he was wearing leather sandals and no socks.

"I had never been to a football game before," he said, brushing at his gray moustache.

"They don't usually end that way."

"I hope not," Einstein said, a smile crinkling his face into a hundred lines. "I hope not. Still, I do not think that I will go to another game very soon."

Of all the things Lucas might have expected, this was not one. Over the next few minutes, he found himself more and more relaxed in Einstein's presence—the professor was plainly a man accustomed to, and adept at, putting other people at their ease, and he showed a genuine interest in who Lucas was, where he was from, what he had done in the war. The mention of the art recovery work conducted by the CRC, of which he had never heard, seemed to particularly intrigue him. He was clearly a cultured man, as even the violin and bow, resting on the window seat, attested.

More than once, however, Lucas saw his eyes alight on the breast pocket of his shirt, where a packet of Camels rested. Finally, unable to restrain himself any longer, the professor glanced at the closed door of the study, then leaned forward and, gesturing at the pocket, said, "You have cigarettes?"

"Yes," Lucas said. "Would you like one?"

Einstein nodded vigorously, and as Lucas took one out, he got up and lifted the sash of the window looking onto the back garden. "Do not tell Helen. It is against the doctor's orders."

Lucas hesitated.

"But doctors, they do not know everything."

Who was he to argue with Einstein? They settled back into their chairs. Einstein pinched his cigarette between his thumb and index finger, and inhaled deeply, eyes closed, savoring the taste and smell. A bit of ash trickled down the front of his sweatshirt.

Looking around for an ashtray, Lucas couldn't help but notice the official military stamp on some of the papers that Einstein had thrown on the desk. Next to them, there was also an empty can of baked beans with a spoon sticking up out of it. Removing the spoon, he tamped the end of his cigarette into the can, then held it out to the professor, who did the same. Lucas left the makeshift ashtray perched, somewhat precariously, on the ottoman.

"A terrible thing," Einstein said. "Monte Cassino."

For a moment, Lucas didn't follow. Why had this just come up? Monte Cassino, a Benedictine abbey about eighty miles southeast of Rome, had been destroyed in a pitched battle a few months earlier.

"Especially for a man whose job is to preserve great art."

And then he understood. A beautiful structure in its own right, dating from the sixth century AD, the ancient monastery had held an irreplaceable library of papal documents and treasures dating from the Middle Ages and Renaissance. "Yes, it was."

"It is as if mankind is trying to . . . obliterate itself, and every beautiful thing that it has made."

The professor's eyes, so full of cheer a few minutes earlier, had clouded over with sorrow, and Lucas's mind flashed back to Strasbourg, and the Nazi plunder secreted in the iron mine. At least that particular cache had been salvaged from the wreckage of a ruined continent. He wished he was at liberty to share with Einstein the story of the ossuary and its miraculous odyssey—he sensed that it would be appreciated—but he did not dare. He could feel the spirit of Macmillan glowering in the air.

"Even if one fights on the side of angels," the professor continued, "it can feel as if one is doing the Devil's work. For years now, every day, it is all bombs and bullets, guns and planes, tanks and cannons, death and more death . . ." He trailed off, taking one last draw on the butt of the cigarette before leaning forward to drop it into the tin can. There was a tiny sizzling sound. "One must wonder, where will it all end?"

"It's just a matter of time," Lucas said. "The days of the Third Reich are numbered."

"And the Fourth? What is to keep that from happening?"

For that, Lucas had no answer. No one did.

A breeze from the open window blew back the curtains and toppled the can onto the floor, spilling ash onto the rug.

"*Ach*, now Helen will know we have been smoking."

"I'll take the blame," Lucas said, squatting down to brush the evidence back into the can.

"And I will let you take it," Einstein said, flashing a crooked smile once again. There was something so beguilingly contradictory about him—a weathered, white-haired man who nevertheless retained in his demeanor the mischievous air of a child. In the bat of an eye, he could go from sage to schoolboy. "I can hide nothing from Helen," he said, going to the window and fanning the air.

After righting the can, Lucas blew the remaining ash off some of the papers and gathered them up. Again, his eye skipped across the red TOP SECRET stamped atop several of the cream-colored pages, along with a simple letterhead emblazoned on the top sheet: THE WHITE HOUSE.

His eye jumped to the bottom, where he saw, below the warning "I fear they are close to success," a hastily scrawled signature in bright blue ink. *"Franklin D. Roosevelt."* He laid the letter carefully on the desk with all the others, just as Einstein shut the window and a firm knock came on the door.

"You are not smoking in there, are you, Professor?" Helen said.

"No, no," Lucas volunteered. "It was just me."

There was a pause before she replied, "You are a brave man, Mr. Athan. We knew that much already. But you do not lie well."

Einstein whispered, "I told you so, *ja*?"

"*Ja*," Lucas replied softly.

Einstein sat back, nodding, with a grin lifting the ends of his moustache. "She knows everything, that woman."

Chapter TWENTY-FIVE

"And this!" her father was saying, pulling several photos and reproductions from the blue folder he never let out of his sight anymore. "Look at this!"

"Lower your voice," Simone said, glancing around the taproom, where several patrons had looked up from their drinks and meals. The only one who didn't stir was the small man slouched in the wingback chair by the fire, his collar pulled so high and his cap so low there was no telling if he was dead or alive.

"Look at these and tell me they do not corroborate the injuries sustained by the bones in the ossuary!"

Simone had seen these pictures and photographs before. On a trip to Alsace, she had viewed the Isenheim Altarpiece itself; painted by Matthias Grünewald in the early sixteenth century, the masterpiece hung in the monastery of the Antonian monks, who were known for their care of those who suffered from the plague and other diseases of the skin, such as Saint Anthony's fire.

"Look at this one in particular," her father said, placing on top of the pile a photograph of a panel depicting the holy hermit tormented by demons. According to the legends and patristic literature on which Simone had been virtually raised, Satan and his hordes had tempted and tortured Saint Anthony his entire life. His purity and faith were considered a stubborn and vexing rebuke to their powers. But he had fought valiantly, wielding his staff with the crooked iron handle against them. In this particular panel, he was seen raising his staff to the Heavens for help, his body bloody and mutilated from the creatures' claws and fangs.

Though she did not doubt her father's conclusions—that the ossuary bones belonged to the ancient and persecuted saint—she did not see that these photos and etchings would help convince anyone else. "These are just paintings," she said. "No one will lend them any credence."

"But they are paintings that perfectly accord with the anatomical evidence your professors Athan and Delaney have uncovered."

There was a glitter in his eye, a slightly feverish look, which Simone did not like to see, and his cough had not abated. She worried that he had caught a chill at the football stadium. She worried, too, that the shock of witnessing the knife attack on Einstein, by an assailant shouting an Arabic curse that no American would have had any way of knowing, had further disturbed him. How could it not? It had haunted her own thoughts ever since.

"And didn't you tell me that those isotope tests, or whatever they are called, also confirmed the correct dates?"

"Yes," she admitted, feeling guilty all over again that she had broken her vow of secrecy and shared all of the current findings with him. But it seemed impossible, and even unethical, to leave her father, without whom none of this would even be under discussion, out of the loop. No one deserved to know what was going on more than he did, and no one was owed her loyalty, and love, more than he was. "At least, most of the bones conformed."

"Most?"

"The human bones dated from the third century or so. But the others, as I said, were indeterminate."

"Of course they were," he said. "They're not human—they're the bones of one of these," he said, tapping an image of a creature in the Grünewald painting. "Listen," he said, riffling through the blue folder and withdrawing a yellowed page. "This is from a biography of Saint Anthony, written by Ambrose in the fourth century." His finger underlining the words, he read aloud, " 'And Anthony told the monks that followed him, "When, therefore, the demons come by night to you and wish to tell the future, or they say, 'We are the angels,' give no heed, for they lie . . ." ' "

Similar words, Simone knew, to some that Lucas had found on the ossuary itself.

" ' "And if they shamelessly stand their ground,

capering and changing their form or appearance, fear them not, nor shrink, nor heed them as though they were good spirits. For the presence either of the good or evil, by the help of God can easily be distinguished." ' " He paused, pressing his knuckles to his mouth to stifle a cough.

Behind her chair, Simone could hear the waitress asking the man slouched by the fire if he would like to order something now, but he snapped back at her to go away and leave him alone; judging from his guttural voice, he was not only someone who could barely speak English, but someone who could hardly speak at all. And to think that she and her father had been the ones nearly refused a room here.

"There is no question," her father was saying, "that the thing is loose. But where? And how is it getting about?"

"What?" Simone said, refocusing and checking her watch. She was due—overdue now—at the art museum to see the film she had shot there.

"The demon may take any form, it says so right here, but how can we determine what host it has chosen?"

"You mean, who has been possessed?"

"Who, or what. Anything animate, anything with a corporeal form, will do. It needs a vehicle, as it were, to get around in."

Simone's head was spinning, though the sight of the would-be assassin, trudging like a zombie down the stadium aisle, did spring unnervingly to mind.

"Right now," her father said, waving a hand around the taproom, "it could be anywhere."

Simone heard a voice close behind her, and turned to see the restaurant manager looming above the man slouched in the armchair.

"Sir," he was saying, "are you a guest of the inn? Sir?" After getting no reply, he said, "If you're not going to order anything, you will have to leave."

Though the man made no reply, an errant flame suddenly shot, like an arrow, out of the grate and singed the hem of the manager's trousers. "Jesus!" he exclaimed, jumping back and batting it out.

"Come on," Simone said to her father, "let's get you up to the room." She wouldn't mind putting some distance between them and the surly stranger in the wingback chair, either. "What you need is a hot bath and a good night's sleep."

"A hot bath? That's all you have to say in response?"

She was tempted to tell him that she was leaving for the art museum, but she knew that that would only lead to another argument. He would insist on going, she would refuse to take him out into another wet and blustery night, and things would go from bad to worse.

After signing the bill to their room—as usual,

her father had had nothing but some noodle soup and tea—and helping replace his papers in the blue folder, she handed her father his walking stick, then held him by the elbow as they turned to leave the taproom. The unwelcome guest hadn't budged from his chair, though Simone left him plenty of leeway as they passed by. Another burning log sputtered in the grate, and the faint smell of wet turf tinged the air. It reminded her of an autumn hike she'd taken through the Scottish Highlands.

"I'll be back in a couple hours," she was saying to her father, "and I want to find you fast asleep when I get here."

"Where are you going at this hour?"

"To see Lucas," was all she said, but it was enough to elicit a harrumph.

"He's a good man," Dr. Rashid grudgingly admitted, "but he's been damaged, in more ways than one, by the war. Anyone can see that."

"I do."

"Tread lightly."

Behind the bar, she spotted the manager dialing a phone while the waitress said, "I don't care if you fire me—I'm not going back there."

Simone didn't blame her, especially as she had the distinct, and unsettling, impression that the man in the armchair, his head still tucked down into his coat like a turtle, had roused himself enough to turn and watch them go. She considered turning around to see if her suspicion was correct, but she didn't want to give the nasty bastard the satisfaction.

Nor, if she was totally honest with herself, did she dare.

Chapter TWENTY-SIX

"You're sure you don't want me to run the film for you?" the elderly projectionist said. "I don't mind at all, Professor."

For the third time, Lucas assured him that he could do it himself, so long as the projectionist gave him a quick tutorial.

"Okay then," the man said, adjusting various switches and knobs. "Let me at least load it for you and get it ready to run."

As he did so, Lucas looked around the cramped booth with the sagging acoustical tiles, the fire extinguisher in the dusty case, and the metal racks jammed with film canisters and slide boxes and, of all things, mousetraps.

"You have a problem with mice?"

The projectionist grunted. "No matter how many times we tell the students not to bring food into the auditorium, they do anyway." Brushing the palms of his hands together, he said, "I'll leave it to you then." Inching around Lucas, he slipped out of the booth.

No sooner was he gone than Lucas heard Delaney, sitting beside Simone in the auditorium, clap in mock frustration and shout, "Let's get this show on the road!"

From inside the projection booth, all Lucas could see of them was the backs of their heads. "Keep your shirt on!" he hollered, turning off the house lights and fumbling to start the projector. The sound reminded him of his mother's sewing machine, clicking and ratcheting along as the film first displayed its numerical countdown, and then cut to a shot, in crisp black-and-white tones, of himself announcing the time and date—in a voice he could barely recognize as his own—and introducing the members of the investigatory team. He had never seen himself on film like this before, and it came as quite a shock to see how forbidding a presentation his five o'clock shadow and eye patch made; his first thought was that he looked like a pirate. Delaney, on whom he had turned the lens for a few seconds, appeared like a good-natured grizzly bear, and Simone, who had stepped in front of the camera next, radiated apprehension.

But beauty, too.

Seeing her on the screen, even in this context, Lucas was struck by her distinctive, even mysterious, features—her luminous eyes and arched brows, and the way her raven hair framed her face. There were moments like this, moments when he felt a certain tugging at his heart, that he regretted ever having allowed her to become involved in this project—though he knew full well he could hardly have stopped her. She was as determined as she was attractive. And if not for her and her father, the ossuary would still be languishing in a hidden tomb somewhere in the Egyptian desert.

There were a few blank frames in the film at the point where Lucas had paused to turn the camera over to Simone.

And then the movie began again, the lens trained on the closed lid of the ossuary. Lucas could see the various creatures incised there, brandishing their claws and baring their fangs at the figure of the shepherd—swineherd, he corrected himself—with the crooked-handled staff. Somehow the threat from the gamboling beasts was more noticeable on the film than it had been on the actual sarcophagus. Despite the complaints from the technician at Fort Dix, Lucas couldn't see anything on the film so far that suggested Simone had done anything but an admirable job behind the camera.

A pair of gloved hands protruded into the frame—his own, as he recalled—holding up a length of rusty chain that was bound around the box. Delaney's hands, also gloved, wielded the hacksaw that quickly reduced the links to powder. The removal of the remaining chains took several minutes, and then the ponderous lid—he could remember just how heavy, and cold, the alabaster had been—was sliding the length of the box. Simone had adroitly directed the camera to follow its progress onto the thin mattress, where it had been laid to rest.

And then, for a split second, something blurred the lens before clearing again.

The focus changed, as Simone had swung the camera to take in a new view. She could be heard saying, "Oh my God."

The lens was pointed at the interior of the sarcophagus, at the jumbled bones and artifacts. And the pair of skulls. Lucas's gloved hands could be seen reaching into the box and lifting the stranger of the two; he remembered thinking that it was like enacting the scene from Hamlet.

But he did not remember the rest of what he now saw on the screen. It was as if some unseen agency had clouded the film, deliberately obscuring the image of the skull. From the empty eye sockets, there was an unmistakable gleam of something bright, like a spark from a fire. Had he looked away at precisely that moment? Surely he would have remembered that. How had the camera captured something that had gone unnoticed by the eyewitnesses in the room?

Simone's voice on the soundtrack was saying, "Something's going wrong with the camera," and from that point on, all hell broke loose. The audio picked up a rising wind; the picture became scratched and jerky. Delaney was heard warning him to "put it back," and Lucas could see his hands replacing the deformed skull in the box. He remembered that Simone had abandoned her post on the cinder block, and left the camera swiveling atop the tripod. The pictures turned wild and random, as the camera gyrated in the wind. Its lens roamed the conservation room, and every-where it looked there was a swirling mist that had been all but invisible to the naked eye. Or had the film stock simply been defective? The lights in the room went on and off, on and off, and each time, the picture changed. Buried in the fog, a strange shape coalesced and then dissolved, loping on all fours with its snout raised and stubby wings flapping, then vanishing again into thin air. Some frames went blank, others were smudged or striated. Glass cracked—the clerestory window, just replaced, had been splintered as if hit by a hardball—and a scream erupted from somewhere behind the tumbling easels. The door at the rear of the room was flung open, and a different shape—this one distinctly human, but crouching low—scrambled out.

Although the film rolled on for a few more seconds, the picture blurred, and then abruptly stopped. Lucas fumbled for the switch, but in the dark, he couldn't find it. A smell arose—something burning—and he groped again for the switch to turn off the projector. Again with no luck. The machine kept humming.

Turning quickly, he ran his hand along the wall, finding the overhead light and turning it on. A thin gray rat, caught out in the open, squeaked in alarm and squirmed under the door. The smell was much worse—the film had now caught flame. He yanked open the glass case and grabbed the fire extinguisher, raised the nozzle and sprayed a tide of white foam, up and down, up and down, over the entire mechanism. Despite the caustic fumes, he didn't stop until the extinguisher was empty.

Delaney threw open the door to the booth. "What happened?" he said, as Simone cried, "Are you all right?"

Waving away the smoke and stench, Lucas stumbled out. Delaney slammed the door behind him and, patting his back, said, "Take slow breaths. Slow breaths."

Lucas tried to do it, but his throat burned from some chemical in the celluloid stock, or maybe the extinguisher foam. His one good eye was streaming tears. When he was finally able to get his wind and straighten up, he saw that the immediate alarm was fading from his burly colleague's face, but taking its place was the shock he had felt at watching the film.

"At least I know what that guy at Fort Dix was talking about," Delaney said.

Lucas, still unable to speak, simply nodded. Simone appeared with a paper cup of water.

"Drink this."

He took it gratefully.

"You sure the fire's out in there?" Delaney said.

"See for yourself," Lucas croaked.

Delaney had barely cracked the door open when Simone jumped back—"Look out!" she cried. A flock of gray mice scampered out, scattering to all corners of the auditorium. Sauntering out behind them, unalarmed and unafraid, a fat brown rat sniffed the fresh air with twitching whiskers and tail. Delaney tried to stomp on it, but missed, and the rat adroitly ducked under the auditorium chairs.

"Time to call in an exterminator," Delaney said.

Lucas, raising his bleary vision to Simone, saw that she was clutching something concealed beneath her blouse, just as she had at the opening of the ossuary. The look on her face, however, perfectly confirmed his own thoughts.

There wasn't an exterminator on earth equipped to deal with what was happening here.

Chapter TWENTY-SEVEN

"The paratroopers have landed," the voice on the radio said, "and all around me, they're freeing themselves from their chutes."

Dr. Rashid leaned forward, hanging on every word. Tonight's broadcast was coming all the way from Holland, where soldiers from the 101st Airborne had been dispatched to capture the bridges along the Dutch/Belgian border.

"There's a full moon tonight, and the chutes are blowing across the farms and fields that surround us." There was both urgency and trepidation in the reporter's tone. "Make no mistake, this is still dangerous ground."

These broadcasts from the war in Europe routinely held millions of listeners captive, and this one was no exception; there was an immediacy to the reports, an on-the-scene aspect that most of the other newsmen, bound to desks in Washington —or to telex machines in New York—could not touch. Knowing that the reporter was actually there, risking his neck along with the soldiers whose dangerous missions he was reporting on, lent the broadcasts both credibility and nerve-wracking suspense.

Rashid put his blue folder to one side, untied

his shoes—bending over was getting harder on his back all the time—and summoned up another volley of coughs. As the broadcast continued, he began to undress. His daughter had escorted him up to their suite and then gone off to see that fellow Lucas; it was only natural, and at least the man had already done his service and come back in one piece, or nearly one. No matter what came of it, she wouldn't wind up a war widow. There was that.

He regretted getting so worked up in the tap-room. It never did any good to let your passions cloud your arguments. And he knew what he sounded like. Like most of the others in his field—even his own daughter—he had started out as a strict empiricist, unwilling even to listen to the babblings of monks and mullahs, priests and so-called prophets. Scriptures, of any sort or origin, were nothing more than ancillary tools to help him in his scholarly research.

But time, enhanced by experience, had altered his views. Too often he had felt the inexpressible presence of something greater, too often he had had to discount his own intuitions. Like the physicists, whose theories and discoveries he did his best to understand and follow, there were things he could not account for, things that he was forever having to rejigger his philosophy in order to accommodate. Even Einstein's theory of relativity, from what he could fathom of it, did not square with some of the more recent revelations of something else called quantum mechanics. Apparently, on the atomic level, it was impossible to pinpoint a particle's velocity and location at the same time, without altering one or the other in the process. It was precisely that sort of slippery and irrational problem he had encountered in his own work. He was trying to mix fact and faith, science and sorcery, into one palatable, if volatile, brew.

If only he had before him more time to unravel the mysteries of the ossuary, but his health was failing—far more precipitously than he ever let on to his daughter—and his fondest hope now was to live long enough to see Simone safely ensconced in a tenured university position in a world that had, at long last, found peace again.

"We're strung out now along the banks of a canal that cuts across the fields. Every eye and every ear is on alert for Nazi snipers who might be lying in wait."

Rashid turned the radio volume higher as he went into the bathroom, where he pushed the shower curtain to one side and started the hot water running. He leaned his cane up against the door, then finished undressing. In the medicine chest, he found, and took, the nightly pills for his heart, then put his hand under the faucet to test the water temperature. He would say that much for the Nassau Inn—they might not welcome guests of the wrong skin color (oh, he hadn't missed that insult at the reception desk), but their boiler was a good one. The steam building up in the room already was soothing his sore throat.

"There's a body floating by me in the canal," the reporter said, solemnly. "It's not one of ours, though. He's still got his helmet on. His arms and legs are spread out wide like he's about to make an angel in the snow."

Turning off the water, and holding onto the edge of the claw-footed tub, Rashid eased one leg into the water, and then the other. With one hand bracing himself against the white tile wall, he sat down, dipped a bar of soap in the water and lathered his face and shoulders. Then he settled back, with the nape of his neck resting comfortably on the lip of the tub. The bunched-up shower curtain obscured his view through the open door, but did nothing to hinder his ability to hear the radio.

"The moonlight is glinting off the white arms of a windmill not far away. Under normal circumstances, this would be a beautiful sight on an equally beautiful night."

Over the broadcast, Rashid thought he heard the front door to their suite being opened. *Is she back already?* he thought with relief.

"Simone?" he called out, but there was no answer.

"This, however, is not a normal night," the reporter said, keeping his voice low.

There was a slight but sudden draft, and Rashid called out again, "I'm in the tub. Please turn the radio down and close the bathroom door now."

Still there was no reply. He must have been wrong. Closing his eyes, he concentrated again on the broadcast.

"Wait—did you hear that?" the reporter said. "Off in the distance?"

Rashid thought he smelled something, like damp sod, and opened his eyes. As he did so, the light in the front room winked out.

"It was a rifle shot."

Why had the light gone off? Was there an electrical short? No, that couldn't be the reason. The radio was still working.

The draft grew stronger, as did the odor.

"Simone?" he tried one more time. A fleeting shadow appeared just outside the door, but whoever was casting it clung to one side, the side Rashid could not see past the plastic shower curtain.

For the first time, he felt fear—a cold fear gripping at his already weakened heart.

"Who's there?"

"It came from the windmill," the radio relayed.

Something dark and crouching low slipped into the bathroom with him.

He sat up and shoved at the curtain pleats,

trying to clear his view. "Who are you?" Rashid demanded.

The room smelled like a marsh.

"Get out of here!"

Instead, the figure moved closer. Through the filmy plastic, he watched an arm reach out, take hold of the curtain, and with one pull, rip the whole thing loose from the rings.

He recognized the hat, and the coat with the upturned collar. But the face nestled deep in its folds was like nothing he had ever seen before. Though plainly alive, it looked like it had died a thousand years ago. His mouth opened in a silent scream as he felt its hand clamp down on the top of his head, and with surprising ease, push him down into the water and hold him there. He struggled to free himself, his fingers scrabbling at the slippery lip of the tub, his heart beating like a trip-hammer, but the hand held steady. His legs kicked, splashing water all over the floor, but through the sting of the soapy water, he could see no more than a glint of gold in a pair of evil and unyielding eyes.

Nor could he hear the final words of the broadcast, as the kicking of his legs subsided and the bubbles of his last breath escaped his lips. "The paratroopers have fanned out, and they're shooting back." There was the crackle of gunfire, as his heart gave way. "I can't tell if anyone has been hit, but one of the soldiers has made it close enough to throw a grenade up top." There was the sound of a distant explosion. "Holy smokes—that was a throw worthy of Dizzy Dean," the reporter shouted, as if he were recounting a baseball game. "The windmill's catching fire now. And let me tell you one thing, there aren't any more shots coming from it. Not a one."

Chapter TWENTY-EIGHT

The sudden death of her father left Simone feeling more bereft and alone in the world than words could ever express. She had known that such a day was bound to come—lately, she had seen the shadow of death steal across his brow more than once—but to have it happen here, in a place where she already felt so alien and alone, only made matters worse.

If that was even possible.

As she walked to the end of the dock, with Lucas and Delaney supporting her between them, it was all she could do to put one foot in front of the other and not get the heels of her shoes caught in the gap between the wooden boards. She wondered how long it would be before she stopped feeling the void every hour of every day. She wondered, in fact, if that time would ever come.

In her hands, she held the urn carrying her father's cremated remains. It was heavier than she'd thought it would be.

The afternoon was a crisp and sunny one, and the leaves of the trees around Lake Carnegie had turned bright crimson and gold. As if to complete the postcard view, a small blue boat with a yellow sail drifted along the far shore. Her father couldn't have wished for more—apart, perhaps, from having his ashes scattered in the dunes of the Sahara. The desert, curiously, was always where he had felt most alive. But it would have been reckless for Simone to attempt another trans-atlantic crossing in the midst of the ongoing naval warfare, and she knew that her father would have wanted this business disposed of in as expeditious a manner as possible. In his view, a corpse was merely an empty vessel for the spirit it had housed.

"The soul," he'd said one night by a campfire in the Valley of the Kings, "is like a falcon. Despite its loyalty to the falconer, it longs to fly free. When my time comes, let my soul soar into the wind and the sky. Wherever its natural home is meant to be, that's where it will go."

Although she had found such thoughts morbid, her father had not. He was reconciled to his place in the cosmic scheme—if scheme it was—and could face even the worst fear, as he had in the tomb of Saint Anthony, with courage and dignity.

She wondered if she would be able to do the same.

When they arrived at the end of the pier, she closed her eyes and let herself feel the breeze blowing her hair over her shoulders. Delaney stepped, respectfully, a few feet back, but Lucas remained at her side. Without him, she could not imagine how she would have made it through all that had happened. After walking her back to the hotel on the night the film had gone up in flame, it was Lucas who had found her father's body in the bathtub. Lucas who had called the ambulance. Lucas who had handled the police and the coroner's inquiry. As for the cause of death, it was ruled accidental—an old man had slipped getting out of the tub, cracked his head, and drowned.

Even Simone would have believed it, were it not for the fact that everything in the room was where it had been, except for one thing—the blue folder. The folder, the one thing her father never let out of his sight, was nowhere to be found.

"Do you want to tell the police about it?" Lucas had asked.

She'd said no. What good would it do? They'd think she was crazy, and there was a risk that the work she and Lucas were doing on the ossuary would be compromised during the investigation. Besides, who could she suggest as the culprit?

"What about that man in the taproom, the one you said had given you the creeps?"

"If I had sixpence for every man who'd ever given me the creeps in a barroom . . ." she said, and he'd let it drop.

What she *didn't* say was that the thought had occurred to her, too.

Hovering close beside her now, the wooden planks of the pier creaking beneath his feet, Lucas asked, "What would you like to do?" His voice was as gentle as the breeze off the water. How long, she wondered, had she been standing there, urn in hand and lost in thought? "Would you like me to say a few words?"

"No, that's all right," she said, opening her eyes to the brilliant sunshine again. The sailboat, though still far off, was tacking toward the boathouse pier on which they were standing.

"Would you like to say something yourself?"

But what could she say at this moment that she hadn't said already, a hundred times, in her heart? *Good-bye?* She'd said that. *I love you? I will miss you every day of my life?* If the dead could hear the living, then he had heard her.

"You might want to do this," Delaney suggested softly from the rear, "before that boat gets any closer."

Simone looked down at the urn in her hands. True, it was heavier than she'd expected, but considering all that it held, lighter than it should have been, too. An entire life was contained inside it. A life now reduced to ash and bone. Bone and ash. An ossuary of its own.

Unable to budge the lid, she handed it to Lucas, who twisted off the top, then gave it back to her. Gauging the direction of the wind, she held the urn over the end of the pier, and then turned it upside down. A light powder filtered out, but nothing more, and she had to shake it several times before the bottleneck was loosened and a full cascade—bits of bone, gray cinders, white ash—tumbled out, the larger pieces, some the size of acorns, dropping into the water, the rest snatched up by the wind and carried off. She shook it until it was empty.

What, she wondered, had she truly released?

As if its captain had become aware of what was happening and elected to give them their privacy, the little boat with the yellow sail veered off in the opposite direction.

Were they merely mortal remains? she thought, as the air cleared and a billowy white cloud momentarily obscured the sunbeams. Was that all she'd let go, or had she, as her father promised, allowed a falcon to take flight?

Chapter TWENTY-NINE

After returning Simone to the Nassau Inn—which had, obligingly, relocated her to a much nicer room on the top floor—and making sure she had finally fallen asleep, Lucas set out for the junior faculty housing on Harrison Street.

So much of what he'd seen in the film—the weird shapes cavorting in the mist, the gleam of light from the empty eye sockets of the skull—was inexplicable, but one image, appearing in only the last few frames, was not.

Someone real had run from the conservation room—the same someone upon whose heels another of the apparitions had followed like a faithful dog—and that someone, he strongly suspected, was Andy Brandt.

It was only a suspicion, but one thing he had learned in the war was that his suspicions were often spot-on. The guy was definitely a snoop, insinuating himself into Delaney's lab whenever he could, always asking about the advancements in the radiocarbon processes, or kidding with Lucas about what he did all day, holed up in the art museum. "You'd think you had some top-secret weapon in there," he'd joked, though he had also waited for an answer, which never came. But why had Brandt been in the conservation room in the first place, and what, if anything, did he know that Lucas did not?

Dusk had fallen and a light rain had begun by the time Lucas arrived at the barracks-like structures, built decades before and coming apart at the seams, that most of the young faculty and grad students inhabited. Not for the first time, he thanked his lucky stars that he had again landed his spot at Mrs. Caputo's; if, as he imagined, strings had been pulled behind the scenes, by President Dodds or the OSS or whomever, he was grateful they had been.

Stepping into the open stairwell and shaking the rain off his leather bomber jacket, he scanned the tenant roster. Hand-lettered labels had been taped up on the board. "A. Brandt" was listed in apartment 2B, one of the upper units, and he climbed the darkened stairs cautiously. Although there was a light fixture in the ceiling, someone had made off with the bulb; they were in scarce supply these days and highly coveted as a result.

At the door with a metal "2" on it, and a "B" hanging by a thread, he raised a hand to knock, then paused when he heard a voice within. Bending his ear closer to the door, he heard the voice—Andy's—continuing to talk, but nobody was talking back. He waited, but it was still only Andy talking, and in subdued tones at that—too subdued for Lucas to make out what he was actually saying. The chances of these apartments having individual phone lines was pretty much nil.

It sounded more like he was transmitting via a ham radio.

Was Andy a ham radio operator? He'd certainly never said anything about it that Lucas could recall, and even if he was, why would he be speaking in such a clandestine way?

Holding his breath, Lucas eased himself away from the door. His wet shoes made a sucking noise on the floor, and he stopped—but the broadcast went on.

One by one, Lucas went down the steps, backward so as to keep an eye on the door, and once outside again, he ran around to the back of the building, where a rusty fire escape rose to the second-floor units. He climbed the squeaking rungs as quietly as he could and then crouched in the rain outside Andy's apartment. The blind was drawn, but like everything else in this housing block, it hung imperfectly, slanted to one side. Lucas peeked inside the room.

Andy was sitting on a wooden chair, with a radio transmitter on the table, speaking into a handheld microphone. Lucas recognized the radio—it was a standard issue, BC-1000, the same kind he had employed in Europe. He surveyed the fire escape for an antenna. There it was, fixed flush with the window frame, its customary olive green painted the same brown as the wood, presumably to camouflage it. He peered in again, and now he could see that Andy was consulting a batch of papers and reciting what he read there into the microphone.

Papers that were gathered in a blue folder—just like the one Simone said was missing from the suite.

Whatever he was up to, Lucas thought, it was time to put a stop to it. Digging into his pocket, he found his key ring, and picking the one with the bluntest end, he wedged it, as quietly as he could, under the antenna, until he had pried it loose from the window frame. At one end was a loop of wire, just long enough to coil around his wrist. He pulled hard, snapping it in two.

He didn't wait to see what would happen next. He clambered down the escape, antenna in hand, and had just reached the muddy ground when the window sash rose, and Andy poked his head out into the drizzle. Lucas hid in the shadows of the building while Andy looked to the right and left, then ran his hand along the side of the window, feeling for the missing antenna. He craned his neck out farther and found the split wire. For a second, he looked puzzled, and then, after another quick look around, ducked his head back inside.

He would know it was no accident.

But what would he do next?

Running back around to the front of the building, Lucas concealed himself in the neighboring stairwell and waited. The rain had not let up, and the temperature had dropped into the forties. The wound on his arm, where Wally Gregg's knife had slashed him, throbbed. Running his hand along his hair to brush the water off, he debated what his next move should be. Should he continue to wait here, or find a way to get to a telephone and call his contacts at the OSS, and then leave it to them to sort it all out? Was it possible that Andy Brandt was more than an annoying brownnoser? That he was actually an enemy mole?

While it seemed impossible at first, the more he thought about it, the more the pieces fell into place. By the time Lucas had arrived at Princeton, hadn't Andy Brandt already secured a place for himself in the same science building as Professor Delaney, who was in the midst of conducting top-secret isotope testing? And since then, hadn't Brandt done everything in his power to ingratiate himself with Delaney—which might have worked for a spy gifted with a better personality—and used every opportunity to penetrate the upstairs lab and procure its latest findings?

Could it have been Brandt who had stolen into Dr. Rashid's suite at the Nassau Inn and made off with his papers? The blue folder was right there in plain sight on Brandt's desk.

A wind ripped the treetops, sending a cascade of wet leaves onto Harrison Street.

The next question, however, was the most terrifying of all, for if Lucas followed the train of logic, it led to one conclusion alone. If Brandt had broken into the hotel room, had he been there when Dr. Rashid had suffered his fatal accident in the tub? Was it an accident at all? Or had Simone's father been deliberately drowned?

He heard a door close, then footsteps descending in the next stairwell over. As Lucas kept watch from his hiding spot, Andy, wearing a long black rain slicker with a hood, stepped out into the rain, looking all around. Like some ghastly caricature of Santa Claus, he carried a canvas rucksack over his shoulder, bulging with something that made a clatter. Satisfied that he was unobserved, he walked up the street, staying out of the light of the occasional streetlamp, and stopping periodically to turn and look behind him.

Trailing him from a safe distance, Lucas watched as he skirted the little campus train station, built to resemble a Cotswold cottage, crossed the tracks, and entered the lower reaches of the campus. Lights were on in the dormitories, and lampposts glowed along the main walkways, but most of the grounds were black as pitch, and Lucas had a hard time just keeping Brandt in sight. The rain didn't help. Fortunately,

Andy was moving slowly, and whether it was due to the galoshes he wore or some kind of sprain, Lucas was grateful.

Nor was it long before Lucas could guess his destination. He was weaving his way through the dorms and classroom buildings, past the gardens of President Dodds's house, and heading for the rear of the university art museum.

Where the conservation room was located.

The rucksack took on an ominous cast. But what was he planning to steal? The bones and artifacts had been removed to the labs, and he could hardly be planning to carry off the sar-cophagus itself.

Lurking in a grove of trees, Lucas watched as Brandt, whose gait grew worse with every step, hobbled up to the ivy-covered wall of the museum. It was a sheer thirty or forty feet high, surmounted by the clerestory window. The glass had cracked on the night they had opened the ossuary, but as the pieces had held together, the grounds crew had not gotten around to fixing it yet. He saw Brandt tilt his head back, the rain running down his face, but there was something different about him. A firmer set to the jaw, a furrowed brow, an expression of what could only be called . . . fury. As if the brick wall had dared to thwart him, though not for long.

As Lucas wiped the rain from his eye, he saw Brandt loop the rope handle of the sack around his neck like a cape, then reach out to the ivy tendrils, and as gracefully as a chimpanzee, swing himself six feet up the wall. Clutching the vines, hand over hand, he scuttled up what had seemed only moments before to be an impregnable barrier, making his way, smoothly and swiftly, toward the window up top. Lucas watched in astonishment; it was a performance worthy of a circus acrobat, loose and easy and assured. Andy was swinging open the clerestory window when one of his galoshes came loose and tumbled to the ground. By then, Lucas knew that there was no time to lose. It would be impossible for him to match Andy's feat, much less with his injured arm.

But he could still stop him, if he moved fast.

Barely catching his breath, he raced around to the front of the museum and, panting hard, unlocked the doors and quickly turned off the alarm panel, lest it provide Brandt with any warning. He wanted to catch him red-handed.

The galleries were only faintly illuminated by the night-lights along the baseboards, but it was enough to help him avoid the various statues and pedestals and display cases. The bigger problem was navigating with only one eye; he was constantly having to turn his head this way and that, in order to make sure he hadn't missed something that was just out of his limited range of vision. The ancient Greek and Roman figures glowered down at him, as if he were disturbing their repose, and even the decorative vessels and vases reminded him now of the funeral urn for Dr. Rashid.

He had rounded the corner of the main gallery and was hurrying toward the conservation room when he heard the noise. A clunk, as if from a hammer or chisel, followed by a scraping. It wasn't much, and he wondered if he'd actually heard it at all. Maybe it was just a noise in the pipes. It didn't come again.

What did was a scuffling sound, accompanied by the rustle of something being dragged along the marble floor. He ducked behind the base of a massive kouros, three meters high and over two thousand years old, and waited. The limestone figure towered above him, like a guardian angel, but Lucas knew full well that he was on his own here. If he let Andy get away with whatever he was carrying, the fault would lie with him—and it was doubtful that Andy Brandt, or his purloined treasures, would ever be seen again.

The sound grew nearer, and now he could hear labored breathing. If he hadn't known better, he'd have guessed it was an animal—a wild boar, or a lumbering bear—snuffling and snorting its way through the museum. A shadow passed in front of the kouros, but Lucas held still. He wanted to see exactly what he was up against— was Andy armed? And how was he toting the sack? A CRC man to his core, Lucas needed to ensure that, in any fracas that might ensue, he wouldn't destroy some artifact that he had come there expressly to save.

Then the shadow had moved on, and Lucas still couldn't quite make sense of what he was seeing. It was Andy all right, but he was almost doubled over, his head bent low beneath the hood of his black slicker, one arm dragging the filled rucksack behind him.

If Lucas had still harbored any doubts, they were resolved now. From the clattering alone, he knew that the sack was filled with the contents of the ossuary. But why would Andy have taken them from the lab and brought them back *to* the museum, before leaving with them again? He must have been up to something else. But what?

Like prey that had just caught the scent of a hunter, Andy suddenly stopped and lifted his nose in the air. He sniffed, turning his head to look all around. Lucas ducked back out of sight and held his breath. He was still trying to reconcile this strange creature in the corridor with Andy Brandt, the young anthropologist. After a few seconds, the sound of the rucksack being hauled along the floor resumed, and when Lucas dared to look again, he saw a wet trail and the second of the galoshes lying upside down.

Where, and when, Lucas wondered, should he confront him? Right here, there were several other display cases, containing extremely fragile terracotta amphorae. If a struggle ensued, this would not be a good place for it to occur.

Moving from the cover of one statue or display to another, Lucas kept pace, and in another minute or two, Andy had made his way out of the gallery and into the broad museum lobby. Once there, he stopped again, and as Lucas watched, he ripped off his shoes, too, and threw them to one side. His legs, like his arms for that matter, were cocked at an odd angle, and the hard breathing seemed now to be associated with some kind of pain, rather than exertion.

Whatever was going on, Lucas couldn't wait any longer. As Andy looped the rope handle of the sack around his neck again, Lucas stepped out of the shadows and said, "Leave it there."

Paying no attention at all, Andy straightened up and shifted the sack to fit neatly between his shoulder blades.

Had he heard him? "I said, leave it there."

This time Andy glanced up from under the hood, but the look in his eyes was of utter incomprehension. For Lucas, it was like staring into the eyes of a beast, not a man.

Lucas repeated his order a third time, and Andy tilted his head to one side, as if out of curiosity. His eyes blinked furiously, uncontrollably, and then a light seemed to flicker on behind them. A yellow gleam, like a bolt of sunlight glancing off tarnished bronze. A gleam like the one Lucas had seen in the empty eye sockets of the skull.

As he watched in horror, a smile creased Andy's lips, widening until it seemed almost to split his face, baring his teeth and projecting no mirth at all, only malice. Then he turned around and jumped with blinding speed directly at the doors to the museum, wrenching them entirely off their hinges and shattering the glass into a thousand pieces. As the shards, tinkling like tiny bells, rained down on the floor around him, Lucas saw Andy land on all fours on the walkway outside, shake the fragments of glass loose from the rain slicker, and then scramble with his rucksack into the night.

Lucas leaped through the jagged hole where the doors had been, and ran after him. In the dark and the rain, it was hard enough just to see him. To make matters worse, his quarry was loping along, close to the ground, like a wolf, dodging from one side to another, following no clear course, but gradually making his way up campus, and toward the lights of the town. There was a scream of terror as an unsuspecting student, heading home from the library, was bowled over. Lucas found him lying on his back in a puddle, his wire spectacles twisted on his face, mutely pointing in the direction that his attacker had fled. Lucas hurried on, gaining ground slowly but surely. In the distance, he could hear the commotion of traffic in town, and he could see that Andy was losing steam. Lucas picked up his own pace, and when he found himself within striking distance, lunged for the bottom of the rucksack. He tugged on it, hard, and Andy lost his footing on the damp grass, slipping onto his side. In the light of the lamppost, his face now was unrecognizable—it was a mask of pure depravity, frozen in the rictus of that agonizing smile.

"Stop!" Lucas shouted as he felt the stitches in his arm pop loose.

Then Andy was up on his feet again—or was it his paws?—and galloping with the sack toward a low stone wall that ran along the perimeter of the lawn on Washington Road. Lucas expected him to change directions and stick to the darkness of the campus, but instead, he took a mighty leap over the wall and skidded on all fours into the busy lanes of the street.

The first car he dodged, and the second, too, but a moment later a yellow bus slammed into him, sending his body flying, the black slicker spreading like the wings of a bat. The bus careened into a flimsy newsstand that disintegrated like a pile of twigs. Horns blared, people screamed, loose newspapers were picked up and blown around in the wind and rain. By the time Lucas got there, the bus driver was standing in the wreckage, saying, "Where'd he go? I know I hit somebody." He bent down and ran his finger along the dent in his front fender. "And see? There's blood."

Lucas looked up and down the street, blazing with the headlights of stopped cars. Shielding his one good eye from the rain, he searched for any sign of Andy.

But the man and his rucksack had vanished into the night.

Chapter THIRTY

Edward R. Murrow was doing his regular 8:00 p.m. broadcast on the radio, reporting this time from a pitched battle in a place called the Hürtgen Forest, when Simone heard a knock on her hotel room door. More cautious now than she had ever been in her life, she didn't remove the chain or even look through the peephole before asking, "Who is it?"

"It's me."

Sliding back the chain and turning the lock, she threw the door open to find Lucas, soaked to the skin in his bomber jacket and leaning against the doorjamb as if too exhausted even to stand. He was holding his left arm with his hand.

"What's happened to you?" she said, drawing him into the room and locking the door behind him.

"I just wanted to make sure you were okay."

"Why wouldn't I be?'

But he didn't answer—he sounded as if he barely had the breath to speak.

"Let me get you some water."

"You wouldn't have anything stronger, would you?"

She was about to say no, when she remembered that the hotel management, still trying to make amends for all of the tragedy that had befallen her under their roof (though how could they?) had sent up a basket of fruit and a decanter of fine brandy. She poured him a glass, and he tossed it down, wincing.

"Is it your arm?" she said, and he nodded. She helped him to remove the wet jacket, and then his shirt, draping them on the radiator to dry. The bandages were pink where several of his stitches had popped. "Oh my God, let me take care of this."

Of the many things she had learned from her late father, one was never to travel anywhere without a first aid kit. Retrieving it from the bathroom cabinet, she poured him another generous shot of the brandy, then sat him down in the desk chair and said, "Now stay still."

"Yes, Doctor."

"How did you do this?" she said as she knelt in front of him, intent as any surgeon, using Q-tips and antiseptic and fresh washcloths to clean up the area. She had never been this intimately close to him, never seen his bare chest or arms, never smelled his sweat or felt his breath on the back of her neck as she bent to her task. She tried to concentrate on the work at hand, dabbing at the wound, cutting and applying a strip of sterile bandages, but she was finding it hard to focus.

"I went by Andy Brandt's apartment," he began, and when she looked up inquiringly, he continued, telling her about his suspicions and what he had seen there, including the missing blue folder. He told her how he had chased Andy to the art museum, and from the museum, across the campus and on into town. The bus accident, the absent body. And now, here he was, making sure that she was safe and sound.

"I had to see for myself," he said in a tight voice, "that you were all right."

Simone, sitting back on her haunches, was moved by the emotion evident in his tone, and stunned by all that he had just told her. Although she realized that the accident with Brandt should have been the most troubling part of Lucas's story—the man could be lying dead somewhere—that wasn't the part that truly mattered to her. "How do we get the folder back?" she said.

"I had to give a police report at the scene," Lucas said. "The cops know who was hit."

"But even if they go to his apartment, that doesn't mean they'll surrender any of his property to us—even if we say it was stolen."

"Actually, it does."

"Why?"

"Because I made a call from the lobby. To Colonel Macmillan."

"Oh," she said, "of course. You had to." Their entire mission had just gone up in smoke. She gathered up the supplies and stood before his chair.

"I had to tell him that the bones and artifacts had been stolen."

Simone could well imagine the kind of reaction that the colonel, ill-tempered under the best of circumstances, had displayed. "Was it bad?"

Lucas cocked his head and gave her a wry smile. "Let's just say I won't be getting any medals soon. But he'll have started the wheels turning, that much I can guarantee. Do you think I could have another shot of that brandy?"

She handed him the glass and the bottle, and went to the bathroom to put the first aid kit away. Resting her hands on the sides of the sink, she stared at herself in the mirror of the medicine chest, wondering who she was, who she had become over the past few weeks. She had circles under her eyes from lack of sleep, her long black hair was tangled and unbrushed. Her father was gone forever; she was staying in a strange hotel in a foreign country in the middle of a war. All of her possessions were stuffed into a couple of battered suitcases. And she didn't seem to be any closer to figuring out the ossuary's secrets or ensuring its return to Egypt. Even on a desert island, she doubted she could have felt more marooned.

Compounding the problem was the shirtless, wounded, and weary man sitting at her desk in the next room. *What did she want from him?* she asked herself. *What could he give her?*

And what was she prepared to offer in return?

In the mirror, she saw his face appear over her shoulder. His chin was sooty with stubble; his black patch glistened from the rain. She felt his hands turning her around, then pulling her close. His fingers went under her chin, tilting her face up toward his own, and though she knew full well what was happening, she felt immobilized, unsure, confused. She simply let him touch his lips to hers. She let him steal her breath as if it were his own. She let his scruffy face scratch her cheek.

Then he kissed her again, harder. Longer. More insistently.

She felt his hands coursing down her body, as if sculpting every inch, and before she could stop it—even if she had wanted to—something inside her, like a dam too swollen to hold fast, gave way, bursting wide open. Her lips pressed against his, tasting the sweet burn of the brandy, and her arms went up around his bare shoulders.

On the bed, he laid her sideways, her shoes thumping softly onto the carpet, her tousled hair fanning out on the cream-colored coverlet. Flicking off the lamp, he knelt beside her, his hands roughly unfastening the buttons of her blouse and tossing it aside, followed by the rest of her clothes. Above the drumbeat of her heart, she heard Murrow's voice, scratchy with static, and the hissing of the radiator. Wherever Lucas touched her—and it was as if he were touching her everywhere at once—his fingertips left an electric trail. She let her mind follow that trail, let her thoughts evaporate, let her hands and lips go where they wanted . . . and when she felt his body on top of hers, firm and urgent and all enveloping, she could no longer tell where her own skin ended and where his began.

Chapter THIRTY-ONE

"*Nein, nein*," Gödel said, impatiently wiping a string of figures off the blackboard with the sleeve of his tweed jacket. "How did you ever pass the polytechnic exam?"

"Easy," Einstein replied from his easy chair. "I took it twice."

"*Ach.*" Gödel quickly scrawled a new sequence of numbers and mathematical symbols on the cleared corner of the blackboard. "I'm surprised that was all."

The rest of the board was still cluttered with

complex field equations that Einstein had been working on for weeks. He knew that his calculations sometimes needed review by some fresh eye, but it was difficult to find anyone up to the task. Gödel, thank God, was perhaps the premier mathematician in the world—purer, in a way, than even the brilliant John von Neumann—and it was why Einstein had lobbied so hard for him to be allowed into America, and to join him in Princeton. Still, if Oppenheimer knew that even Gödel had been privy to some of this work, he'd throw a fit. It was all as highly classified as any information could be.

While Gödel silently assessed his own corrections, Einstein went to the window, streaked with rain, and peered out at his rear garden. Night had fallen hours ago and a lonely light in the alley revealed a swarm of brown leaves swirling against the doors of the old garage; as neither Einstein nor Helen Dukas could drive and relied upon friends to take them anywhere a bus didn't go, the garage was used instead to store boxes of his unsorted papers from the Berlin Institute.

"So, what do you think now?" Gödel said, standing back. "Does this not resolve the difficulty you were in?"

Einstein studied the blackboard, squinting in the inadequate light from the torchiere by the door.

"Yes, that's better. Thank you, Kurt. I should have seen that myself."

Although Einstein had long prided himself on his thought experiments—his ability to imagine fantastic scenarios and, by doing so, arrive at remarkable conclusions—it was in the more mundane areas of mathematics that he sometimes tripped over his own feet. Once he had achieved some illuminating insight, he was not so interested in explaining the thousand steps by which he had come to it. He wasn't even sure he knew. His mind was already extrapolating from the new concept—which he accepted intuitively to be right—and racing onward.

From downstairs, he could smell spaghetti sauce simmering in the pot, and hear the chatter of Helen talking to Adele Gödel as they prepared the meal and set the table. He glanced at the clock; it was nearly nine. No wonder he was hungry. As if on cue, Adele called from below, "Enough, you two. This is not Berlin—in America we eat at a decent hour."

Gödel, still focused on the blackboard, didn't move, and Einstein had to get up and put a hand on his narrow shoulder to get his attention. Even a gesture that small, and coming from his closest friend in the world, made the man flinch.

"We can finish later," Einstein said gently. "Let's have some dinner."

He shepherded Gödel down the creaking steps and into the dining room, where the anxious Austrian sat down in his chair like a man about to undergo a Gestapo interrogation. His wife made a show of helping Helen to bring in the bowls of pasta and sauce, and then ladling them herself onto Kurt's plate. He watched her like a hawk, and Einstein exchanged a quick and subtle glance with Helen, who, equally familiar with the couple's strange protocols, pointedly paid no attention while lifting the lid off a tureen of steamed asparagus.

Even so, Gödel waited until he had seen Adele dig into her own dinner before he cautiously lifted his fork.

"Eat, *mein strammer bursche*," she said, using her pet name for him. *Strapping lad,* it meant, and it always brought a tiny smile to his thin lips. "I made this sauce myself, from the tomatoes from our garden."

Adele, who wore her hair in curly gold-and-red ringlets, was as natural and outgoing as her husband was reserved. But she doted on her husband, and fiercely protected him from as many of the vicissitudes of life as possible. Back in Vienna in 1937, she had even fought off some teenage Brownshirts who, mistaking Kurt for a Jew, had attacked the couple on their way home from the *Nachtfalter*, the popular club where she performed. She had kicked and beaten them with her furled umbrella until they ran for cover. Kurt had been traumatized for months.

"You two boys work too hard," Adele said, putting some asparagus on her husband's plate, and then cutting the stalks into shorter segments. "I am going to get you some marbles to play with," she said with a laugh that made her earrings jangle.

"Ah, Kurt will win every time," Einstein said. "He is the sportsman, not me."

Gödel, inspecting a bit of the asparagus, beamed; he enjoyed this kind of banter, as it made him feel included without his having to make jokes himself. And he plainly knew it was all in good fun.

Einstein nursed a paternal feeling toward his younger colleague, in part because he had a son of his own, Eduard, who suffered from mental illness. Like Gödel, Eduard had immense talents —he was a technically accomplished musician and a fine writer—but his abilities were so entangled in a skein of neuroses and phobias, fears and delusions, that he could not function outside the confines of the Swiss facility where he lived. It was the greatest sorrow of Einstein's life that he could not help his son, and it made watching over Kurt seem like a kind of penance.

"Kurt has been trying to convince me—again—that there are psychic elementals that are as real as any physical properties," Einstein said, as he could not share what they had actually been doing. "If we're not careful, he will be able to use his mental energy to levitate this table."

Adele planted her elbows on the cloth. "He'd better not try. Helen has put out her best china."

Helen smiled, and Gödel, dabbing at his lips

with the linen napkin, launched into another of his ontological proofs. Even as far back as his days in the Vienna Circle, he had rejected the positivism of Bertrand Russell and his cohorts for taking much too dim a view of intuition. Gödel freely admitted that the intuition of a concept was not proof; he argued that it was the opposite. "We do not analyze intuition to see a proof, but by intuition we see something without a proof." Recently, however, he'd gone beyond that conclusion, too, and asserted that there must then logically be a realm unknowable to our simple senses, where ultimate truth resided. Although Einstein found such mystical speculation unpersuasive, its proponent was not so easy to dismiss out of hand. After all, whose portrait did he himself have hanging on a nail in his study upstairs? Isaac Newton, who had devoted countless hours to the lunatic aims of alchemy.

"If the world is rationally constructed and has meaning," Kurt said, his head down as he carefully lifted a single strand of spaghetti from his plate, "then there must be such a thing as an afterlife. Otherwise, what is the meaning of this one?"

"Oh, Kurt," Adele said, "why must everything have a meaning? Maybe we are just here to eat spaghetti and talk and laugh and," she paused, replenishing her glass and raising it to her host, "drink good wine."

"You said it yourself, Albert," Kurt persisted.

"What did I say?"

"That God does not play dice with the universe. The cosmos cannot simply be a game, designed at random and made without reason."

"But perhaps He is playing some other game," Einstein said. "A game we don't know yet, with rules we can't understand."

"But every game *has* rules—you will concede that much, *ja*? Let us take this quantum physics."

"You may have it."

"You do not like it because you cannot accept this notion of—what is it you wish to call it?— spooky action at a distance."

"A particle, in two places at one time? No, I am not yet convinced of that."

"And I will not try to convince you. Still, there must be a consistency to it all. The problem is simply that we have not been able to discover— at least not yet—the invisible hand that moves these particles about."

"Is there an invisible body to go with this invisible hand?" Einstein joked, but once Gödel was on a tear, it was tough to distract him.

"At present, they may seem to move in a fundamentally illogical way—"

"That they do."

"And thus you regard this as less than optimal."

"I do."

"But what might appear to be optimal to you may not appear to be optimal to such particles, operating as they do in a system we do not comprehend."

"Now there I do agree," Einstein said, twirling a thick clump of the spaghetti around his fork. "It is a system I do not comprehend. And that is why, like Don Quixote with his lance, I will continue my quest."

"For your Dulcinea?" Adele interjected.

"Yes. And the unified field theory will prove just as beautiful. Oh, I know what all the young Turks think of it, and of me. But I have always proceeded as much by what I feel here," he said, patting his belly, "as I do here." He pointed at his temple with the loaded fork.

"My point exactly," Gödel said. "Intuition, you feel it in your gut."

"Albert, you're going to get spaghetti in your hair," Helen clucked.

"Too late," Adele said, reaching over with her napkin to disengage an errant strand.

"You're as bad as a child," Helen said, and Einstein laughed.

"I think I need to start my life all over again," he said. "I should have learned better manners as a boy."

"According to your own theory, you still can do that," Gödel said, but before he could elaborate, there was a scratching at the dining room window, and when they all looked, a pair of green eyes flashed behind the glass.

"Oh, my," Helen said, swiftly rising from her chair and going into the foyer.

"What is it?" Kurt asked nervously.

"It's nothing," Adele said. "Eat your dinner before it gets cold."

The front door opened, and a gust of autumn air blew into the house, then it closed again and Helen returned with the tabby cat in her arms. "It's my fault," she said. "I've been leaving a bowl of milk for her after Albert leaves for work."

Although he hadn't been aware of this particular phobia, Einstein realized that he should have guessed—Kurt was frozen in his chair, staring at the cat as if it were a tiger about to pounce. What wasn't the man afraid of?

"Now, Kurt, it's just a little pussycat," Adele said, smoothing his arm with the palm of her hand. "Remember how much you liked the cat I kept at the nightclub?"

"I'm sorry," Helen said, "I didn't know—"

"But maybe you could take the cat into the kitchen," Adele urged, hoping to avert a crisis.

As Helen did so, Einstein asked, "Why did you say that my theory could help me to learn better manners?"

"That is not what I meant," Kurt said, still plainly perturbed.

"So, you approve of my manners? That is good to know."

"What I meant," Kurt said, taking slow breaths

and keeping his eyes riveted to his plate, "was that if you accept the premises of general relativity—"

"I certainly do."

"—and if you succeed in wedding them to the gravitational field equations on which we have worked—"

"Go on. Go on."

"Then you must, logically, assume that it would be possible to travel in time . . . and in that way to go back to your own boyhood."

"*Ach*, I'm too old for that. Once was enough."

"What have I missed?" Helen said, returning to her seat.

"My Kurt is explaining how we can grow younger," Adele said.

"Then I am all ears."

"If the universe and everything in it rotates, like a vast cosmic whirlpool, then it follows that time cannot be a straight linear sequence of events—first this happens and then that—no, it must instead bend like the universe itself. It must follow the curve, *ja*, and space-time projectories must therefore be able to loop back on themselves. How could they not? In theory, they must be able to return to the very places that they have already been."

"So how do I get back to my sixteenth birthday?" Adele said. "That is what I'd like to know."

"You would need a rocket ship," Einstein said,

joining in the speculation. "And it would have to travel very fast indeed."

"But, theoretically, if you went fast enough, and if the curve was wide enough," Kurt said, "you could visit any time at all—past, present, or future."

"Oh, no," Adele said, "the future can wait. I don't want to get older any faster than I have to."

"Nor do I," Helen said, starting to clear the table. "Who wants coffee?"

As Helen and Adele prepared coffee and dessert, Einstein questioned Gödel further—he did not agree with all his conclusions, in part because they could never be empirically proven, but he was fascinated, as always, by the manner in which a mind as astute as Kurt's could tease out such implications from his own theories. He would have to think on it, hard, if he wished to find the fallacy or fault in Gödel's logic.

By the time Kurt and Adele took their leave, it was nearly midnight and Helen, exhausted from the long day, went up to her room. Einstein was ready to turn in himself, but as was his ritual, he went into the kitchen first, to have a glass of warm milk. Looking in the icebox, he found only an inch or so left in the bottle.

When the cat rubbed up against his pant leg, he understood why. "Ah, so you're the one who's been drinking my milk."

He bent down and rubbed his knuckles under the cat's chin, and said, "Where are you going to sleep tonight?" His former wife, Mileva, had had a cat that looked like this. But by now it was surely gone. And even Mileva, judging from her last letters from Zurich, was in declining health. Time was no illusion; it was a relentless force, and he felt its sharp fingers digging into the small of his back as he tried to straighten up.

The cat trotted to the back door and waited there.

"It's a cold night," Einstein said, but the cat stayed put, turning its head and meowing loudly.

"All right then," he said, opening the door, "if that's what you want."

The cat bolted out into the yard, and Einstein stood in the doorway looking out at the tree branches bending in the wind. Dead leaves scuttled across the back steps, and the wooden doors to the garage banged and rattled. He was just about to go back inside when they banged again, and he realized that the latch must have slipped. If he didn't resecure it, the noise would keep him up half the night.

Descending the stairs with one hand on the rail—his back complaining with every step—he shuffled across the yard. The harvest moon hung low and yellow in the sky. At the garage, he found that the latch had indeed been thrown. Before closing it again, he pried the door open and had a glance inside.

Boxes were stacked to the rafters, along with

rusty rakes and shovels. But the darkness was nearly impenetrable.

"Anyone there?" he asked. "Last chance."

Then he pushed the door closed, dropped the latch into place, and picked his way through the dead leaves and up again to the back door. It was only as he took one last survey of the yard, checking to see if the cat had changed her mind, that he thought he saw, at the tiny smudged window of the garage, a flicker of life. Of movement. As if something had been watching him, and ducked out of sight a fraction too late.

Was this, then, the cat's lair? Well, if she could find a way in, he thought, then she could find a way out again. And it was too dark and cold to make another trip across the yard. He would check in the morning. For now, he would drink what milk was left in the bottle, and go to bed. Dinner with the Gödels was always stimulating, but seldom ended early.

It was only hours later, long after he'd retired, that he was awakened by a strong wind battering the windows, and thought he heard a screech in the yard. He stumbled out of bed and closed the window tight before peering out into the darkness. Apart from the fact that the garage door had blown open again—the latch must need to be replaced; he would have to tell Helen in the morning—there was no sign of anything amiss, and he put it down to a bad dream.

Chapter THIRTY-TWO

"I was hoping I'd never see you again," Police Chief Farrell said from the top of the stairs.

"Nice to see you, too," Lucas said as a uniformed cop standing sentinel stepped aside to let him pass. The last time he'd climbed these stairs, it had been dark out, but even at this time of day, they were dim.

Farrell was holding a cardboard cup of coffee in one hand, and with the other pushed the door to Andy Brandt's apartment open wide. "You must have friends in high places," he said as Lucas edged past him and into the room.

Someone whose back was turned was seated at the makeshift desk, his fingers rapidly combing through a blizzard of papers, including, as Lucas could see, a corner of the blue folder that had belonged to Simone's father.

Lucas wasn't surprised at all by the quick action. A call to Colonel Macmillan, with the suggestion that the still missing Andy Brandt had been engaging in espionage, was bound to kick-start the local authorities. Lucas had found a summons to the Harrison Street apartments waiting in his university mailbox.

"So, you worked with this guy Brandt?" Chief Farrell asked him now.

"Not much. He was in another department—but, yes, I knew him."

"He sure as hell knew you," Farrell said, and when Lucas asked him what he meant by that, the man at the desk turned around in his chair and said, "A picture's worth a thousand words."

To his astonishment, Lucas recognized his fellow boarder, Taylor. The factory worker, or so he'd said.

"Take a gander at these," Taylor said, holding out a batch of photos.

In the pile were at least a dozen shots, all snapped surreptitiously: Lucas, walking on Nassau Street with Delaney or standing in a museum gallery surrounded by students or smoking on the front steps of Mrs. Caputo's house. In one, he was in the lobby of Guyot Hall, where Andy's lab had been, contemplating the Caithness Man.

"Oh, and he's got a few of your girlfriend, too," Taylor said as Lucas looked up from the photos, dumbstruck. "Go ahead. Ask me anything."

"Okay," Lucas said. "First of all, what are you doing here?"

Taylor reached into the breast pocket of his Windbreaker, removed his wallet, and held it open. Under the plastic sleeve was an FBI identification card.

"Now you can answer a question for me," Taylor said. "Why was Brandt taking pictures of you? Did he have a crush on you or what?"

Lucas wondered if this was some kind of trap. Was it possible that the FBI didn't know what the OSS was up to? He didn't dare say anything that might foul him up any further with Macmillan. "You'll have to ask him."

"I would if I could. Everybody wants him, but nobody can find him."

Taking the photos back and tossing them on the desk, Taylor leaned back in the chair, reappraising him. "Well then, maybe this will be more up your alley, Professor—if it isn't too much trouble, maybe you could tell me what all of this stuff is about?"

He opened the blue folder and spread some of the papers out on the table. Lucas saw Arabic writing, and illustrations of hieroglyphs and Christian iconography. "For starters, who's this guy?" Taylor said, picking out a dog-eared antique print. "He shows up in a bunch of these."

Lucas studied the print. It depicted a bearded man in a long robe, swinging a crooked-handled staff at a cringing devil with stubby horns. "That's Saint Anthony."

"The patron saint of travelers?"

"No, that's the Saint Anthony of Padua. This is an earlier one—Saint Anthony of Egypt." Recalling everything Simone had since filled him in on, he added, "He was a hermit who lived in the desert and, according to Scripture, wrestled with demons who tried to get him to succumb to worldly temptation and renounce God."

"Did he win the wrestling match?"

"Legend has it that he did."

"Just in case I ever need to know," Taylor said, bemused, "how the hell do you beat a demon?"

"See that staff, with the odd handle?" Lucas said, trying to recall what Simone had once told him. "He raised it to the sky and the Lord sent His power through it."

"Huh. I'll have to remember to put in a requisition slip for one of those." He took the print back and tossed it on top of the others. "Why would a spy, if that's what we're talking about here, take any interest in crap like this?"

Why indeed, Lucas thought, unless he had received explicit orders to do so. Those orders could only have come all the way from Berlin, from the highest levels of the Third Reich. How much did the Germans really know about the ossuary? The ossuary had never made it to the capital, much less to Hitler's private retreat.

"First, you can answer a question for me," Lucas said, in an attempt to redirect the conversation. "Why have you been keeping me under surveillance?"

"What are you talking about?"

"Are you going to tell me that it's just a coincidence that you live in the same boardinghouse that I do? That you've lied to me about who you are, and what you're doing in Princeton? And how about turning up a few rows away from me at the football game—another coincidence?"

Taylor paused, then said, "Chief, could you leave us alone for a few minutes?"

Farrell stepped outside reluctantly, and closed the door.

"For starters," Taylor said, "in case you forgot, I was boarding in that house before you were."

"But you must have known I was moving back there."

"And second, you've got an inflated opinion of yourself."

Lucas waited.

"You're not the reason I'm living there, you're not the reason I'm in Jersey, and you're not the reason I was sitting in the stands."

"Then why?"

Taylor shook his head and said, "For an Ivy League professor, you can be awfully slow."

Lucas still hadn't grasped what he was getting at.

"Ask yourself. Who else lives on Mercer?"

And then Lucas thought of the view from Taylor's front window . . . and how his light went on or off in keeping with what was happening directly across the street . . . and of his proximity to someone else at the stadium that day.

"You're keeping watch over Einstein?"

The agent didn't answer.

"You're his secret bodyguard?"

"Something like that."

So many things were falling into place.

"Do I need to tell you that that's highly classified information?" Taylor said.

"No." But then why had he divulged it?

"And that you're in a position to do your country a great service?"

Ah, here it comes, Lucas thought. "What service is that?"

"Ever since that incident at the stadium, you and Dr. Einstein have become acquainted."

"Barely."

"It would really help us out if you could tell us what you talk about."

"What we talk about? I've met with him once. You really think we discussed the theory of relativity?"

"No. I don't. But does he ever say anything about, say, the war?"

"He says he hopes we win very soon."

"What's he say about our allies?"

"Our allies?"

"Yeah, you may have heard of them. England. France. Russia."

The penny dropped. For years, Einstein had been accused by some newspapers and radio commentators of being soft on the Soviets and Communism. Now Lucas knew what Taylor was fishing for, and what he was being asked to do.

"You really want to know what we talked about? We talked about the Battle of Monte Cassino."

"Why that one in particular?"

"Because I'm an art history professor, and the destruction of the monastery was a tragic loss to the art world."

"Anything else happen?"

"Yes."

Taylor looked hopeful.

"He bummed a cigarette. It's against his doctor's orders." The letter he'd seen from President Roosevelt, hinting at Nazi progress on some dangerous scheme, he decided to keep to himself. There *was* one thing, however, that Lucas wanted before he left.

"But I'll tell you what I can do. I might be able to help you out with those papers," he said, casually gesturing at the contents of the blue folder. "If there's anything important in them, I can let you know."

Taylor seemed to mull the offer over from every angle before saying, "Okay," and handing them over. "They're sure as hell unintelligible to me."

On his way out, Taylor warned him not to leave town without notice, and the police chief chimed in. "I'll be keeping an eye on you."

"Good, I could use a spare."

The cop at the bottom of the stairs laughed, then stopped when Farrell glared at him.

Chapter THIRTY-THREE

Because there were no spare offices on campus—some of the buildings had been closed to conserve fuel for the war effort—Simone had been assigned a carrel in the sub-basement of the main library. It was not much bigger than a clothes closet, with a gray metal desk bolted to a gray metal wall, surmounted by gray metal bookshelves. Even the wooden chair was dreary, with a worn-out padded green seat. To make it all a tiny bit more con-genial, she'd taped some family photos, faded and curling up at the edges, to the walls. The sliding door, with a narrow window the size of a shoebox, opened onto a long, poorly lit corridor, lined with racks of books from floor to ceiling.

Slumping back in her seat and stretching her arms, she surveyed the dusty volumes and mono-graphs and scholarly publications cluttering her desktop. Every one of them had been something her father was consulting, and while it was comforting to know that his eyes had coursed across these same texts and his fingers had turned these same pages, it was also maddening. Somewhere in all of this, there were answers— answers to what the ossuary had held, to what powers it might still retain, and even to what might have caused her father's death. So long as the critical blue folder was unaccounted for, however, Simone had her doubts about the "accidental death" ruling, and she was determined to follow every lead to its logical, or even illogical, conclusion.

No matter how weary she became—and there were times she found herself staring blankly into space—she would not give up.

Several times already she had found little scraps of paper that contained notes written in his distinctive hand, slipped into one of the old leather-bound volumes, revealing that he had intended to begin work at that spot again the next day. Each one of these notes she kept in a separate binder, though the most striking of all was a transcription of a prophecy from an ancient account of Christianity's earliest saints; the book itself had come from the personal library of one of the university's eighteenth-century presidents, the Scottish clergyman and theologian, John Witherspoon. Though the sentiments sounded like something from the book of Revelation, the words were attributed to none other than "the Holy Desert Anchorite," a reference, quite plainly, to Saint Anthony of Egypt.

"And there, in the barren soil of sand, home to snakes and scorpions, the seeds of destruction shall be planted and grow."

The next few lines were smudged beyond deciphering, as a blue mold had infected the book, and it appeared her father had given up trying to parse them.

But then the transcription had resumed with ". . . rising from the desert, like a pillar of fire, burning the eyes of those who behold it and laying waste to all that lives upon the earth and to all that ever will, unto the tenth generation." Again, there was a missing phrase or two, followed by, "And even the clouds shall burn."

Despite its poetry, the passages were similar to what could be found in much of the patristic literature, the dire warnings and apocalyptic visions of the early prophets and martyred saints. Her father had scrawled "St. A's Fire?" at the bottom of his transcript, and though Simone knew that this term normally referred to the skin disease associated with the swineherd, she wondered if her father had not uncovered a second, and possibly even more powerful, meaning.

One other thing grew plain, too. Her father had evidently become fixated on the idea of demonic transmigration. There were the expected Catholic texts from the *Rituale Romanum*, containing the rites and guidelines for major exorcisms, but also a host of more arcane materials whose origins ranged from India to Egypt. She found passages copied from the Zohar, the Jewish mystical text of Kabbalistic teachings, describing the ways in which a demon could secretly slip into a victim's soul, and how it could only be dislodged by a minyan reciting Psalm 91 three times; if the rabbi then blew a certain melody on the shofar, or ram's horn, the sound would in effect "shatter the body" and shake the evil spirit loose.

Even the Muslims had their methods for disposing of wandering demons. The prophet Muhammad instructed his followers to read the last three suras from the Koran—the Surat al-Ikhlas (the Fidelity), the Surat al-Falaq (the Dawn), and the Surat an-Nas (Mankind)—and drink water from the holy well of Zamzam.

What none of these faiths—even the Hindu—did was doubt for one moment the existence of dark spirits, or their ability to jump from one living presence to another.

Demons were considered parasites, infinitely malleable and indefatigable, hitchhikers of the soul, and as she read, Simone could see that her father had been trying to unify all this material in some way, with many arrows and notes and cross-references. Just seeing his handwriting on various scraps of paper, stuck inside some of the books, stiffened her resolve to complete the work that he had begun. Inadvertently, she found herself clutching the medallion she now wore around her neck.

She was just about to start in again—what had he meant by writing "sigil/Saturn/

containment" and underlining it three times?—when she thought she heard a noise in the corridor.

The creaking of a library cart's wheels.

She had put in a request for a twelfth-century map of Mesopotamia, kept in the Special Collections Department, and she hoped that this was a library assistant finally delivering it to her carrel. But the creaking seemed to pass her by, and it was already receding into the stacks when she unlocked her door and popped her head out into the corridor. She could just see the back of someone in a long overcoat—small and dark, with his head down—pushing the cart into an aisle down the way.

"Hold on there!" she called out. "Did you have something for me?"

The man and his cart disappeared altogether, and she called out, "Do you have the map I requested?"

Again, there was no answer. Annoyed, she slipped on the shoes she had kicked off under the desk, and muttering under her breath, closed the door of her carrel without bothering to twirl the combination lock, and went off to find him. Only one other carrel, at the far end of the row, showed any light through its little window.

But by the time she got to the end of the stack where the cart had disappeared, there was no sight of it.

She stopped to listen, and she could hear the

rattle of wheels a couple of aisles across, and deeper into the gloomy stacks. Lighted by only forty-watt bulbs, the bookshelves seemed to go on forever; in fact, Princeton had one of the largest open-access libraries in the country, with over two million books on display, and though she was normally grateful for that, right now she might have wished for a less expansive space. Every time she thought she'd spotted the corner of the cart, it vanished into the maze again, and she had to follow it down another aisle.

"Excuse me," she called out. "Could you hold still for a moment? I think you have something I want."

The assistant was either deaf, obtuse, or both. Whatever the reason, she got no reply. She began to wonder if she was on a wild goose chase. Maybe she should just go back to her carrel and put in a fresh request with the head librarian on the main floor on her way out.

A solitary student, his nose buried in a book, passed her by without even looking up.

Then, just as she was about to give up, the creaking of the cart came again, almost as if it were trying to tease her, and she couldn't resist going a little farther. More and more, it was like swimming through some murky underground sea, moving from one pool of light to the next, around blind corners and down towering rows of books. Simone's eyes scanned the titles as she went, many of which were in foreign languages. Some of the books were so old that the words imprinted on their spines had become illegible. They looked as if they'd been there since the college was founded in 1746, and it was a miracle that they were still in circulation. Lucas had once joked to her that he'd found George Washington's name on a check-out card.

Ever since the night he had come to her hotel room, she had struggled to keep herself focused on her work. Sometimes, she was able to carry it off, for half an hour, maybe a bit more. But try as she might, she'd find her thoughts turning to that night at the inn. Minutes would pass and in her mind's eye all she could see were his arms lifting her up and laying her on the bed, all she could feel were his hands, tearing at her clothes, caressing her body. It had been years since she had felt anything like it. No, she thought, that wasn't true, either; she had never felt anything like it at all.

As she turned into the next empty aisle—no surprise there—she picked up a faint loamy scent. Like wet soil that had been recently turned.

"Hello?" she said, swiveling in all directions. "Can you hear me?"

At the distant end of the stacks, she now saw something sticking out, and she promptly marched toward it. "Ah, so there you are." It wasn't until she got closer that she realized it wasn't the cart, but only one of the footstools that the library left here and there for the benefit of its shorter browsers.

Finally, she had reached a dead end. The basement went no farther than this, nor did her patience. Turning to thread her way back, she thought she saw a shadow move on the floor.

"Hello?" she said. The shadow shifted, but no one answered.

She peered over the top of the books and into the next aisle. "Hello?"

This time, when there was no answer again, something told her to stop asking.

To stop advertising her position.

As stealthily as she could, she slipped into the next aisle. And then, when that one proved clear, into the one beside that.

But she could sense the presence of another living thing. Close by.

The smell of sod grew stronger.

She placed each foot on the floor with the greatest deliberation, though her heels still made a noise.

She thought she could hear breathing. A snuffling sound, like something whose mouth was crowded with too many teeth. She flashed on the old etchings of the beasts assailing Saint Anthony.

Leaning against the end of a bookshelf, she slipped off one shoe, and then the other, and holding them in her hands, crept in the direction of the stairwell that led to the main floor.

The labored breath came again, closer than before. Lowering her head, she peeked through the stacks into the neighboring aisle. Something moved there, dark and indistinct, its back to her.

Ducking down, and swallowing hard—her mouth was suddenly as dry as the Sahara—she inched away, down the narrow passage between two rows of books, and when she thought she'd put enough distance between them, stopped to take another glance back.

Over the top of a collection of atlases, she saw a pair of eyes staring back at her. Sunken, black, buried deep in a face the color of mud.

She bolted. Throwing the shoes behind her, she raced down the aisle, turning left at the end, then racing down another and turning right. She could hear the sound of padding feet—or was it paws?—keeping pace with her.

She ran harder, desperately trying to orient herself. Was she heading toward the stairs or another dead end? She had the vague notion that she was being deliberately stampeded, that her pursuer had no intention of overtaking her yet— that it was only playing with her, like a cat with a mouse. Trying to scare her to death.

Her elbow caught on a volume, knocking her off balance, and the sleeve of her blouse ripped on the sharp end of a metal shelf. Several books toppled to the floor. She slipped on one, then took off again, the sweaty soles of her feet sticking to the linoleum. A red Exit sign glowed ahead, its arrow pointing to the stairwell and elevators.

Somehow the hunter seemed to have gotten ahead of her. Even before she saw its looming shadow again, she could sense that it stood between her and the stairwell. It was as if the damn thing could be in two places at once. She changed course, racing instead toward the carrel, where at least she could throw the sliding door closed, and lock it from the inside.

She burst into the wider corridor that ran along one wall of the basement and followed it down, past the ends of one stack after another, all of them nearly identical, until she finally rounded a corner and saw the lit island of her carrel straight ahead.

But that was when she skidded to a sudden halt, the breath ragged in her throat.

There was something in the carrel already.

How could it always be everywhere? Through the narrow window in the sliding door, she could see something moving, and she could hear the sounds of papers being ripped to shreds, books torn to pieces. The light from inside wavered as the intruder crossed in front of the desk lamp, back and forth, tending to his destructive work.

Reversing course, she headed back toward the stairwell, expecting at any minute to see the shadow blocking her way, but this time there was none. Her hands shaking, she threw open the steel fire door and scrambled through; the door clanged shut behind her, and she was halfway up the first flight of stairs, her head down like one of those football players she had seen, when she crashed into someone or something on the landing. She looked up, wild-eyed, as it snatched her by the arms and held her there.

She was about to scream when he said, "Hold on!"

And she saw who it was.

"What's wrong?" Lucas said, gripping her more tightly.

She gasped, and fell against him so hard he nearly toppled over the railing.

"What is it, Simone?"

A folder—blue—fell from under his arm, scattering papers on the stairs.

"Why are you running?"

She couldn't answer; she had no breath yet. She turned her head to watch the stairs below.

"Where are your shoes?"

But all she could do was cling to him, and listen for the sound of the fire door being thrown open again.

It didn't come.

"Simone, talk to me. Tell me what's wrong!"

How could she explain? Instead, she clutched his arm and dragged him up the stairs, over his protests—"Wait, I need to retrieve those papers" —and toward the light and safety of the main reading room. Once they got there, she collapsed in a chair at the nearest table. A few students, annoyed at the commotion, looked up from their studies.

Lucas knelt beside her, holding her hands in his own and murmuring soothing words. A librarian hurried over to ask what was wrong. Lucas said, "I'm not sure yet."

Neither was Simone, although, as her thoughts cleared and her heart slowed, she began to form, however reluctantly, a terrifying idea. It was the destruction in the carrel that gave it to her. Someone, or something, seemed intent on erasing its own trail, on eradicating all the evidence that had been amassed over the centuries, from all around the world, of its very existence. But to what end? Did it have some new and more monstrous havoc yet to wreak?

Chapter THIRTY-FOUR

All morning, Einstein had been poring over the latest notes and internal queries that Oppenheimer had sent by secret courier. There was no escaping the sense of urgency. Apparently, some communiqués from the highest echelon of the Nazi command had been intercepted and decoded at Bletchley Park, and unless they had been deliberately devised to be leaked and thereby mislead the Allied scientists (which was always a possibility), the German physicists were honing in on the last steps necessary to create a nuclear reaction. The race to unleash the unparalleled power of the atom was picking up speed, and Einstein knew that if the Third Reich got to the finish line first, the civilized world would cease to exist. Washington, New York, London, Moscow —all of them would be consumed in balls of fire overnight, and Hitler would rule the globe unchallenged. Evil, in its purest distillation ever, would reign triumphant.

President Roosevelt himself had acknowledged as much in a phone call at dawn that day. "Even your friend Bertie Russell has come around and made some comments helpful to the war effort."

For the world's most renowned pacifist to do so, Einstein recognized, was newsworthy. Although no one concurred, he still believed that it might have been Russell who was the target in the stadium that day. They had once compared hate mail, and Russell had won by a mile.

"But those bastards in Berlin are breathing down our neck," Roosevelt had explained, "and I don't need to tell you, of all people, what it will mean if they crack this before we do."

"You do not, Mr. President."

He could hear another voice, insisting that the president come to a meeting.

"Duty calls," he said, "but if there is anything you need, Albert, just say the word."

The phone had clicked off, and after Einstein had calmed down Helen—it wasn't every day that the White House telephoned—he'd gone straight back to work. Now, he could hear her in the yard below, calling for the cat.

That, at least, was one problem he could immediately address.

Lifting the window sash, he poked his head out—the autumn air was bracing—and said, "I know where she is."

"Where? I put out fresh milk for her, but she hasn't touched it."

"Wait. I will come down." A walk in the yard might clear his head.

Helen was at the back steps, by the bowl of untouched milk, when he came through the kitchen.

"She went into the garage last night," he said.

"The garage is locked."

"There is something wrong with the latch. Come, let's get her out."

The ground was uneven and matted with a brown carpet of damp leaves. Helen stayed close to his side, making sure he didn't slip and take a fall. He didn't know what he would do without her. When he had first employed her, seventeen years ago now, he'd had no idea how much he would come to rely upon her, for everything from household chores to protecting him from intruders and interruptions to his work.

When they got to the garage, the latch was again hanging loose, and the wooden doors, their white paint chipped and flaking, were rattling in their frame. He pulled one of them open, and the autumn sunlight fell on the clutter of cardboard boxes packed with papers, and some old office furniture he should have discarded long ago.

And on what looked, to his surprise, like a blanched and brittle femur.

"Is that what I think it is?" Helen said in wonder, as she inched past him to pick it up.

Now he could see that it was one of several bones, scattered around the dirt floor. Had some wild animal been making this its lair, dragging its prey inside for a leisurely meal?

"Oh my God," Helen said, drawing back with one hand to her mouth and the other pointing with the bone into the darker recesses of the garage.

A pair of bare feet stuck out from behind a pile of cartons. Einstein put out an arm to hold Helen back, then stepped forward. Something told him that the man, whoever he turned out to be, was dead.

"Open the other door," he said to Helen. "We need more light."

She pushed it back as he came around the boxes.

The man lay sprawled on the ground, face-down, his arms flung out to either side like a skydiver in free fall. He was wearing a long black

338

slicker, its hood drawn up over the back of his head. A canvas sack lay beside him, along with a sharpened chisel. He was utterly still.

Bending down, his back creaking, Einstein touched the man's shoulder, then shook it gently. The motion went no farther down the body than the arm. He shook it again, expecting no response and getting none.

"Who is it?" Helen asked, without coming close enough to see. "Is he . . . all right?"

"No."

"Should I call for an ambulance?"

"Too late. I think you must call the police."

Helen scurried off to the house.

Was it a hobo, he wondered, who had taken shelter for the night? The poor soul, Einstein thought . . . to die like this, alone, on a dirt floor. With all of his earthly possessions in a canvas bag.

But what accounted for the bones? They appeared ancient. Why would he have been carrying those?

Delicately, Einstein drew the hood aside, revealing a thatch of dark blond hair, the kind only a young man might possess. And then, curiosity getting the better of him, he gently pushed the body onto its side . . . and instantly regretted that he had.

The skin of the face was puckered, as if it had been sucked dry, the lips were raised so tight the gums were showing, the eyes were open, empty, and staring into infinity. It was hard to tell if he had been twenty, or two hundred.

"I am sorry," Einstein said softly. The man smelled like a swamp. "Very sorry." He let the body roll back into its previous posture, and kept vigil beside it until Helen could return with the police. It would be wrong to leave the poor man alone again. Not knowing what else to do while he waited, he laid a hand gently on his shoulder and recited, under his breath and with his head bowed, an ancient Hebrew prayer for the dead.

Chapter THIRTY-FIVE

Would wonders ever cease? Lucas thought.

He was hardly able to believe that he had the bones and relics back, that the police had been willing to relinquish them to his care. He carried the sack as gently as if it were a baby he was cradling in his arms. Never again would he let its contents be kidnapped.

Passing under the grinning gargoyles that cavorted along the roofline of Guyot Hall, he looked up at them with a newfound, and wary, appreciation. Although they were much eroded by time and the elements, he could still see the protuberant horns on their brow, the grasping talons, the pointed teeth and furled wings, and he was struck by how closely they resembled the shapes and shadows he had seen in the film made the night the ossuary had been opened. For the first time in his life, a thought crossed his mind—an unwelcome one that he would never before have entertained. Could these fantastical creatures, their visages so familiar from cathedrals and castles the world over, have been modeled on something other than the fever dreams of independent stone carvers? Could they have been cast from living specimens—or, perhaps, from the atavistic memories of such beings, harbored deep in every human soul? Could there be, as the Swiss psychoanalyst Carl Jung had claimed, a "collective unconscious," where such fears and apprehensions lurked? As children, weren't we all afraid of the dark?

Maybe, he thought, we had reason to be.

In the lobby, a janitor was down on his knees with a screwdriver in front of the display case containing the Caithness Man; glancing back over his shoulder, he said, "If you ask me, this place should be off-limits to townies. Kids in particular."

"Why?"

"They snapped the damn lock."

"Was anything damaged?"

"You tell me," he said, going back to screwing in the replacement.

Lucas stepped closer and looked into the case.

The ancient figure's lips and eyes were still sealed shut, its back was still pressed hard against the stake where it had been slaughtered. The leathern cap, its muddy color indistinguishable from the weathered brown skin, was right where it had always been. Lucas was about to turn away when something caught his eye.

A loose strip, hanging away from the pole.

He leaned over the kneeling janitor's bald head to get a closer look.

"Something wrong, Professor?"

"I'm not sure yet." He peered at the other side of the specimen, and saw that the strap that had held the prisoner in place had been severed there, too. Whoever had broken into the glass case had been trying to dismantle the display, either as an act of vandalism or, even worse, theft. Thank goodness the thing was still there at all. But Lucas couldn't help but wonder if this particular crime wasn't somehow connected to the stolen relics, or the destruction of the research materials in Simone's carrel.

"The hall ought to be locked at all times," the janitor said, packing up his tools.

"Students, and faculty too, have to get in and out all day."

"Give 'em all keys," he replied, lumbering to his feet again.

Lucas didn't comment on the impracticability of dispensing hundreds of keys to the front door.

He headed for the lab upstairs, where he was expected.

The door was already open, and as Delaney raised his head from a microscope, his eyes went straight to the sack of bones Lucas had told him about on the phone.

"Strange doings," he said solemnly. "I never would have guessed it of Brandt."

"Neither would I," Lucas said, as he laid the bag on a countertop.

"Why the hell would he have done something like that?"

Lucas could not divulge, even to Delaney, what he knew. "Maybe he thought he'd make some great discovery and catch the fast track to tenure."

"By stealing artifacts that even the OSS is keeping tabs on? Makes me wonder if the guy was dealing from a full deck."

"I don't think he was."

"I mean, I'm not saying that he wasn't a pain in the ass sometimes, but I still wouldn't have wished what happened to him on anyone."

And Delaney only knew the half of it. Lucas felt it would be unnecessary, and unwise, to share the gorier details of what he'd seen, only hours before, in that garage on Mercer Street. It was the FBI agent, Ray Taylor, who had summarily hauled him out of a lecture hall and driven him straight to Einstein's house. The professor was in the yard, in a sweatshirt and a pair of rumpled trousers, holding an unlit pipe.

"This is a sad business," Einstein said. "A sad business."

But it was only when Lucas was ushered into the garage that he understood what the professor had been alluding to. The missing bones and relics were strewn around the dirt floor, as were a couple of other items—a chisel and a worn hammer. Toward the back, between teetering stacks of cardboard boxes, he saw a man in a jacket labeled "Coroner" bending over a corpse.

"It's that guy Brandt, right?" Taylor said.

Lucas nodded, but at the same time he would hardly have recognized him—it looked more like the husk of a man than an actual corpse.

"And this is the other stuff that was missing? From the university?"

Looking around, Lucas said, "Yes."

"Pick it all up, make an inventory, and give me a copy. Then do me a favor—lock it all up, someplace safe for a change."

Trying to avert his eyes from the coroner's grim work, Lucas gathered the things together—even the staff with the crooked handle—and slipped them into the canvas sack he had last seen looped around Brandt's shoulders. On his way back through the yard, he was stopped by Einstein, who said, "You will come and talk sometime, *ja*? Afternoons are good." There was an even more doleful look in his eyes than usual. "In times like these, it is good to talk about other matters. Art . . . music . . . the higher things."

"I promise," Lucas said.

"And maybe," he said, in a low voice tinged with embarrassment, "you can bring with you some tobacco?"

"For sure," he'd replied, as Einstein patted him on the arm and, head down, shuffled back through the screen door Helen was holding open for him.

"Here," Delaney said, going to the green metal locker, twice the width of a normal locker, bolted securely to the wall. He threw open its door. "You can stash that stuff in here," he said. "It's where I keep my reports and the radiocarbon data for Macmillan. It's got a padlock, and the door to the lab has a dead bolt on it, too."

"Do you also sleep in here?"

"Occasionally, yes."

Although he'd been kidding, Lucas wasn't surprised. He deposited the bag, the crooked end of the staff poking out of one end and barely clearing the top shelf. Delaney closed the locker again, clamped the steel padlock shut, then yanked down on it for good measure.

"How's Simone doing?"

"I called her this morning, and she sounded like she was still pretty shaken up."

"Who wouldn't be? First her father drowns in a bathtub, then she gets chased by some weirdo in the library. It's a miracle she's still standing. They figure out who did the damage to her carrel, by the way?"

"Not yet." Lucas had originally suspected Andy Brandt, but now he knew that he'd guessed wrong. And when Agent Taylor had asked him, pointedly, why Brandt might have made his way—badly wounded by the bus—to Einstein's house, of all places, Lucas had said it might have been dumb luck.

"Some dumb luck," Taylor had replied. "A hundred garages between here and Washington Road and he picks this one to die in?"

Lucas was wrestling with his own suspicions. Could Brandt, like Wally Gregg, have possibly intended to attack the professor? Or—and this struck even closer to home—could Brandt have been on the way to the boardinghouse across the street, to silence the one man who knew his secret, Lucas Athan?

For the next hour or two, Lucas and Delaney went over the latest lab data—the radiocarbon tests were being better refined, it seemed, every hour, but it was unclear how much use they would be to Colonel Macmillan. When the janitor came in to empty the wastebaskets and to say that he would be locking up in a few minutes, they made sure that everything of importance was sealed in the green locker, then headed down to the exhibit hall. As Lucas stopped to turn up the collar of his coat, he happened to glance over at the Caithness Man, now locked away again in his display case; the low light at its base made it appear, for a split second, as if his eyes, sealed shut for centuries, had opened just a slit.

The campus was quiet, except for the tolling of the carillon in the chapel, and nearly deserted, apart from a few students charging off to commons for dinner, or to the library for a study session. Lucas was glad when the lights of the town came into view, the Nassau Inn presenting an especially cheery sight, with an amber glow emanating from its windows and a lazy curlicue of wood smoke drifting from the taproom chimney.

"I don't suppose I can cajole you into one drink before you go upstairs?" Delaney asked.

Lucas, with another plan in mind, fumbled for a reply.

"Come on, pal, I can read you like a book."

"Maybe we'll both come down and join you," Lucas said.

"I won't be holding my breath," Delaney said as he crossed the lobby. "Hope she's recovered from that scare in the stacks."

Lucas hoped so, too, and as soon as the creaky elevator had taken him to the top floor, he rapped gently on her door—twice, then twice again. A signal that they had agreed on.

Even so, he heard the latch on the peephole slide open, then the locks being turned. The door opened only halfway, and she said, "Quick—come in."

Lucas ducked inside, turning to embrace her, but Simone was slamming the door shut and throwing the locks. Then she peered through the peephole again, twisting her head to see as much of the hallway as it would allow.

"Trust me, there's no one else out there," Lucas said. She looked, if anything, in worse shape than she had the night before when he'd accompanied her back to the room, waited while she took a sleeping pill, and then left her, still dressed in all but her shoes, under the quilt.

"Have you been out today?" he said.

"Why?"

"Because you look like you could use some fresh air." Her white blouse was untucked, her skirt wrinkled, and her face drawn and pale. "The room could use some oxygen, too." The little writing desk by the window was covered with papers and prints, a room-service cart was pushed up against the radiator, with a black fly—surely the last of the season—buzzing around a dirty plate and an upturned silver lid. Lucas went to the window and started to lift the sash, but noticed that an index card, wedged under it, had slipped free. Picking it up off the carpet, he saw a strange sign—a diamond tilted to one side, with a diagonal line crossed through it—drawn in pencil, and underlined three times.

"No, don't do that," she said, quickly replacing the card and pressing the window down on it.

But where had he seen that symbol before?

"Did you recognize it?" she asked, nervously.

"The sign?" Then, snapping his fingers, he remembered. "It was carved on the lid of the ossuary. Under the last chain we removed."

Simone nodded. "It's an ancient sign. It also appears on the Coptic papyri that we removed from the tomb. My father was studying it, just before . . ."

To keep her from having to complete the thought, Lucas said, "So what does it represent?"

"It represents the forces of containment."

"So it's a seal?"

"Correct."

Now he could see where this was going. "And we broke it when we opened the ossuary."

"Yes."

Looking around the disorderly room, he asked, "But aside from the aroma of the food trolley, what are you trying to contain in here?"

"I'm trying to contain—I'm trying to *protect*—everything we've learned. To begin with, everything my father had collected in that blue folder."

"Who do you think is coming to take it away?"

"The same thing that killed him."

He knew she harbored doubts about her father's death, but he had never heard her put it so bluntly.

"He was studying these pages just before he died," she said. "It's why they were stolen."

He waited, not wanting to say anything that might increase the strain she was evidently laboring under.

"And they reveal the name of his murderer."

"He had written it down?" he said, incredulously. "Before it even happened?"

"He didn't have to. It's all right there."

"What is?"

" 'My name is Legion: for we are many.' "

Though he couldn't have given the chapter and verse, Lucas recognized the line.

"Mark 5:9," she said. "It's the story where Jesus casts the unclean spirits out of the raving man, the Gadarene, who had been haunting the tombs and cutting himself with sharp stones."

"Yes, I know the passage," Lucas said.

"But do you remember what happens to the demons that Jesus casts out of the madman?"

"To the best of my recollection, they enter into the bodies of swine."

"Demons can do that."

"Enter swine?"

"They can enter anything. They can jump, like ticks, from one host to another. My father was documenting it. In fact, they have to do that. To function in this world, they have to find some physical form to get around in. Otherwise, they're just disembodied and ineffectual."

The fly from the cart circled lazily around the rim of a teacup before landing beside another insect that had just crept out from under the saucer.

"The pigs were driven mad by them," Simone continued.

"And then the whole herd ran off a cliff and drowned in the sea," Lucas said, the rest of the story coming back to him now.

"Saint Anthony was a swineherd," she observed, as if simply stating the next irrefutable corollary. "It's his ossuary we opened."

Lucas was finding it hard to keep up, or guess where this was all going. Idly, he waved a hand at the flies, which flew off, then quickly returned. Three of them now. Where the hell were they coming from?

"We've let this evil—whatever it. is—loose," she said, finally looking straight at him. "Only instead of running off a cliff and drowning in the sea, it's managed to stick around long enough to cover its tracks."

"Okay," Lucas said, in carefully measured tones, "but how would it do that?"

She frowned like a teacher whose student is proving slow to grasp a simple lesson. "By stealing its own bones back, for a start," she said, raising one finger. "By incinerating the film," she said, raising another. "By murdering people like my father"—a third—"and by killing even its own servants, once they've outlived their usefulness."

Andy Brandt.

"And, finally, by luring me out of my carrel, chasing me through the library and trying to scare me to death, before destroying all the proof I'd gathered in there."

Lucas was torn. On the one hand, there was his lifelong allegiance to everything rational, to everything he believed true about nature and the universe, everything empirically provable. He had never been one to engage in the paranormal, in clairvoyance and telekinesis and astrology, or anything having to do with the so-called science of the occult.

On the other hand, there was the increasingly substantial, and persuasive, body of evidence Simone was amassing. Evidence that he himself could supplement, if he chose. There was Brandt's corpse, for instance—sucked dry like a piece of discarded fruit. (That was one detail he had spared Simone.) In addition, there was everything he had seen for himself in the conservation wing . . . and watched on the film that had mysteriously self-destructed.

"Accepting, for the time being, your premise," he said, "what would keep this demon, this unclean spirit, here? In a little college town, in the middle of nowhere?" He had his own suspicion, but he didn't want to voice it yet. He didn't want to plant any idea in Simone's head. "What's here?"

"Instead of asking yourself *what's* here, ask yourself *who's* here. That one is easy."

It was.

"Who did Wally Gregg attack?" she said. "Where did Brandt go on the night he died?"

Now he knew that she had indeed been thinking along the same lines that he had. "But why Einstein?"

"That's what I have been asking myself." Riffling her fingertips through some of the pages on the desk, as if the answer were in there somewhere and she'd simply overlooked it, she asked, "Why send your minion to attack an elderly professor who spends his time fussing over equations almost no one can understand?"

Lucas remembered the day he'd first visited Einstein in his study, and the letter he had seen on White House stationery—the letter from the president, warning, "I fear they are close to success." It was no great leap to surmise that Einstein, whose momentous discoveries were considered long behind him, who was regarded more as an icon than a working scientist, might not be retired after all. Could he be more engaged in the war effort than anyone knew? Was it possible that his genius was being employed, in some unknown way, to tip the balance in America's favor?

Only those in the highest government circles—such as the Oval Office—would know for sure.

But if it was true, could that be why the Germans had wanted the ossuary in the first place? Did they know that it contained a spirit so powerful that it could serve as the ultimate weapon—a weapon that they had cleverly deployed against the one man on earth who could foil their plans for world domination? Had they planned this all along? Had they deliberately sent the incriminating telegrams, setting the ossuary aside for Hitler himself, knowing that the missives would be intercepted, knowing that the OSS would rescue the ossuary at all costs, and that it would then find its way to the one spot in America where the nascent isotope research would be used to verify its authenticity? Hadn't Brandt already been put in place to relay the findings? Wasn't this where it would most probably be opened, and its evil thus released on an enemy shore?

Lucas found his head spinning with all the possible schemes and scenarios, questions and conundrums. It was as disorienting as the hall of mirrors at the Coney Island amusement park he'd gone to as a child.

"I want to find this thing that killed my father," Simone said in a calm but implacable voice. "I want to find it, wherever it's hiding, and I want to kill it."

A look of cold resolve gleamed in her dark, lustrous eyes, a look that Lucas might well have imagined on the face of some storybook heroine, an Arabian princess, sitting astride a noble stallion.

"I need your help, Lucas."

What help he could offer, he did not know. How did you capture, much less kill, a spirit as old as time? But he was not about to abandon her—not now, not ever. Without a word, he enfolded her in his arms. "Anything," he said. "I'll do anything you need me to."

At first, she remained as stiff as a sentry, unyielding, still caught up in her anger and determination.

"I'm with you, Simone," he reassured her.

He felt the tension in her shoulders relax.

"I will always be."

She virtually melted in his arms, her head resting against his chest, all the energy draining away so swiftly it was as if he were catching her in free fall.

"I need you, Lucas. I need you so much."

She was speaking of more than the ossuary, he knew. He knew it because it was precisely how he felt, too. He needed her. He turned off the bedside lamp.

This time, their lovemaking was more tender than torrid. This time, he tore no buttons from blouses, ripped no stockings, scratched no cheeks with his stubble. This time he allowed himself to undress her slowly, to kiss and savor each inch of skin revealed. My God, he thought, she was such a wonder. Never had he wished more fervently to be rid of the black patch, to have two eyes rather than one to take her all in. When he leaned above her to kiss her breasts, she gripped his arm so tightly the bandage threatened to unravel.

"Oh, Lucas. Did I hurt you just now?"

"No."

"You're sure?"

He reassured her with a kiss, and then another, losing himself in the realm of pure sensation. Here there were no demons to catch, no boxes of bones, no nightmares of land mines and battles and blood. All of that—the horrors he had witnessed, the things that haunted him still—all of that was banished. Now there was only this, her tawny limbs entwined with his, her head thrown back with eyes closed and mouth open, her hair spread across the white pillows, her breath growing as hot and ragged as his own. There was only this moment—and in this moment there was everything he could want.

When it was finished, Simone pressed her lips to his throat and murmured something in Arabic.

"What's it mean?"

"Ask me in the morning," she said, then rolled over, falling instantly into a deep and silent and motionless sleep. Lucas lay back beside her, his own body cooling off like an engine that had been running too hard. Apart from the low hiss of the radiator and the muffled thump of doors being closed down the hall, the room was silent. He let his fingers graze up and down the gentle swell of her back, let his mind drift. The sweat evaporated on his skin. He must have fallen asleep because it was only later—how long, he couldn't tell—before he became vaguely aware of a tickling sensation on his face. Brushing it away, he heard the buzzing of a fly.

Minutes later, he felt the tickling again, and again brushed it away.

When it happened once more, he knew that if he didn't get up and swat the damn fly, he would never be able to get any rest.

He opened his eye, but his vision was blurred by sleep, and the only light was provided by the streetlamps outside. Trying not to disturb Simone, he groped for the switch on the bedside lamp. His hand flailed about, unable to find it, but when he did, he drew his fingers back instantly. The knob was soft as velvet . . . and animate.

Snapping awake, he sat up, swinging his legs off the bed.

There was a constant humming in the room, a sound that in his sleep he might have mistaken for some ambient hotel noise.

Going to the window, he yanked the curtains back, enough that he could now discern the shape of the lampshade, and reaching under it again, he found the switch—unaltered this time—and turned the lamp on.

The light only made the scene more confusing. His brain could not process what he was seeing: The whole room was seething, like a pot boiling over. The walls and ceiling were so black with movement, punctuated by glints of iridescent green and indigo, that they merged into one vast undulating surface. The desk was as thick and black as an anvil, buried under an army of flies so dense its legs and drawers couldn't even be seen.

The swarm didn't seem to like the light, growing more agitated, churning and surging and buzzing.

Stealthily, Lucas nudged Simone's bare shoulder.

She was so fast asleep, she didn't budge.

He shook her harder, and whispered, "Simone, wake up."

"What?" she mumbled.

"Wake up. Go into the bathroom." He prayed that the flies were not already in there, too. "Lock the door."

"Why?" she said, raising her head a few inches from the mattress.

"Do it."

Then, looking around, she must have taken in the horror surrounding them. He heard a fast intake of breath, saw her back stiffen with fear.

"Don't make any noise. Just go."

She slid off the far side of the bed, but must have stumbled over the clothes strewn on the floor. As if it were all one organism, the tide of flies shifted from the walls and ceiling, and Simone screamed as they descended upon her naked body.

Lucas leapt over the bed. She was down on all fours, trying to swat them away, but there were too many, and they were too intent. Grabbing her under one arm, he dragged her toward the bathroom and shoved her inside. Her hands covering her head, she scuttled under the pedestal sink, but before he could follow her in, the door banged shut in his face, so hard it nearly broke his nose.

"Lucas!"

Answering her was impossible—the flies had descended upon him now, coating his cheeks and lips and forcing him to close his one good eye. He staggered backward, blind, around the foot of the bed, and groped for the door to the hall. But the wall was so carpeted by the horde that he couldn't even find the handle. Opening his mouth to catch a breath, he was instantly choked by a clutch of flies. He spat them out, and wiping his eye and holding his head down, lurched across the room, bumping into the room-service cart and sending it careening into the bedside table. Though the light stayed on, the lamp toppled to the floor, emitting a sinister glow as it rolled back and forth on the rim of its dented shade.

The wooden desk chair was covered, too, but Lucas picked it up and slung it at the window, shattering the glass. The chair clattered out onto the fire escape, as the curtains billowed out in the night wind.

The index card under the sash fluttered in a circle, then flew away as if it were a bat taking wing.

Instead of entering the room, the wind drew the air out in a kind of vortex, sucking out the flies in a swirling black funnel that enveloped Lucas, churning around his shoulders, over his head, under his arms, and between his legs. It was all he could do to remain upright. Once above the moonlit street, the flies, like an army deserting en masse, dispersed in every direction.

Lucas planted his hands on his knees, and took deep, labored breaths. He heard the bathroom door creak open, and a moment later felt Simone's arms around him.

"Are you all right?" she asked, but all he could do was nod.

With the curtains rustling and the overturned lamp casting its eerie glow, they stayed just as they were, holding each other tight, naked and cold and alone. Adam and Eve, expelled.

A tattered remnant of the blue folder blew across the floor, stopping at Simone's ankle.

Though not a word passed between them, Lucas knew what Simone was thinking. Just as she had predicted, their ancient adversary had assumed one of its countless disguises, and paid them a visit. He, too, knew that it wouldn't be the last.

Chapter **THIRTY-SIX**

Back when he was in training in Fort Meade, Maryland, Ray Taylor had earned the nickname Hawkeye. His eyesight was exceptional—his scores on the rifle range were among the highest ever recorded—and his hearing was equally acute. Even when sleeping, as he was now, he remained more aware of his surroundings than some people were when they were wide-awake.

At the sound of a car pulling up outside now, he abruptly lifted his head from the pillow. In his T-shirt and boxer shorts, he went to the window; crouching down, he pulled the curtain to one side and saw the back door of a cab swing open and Lucas get out. A second later, a girl got out, too—that Egyptian girl who'd shown up in several of Brandt's photos, the one who worked at the university. Simone Rashid. He'd been sent a thorough report on her from headquarters, and he'd read it twice. An impressive résumé, especially for such a knockout.

Right now, however, she didn't look so hot. Right now, she looked like she was barely holding herself together.

After unloading a couple of suitcases from the trunk of the cab and leaving them at the curb,

Lucas put an arm around her shoulder and escorted her unsteadily up the front steps. The front door closed behind them as softly as possible, and as they mounted the staircase to Lucas's apartment at the top of the house, he could hear their footsteps passing his own room. By the time Lucas had crept back down to retrieve the suitcases, Taylor had thrown on some clothes and followed him outside. From force of habit, he'd also slung his shoulder holster and gun under his Windbreaker. The cab was long gone.

It was cold and dark, with a wet wind blowing, and Taylor had to come up right behind him and put a hand on his shoulder before Lucas even knew he was there. The man whipped around, fists clenched, head down, ready for a fight.

Taylor lifted his hands and took a step back. "Whoa there, pardner. I came to help with the bags."

Lucas raised a dubious eyebrow.

Taylor picked up one of the bags by its handle—judging from the weight, it had to be filled with more books than clothing—and carted it to the front steps. When Lucas arrived with the rest, Taylor stopped him before going inside, and said in a low tone, "So, you want to tell me what the hell is going on?"

"Simone had a problem at the hotel. She's staying here tonight."

"What kind of problem?"

"They overbooked."

"Yeah, right." He'd pursue this tomorrow, with a stop at the hotel desk. There was something else more important. "What about the bones? Did you find a safe place to store them?"

"Yes."

"Where?"

"Delaney's lab. Half the time, he sleeps there."

From what he'd seen of the guy shambling around the campus, Taylor could believe it. "Anything else you want to tell me? Before I find out later?"

Lucas shrugged and mounted the steps, then turned.

"Yes," he said. "Keep a close eye on Einstein's place."

"I already do."

"Keep it closer."

"Why?"

"You asked for my advice," Lucas said, opening the door and holding it with his foot while he wrestled the suitcases inside. "Now you have it."

The door swung closed behind him.

Taylor was in no mood to go back to bed now, and he sure as shootin' didn't believe the warning had been issued for no reason. Lucas was still laboring under the mistaken impression that Taylor was there to *guard* Einstein. Guard duty had most certainly not been J. Edgar Hoover's intention in dispatching his agent to

Princeton. Hoover wanted Taylor to shadow the man and dig up any dirt he could find.

"The man's a Red," Hoover had blustered from behind his immense desk. "Anything he knows, and anything he learns about our top-secret projects, he's going to share with Moscow."

"But the Russians are our allies," Taylor had managed to get out, before Hoover blew his top.

"If you believe that, you believe in the Easter bunny, and you have no business serving in the bureau."

Taylor had fallen silent; he'd worked too long and hard for this job.

"Once we're done with the Nazis—and trust me, we will be—we'll deal with the Soviets." He'd stopped to growl an order into his intercom, then resumed where he'd left off. "And we'll also deal with their sympathizers here in the United Sates. I've got a list ten yards long."

Taylor didn't doubt it, and lest he wind up on Hoover's shit list himself, he had hunkered down in the boardinghouse right across from Einstein's home on Mercer Street. In all the time he'd been there, the only thing he'd seen of a remotely suspicious nature was a car carrying what looked like J. Robert Oppenheimer. Hoover didn't trust Oppenheimer, either; everyone in the bureau knew that. Taylor sometimes wondered if it wasn't because both men were Jews. Anyway, he'd dutifully relayed the license plate number to headquarters, but they had never even bothered to let him know if his guess had been correct.

Zipping up his Windbreaker, Taylor crossed the street, keeping out of the feeble pools of light cast by the streetlamps. It was colder than he'd thought; he should have grabbed a scarf, or gloves. But he didn't plan to be outside long; he'd make a quick circuit of Einstein's place, check to see that the garage was still locked up, and then head back to bed.

Vaulting the low wooden fence and rounding the side of the house, what he didn't expect to see was the yellow glow of a desk lamp in the upstairs study. He instinctively stepped back into the shadow of the trees, while moving closer to get a better look.

He saw a silhouette pass in front of the window, and then pass back again the other way. It was Einstein, pacing with a pipe in his mouth.

Taylor crept a little closer. From this angle he could see, through the half-open window, a blackboard covered with equations that he could never have made sense of in a hundred years. Thank God the FBI had placed a greater emphasis on marksmanship than math.

As stealthily as he could, he made his way across the yard and when he reached the garage, tested the new padlock to make sure it was still secure. He was about to head back home when he heard the back door creak open, and saw

Einstein in a ratty bathrobe and moccasins step outside. In one hand, he held the pipe, upside down and unlit. In the other, he held a bowl of milk, which he put down on the stoop and then, pressing a palm to the small of his back, straightened up as Taylor ducked behind a bush.

"Dinner is served," Einstein announced to the darkness. "Come and get it."

Then, after waiting a few seconds, he went back inside, and Taylor breathed a sigh of relief. If Einstein had spotted him, and he'd had to concoct some excuse for hiding out in his yard, he'd have been pulled from this job, and he'd have had his head handed to him, personally, by Hoover.

Rather than risk it, he decided to return by way of the alley.

He hadn't gone far before he began to reconsider. The alleyway was so damn dark he tripped over every rut and puddle, and three or four times dogs penned up in backyards rushed the fence, barking ferociously. Once a man called out, "Shut up, ya lousy mutt!"

Then he noticed something odd. The dogs would stop barking as abruptly as they'd started. The moment he'd passed by, they'd stop, and once or twice he could hear them whimper before retreating back toward their kennels. In his experience, once dogs got riled up enough to start barking at night, nothing short of a miracle could get them to quit.

It was as if they were scared of him . . . or of something else.

He stopped in his tracks, a row of garbage cans on one side, a dilapidated garage on the other.

Something told him to turn around, at the same time that something else told him not to, told him to run like hell to the end of the alley, where a streetlamp shone, and never look back.

He turned around.

And breathed a sigh of relief. There was no one trailing him, and nothing but an empty alleyway.

Oh, and a tabby cat, sitting quite still in the middle of a pothole, its head erect, tail twitching.

"Get going," he said. "You've got a bowl of milk waiting for you."

The cat, however, didn't budge.

"If one of these dogs gets loose, you're a goner."

He moved on, but the same thing happened at the next backyard he passed—a yapping Doberman rushed the fence, then ran away just as swiftly—and when he turned his head, he saw that the cat was padding along right behind him.

A Doberman afraid of an alley cat?

You had to hand it to this one, though—every time Taylor turned, the cat was still on his heels. But it didn't feel as if it were keeping him company.

It felt more like it was stalking him.

"Is there something I can do for you?" Taylor

joked. Even the sound of his own voice in the moonlit alleyway faintly unnerved him.

That, and the way the cat was looking at him. More intently than any cat or animal ever had. Its green eyes flashed, and it seemed absolutely unafraid of him. If he could imagine feeling a direct challenge from a feral cat, then this was it.

How crazy was this? He was an armed FBI agent, confronted by a cat in an alleyway, and he was going to do what? Back down? Run away?

Instead, he reached into his Windbreaker, unsnapped his shoulder holster, and pulled out his gun. Just pointing it at the creature would probably do the trick; the animal kingdom had long ago figured out what firearms betokened. How they'd done that, Taylor had never been able to quite figure out. How did one animal pass along, or instill in another, a fear of something so inexplicable as a gun? Was it some kind of telepathy, or a group mind, like bees in a hive seemed to possess? Or were they just gifted, like humans, with an innate understanding that the world is a dangerous place, and that whenever you were confronted by something you couldn't quite grasp, it was best to turn tail and run for your life?

Whatever the answer, this particular cat had not gotten the message.

Taylor waved the gun in the air, then pointed the muzzle directly at its head.

The cat stared down the barrel unmoved.

"Yeah, you're right," Taylor said. "If I shoot you, the whole damn town wakes up, and I get demoted tomorrow." Reaching into his jacket again, he said, "However . . . there are ways around that."

He withdrew a short cylinder—a silencer—and screwed it onto the barrel of the gun.

The cat watched the maneuver with interest, but no fear.

Taylor wondered why he was bothering with this at all. Was he trying to scare a cat with the sight of a silencer? Why didn't he let the damn thing alone and go back to his nice warm bed? He'd fired his revolver in the line of duty only once before, and that was in an armed chase of an enemy agent in Philadelphia; he'd brought his target down with a single shot.

But this? This was stupid; it made no sense.

For some reason, he was angry, however. There was something about this animal that pissed him off, something about it that seemed both preternaturally intelligent and downright insulting. It felt no different than if some guy had prodded him into a bar brawl. Taylor was mad, and weirdly enough, he was frightened, too. Of what, he couldn't say. The air seemed to crackle with menace.

Yeah, this time he was gonna use the gun, one more time, and who would ever question a dead cat in an alley, anyway? If he tossed the carcass in a trashcan, who would even notice it?

He clicked off the safety, and the cat's ears pricked up at the sound.

"What," Taylor said, "now you get it?"

The cat didn't move.

"Last chance. Take off."

He pointed the gun at the cat, but instead of racing away, the cat sauntered toward him, back arched, hissing.

Taylor was so surprised, he retreated.

"Are you really this dumb?" he said.

The cat kept coming, and Taylor suddenly tripped over a fruit crate crumpled in the alley. He stumbled, shook his foot free from the crate, and by the time he had looked back again, the cat had somehow grown . . . bigger.

That wasn't possible.

When it opened its jaws now, he saw bright white teeth, sharp as daggers, and it hissed so forcefully he could feel its hot breath riffling his pant leg.

He squeezed the trigger and a shot went so wild it pinged off a trash can.

Whether it was a trick of the shadows and the moonlight, or simply his imagination running wild, the cat seemed to be taking on the proportions of a panther, and moving with the same deliberation and lethal intent.

Taylor walked backward faster than before,

and when he saw that emerald flash reappear in the animal's eyes, he knew, in the coldest depths of his soul, that he was confronting something unimaginable. Something bullets weren't going to deter. He turned around. The end of the alleyway, lit by a lamppost, was only fifty yards or so off. He started running, the pounding of the blood in his ears so loud he couldn't even hear his own feet. He didn't look back to see if he was being pursued—he didn't need to. He could sense the creature's presence. When he felt something snag the cuff of his trousers, he whipped the gun around and shot blindly. Once, twice. He couldn't hear the *pfft* of the shots either, but he felt the gun jerk in his hand, and his trousers rip.

There was only another ten or twenty yards to go—he could see a laundry truck rumbling by on the street—and he prayed that once he got out in the open—into the light, onto the sidewalk— the chase would end. Already, he was getting winded, not from the distance, but from the sheer overload of panic and fear.

He staggered over some old refuse littering the ground, and as he straightened up for the final sprint, something landed on his back so hard it was as though a sack of cement had dropped from a roof. The gun flew from his grip as he sprawled headfirst on the hard dirt and loose gravel. The air was jarred from his lungs, his front teeth cracked in half, and the weight, instead of letting up, bore down even harder, grinding him into the earth. Hot breath scorched the back of his neck—it felt like the blast from a blowtorch—and claws digging deep into his skin pinned his shoulders flat. He was no more able to breathe than he was to flip over and see, with his own eyes, what was even then squeezing the last bits of life out of him.

Chapter THIRTY-SEVEN

Lucas awoke to a ray of pale sunshine falling across his face. Reaching over Simone's sleeping shoulder, he was able to snag his wristwatch from the bedside table, hold it up, and see that it was almost eight o'clock already.

From the kitchen downstairs, he could smell pancakes, coffee, and bacon frying in the pan.

He lay back, with Simone's body, clad only in one of his flannel shirts, snug against him beneath the quilt. Her suitcases were stacked by the door. The events of the night before had left them both so shaken that as soon as they had crept into his room, hoping not to disturb Mrs. Caputo or Amy on their way upstairs, they had simply fallen into each other's embrace. The narrow bed had creaked and groaned, but its very narrowness had served them well; they wanted not an inch of space between them. When Lucas kissed her good night, Simone's arms wrapped around his shoulders and pressed him down, holding him there. Separating, his eye patch came loose, and as he fumbled to reposition it, Simone whispered, "Leave it."

"No, it's best if you don't—"

"I know what's best," she said, "not you."

She slipped one finger under the loop and drew the patch over his head, then dropped it on the quilt.

He was painfully aware of what she could now see—a glass eye of a murky brown, badly fitted, and staring sightlessly straight ahead.

"There," she said.

"There what?"

"I've seen the worst of your secrets."

She leaned her head up and tenderly kissed his brow.

"And lived to tell the tale," she said.

For the first time in his life, he had been overwhelmed with the urge to share all of his secrets, to reveal himself to this woman in a way he had never revealed himself to anyone. In return, he wanted to know her, too. He wanted to comfort her, and cradle her, he wanted to protect her from the evils that he now knew, in a way he never had before, existed in this world. He doubted if even his famous neighbor across the street, whose thoughts had traveled farther than anyone's since Newton, could have accounted for the catalogue of horrors he had witnessed since the arrival of the ancient ossuary. But Lucas knew, and Simone knew, and sharing that knowledge bound them together in a way that nothing else could have done. He wanted to ask her everything, and then listen to her voice, with its exotic lilt of English and Arabic, reply.

As she stirred awake now, he whispered in her ear, "So, what was it that you said to me in bed, back at the hotel?"

"What?"

"You know, before all hell broke loose?"

She blushed, but before she could answer, there was a thumping on the bedroom door, and Amy's voice shouting, "Get up! Get up! It's pancake time."

Simone's eyes went wide, and even as she pulled the quilt up to her chin, the door opened, and Amy poked her head inside. "Mom wants to know how many you want."

That was when Amy's eyes met Simone's, and everything just sort of stopped.

"Amy, close the door now," Lucas said. "I'll be right down."

But she didn't move.

"This is my friend Simone. Now scat."

Amy pulled the door closed again, and he could hear her feet scampering, as fast as they could take her, back down the stairs.

"I hope I haven't broken the house rules," Simone said.

"We'll find out," Lucas said, easing himself up and over her on his way to the bathroom. When he came back out again, tucking his shirt into his pants, Simone was still in the bed—where else was there to go in a room this size?—staring absently out the window. He feared she was reliving the horrific events at the hotel. "I'll go down and get the lay of the land."

She turned her head toward him. "Should I leave?"

"And go where?" he said, crouching down beside her. "I want you to stay with me."

"So do I."

"Is that what you said in Arabic?"

"It was close," she said.

He waited for the rest.

"It's just an old Bedouin saying."

"Give me the rough translation."

"I would not trade you for a thousand goats."

Lucas laughed. "I'm glad to hear it." Then he leaned forward, kissed her, and said, "Be advised —the hot water never lasts more than two minutes. Plan accordingly."

On his way downstairs, he stopped at Taylor's door on the second floor and listened for any noise within. There was none. And not much more in the kitchen, either. Amy was sitting at the Formica table, plowing her way through a plate of pancakes while her mom sat sipping her coffee over the morning newspaper.

"Morning."

Mrs. Caputo got up, lips primly sealed, and fixed him a plate of pancakes and bacon. She set it down opposite Amy, who looked up long enough to push the syrup bottle toward him. "Who's that girl?" she asked around a forkful of pancakes. "Is she going to live with us?"

"Amy," her mother said, "why don't you go upstairs and make your bed?"

"I already did."

"Lucas and I have some grown-up things to talk about."

This time Amy grudgingly took the cue, and when they were alone, Lucas said, "I can explain."

Mrs. Caputo looked at him, not entirely unsympathetically, over the rim of her coffee cup. "I don't want to sound like a prude, Lucas—"

"You don't."

"But you know how it is. I don't want to set a bad example for Amy."

"I get it," he said, but before he could explain anything more, they were interrupted by the tromping of heavy feet on the front steps.

"Who can that be," she said, "at this hour?"

When Mrs. Caputo had finished wiping her hands on her apron and opened the front door, Lucas saw a couple of cops, led by Police Chief Farrell, holding empty cardboard boxes. Farrell thrust an official paper at her and said, "We have orders to remove all private belongings from Mr. Raymond Taylor's room."

"What? Why?"

"Which room is it, ma'am?"

"Second floor. Front."

The two cops maneuvered around her, dutifully wiped their shoes on the floor mat in the hall, and headed up the stairs.

"What's going on?" Lucas said.

"Maybe you can tell me," Farrell said, motioning for Lucas to step out onto the porch with him. Once he had taken him aside, he said, "It's about your fellow boarder, Ray Taylor."

"What about him?"

"He's dead."

Lucas was stunned into silence.

"His body was found a couple of hours ago. In the alley across the street. That part of town is getting to be mighty dangerous."

Fallen leaves, driven by a chill wind, tumbled across the front yard.

"What happened to him?" Lucas asked, dreading the answer.

"You might as well ask what happened to that young prof Andy Brandt," Farrell countered. "Or why some janitor, also from the university, would attack Einstein with a knife. All I know is this, my friend—anytime something bad happens, you're connected to it somehow."

Lucas's mind was already churning. Why

Taylor? Had he, too, presented some obstacle to the malevolent force Lucas had seen at work in Simone's hotel room?

"So, for the record, where were you last night?"

"The Nassau Inn."

"With that Rashid woman?"

There was no use in lying about it, and even less in telling him she was upstairs right now. "Yes." There was something else, however, he wanted to know. "How did Taylor die?"

Farrell gave him a long, appraising look. "That's a good question. Come and see."

By the time Lucas had retrieved his coat—and found that Simone had fallen right back to sleep, curled up under the quilt—Farrell was already at the curb, jotting in a notepad. Together, they walked around the corner, then a short distance down the alley.

Taylor's body hadn't yet been moved any farther than the back of a morgue ambulance. It was parked in the alleyway, back doors open, in an area marked off by two black-and-yellow-striped sawhorses. The coroner pulled back the sheet and let Lucas see the mauled corpse.

"Whatever got Brandt, it got Taylor, too," Farrell said.

The coroner started to replace the sheet, but Lucas stopped him to make a closer examination of Taylor's neck and shoulders, where there were visible claw marks.

Farrell, taking note of his interest, said, "Yeah. It's got talons, or teeth, or fangs. Whatever the hell it is. But last I checked, we don't have a lot of lions and tigers in New Jersey."

Lucas hated to think what they might have instead.

"We found a few bullet casings," Farrell said, "but who knows if he hit the damn thing."

Lucas looked down the alleyway, past the battered trashcans and potholes, noting their proximity to Einstein's backyard. And his concern grew, as did his guilt—hadn't he been the one who advised Taylor to keep a close eye on the place?

After a few more minutes of questioning, during which Farrell acted as if he smelled a rat but was at a loss to catch it, Lucas managed to excuse himself, and then headed down the alley, as if taking a shortcut home.

All along the way, he was on the lookout for any sign of Taylor's having passed this direction. The chances of finding a footprint, or much else, were awfully slim, however, and Lucas got all the way to Einstein's garage without spotting a single clue. Glancing back toward the crime scene, he made sure that the police chief was looking the other way when he ducked into the professor's back-yard.

The grass had long since gone brown, and he saw that a shiny new padlock had been affixed to the garage doors. In the upstairs study, he could see Einstein himself hunched over his desk, scribbling something down, and looking perfectly all right. At least, Lucas thought, his worst fears were assuaged, and he was just about to retreat from sight, when, as if pausing to ponder some problem, the professor raised his eyes from his work and saw him there in the yard.

For a moment, they both just looked at each other, then Einstein, cocking his head to one side, raised a hand and waved him toward the back door of the house.

Now it was too late to make a clean getaway.

Lucas went to the stoop and waited there until, a minute later, Helen Dukas, looking puzzled, opened the door.

"What are you doing out here?" she said, standing to one side to let him in.

How, Lucas wondered, should he answer that?

"Let the man come in first," the professor said from the kitchen. "Then we can find out why he has come to visit."

As Helen closed the door, Lucas shook hands with Einstein, who was wearing an old terrycloth bathrobe, pajamas, and below his bare ankles, a pair of moccasins embroidered with red and yellow beads. Einstein saw that he had noticed the footwear.

"A gift, from the Navajo tribe," he said proudly, wiggling his toes. "The Navajo tribe."

"And he won't take them off," Helen said, pulling a chair from the kitchen table and gesturing for Lucas to sit. "I think he sleeps in them now."

"They are very comfortable."

Einstein drew up a chair, too, and Helen poured them tea and put a plate of muffins on the table. "They're poppy seed," she said, "and only from yesterday."

Out of courtesy, Lucas helped himself—the muffin was so dry, he washed it down quickly with a gulp of the hot tea—while Einstein looked on approvingly. Although Lucas had only seen him up close on a couple of occasions, Einstein appeared unusually animated and alert today. Perhaps he was happy to take a break, and perhaps he was hoping that Lucas was there to smuggle him some tobacco.

"He has been up all the night," Helen said, "pacing up and down." She blew out a sigh of resignation. "Maybe you can tell him that he must take a rest now and then. He is no spring chicken."

"But when the ideas come, you must take hold of them," Einstein said, clenching his fist. "Or sometimes they do not come again."

"They can come after a good night's sleep, too," Helen replied.

They bickered, Lucas thought, like an old married couple.

"And last night," he said, directly to their guest,

"they were coming very well. *Ja*, this old brain of mine was young again."

"What were you working on?" Lucas asked, though anything but the most cursory answer would probably make no sense to him.

"It was a problem that was practical, and not so much theoretical," he said. "It was something I had promised I would do, but that I could not solve. Round and round I went. For weeks, I could not solve it."

"I hope you have now," Helen said, as she dried some dishes and put them in the rack.

"I have," he said, almost gleefully. "I have written the answers down, and I have put them in an envelope, and now I may relax a bit. Maybe I will take the *Tinef* out on Lake Carnegie. To celebrate."

"No sailing today," Helen said. "The weather forecast is for rain."

"The forecast in New Jersey is always for rain."

"We are playing bridge at Kurt and Adele's tonight."

"I am taking a walk with him this afternoon. We can play the game later."

Plainly, they liked going back and forth like this, and might have kept the volley going if the doorbell hadn't rung.

"There they are already," Helen said. "They don't waste any time."

Looking down the hallway, Lucas saw Helen

take an envelope from the hall table and, opening the front door, hand it to a burly man in an army uniform. At the curb beyond, Lucas glimpsed a jeep idling at the curb, its exhaust fumes pluming in the autumn air.

This was not university business; this was, as the professor had said himself, something practical. Something big enough that the army would dispatch a courier, on short notice, to get the results. He was reminded of that letter he'd seen, the one from the White House, in Einstein's study.

Einstein was intently, though silently, watching the transaction from his own chair, too. The lines on his face were deeply etched, and his white hair, as always, looked like it had been styled with an eggbeater. Many people said that in his company, they felt they were in the presence of an other-worldly being, someone who existed on a slightly different, and more elevated, plane than the rest of humanity. His gaze, according to a magazine article that Lucas had recently read, "extended to the frontiers of eternity." Yes, he was a little old man, with a funny accent and a thick mustache, but he was also, in an odd way, like some kind of ancient ascetic, one of those hermits, or holy men—a Saint Anthony—who had experienced great solitude, high on a mountaintop, and from that vantage point seen things no one else ever had, done things no one else could have done. Even in a ratty robe and beaded moccasins, he radiated fortitude and wisdom and benevolence.

Which was why it seemed so strange, when the door closed on the courier and he turned again toward Lucas, that his brow should be so furrowed and he should look, for a second or two, like someone awakening from an awful dream. He fidgeted in his seat, and Lucas thought he was about to jump up from the chair, call the soldier back, and retrieve the envelope.

"Are you feeling all right, Professor?" Lucas asked.

Einstein simply shuddered and passed a hand across his eyes. Helen, spotting the shiver, said, "I told you to put on some socks. You are going to catch the flu."

"*Ach*, I have not had the flu since 1938."

She poured some milk into a saucer, and placed it on the floor by the stove. "Well then, don't complain to me when you do."

As she lifted the teapot to refill Lucas's cup, he held up a hand and said, "I really have to get going."

From the front stairs, he saw a cat mosey around the banister, then saunter toward the kitchen and the waiting saucer of milk. When it saw him, it stopped in its tracks. Turning in his chair, Einstein said, "Ah, there she is—my little muse."

But the cat stayed put.

"Here kitty kitty," Helen called to it. "Come have your breakfast."

"Late last night," Einstein went on, "the cat came to keep me company. How she made it all the way up to my window, I do not know. But she scratched on the glass, and I let her in. She must have known I could not sleep."

"Warm milk," Helen told him, "tonight you are going to drink a glass of warm milk before you go to bed."

"Sometimes," Einstein said, "she watched me write on the blackboard, and sometimes she just sat in my lap, helping me with my equations."

"Come on," Helen said to the cat, bending forward and clapping her hands. "Come and eat. The professor says you have earned it."

The cat went to the bowl, and after a sniff or two, began lapping at the milk.

"The solutions," he said, "they came to me like I was twenty again."

The cat's ears twitched, as if it knew it was being talked about.

Lucas, getting up, thanked them for the tea and muffin, and Einstein said, "You must come and have a sail with me sometime."

"I'd be happy to," he said, though from what he'd heard of the professor's seamanship, it would be best to wear a life preserver at all times.

Opening the door, he saw the ambulance from the morgue rumbling down the alleyway, its light flashing but the siren off.

"Quick—the draft," Helen said, motioning for him to close the door again.

The last thing he saw inside was the cat, contentedly licking its whiskers and watching him go, as if he were the luckiest mouse alive.

Chapter THIRTY-EIGHT

He'd been right about the hot water, Simone thought. She had barely soaped up in the shower before the water ran cool, then cold. But how, she wondered, did Lucas even maneuver in this cramped stall that had been jury-rigged under the eaves? She rinsed off hastily, got dressed, and tried to make herself look as proper as possible before daring to appear downstairs. It didn't make it any easier that, apart from the medicine chest, the room had no mirror. She fixed her hair as well as she could, and was pleased to see that the extra few hours of sleep she had just had—the clock said it was almost noon already—had restored some of her normal skin color.

Now if only she could clear her thoughts as well. The ordeal at the Nassau Inn was something that she simply had to keep at bay.

Closing the door of Lucas's room and tucking a scarf under the lapels of her coat, she stopped to listen for sounds downstairs. Earlier, she thought she'd heard men's voices—and in her sleep, she'd dreamt of helicopters buzzing overhead—but now it was only the whine of a vacuum cleaner on the floor below. When she got there, and glanced into the front room, she saw what had to be the land-lady, her hair tied up in a blue rag, pushing a Hoover back and forth across the floor. The drawers of the desk and dresser were all opened and empty, as was the closet; Simone saw nothing inside but wire hangers. The bed had been stripped of its linens.

"Hello," Simone said, but the vacuum racket swallowed her words. She said it again, adding, "You must be Mrs. Caputo."

This time the landlady did hear, and looking up, she shut off the machine, and said, "Oh, hello."

"I'm Simone . . . Rashid."

"Yes, I know."

The two of them stood where they were awkwardly, wondering who should speak next.

Finally, breaking the silence, Mrs. Caputo said, "You and Lucas work together?"

"Yes, at the university."

"You're a professor there?" she asked, sounding a bit awestruck, perhaps at the notion of a woman —much less such a young one—holding that post.

"Oh, no, I'm just there temporarily—helping out with one project."

Mrs. Caputo nodded nervously and glanced

around as if looking for something other than the elephant in the room to discuss.

"Looks like someone has moved out," Simone remarked.

"Yes, only this morning," she said, averting her eyes altogether. "It was very unexpected."

"I do want to thank you for allowing me to stay here last night. I was in a bit of a bind, to put it mildly. I know it won't do for me to stay on."

"No, that's right, I'm afraid," Mrs. Caputo agreed. "It's just that there are city codes, you know, about unmarried people living together, and then there's my daughter to think of. I wouldn't want her to get the wrong—"

"No need to say anymore," Simone assured her. "I understand completely."

"I'm so sorry, but—"

"I'm sure I'll find something in town."

"I'm sure you will. In fact, I can recommend—" And then she stopped, her hand still on the vacuum cleaner, just as the same thought occurred to Simone. For a second or two, it hovered in the air like a hummingbird. "Of course, if you wanted to stay close to this neighborhood—"

"I do."

"—and if it would be helpful to you to live near Lucas—"

"It would."

"Then, well, perhaps," Mrs. Caputo said, looking around the room that was even then in transition, "you might want to rent this room? It's all cleared out now, and I'll be making the bed up fresh this afternoon, as soon as the sheets have been ironed."

For Simone, it was as if an enormous wave of relief washed over her. "Yes," she said eagerly, "yes, I'll take it. You are too kind."

"Would fifteen dollars a week be okay?"

"Absolutely. This room is perfect, and it will allow me and Lucas to continue to easily confer about our work." She wondered if she had just gilded the lily with that last bit.

Mrs. Caputo was plainly happy to stick to that fiction, too. "Yes, I think if you're down here on this floor, and he's up there, everything will be fine. There'll be no questions about propriety and all that." She beamed at her new tenant. "Well, welcome to the house."

"Thank you."

"I'll have to get new keys made."

"No rush. I can get Lucas to make a copy of the front door key."

"Of course. That would be a big help."

"That is, if I can find him. Did he say, by any chance, where he was going?"

"Oh. I'm afraid he didn't. His study, on campus?"

"I'll try there," Simone said. And waving a hand cheerily, she bounced down the rest of the stairs and out the front door. Five minutes earlier, she'd been trying to figure out where she might find a safe harbor for that very night—or as safe as any harbor could be for her—and now she'd just found it . . . only one flight away from Lucas. It was ideal.

As was the day. Crisp, the sun breaking through great banks of snow-white clouds, a strong breeze stirring the fallen leaves. She wasn't the only one out taking advantage of the clear weather—on the other side of the street, she saw the familiar figure of Professor Einstein in his battered leather jacket, hands clasped behind his back, walking along with another man wearing owlish glasses and a long winter overcoat. That Austrian mathematician, if she wasn't mistaken. They appeared to be engaged in an intense and animated conversation, and as they turned down the street leading to the woods surrounding Lake Carnegie, she saw Einstein tilt his head back and laugh out loud. He clapped his scrawny friend on the back and said something so tangled it had to be in German.

She'd have loved to know what they had been discussing.

Once she'd passed through FitzRandolph Gate, she headed for Lucas's office, but as she passed by the art museum, she saw the incongruous sight of an army helicopter—a long one, painted in green-and-brown camouflage—parked on the open plaza in front of the main doors.

So she hadn't just dreamt of helicopters—it had been real.

A campus security guard, one she knew, was at the doors, and when the military sentry tried to bar her entrance, the guard waved her through. Inside, she found the galleries deserted, but a great deal of noise coming from the conservation wing. Voices were raised, hammers were striking, wheels were rolling on the concrete floor. When she stopped in the doorway, she saw a stocky army officer in full uniform, with spangles on his hat and chevrons on his sleeve, barking orders at several soldiers who were bustling around the platform on which the ossuary stood.

"The chopper waits for no one, gentlemen. That means you had better get this job done a lot faster than you are doing it."

"If they go any faster, Colonel, they'll do lasting damage," she heard, as Lucas's head appeared on the other side of the sarcophagus. He had a roll of heavy-duty duct tape in one hand and a yardstick in the other. "We're not moving a refrigerator. We're moving a priceless artifact, thousands of years old."

"Damn straight we are," Macmillan replied. "We're moving it because you and your colleagues couldn't keep the thing safe and secure."

"But our work isn't done," Simone said.

The colonel and the others suddenly took notice of her.

"Where are you taking it?" she said.

"Miss Rashid, I presume?" the colonel said.

"Yes."

"I'm planning to take it where nobody but me and the OSS knows."

The lower half of the ossuary had been wrapped in plastic sheets; braided ropes, waiting to be tied, were draped loosely over its lid. A steel trolley had been wheeled to the bottom of the short ramp on which it still rested.

"For starters, then, you'll have to be more careful with the placement of those ropes," she said. "Wherever they come into contact with the contours of the stone, you risk rubbing away some of the faintest carvings."

"That's right," Lucas said, carefully planting his hand smack dab on the center of the lid, and with a flick of his eyes, directing Simone's attention to the spot he was touching. "That's exactly what I was telling him."

The alabaster, she could see, was nicked and gouged there, as if someone had gone at it with a chisel or a spike.

"The diamond sign," Lucas murmured, "it's gone."

"What'd you just say?" Macmillan demanded.

"I said, we need to use more padding under the ropes."

Simone nodded. Removing the sigil of containment made perfect sense. The demon had vandalized the ossuary to make sure it could never be used to imprison it again.

Holding out one hand toward an adjutant, the colonel said, "The inventory," and a clipboard was slapped into his palm. He glanced at the pages attached. "We've got the box itself accounted for, but I see we still have to round up a bunch of stuff—bones, a cross, a stick or staff of some kind. We'll want those, too."

Of course they would, Simone thought. The ossuary itself was merely the vessel for the powers, both evil and good, that it had held. Without them, it was only an alabaster box with a gabled lid and a hodgepodge of symbols and inscriptions carved all over it. Although it had cost lives, including her own father's, she regretted losing it. As far as the colonel was concerned, she and Lucas had had their chance, and they'd bungled it. Once it was loaded on board that helicopter, she knew that she would never see the ossuary again. Would anyone? she wondered.

So," Macmillan said, looking around at all the other crates and cartons and easels littering the conservation room, "where are they? Which boxes do we take?"

"What you want isn't here," Lucas said, laying the tape and yardstick on a worktable, and brushing some dust from his hands. "But I can get it for you."

"Then what have you been waiting for? I want everything on this list," he said, rapping his knuckle on the clipboard, "and I want it by the time we load this damn sarcophagus into the cargo hold. Do not make me come back again."

As Macmillan ordered the adjutant to continue wrapping the ossuary, Simone left with Lucas, down through the unlit galleries and out into the daylight. The sky, so bright and clear when she'd gone inside, was already becoming overcast; New Jersey weather, she had discovered in her short time there, was fickle in the extreme.

"I tried everything," Lucas said, "but the decision to take it had already been made. It's out of our hands."

"Maybe it's just as well," Simone said.

"I never thought I'd hear you say that."

"I never thought any of this. I never thought I'd be here, or that one day I'd be scattering my father's ashes at the end of a pier. Let the OSS bury the ossuary in a salt mine or a bank vault or wherever else they've got planned."

"And the relics?" he said, as they followed the winding path toward Guyot Hall.

"That's all they are now."

"When did you become so fatalistic? The last time we talked about this, you were on the warpath."

"I still am. But whatever was in that box isn't in it anymore. And if it's done with us, then, as far as I'm concerned, this whole business is done."

"What if whatever was in the box doesn't see it that way?"

"Then it could be lying in wait for us anywhere. It could be lurking in that squirrel," she said, gesturing at the bushy-tailed black squirrel foraging for nuts, "or in those birds in the trees. Evil is everywhere and nowhere at the same time these days. You only have to read the papers to know there's no escaping it."

As they approached Guyot Hall, she heard the squawking of crows and saw a flock of them arrayed among the grinning gargoyles guarding the parapets. The building looked unoccupied, though the windows were open, and the lights were on in Delaney's lab.

"Thank goodness he's there," Simone said.

"He's always there."

The exhibition hall was as gloomy as ever, and they were halfway across it before Lucas stopped abruptly, his jaw dropping.

Turning around, Simone saw that one of the display cases was damaged, its door hanging from one hinge and swinging back and forth.

"Oh no, not again," he said, under his breath.

Joining him beside the case, she saw a pair of straps hanging limply down, like strips of beef jerky. This time, though, whoever had tampered with the case had not only left a bloody impression on the glass—it looked to Simone like a frenzied paw had been scratching at the lock—but had fully severed the Caithness Man from his stake before making off with him altogether.

Chapter THIRTY-NINE

"But if a deity, as I have proved, *can* exist in any universe, then it follows that He *must* exist," Gödel was saying, "and in *all* of them."

So focused was he on explaining his proof, that it was Einstein who had to pull him back onto the curb of Washington Road before he was run over by a speeding Studebaker. Usually, Einstein was the one who needed rescuing; indeed, on one occasion he had been so absorbed in thought that he had fallen into an open manhole, and clambering out, had begged a passing photographer not to release the picture.

"And all of these universes are rotating, *ja*?"

"Of course," Gödel replied, tucking his woolen scarf even more securely into the top of his coat. "I thought we had agreed on that."

"But doesn't your God get dizzy then?" Einstein said, resorting to jokes, his usual ploy, to get Gödel off his hobbyhorse. Gödel, he knew, tried to pass off his obsession with the spiritual realm, and most pointedly the afterlife, as an intellectual pastime and no more, but Einstein understood his friend too well—Gödel was a man who feared that death lurked in anything from an uncovered sneeze to a tuna fish sandwich. The thought of extinction was so overwhelming to him that he devoted countless hours—hours that might have been better spent on pure mathematics—to proving that life had no definitive end, but that it was merely shifted to another plane or dimension. Einstein did not share his optimism (if optimism was what it could be called). He had already left blunt instructions with Helen to the effect that, when his time came, he should be cremated and his ashes distributed to the four winds. "Why waste a good plot of earth," he'd said, "when someone like Adele could be growing tomatoes there?"

As they quit the main thoroughfare for the rural path that led through the woods and down to the shores of Lake Carnegie, his thoughts turned to the work he had done, in an uncanny passion, the night before. It was as if all the powers he had once possessed, almost forty years ago, when he was constructing his theories on everything from relativity to the photoelectric effect, had returned to him in spades. It was all he could do to keep up with the cascade of insights and equations that entered his mind and had to be scrawled on the blackboard, and then, once ironed out, transposed to the notebook that he could dispatch by courier to an anxious Oppenheimer in New Mexico. It was as if a voice, a strange voice he could barely hear, was whispering answers, and encourage-ment, in his ear.

There had even been moments when he felt that his hand, too, was being guided by some unseen force, some invisible presence, an angel, or, given the nature of the work, perhaps a devil, whose mission it was to guarantee that the last intractable problems were solved, and that the most lethal weapon ever conceived was brought into its full, destructive existence. That he, a man so opposed to war that he could not watch a marching band without instinctively recoiling at its martial air, should have, however unwittingly, laid the groundwork for such a thing as this, was ironic enough; the fact that he had been secretly instrumental in its actual construction was positively astounding.

"Adele tells me we are playing bridge at your house tonight," Einstein said.

"Yes. That is so."

"I am going to leave my wallet at home," Einstein said. "Last time I lost almost two dollars."

"It is how we pay our rent," Gödel said, and Einstein laughed. Kurt seldom made jokes—he must be in an especially fine mood today.

A light breeze kicked up some leaves across their path, and Gödel gathered his long coat around himself. "You do not dress warmly enough for the weather, Albert."

"I dress not as the weather is, but as it should be. And it should be a good day for a sail around the lake."

"I do not think that I will join you today."

Einstein laughed, and said, "No, my friend, I will not put you through that ordeal again. Not again."

"I will wait for you in the boathouse."

"That's a good idea. You'll stay nice and warm and dry in there," he said, "and you already know where the towels are kept."

"I hope I do not need them this time," Gödel said, looking up at the sky, "though it is possible that you might."

Einstein had seen them, too—great banks of puffy clouds far off to the east. "We will both be back in my study, enjoying a pot of Helen's tea, long before we lose the sun."

By the time the boathouse came into view, Einstein was eager to get the *Tinef* out on the water, and Kurt looked equally eager to get out of the wind. Inside, Kurt took a seat in an old rocking chair, right beside the cabinet holding the binoculars, starting pistol, and first aid kit, and settled in. From the voluminous pocket of his coat, he removed a book—Einstein suspected it was his worn copy of Kant's *Critique of Pure Reason*—adjusted his spectacles, and prepared to lose himself, as usual, in the realms of higher thought.

Einstein thought he saw something dart by the window, and was reminded that the occasional black bear was spotted in these woods. He hadn't mentioned it to Kurt, lest the man faint from fear. "I shouldn't be too long," he said, going to the window to take a look. But all he saw was a gray owl, head down, wings furled, sitting silently, pensively, on a high branch. "You and I, we are kin," he said, so softly it did not disturb Kurt's reading. "A couple of wise old birds." Then, leaving his door keys on the table—more than once they had slipped out of his pockets when the boat heeled—he said, "Then you are comfortable, Kurt?"

"Quite."

Closing the squeaky door of the boathouse, he walked down the wooden pier to the spot where the *Tinef* had been tied up after his last outing. He could tell from the rigor with which the knots had been tied that someone had come along after him and done the job properly, and he smiled. Sometimes it seemed that the whole community—the university, the institute, the townspeople—took a friendly interest in his well-being and watched over him. When he had first immigrated to this small, provincial town from the intellectual and cultural ferment of Berlin, he had thought he might feel stifled—and at first he had, oh how he had—but over time he had come to feel at home here, to appreciate the quiet charms of its very insularity.

Stepping down into the boat and pushing off from the pier, he almost lost his balance and toppled overboard into the water. How amused Kurt would have been to see his bedraggled figure in the boathouse doorway—soaked to the skin, just like when they'd been caught out in the rain.

Once away, he dropped the center board, unfurled the yellow sail and, while raising it, noticed that another canvas sheet had been sloppily stowed in the bow. Had he left it that way himself? He certainly didn't remember doing so, and it seemed unlikely that his mysterious benefactor, the one who might have fixed his knots, would have left such a rumpled heap there. It didn't even seem that it belonged to this boat at all; it looked more like one of the canvas covers used to protect the rowers' boats.

Who could have put it there, of all places?

A cool breeze filled the sail and carried him out onto the deep blue-gray waters of the lake. Einstein zipped his leather jacket up to the top of his throat—perhaps Kurt had dressed more sensibly for the coming weather than he had, after all—and took the tiller in one hand and the rope in the other. As always, he felt that he was leaving all the mundane and often vexing concerns of daily life behind, and passing into a world where no telephones could ring, no doors could be knocked on, no breathless couriers could arrive with out-stretched hands for his latest packet of diagrams and calculations.

His eye wandered to the eastern sky, where the towering white clouds looked like a lop-sided wedding cake, and then to the thickly wooded shores. While some of the trees had entirely shed their leaves already, others were still bedecked in red and yellow leaves that gleamed in the light of the afternoon sun. A couple of boys on the bank, holding pails and fishing poles, waved to him, and, securing the tiller in place, he waved back. His little blue boat with its distinctive yellow sail was well-known on the lake.

The wind picked up, and rustled the crumpled canvas in the bow. He should have stowed it away under the seat where the life preserver was kept, but it was too late for that now. Despite all the sailing he had done in his life, he knew that he remained a wretched sailor—once he had absentmindedly run his craft onto the shoals, another time into a buoy—and to make matters worse, he could hardly swim a stroke. It was a skill that he had always meant to acquire, but never managed to find time for.

To his surprise, the canvas pile rustled again. Glancing down, he could swear that the fabric bulged, as if something lying beneath it had moved. Could it be wharf rats? The fabric shifted again, and now he was quite certain that something was hiding underneath the cloth. For a second, he considered turning around and heading back to the pier, but even a rat, he knew, would do its best to keep clear of him. Maybe it was some more benign creature, a chipmunk perhaps, that would simply hide out until it could scamper back onto the pier.

The boat heeled, and he had to pull in on the sail. Water splashed over the side, sloshing under the floorboards and soaking the bottom of the canvas hcap. Whatever was lurking under it reacted to the intrusion, jerking the canvas out of its way, then tenting it—higher than any rat or chipmunk could have done—and causing Einstein to rear back in alarm on his seat.

Was there a bear in the boat, for God's sake?

His first clue came when it sat up entirely—and then, to his shock, stretched out one meaty hand, scabbed with blood, from under the wet canvas.

A moment later, it yanked off the cover entirely, shook its head and squared its shoulders, and looked him straight in the eye, like a stoat eyeing a cornered rabbit.

Chapter FORTY

"Come on!" Lucas called to Simone as he turned away from the empty display case and charged toward the stairs. Bolting up the steps three at a time and rounding the landing like a thoroughbred at the last turn, he made it to the top in a matter of seconds. Down the hall he could see the door to Delaney's lab standing open, fluorescent light spilling onto the linoleum floor.

He had a bad feeling, made even worse when he got closer and smelled the clammy aroma of a peat bog.

"Are you in here?" he shouted. The lab looked like a cyclone had hit it—microscopes and other equipment smashed on the floor, papers strewn everywhere and blowing about in the wind from the open window.

"Oh my God," Simone said, coming up behind him.

The big green steel locker—the one that had held the artifacts from the ossuary—had been ripped from its bolts in the wall, and knocked over. It was covered with dents and twisted out of shape, its door wrenched completely loose—but underneath it, Lucas thought he could detect a body, the empurpled fingers of one hand barely escaping from the crushing weight above it.

"Delaney?" he said, crouching down to peer under the wreckage.

But he couldn't see anything more, and if he simply shoved the locker aside with his shoulder, he was afraid of hurting him even more.

"We need a lever," he said, and Simone, looking around, grabbed the steel panel that had been the door, wedged it under the edge of the locker, and leaned against it. The cabinet lifted slightly, and Lucas said, "Yes—keep going!" as he reached under to grab Delaney by the arm. The locker came up another few inches, and Lucas pulled harder, drawing the body, headfirst, out from under its cover.

It was almost completely free before he realized his mistake, and jerked his hand away as if his fingers had been singed on a hot stove.

Simone, too, saw what it was and let the locker drop back into place with a heavy thud, crushing again the calves and feet of the creature she had been trying so hard to release.

The Caithness Man lay there, still as a mummy, its dark brown limbs twisted like tree branches, its body contorted. The head was turned sideways, revealing its beak-like nose, hollow cheeks, and the bloodless slash that was its mouth.

And of course the slit where its throat had been cut for good measure.

Lucas sat back on his haunches, studying the

specimen for any sign of life, before thinking how profoundly absurd that was. It hadn't gotten up here on its own; it was just a museum exhibit, a petrified man who had been tied to a stake and slaughtered, centuries ago, then buried in a bog. Why would anyone have broken into the display case and dragged it up here?

And how had it wound up under the battered, and no doubt burgled, locker?

"Where's Patrick?" Simone said, asking the question that was just then coming to the fore in Lucas's mind, too.

One thing was sure—he wasn't in this lab. But there was every sign of his having put up an enormous fight. Lucas's eye went to the open window. Had Delaney escaped that way? He went to the windowsill and leaned out—there was no fire escape here, just ivy vines clinging to the walls. A few of them, though, were hanging loose, dangling in the breeze, as if they had just been torn loose. Delaney was a big guy—could they have possibly supported him? The bushes below were dense, and unless he was mistaken, Lucas thought he detected a depression in them, where something heavy might have recently fallen into the thicket.

Had Delaney climbed out the window, even as Lucas and Simone had been coming up the stairs?

Why would he do that? It made no sense.

When he turned back to Simone, however, she

had a look of grim certainty in her eye, and said, "It's inside him now."

"What is?"

"It needed a body—it always does—and so it borrowed the Caithness Man. But now it's using Delaney instead."

"To go where?" he asked. "To do what?"

Simone surveyed the ruins of the empty locker. "It's already stolen the last physical evidence of its own existence. We'll never see those things again. So now I guess it's just rounding up and getting rid of the rcmaining witnesses."

Andy Brandt was already gone. So was Agent Taylor. So was the janitor, Wally Gregg. And Dr. Rashid. That left him. And Simone.

And one other target—a target that had already been attempted once.

"I have to get to Mercer Street fast," Lucas said. "Einstein's house."

"He's not there," she replied.

"Where is he?"

"I saw him heading down toward Lake Carnegie. With a friend."

"When?"

"About an hour ago."

He could run down to the lake in minutes. "Do you know where the police station is? On Witherspoon Street?"

"Yes. I had to fill out a report there after my father died."

"Get hold of Chief Farrell and tell him to send a patrol car down to the lake. Then stay at the station where you'll be safe."

"What are you going to do?"

"Find Einstein before Delaney does." He felt disloyal to his old friend even saying it.

Before he could go, Simone said, "Wait," and reaching under the collar of her blouse, removed the pentagram medallion her father had given to her. "Keep this on," she said, looping it over his head and tucking it into his shirt.

"What for?"

"Protection."

"If you say so," he said, touching her cheek as if in a final benediction, before stepping carefully around the splayed figure of the Caithness Man. He hated to leave her there, in such a dreadful spot, but he knew there was no time to lose. He ran from the room, down the stairs, and out into the quad. A group of students scattered as he ripped right through them like a linebacker, zigzagging across the campus under Gothic archways and quiet cloisters until he got to Washington Road and then across it, so haphazardly that a milk truck had to skid to a sudden halt and the driver shouted, "Hey, pal—you blind?"

The woods were cool and gloomy, and he slipped and slid on the fallen leaves and patches of damp moss as he raced toward the lake. Once or twice he had to vault over rotting logs, and he kept losing the trail, then picking it back up again. But he knew that as long as he kept moving through the trees, and down the gently sloping hill, he would eventually hit the lakefront. With only the one eye, he had to keep turning his head back and forth to ensure he didn't collide with anything. Even so, he was swatted in the face, over and over again, by low hanging branches, and several times he nearly tripped over rocky outcroppings. Almost there, he lost his footing on some slick leaves, landed hard on his butt and wound up skidding on the slick forest floor for a good fifteen yards before his fall was arrested by a dense clump of brambly bushes.

Through the remaining foliage he could see, dead ahead, an orange pennant fluttering high above the treetops. Breaking free of the brush, he scrambled wildly down the rest of the slope, until he came up beside the boathouse, with its collection of canoes and sculls lashed to their racks under protective tarps. The bottom canoe was uncovered.

"Professor Einstein!" he called out as he burst through the door. A startled man in owlish glasses turned, his face white with shock, and dropped a book to the floor.

Lucas recognized him as the mathematician, Kurt Gödel.

"Is the professor here?" he said, panting for breath.

"Yes."

"Where?" Lucas said, looking all around the rustic interior filled with oars and plaques and stacks of saggy life jackets. "Where?" he shouted.

Gödel raised a trembling finger toward the lake. "He's sailing his boat."

Lucas didn't know if this was good news or bad—did it mean he was out of danger, or moving right into its path? He ran to the window, and he could just make out, maybe half a mile away, the yellow sail of Einstein's little boat. Looking back into the room, he spotted the binoculars used by the race officials and grabbed them; the last time he had raised a pair of binoculars, it had been to check for snipers in an abandoned and bombed-out church on the outskirts of Strasbourg—and back then he had had the use of two eyes. Now he adjusted the lenses and focused on the boat skimming along before the rising wind. It was tacking, and to his relief he could see the familiar figure of Einstein—in his brown leather jacket and corolla of white hair—sitting up straight, manning the tiller, looking perfectly alone and perfectly in control.

But just as he started to drop the binoculars, the little blue boat came about, the sail shifted, and to Lucas's surprise, he saw another figure sitting on the starboard side.

A man, a bulky one, bundled deep into Delaney's distinctive overcoat.

Lucas adjusted the lenses again, but he couldn't discern anything more. "He's sailing with Professor Delaney?"

"No. No one. We came here together. Just the two of us."

The bad feeling Lucas had had was growing stronger every second. It was the same feeling he'd had on the night that he and another CRC man had stumbled into an ambush outside a school, or the day he'd discovered the ossuary in the underground cavern and the German boy had stepped on the land mine. He feared that something bad—very bad—was about to happen.

What could he do from here, however?

"Is there some danger to Albert?" Gödel asked, with genuine concern. "Is there something that I should do?"

"Come and help me outside!"

The temperature had dropped, and the sunny sky had become pale and overcast. Lucas could think of only one thing to do—pull the uncovered canoe down from the rack and paddle out after the sailboat before something terrible transpired. Although Gödel was the least likely person to help out, he was also the only one around; despite his frailty, he proved able to hold up one end of the canoe long enough to help get it down to the water.

Once Lucas had climbed into it, the canoe wobbling from side to side as he settled onto the plank that served as a seat, he lifted the paddle stowed under the thwarts, and said, "Give me a shove."

Gödel, bravely and uncharacteristically stepping into the cold water, waded a foot or two deep to launch the canoe. As the boat moved away, Lucas shouted, "Now wait there for the police!"

"The police are coming?"

"They'd better be!"

Gödel floundered back onto the bank as Lucas, who hadn't wielded a paddle since a brief excursion in boot camp, took his first tentative strokes. It took a dozen or so before he started to remember how it was done. Dip, with the blade flat, pull back from the shoulder with an even stroke, then feather the paddle to reduce the wind drag as you raised it, dripping, from the water. Switch sides every few strokes, so as to keep the canoe on an even course. But how was he ever going to close the distance between his little craft and Einstein's sailboat, especially with the wind picking up like this? Already he could see a phalanx of dark clouds skimming in from the east.

The water grew choppier by the minute, and the prow of the canoe bounced up and down. His shoes and socks were soaking wet, and his woolen pants' cuffs were stuck to his skin. The canoe tilted this way and that, buffeted by the waves, and often he had to quit paddling altogether in order to let it slow down enough to stop rocking and get settled in the water again. He'd neglected to bring a life jacket, and there was none he could see in the boat.

The sailboat was heading toward the center, and probably the deepest, part of the lake. Although it was still far off, Lucas thought he saw Delaney, or the shell that was left of him, reaching out over the side of the boat once or twice, and dropping something into the water. It wasn't hard to guess what was being discarded.

The eastern sky was growing darker, and the water in the lake went from blue to black. Even the leaves on the trees ashore changed from gold and crimson to a dull copper and a dusky rose. It was as if all the color were being drained from a picture. With every stroke of the paddle, his coat pulled at his shoulders, and he had to stop again, long enough to wrestle it off and drop it in the bottom of the canoe. Despite the cold air, getting colder all the time, he was sweating from the exertion, and he wiped the back of his shirt-sleeve across his brow. The distance between the two boats was closing, the wind from the east driving the sailboat, luckily, in his direction. Paddling against the choppy water, Lucas kept his eye on the yellow sail, and on its sailor, sitting in the stern with one hand on the tiller. His passenger reached out again, dropped something else in the lake.

When he was done with the items in the bag, what would he throw overboard next?

Lucas dug the paddle deeper into the water and pulled with all his might.

Chapter FORTY-ONE

After rummaging around in the bottom of the sack one more time, his stowaway found another relic—a long yellowed bone that the professor could swear he had once seen littering the floor of his garage—held it up for closer inspection, then tossed it overboard like a gnawed drumstick.

Einstein heard the splash, but his eyes remained riveted on his unwelcome passenger. He was a hulking brute, with a dark, vacant gaze and a strange way of moving. All his gestures and actions were herky-jerky, as if he might suffer from multiple sclerosis, or some other neurological disease. Whatever the cause, it lent him the air of a human marionette. Einstein suspected he had seen this man before, not out at the Institute for Advanced Study but somewhere around the university campus. Still, he couldn't exactly place him, and when he'd asked him for his name, the man had made a bad joke of it, replying in a gravelly tone, "Call me Beelzebub."

Lord of the Flies. Mankind's oldest adversary. Clearly, the man was mad—the disease must have already infected his brain as well as his body—but he was just as plainly a deadly menace. He had emerged from under the canvas like a bear coming out of hibernation, dragging a sack after him. His body smelled like a corpse. Perched on the side of the boat, he'd sniffed at the air as if for the first time, and studied the increasingly turbulent sky with eyes so devoid of fellow feeling that Einstein was reminded of the brown-shirted thugs he had seen in the news reels, strutting through the streets of Berlin, or driving in open cars past the burning ruins of the Reichstag that they had set ablaze.

Off to the east, thunderclouds were approaching, but the dangers of being caught out on the lake in a storm were nothing, he realized, compared to what confronted him in the tiny boat. With a thick finger and bloodied nail, the passenger had pointed in one direction, then another—word-lessly—for the purpose, it seemed, of guiding the boat away from any shore. Einstein, a middling sailor at best, had simply done what he could do to comply and keep the man pacified. But how could he ever contrive to get back to dry land safely?

The passenger's head was down as he peered into the open sack, removing one bone or artifact after another, and then, after close scrutiny, plunking it over the side. Einstein, always the most inquisitive of men, wanted to ask him why, but knew better than to challenge him in any way. Maniacs could be as volatile as nitro-glycerin—even his own institutionalized son, Eduard, could go off like a bottle rocket—and his best bet was to humor him until such time as the sailboat could be maneuvered back toward the dock. If only he had listened to his sweetheart Marie Winteler, and all the others throughout his life, who had begged him to learn how to swim . . .

Too late now.

The bag apparently empty at last, the man scrunched it up and tossed it, too, into Lake Carnegie. Einstein watched as it drifted away, bobbing up and down on the churning waves. Only one thing remained in the boat—a long wooden staff with an iron handle. A shepherd's crook, like the ones he had seen the farmers use in the valleys of Switzerland. To this lunatic, however, it seemed to be of especially great interest; he turned it this way and that, testing its heft, running his fingers down the shaft and gripping the crooked handle in different ways.

"There is a storm coming," Einstein hazarded.

The man grunted, as if he had ordered it up himself.

"And I am not a very good captain. We should turn back while there is time."

"It makes no difference. We are done." Why was there such a strange disjunction, though, between the man and the voice that came out of his mouth? It was as if not only his movements, but his very words, were emanating from some foreign source.

"Done with what?" Einstein said, confused now as well as frightened. "What are we done with?"

The man looked up with a feigned expression of surprise. "Our work. We are done with our work."

Now he recognized the man's voice at last. It was the voice he had heard the night before while working in his office with the cat on his lap. He was stroking the animal's back, and puzzling over the last unsolved problems in the creation of an atomic bomb, but the whole time it was as if some mysterious interlocutor had been murmuring in his ear, directing his thoughts, revealing one solution after another and urging him on to completion. What he had taken to be inspiration, he now realized, might have been something far darker. His hand had been scrawling equations on the blackboard in his office, or onto the sheets of the notepad, without hesitation, as if he had simply been a scribe taking dictation.

Who, however, had he been taking them from? Nuclear fission was a remarkably difficult and dangerous endeavor, one that could, according to some physicists' calculations, ignite the very atmosphere. It was a devil's brew, one that he had long warned against, and which he would never have even considered, were it not for the unthinkable possibility of its coming under the control of humanity's worst enemies first. Now he had to wonder: Had his hand been guided by the Devil himself?

The man smiled, for all the world as if he were reading his thoughts. And that was when Einstein realized his greatest mistake—this was no ordinary man, it was quite possibly not a man at all. Hadn't he said as much when he'd introduced himself?

Beelzebub.

A cold spray flew up from the bow of the boat, wetting Einstein's wild white hair and bushy moustache. His hands were so slick, and shaking so hard, they could barely hold the tiller. "So, what more do you want from me?" he asked, using every ounce of his courage to speak in an even tone.

"Nothing."

A bolt of lightning crackled across the sky, and in that split second, it was if a blinding flashbulb had gone off over a newsman's camera. In that minuscule fraction of time, Einstein glimpsed beneath the brute's face another one that was even worse—a face with sunken yellow eyes, a protruding brow, a mouth crammed with sharp and overlapping teeth. He had seen such a visage in antique works of art—from Dürer, Doré, Bosch. It was the kind of face worn by the soldiers of Hell.

The sun was entirely gone, eclipsed in an

instant by a boiling black cloud. The wind made the sails snap like firecrackers.

And in the passenger's vacant stare, Einstein saw the terrible truth. With this creature's unholy complicity, he had been goaded toward the unleashing of Armageddon. The first drops of rain spattered on the deck and the top of his head.

But in doing so, hadn't he helped the Allies to win the war one day? Why on earth would the Devil, or his minions, want to help defeat a scourge as brutal as the Third Reich? Wouldn't a monster like Hitler be Satan's most favored son?

"To us, the victor doesn't matter," the passenger said, again as if it were intuiting his thoughts. "Given the tools, your kind can be trusted to use them to destroy yourselves."

The packet that Einstein had sent off to Los Alamos that morning would help pave the way—which left but one awful question hanging in the air. What further use could there be for one old, cold, and increasingly decrepit physicist?

Especially, he realized with mounting dread, one that had been allowed this plain view of humanity's most ancient foe?

Obscured now by a light veil of gray rain, the creature was appraising him as if he were simply the next niggling detail that needed to be dealt with.

"Not that we are not grateful," it said, rising from its seat and stepping toward him. "We could not have done it without you."

Einstein reared away, but where was there to go other than over the side? Even if he could swim, he'd never make it to shore in these turbulent waters. Still, he was ready to take his chances in the lake—what other choice did he have?—when he heard a voice shouting behind him.

"Duck, Professor! Duck!" A dripping oar suddenly snagged the rope of the sail and yanked it backward over his head.

Something thudded up against the stern of the boat, and when he dared to turn around, he saw Lucas holding a wet paddle and pulling hard on the line while teetering on a rocking canoe.

A moment later, just as the canoe flipped over, Lucas leapt into the sailboat, falling against Einstein so hard that he was knocked off his seat. Before his wet hands could secure a grip on the tiller or anything else, the professor tumbled overboard, arms flailing and legs buckling, into the frigid waters of the lake.

Chapter FORTY-TWO

Crashing onto the deck, the paddle still entangled in the lines, Lucas scrabbled for a hold on Einstein's pants, but it was too late to catch him. And when he looked up, he saw Patrick Delaney standing, legs spread, in the pouring rain. In his hands, he held the saint's crook.

"Patrick!" Lucas shouted. "What are you doing?" Einstein was fast receding in the wake of the boat. "We've got to turn around before he drowns!"

But Delaney—or what was now passing for him—didn't move.

"A life jacket! Is there a life jacket?" Lucas looked all around the cramped shell. Underneath the corner of a canvas tarp, he saw faded yellow fabric. He scrambled on all fours toward it, yanked the life preserver free, and then bringing his arm back, slung it as far off the stern as he could. It sailed a couple of dozen feet, trailing a long rope, then plopped onto the water, well short of where Lucas could see the professor's white head bobbing in the waves.

The only thing he could do now would be to jump in after him, and then try to ferry them both to shore. It wouldn't be easy. He kicked off his shoes to rid himself of the excess weight, but just as he prepared to dive into the lake, he felt an iron hook wrap itself around his neck and drag him down into the boat. He landed hard on his back, his head thumping against a wooden thwart, and before he could gather his senses, a heavy boot pressed down on his chest.

Delaney stood above him, like a conquistador planting a flag on some new territory.

"What are you doing? Patrick, you've got to help me!" But even as he was appealing to his old friend, he knew it was a futile cause. Although the face was Delaney's, as were the body and the clothes, it was something else entirely that he was addressing—something ancient and implacable and evil, something that had suppressed any shred of Patrick Delaney.

And it didn't care a whit if Einstein drowned.

Lucas grabbed hold of the creature's foot and pried it away from his chest, rolling to one side. He felt the boot kick him in his ribs, knocking the breath out of him, and then kick him again. When he tried to get up on all fours, the staff came cracking down on his shoulders with such astonishing force he was surprised it didn't break in two. Or that he didn't.

With each passing second, the possibility of the professor surviving in the stormy waters was diminishing.

Delaney lifted the staff to deal another blow, but stopped for an instant, suddenly fixated on something dangling free from Lucas's bowed neck.

The medallion Simone had given him.

It was just enough of a reprieve for Lucas to scuttle toward the bow, his shoulders aching and skull throbbing.

But it was no more than that. His enemy snorted, and then tried to squirm around the sail, which was swinging wildly, back and forth across the boat. Lucas snapped the leather cord from his neck and held the ancient pentagram out in front of him. He had no idea what power it might possess, but he was fast running out of options. He shook it defiantly, but any protection he had hoped it could afford was dispensed of with the next swipe of the staff. The medallion was knocked loose and flew off into the lake where all of the other artifacts had disappeared.

A clap of thunder, loud as a cannon volley, rumbled across the sky, and the rain came down in a torrent.

"Stop!" Lucas shouted. He knew that at least one of his fingers had just been broken. "Can't you hear me? Patrick, I know you're in there!"

For one fleeting instant, he thought he saw, like a murky image staring up from the bottom of a pond, the actual face of his old comrade, a beseeching look in his bewildered eyes.

"I can see you there! Patrick, come back!"

Then the image was gone, like a slate wiped clean with a wet cloth, and Lucas was once again confronting nothing but an enemy bent on his destruction. In his head, he heard a voice, as if transmitted by a radio wave, gloating, "He's not here anymore." It wasn't even Delaney's voice. "And you, you should have died in that iron mine."

Suddenly it was all before him again—Hansel reaching for the candy bar, the detonation, the shrapnel mangling Toussaint, killing the boy, and gouging out his own eye. All thoughts but one flew out of his head.

He had to kill it, this damn thing that had possessed Delaney, and he had to kill it now.

The sail whipped back again, and the paddle that had been tangled in the lines fell free, clattering to his feet. Grabbing it, he swung the flat blade at the creature's head, but the blow was deftly parried by the iron-handled staff. His opponent didn't even lose his balance in the rocking boat.

Lucas regained his own footing as best he could; the water in the hull was up to his ankles and sloshing back and forth. He pulled the paddle back over his shoulder like a baseball bat and swung again, this time with every ounce of strength that he could still muster. The paddle cracked against the petrified wood of the staff and splintered, a wide fissure running down its length and sending a shudder all the way up Lucas's arms.

Lightning shimmered in the sky.

There was only enough of the paddle left for one more strike, and Lucas took it, but this time the shaft snapped in two and the blade went skimming off into the howling wind like a loose propeller. Lucas gripped the upper half, its end jagged as a knife, and lunged with it. The tip speared the fabric of Delaney's sodden coat and got snared there. Lucas tried to pull it back, but it wouldn't come, and he watched in horror as the ancient staff, with its crooked iron handle high in the air, rose above Delaney's head, about to deliver a fatal strike. The moment of imminent action.

Unarmed, battered, barely able to stand, Lucas suddenly remembered what Saint Anthony had done when overwhelmed by the armies of Diocletian—he had raised the staff and called upon the powers of Heaven. Instead of trying to dodge the blow, or escape the boat, Lucas leapt at his adversary, gripping the wooden staff with both hands, and though his face was only inches from the creature's foul breath, held on tight. He would either die in the next instant, or . . .

The explosion came in a blinding blue flash, the jagged lightning bolt touching the iron handle like the finger of God. A massive charge scorched the air and hurled Lucas flat against the mast.

The creature, its hands seemingly welded to the top of the staff, juddered from head to foot, jaws clamped shut, head snapped back, its entire body wrapped in a frizzling electric light.

Fire from the Heavens.

For several seconds, it managed to remain upright, limbs convulsing and flesh frying, its eyes bulging with a lurid golden gleam, before the surge ended. Smoldering, the staff still clenched in its hands, its legs buckled, and the demon toppled lifelessly over the side of the boat.

Lucas, tingling and twitching from head to foot, peered overboard and saw the charred body—black and sizzling as a hot coal—drift off. It no longer looked like Delaney—it no longer looked like anything but the remains of some incinerated beast.

Then the weight of its soaking clothes dragged it down beneath the water.

Wiping the rain from his one good eye, Lucas turned and scanned the lake behind the boat. To his dismay, he saw that the life preserver, still trailing astern by a long rope, was empty.

"Professor!" he shouted, praying for a miracle. Another one. Hands quivering, he groped for the tiller and the lines, trying to turn the boat around. Never having sailed before, it was all hit or miss, and by the time he had changed direction, he had all but given up hope of rescuing Einstein.

The blade of the broken paddle floated by, and then he saw, off to one side, the upside-down canoe, rising and falling like a cork on the choppy waters.

Sailing closer, searching for any sign of the professor, Lucas felt an all too familiar aching in his heart . . . the ache he had felt after the land mine, or after visiting the gravely wounded Private Toussaint in the hospital ward, or discovering the lifeless body of Dr. Rashid.

Then he spotted an arm, tenaciously thrown over the bottom of the capsized canoe.

And heard a feeble cry for help.

Shoving the tiller to one side so abruptly that

he nearly overturned the sailboat, too, he shouted, "Hold on! Hold on!"

The sailboat came around, and now he could make out the professor's head, the white hair plastered to his skull like wet goose feathers, as he clung to the canoe. Dropping the lines and tiller, Lucas stretched out a hand as the boat skimmed past, snagging the collar of Einstein's leather jacket and dragging him along in the wake. It was another minute or two before he could finally wrestle him up and into the boat, where he landed like a hooked flounder, sputtering and spitting out water.

"Again," Einstein gasped. "You have saved me again."

"Not yet I haven't. I've still got to get us to dry land."

But the driving wind seemed to be pushing them toward the boathouse, and before long, the little sailboat had ground to a wobbly halt on the shore, a few hundred yards shy of the dock. Lucas jumped out, the water still up to his thighs, and extended a hand to Einstein.

"We are safe?"

"We will be once you get out of the boat."

Overhead, he heard the roar of a low-flying aircraft, and looked up to see the military helicopter—no doubt with the ossuary safely stowed in its cargo bay—plowing its way south through the pouring rain and gusting winds.

As he helped Einstein plod onto the muddy bank, Lucas could see the police running toward them. Even Kurt Gödel, throwing all caution to the wind, was picking his way along the shoreline with his arms extended like a tightrope artist.

Ahead of them all, though, and leading the pack by a mile, was Simone.

Chapter FORTY-THREE

August 6, 1945
Ten Months Later

"You look *so* pretty!" Amy exclaimed.

Simone stood before the floor-length mirror in the master bedroom while Mrs. Caputo checked one more time to make sure that the hem of her dress fully concealed the silk slip.

"How does it feel?" Mrs. Caputo said, standing back and studying Simone in the mirror. Instead of the traditional long white dress, she wore a summer dress, in cream chiffon, adorned with tiny pink and white lilacs, and a pair of matching satin shoes—leather was still hard to come by—in the latest peep-toe style.

"It feels wonderful," Simone said, and Mrs. Caputo, who'd done some last-minute tailoring, beamed.

"We're not done yet," she said, and from the top of her bureau she retrieved a white cap with a lacy veil. After pinning it carefully atop Simone's black hair, she ran a hand one last time over the scalloped sleeves of the dress, smoothing out

any wrinkles. "I've never seen a more beautiful bride."

Simone blushed—compliments had always unnerved her—but even she had to admit that she had never felt quite so cosseted. Her tawny complexion was perfectly offset by the creamy colors of the clothes, and she knew her dark eyes shone with the happiness and anticipation of the day. "What do I do now?" she said, glancing at the clock on the wall. "It's still an hour before the ceremony."

"Finish packing for your honeymoon."

"It's already done," Simone said, gesturing at the battered tan suitcase behind the door. She and Lucas were going to spend over a week in Manhattan, a place she had always longed to explore.

"Well, then, just stand right there," Mrs. Caputo said with a laugh. "No sitting, no stretching, no nothing. Pretend you're a statue."

"Is it okay if I pretend I'm a statue on the front porch?"

"Just stay in the shade," Mrs. Caputo warned. "You don't want to perspire."

It was a hot and sunny day outside, but, as was

usual for New Jersey at this time of year, muggy, too, and punctuated by the chirping of cicadas in the trees. Across Mercer Street, where the ceremony was to be held, she could see that the fence in front of Einstein's house had been festooned with red roses—no doubt the flowers had been Helen's idea—and she could hear the strains of a violin, tuning up, on the summer breeze.

It was all like a dream.

If someone had told her, a year ago, that she would be marrying an ex-GI professor, and in the backyard of Albert Einstein's house in America, she would never have believed it. She could hardly believe it now, and yet, here she was, watching a yellow cab pull up across the street and drop off Lucas's parents and sister. She had only met them two or three times—on trips to their apartment in Queens—but they had embraced her wholeheartedly. His mother, in particular, had warmed to the English and Egyptian girl who had now lost both of her own parents and found herself marooned in a foreign country.

Lucas got out last, and dutifully averting his eyes from the boardinghouse, ushered them all down the walkway and up the porch steps. He'd spent the night at the Nassau Inn with his family, so that he wouldn't see the bride before the wedding. As the front door opened, Simone could hear Helen's voice welcoming them. The word "lemonade" was carried on the wind. A fly buzzed around and around her head, and she felt her heart flutter as she brushed it away.

Ever since that terrible night at the inn, she had nursed an inordinate fear of flying insects.

The only one who could understand everything that had happened to her the previous fall was Lucas. He was her rock. He was the only one who would ever understand—who *could* ever understand—what had occurred. Who else would ever believe a word of it?

As for the ossuary . . . she had never laid eyes on it again after it had been flown off campus in the cargo hold of the helicopter.

The greatest discovery of her life—a discovery that would have made any archaeologist world-renowned—was now a secret that could just as well have remained in its tomb beneath the sands of the Sahara el Beyda. Given the toll it had already taken, however, she wasn't sorry to see it go.

"Hello!" she heard from across the street, and she saw Adele Gödel, in a bright purple dress and gold hoop earrings, waving happily at her as she and Kurt strolled toward the professor's house. Even on a day like this, Kurt had a muffler around his neck. "*Du bist schoen!*" Adele called out. "You look beautiful!"

Simone waved back, then turned as the screen door flew open and Amy, in her white pinafore with a pink sash, bounded out onto the porch.

"Slow down," Mrs. Caputo warned. "Flower girls have to stay neat and tidy." After looking over Simone one last time, she said, "Maybe we should go over."

Simone found, to her own surprise, that her feet wouldn't budge. She felt as if she were waiting, waiting for the one thing that would have made the day complete, but which she knew would never come. She longed to feel her father slipping his arm through hers and escorting her across the sun-dappled street and into the arms of the man she loved. Despite all the joy she felt, there was a hollow place in her heart that only he could have filled.

"What is it?" Mrs. Caputo asked.

"I wish my father could have been here."

"I'm sure he would have been very happy that you're marrying someone like Lucas."

"I know. I'm very lucky indeed." Squeezing her arm, Simone said, "Have you heard from Tony this week?"

"I had a letter yesterday, from some Pacific island that the censors blacked out the name of. But it said he was fine, and working on a ground crew." She took a deep breath and stared into the middle distance. "The Germans have surrendered. Why can't the Japanese?"

"They will," Simone assured her. "I'm sure it will be soon."

"It better be," she said. "But no more talk about war. Today is all about peace and love and harmony."

"To peace and love and harmony," Simone said, as arm in arm they descended the porch steps and crossed the quiet street.

At the house, Helen ushered Simone into the front parlor, where Einstein's flimsy music stand teetered beside the grand piano, while Mrs. Caputo went out in the backyard to make sure Amy wasn't creating havoc. Simone was listening to the voices of the guests—only a dozen or so of their friends and colleagues, along with Lucas's family—when Einstein himself shuffled into the room. He was wearing a rumpled seersucker suit, with a red carnation pinned askew to the lapel. On his feet, he wore moccasins with no socks, and his shaggy white hair was whipped into a froth like cotton candy.

To her, he looked as handsome as any movie star.

"It is an honor," he said, taking both of her hands in his, "to give away such a beautiful bride."

His skin was as soft as chamois, and his drooping dark eyes, under Olympian brows, were filled with affection and kindness.

"The honor is all mine, Professor."

Helen poked her head in the door and said, "It's time," then whisked the sheer veil down over Simone's eyes.

From the garden, she heard the opening strains of the wedding march, played by the string ensemble that often assembled in the front parlor. Einstein crooked out his arm, and she took it. The kitchen, which they had to pass through, was filled with platters of food under sheets of wax paper, and something was still baking in the oven. A timer was ticking. Helen held the screen door open as they carefully descended the back steps and then threaded their way down the aisle between the guests, all of them standing now beside the white wooden chairs that had been borrowed from the university. The Princeton president and his wife beamed from the back row.

Directly ahead, in front of the leafy green arbor which had been hastily erected to camouflage the garage, she saw Lucas, standing with his hands folded, in a suit as black as his eye patch. His younger brother, the best man, reached around to straighten his bow tie. Lucas didn't even seem to notice—his gaze was fixed on her as Einstein escorted her into the presence of the university chaplain, who had been enlisted to perform the ceremony. A lace canopy had been erected to shield them from the hot sun.

When the minister intoned, "Who gives this woman to be married to this man?" Einstein cleared his throat and declared, "I do." Disengaging his arm, he repeated, "I do," then retreated to the seat Helen was patting.

The moment Lucas stepped beside her, she felt as if her shelter were complete. The canopy might ward off the sun, but it was having Lucas at her side that made her feel protected, fulfilled . . . loved. She glanced up at him, and though she saw that his tie was still askew, she resisted the urge to straighten it. There would be a lifetime to indulge such impulses.

The minister was extolling Holy Matrimony, "which is an honorable estate, instituted of God, signifying unto us the mystical union . . ."

But she barely heard him; it was as if her ears were stuffed with cotton balls. As he continued— expatiating on the bonds of love, the responsibilities of marriage, the affection and understanding that a man and wife must always show one another—Simone remained in the warm embrace of this comforting cocoon, this sacred place where she felt engulfed by nothing but love. Feeling Lucas's hand search out her own, she wove her fingers through his, only to glance down, beneath her veil, and see that his hands were nowhere near hers at all. They were still folded in front of him.

For a moment, she was puzzled, but, to her own surprise, completely unalarmed. The touch was a tender one, and on the vagrant breeze that stirred the canopy overhead, she'd have sworn that she smelled the familiar scent of her father's sweet Turkish tobacco and sugary tea. Although she knew that anyone else would say that she was just imagining it, or that it was the aroma from the myriad flowers filling the garden, Simone knew better.

Her father *was* there, and he was giving his blessing to her marriage.

Tears welled in her eyes, and under her breath, she said, "I love you."

Overhearing her, even as the minister prattled on, Lucas did take her hand in his, displacing the ghostly touch.

At the minister's request, Amy skipped forward, holding a pink satin cushion to which the rings were affixed with safety pins. The best man detached them, while Amy swirled back and forth in excitement.

"With these rings," the minister announced, "we seal the vows of marriage and represent the promise of eternal and everlasting love." Turning to Lucas, he said, "Please repeat after me."

Then she heard the time-honored words—"to have and to hold," and "for richer, for poorer, in sickness and in health"—and could scarcely believe it when she felt the ring being slipped onto her finger.

After the minister had repeated the vows to her, she took the second ring and placed it on the little finger of her groom; his fourth finger had been broken beyond repair. Looking up at him, she prayed that she would never forget the stray shaft of sunlight piercing the lace overhead, and the way that it threw his face into light and shadow, the silk fabric of his eye patch glistening, the black curls of his hair unfurling over his forehead, the sideburns a stark white ever since the lightning strike. There was a tiny nick on his cheek where he must have cut himself shaving that morning. She longed to kiss it.

"Those whom God hath joined together," the minister declared, "let no man put asunder. By the power vested in me by the state of New Jersey, I now pronounce you husband and wife." There was a short pause before he added, "You may now kiss the bride."

Lucas lifted her veil, bent down, and gave her a quick and self-conscious peck on the lips.

Adele Gödel called out, "*Ach*—you can do better than that!"

And so he did, this time slipping an arm around her narrow waist and drawing her toward him. There was laughter and scattered applause, and she heard the string ensemble starting to play again for her walk up the aisle. They had no sooner joined hands and turned toward the guests—Einstein was clapping, with a big grin lifting his moustache—when several cars came careening down the alley, horns blaring, and screeched to a halt at the garage. A gang of interlopers, clutching pads and pens, piled out, some with cameras slung around their necks, and stampeded into the garden. All of them had press cards stuck in their fedoras, or clipped to the lapels of their sweat-stained suit jackets.

Her wedding? The press corps was going to crash her wedding?

Like a bunch of rowdy rugby players, they descended upon Einstein, elbowing the guests aside, knocking over a couple of chairs in their haste, and all of them clamoring about an atomic bomb and some place with an odd name that she'd never even heard of.

"We've dropped one on Hiroshima," a reporter shouted out.

"What's your reaction?" another one demanded, his pencil and notepad at the ready. "Did you know in advance?"

Flashbulbs popped as the professor, stunned, took a shaky step back. Helen instinctively moved to protect him.

"Without your discoveries, it couldn't have been done," the first one said. "How's that feel?"

"Look this way!" a photographer hollered.

"No, over here, Professor!"

"What do you have to say?"

Einstein looked stricken.

"You think we've finally knocked the stuffing out of the Japs?"

"The Pentagon says we might have killed as many as a hundred seventy-five thousand of 'em, in one shot. That sound about right to you, Professor?"

Confusion reigned. The music stopped, the guests disassembled, a whole row of seats went over like dominoes as the reporters jockeyed for position closer to the beleaguered Einstein.

"When do you think they'll surrender?"

Before her eyes, Simone saw the wedding collapse. Even the canopy, its stakes jostled by the crowd, became unfastened and blew away.

Lucas clutched her hand, and threw an arm around her shoulders.

Einstein, head down, his red carnation trampled underfoot by the pack of newsmen, was shepherded back into the house by Helen, who slammed the door firmly in the reporters' faces . . . which didn't keep them from running to the windows and trying to shout out their questions. A photographer climbed a tree in the backyard, hoping to get an angle into the house, but the branch broke and he thumped to the ground, groaning. No one paid him any attention. Someone else had turned up the radio of a car parked in the alley, and as she and Lucas stood there, equally ignored in all the commotion, she heard the voice of President Truman.

"The Japanese began the war from the air at Pearl Harbor. Today they have been repaid manyfold. And the end is not yet."

Mrs. Caputo was kneeling on the grass, mouth

open and clutching Amy, listening to the broadcast.

"It is an atomic bomb," Truman continued. "It is a harnessing of the basic power of the universe."

Simone saw the shades being yanked down in the kitchen windows.

"The force from which the sun draws its power has been loosed against those who brought war to the Far East."

Loosed, Simone thought, like an evil genie, never to be contained again.

"God help us all," Lucas said, his arm holding her tighter.

The curtains in the professor's office upstairs were jerked shut, too, as if the whole house were being readied for a wake, not a wedding.

Which was suddenly how it felt to Simone.

The radio was playing "The Star Spangled Banner," and from neighboring houses, she could hear shouts of exultation. Dogs were barking. Somebody cried, "Let 'em have it!" Surely, this would end the war—what nation could stand up against the power of the sun itself?

Mrs. Caputo, still on her knees, her arms wrapped around her daughter, was sobbing with joy.

Chapter FORTY-FOUR

August 14, 1945

On the gigantic movie screen of Radio City Music Hall, often billed as the "Showplace of the Nation," Gene Tierney, improbably playing a Sicilian girl, was about to be kissed by John Hodiak, playing the American major entrusted with replacing a church bell stolen by the Fascists. The film was *A Bell for Adano*, based on the best-selling novel by John Hersey, and the minute Simone had spotted the ad in the New York Times, she had insisted they attend.

"What could be more appropriate for a former CRC man?" she'd said that morning while they finished a late breakfast at their hotel. For good reason, all of their breakfasts had been taken late. "Not only that, I'll get to see this famous music hall before we have to go home."

That was fine with Lucas; this was the last day of their honeymoon, and he had already shown her just about every other tourist sight he could think of. They had climbed to the top of the Statue of Liberty and taken the elevator 102 floors to the observation deck of the Empire State Building. They had strolled through the

Central Park Zoo and the crooked streets of Greenwich Village, walked across the Brooklyn Bridge, and taken in a jazz session at a nightclub up in Harlem. For several days, they had virtually camped out in the Metropolitan Museum, where they could indulge their mutual passion for art and antiquities. Unsurprisingly, Simone had been especially enthralled by the galleries filled with Egyptian exhibits, though she'd also been vexed that so many of her country's national treasures had been absconded with and were now on display in this foreign land.

The matinee performance was almost full, not only because the movie had just opened, but because the vast airy auditorium was preferable to the sweltering city outside. The temperatures had been in the eighties, and showed no sign of abating. Simone was scrunched down in her seat, her shoulder resting on Lucas's shoulder, when they heard banging on the doors to the lobby.

Someone in the audience yelled, "Shut up! We're watching a movie in here!"

The banging got louder. A pair of doors flew open, and an usher, in a red suit and braided cap, ducked his head in. For a moment, Lucas thought a fire might have broken out, but then he heard what the usher was shouting. "The war is over! The war is over!"

Other doors opened, and other ushers issued the same proclamation.

As the word filtered through the audience, people jumped to their feet, some hollering for joy, others weeping and embracing the strangers sitting next to them.

Simone straightened up in her seat and looked at Lucas. "You think it's true?"

All week long, rumors had been circulating that the Japanese were about to surrender. The atomic bomb that destroyed Hiroshima had been followed days later by another, this one dropped on a place called Nagasaki. But still, Emperor Hirohito had refused to accept the Potsdam Declaration, and the war had dragged on. The United States faced the prospect of launching a massive land invasion of the Pacific islands, and the enormous number of casualties that such a campaign would incur.

Hundreds, then thousands, of people were pouring up the aisles of the massive auditorium, nearly trampling each other in their haste to get outside and celebrate the news. Lucas and Simone joined them, swept up in the tide like leaves on a rushing stream.

On Sixth Avenue, fire alarms were ringing everywhere, taxi cabs were blasting their horns, office workers were leaning out of upper-story windows, tearing up papers and throwing the confetti to the breeze.

"Now I think it's true," Lucas said, hugging Simone.

Everyone was heading past them, down toward Times Square, where the news would be officially confirmed by the electronic ticker wrapped around the third floor of the towering news-paper building. Holding her by the arm, Lucas navigated through the crowd, threading his way across Fiftieth Street to Seventh Avenue, then down the jammed sidewalk, and into the street—where all the cars and buses were stopped dead, and people were dancing between the lanes—before finally arriving in the square itself.

Always a popular gathering spot for service-men—there were military service posts all around, including the Pepsi-Cola Center where sailors on leave could shave and shower and write letters home—the place at that moment looked like a cross between the deck of an aircraft carrier and a Mardi Gras celebration. Sailors were tossing their white caps in the air, and others were grabbing all the pretty girls who passed by and stealing a kiss. In the open square, one of them had just snagged a young nurse in her white uniform, and, as a short guy armed with a Leica snapped their picture, bent her backward over his arm in a real movie-star clinch. The kiss lasted for several seconds before the sailor let the poor girl up for air, the shutterbug moved on, and a few other spectators gave the pair a round of applause.

Most eyes, however, were riveted on the ticker.

The block letters scrolling around the building read, "VJ! VJ! VJ!" Victory over Japan. And then, in case there was still any doubt, "The Japanese Government in Tokyo Has Accepted the Allied Surrender Terms." The announcement was followed by six asterisks, representing the six branches of the armed forces.

"Amy's going to get her dad back," Simone said, thinking of how jubilant Mrs. Caputo and her daughter must be feeling right then.

"There are going to be a lot of Amy's."

"Can you believe it?" a guy said, clapping Lucas on the shoulder, and in acknowledgment of his black patch, saying, "You did your part, pal!"

A group of teenage girls in the subway entrance sang, in perfect harmony, "America the Beautiful."

A soldier in khakis, clinging to the top of a lamppost with one arm, wildly waved a flag with the other.

An old woman handed out tulips from a bouquet in her arms.

From every bar around the square—of which there were plenty—a chorus of cheers billowed out every time the doors swung open.

"It's going to be a noisy night in New York," Lucas said.

"Even sleepy little Princeton will be up late tonight."

"We'd better go back and retrieve our bags,"

Lucas said, glancing at his watch. "Our train leaves at five."

Arm in arm, they turned back toward the Astor Hotel, where they were staying at the special rate reserved for veterans and active-duty servicemen, then made their way through the rejoicing crowds to the train station. After purchasing their tickets from a grinning clerk who insisted on shaking Lucas's hand, they plopped onto the last pair of seats available. Someone had left behind a folded copy of the *New York Times*. Even on board, the revelry continued, with celebrants parading up and down the aisle, hooting and hollering, passing around cigars and silver flasks of whiskey. It wasn't until the train had left the city and was passing into the flat, industrial hinterlands of New Jersey that everyone finally returned to their seats, and the racket died down. The air in the car was stifling, and Lucas shoved the dirty window open the few inches it would allow.

Simone pinched the top of her blouse and flapped it to cool herself off. "It's like being back in Cairo." Laying her head against his shoulder, she said, "Wake me when we get there."

Opening up the newspaper that had been left on the seat, Lucas saw on the front page a photograph of the Nagasaki explosion, and read the descrip-tion of the mushroom cloud that had erupted over the city days before. "Early estimates," the paper reported, "put the loss of life at forty thousand." What must it have been like, he wondered, to be caught beneath that deadly blast? What kind of horror was it to be engulfed in such an inferno? "A fiery column rose up from ground zero, a burning cloud that filled the sky and billowed out for a radius of no less than five miles." The words seemed familiar somehow, and it took a few seconds before he remembered why. It was the account from Saint Anthony, of the Roman army being defeated by a "mighty pillar of flame, like a red rose with petals that spread in a burning cloud across the sky." When Simone had read it to him one night, it had seemed so fantastical, almost poetic, but here was a picture of that very thing, and it wasn't fantastical, or poetic, at all.

He wondered what Einstein thought of it. On the day Hiroshima had been bombed, the professor had retreated to his study, and only at dusk, when the mob of reporters had dispersed, had he dared to come across the street to apologize for the disruption to Lucas and Simone's wedding. Simone had already fallen fast asleep upstairs, still in her wedding clothes— they weren't leaving for New York until the next morning—and Lucas had stepped out onto the porch for a cigarette.

He had never seen a man look so haunted. He offered him a cigarette, and the professor had gladly accepted, though he said that they had better take a walk so he could enjoy it without Helen spotting him.

"I think I can be forgiven for smoking on a day like this," he said, as the two men ambled down the block. Even at twilight, the dense canopy of leaves overhead cast a pale green light over everything.

"The Japanese will have to surrender now," Lucas said.

"Why?"

"Because it would be madness not to."

"But that is precisely what war is. It *is* madness," Einstein said, pinching the cigarette between two fingers. "Nothing less than madness."

Lucas could hardly disagree—he had seen enough of it to know firsthand. The carnage had not been confined to Europe, or the Far East, though. When he had given the eulogy at Patrick Delaney's memorial service, he had considered describing him as a casualty of war. A hero in the most genuine sense. But the work Delaney had been doing was still classified, and no one would ever know that he was killed by anything other than a freakish lightning strike.

Einstein, of course, knew better. After the terrible events of that autumn day, the professor and Lucas had come to be close friends, bonded by what they alone had witnessed in the boat on

Lake Carnegie. Each of them held the knowledge tight. Einstein had alluded to having glimpsed "the face of pure evil," and though Lucas had been sworn to secrecy—indeed, he still had the sense that Colonel Macmillan was keeping tabs on him—he had shared enough information about the ossuary to suggest where that ancient evil might have originated. Einstein, absorbing the strange tale, had said, "What is the line, from Shakespeare? 'There are more things in Heaven and Earth, Horatio, than are dreamt of in your philosophy.' *Ja*, that is it. More things than are dreamt of." From the solemn expression on his lined face, Lucas knew that even the professor's cosmology had taken a jarring blow.

Putting the paper down, Lucas laid his head back on the worn leather headrest, and closed his one good eye. Before he knew it, the heat and the rhythmic rocking of the train had lulled him to sleep. His mind traveled back to the iron mine near Strasbourg, to the land mine that had maimed him, to the ossuary that had followed him halfway around the world, and to the woman who had come into his life because of it. Somewhere in all of that, he sensed there was a pattern, a design, one that was sitting right in front of his nose but that he was simply too dim to see. In his sleep he was about to grasp it, about to understand his unwitting role in this great cosmic drama, when he felt a hand gently shake him awake, and the dream evaporated. A stringy young man in a conductor's uniform, said, "Tickets, please."

Lucas fished them out of his shirt pocket, and as they were punched, he noticed, alighting on the back of the seat in front of them, its iridescent wings spread wide, a fat and buzzing blue-bottle fly. He tried to wave it off without waking Simone, but failed.

"What is it?" she mumbled, stirring against his shoulder.

"It's nothing," he said as the fly made a lazy circle around their heads, and he rolled the newspaper into a viable weapon. "Go back to sleep."

The fly made one more loop, then landed right back on the seat where it had been, rubbing its wings together. When the right moment came, Lucas struck.

"Gotcha," he said, but when he looked at the paper for some telltale sign that he'd hit it, there was none.

Epilogue

At 1:15 in the morning on April 18, 1955, Albert Einstein, suffering from a ruptured aneurysm in his abdominal aorta, abruptly sat up in his bed at Princeton Hospital and blurted out several words in German. Unfortunately, it was a language that neither of the night nurses understood. Then, he gasped for breath, twice, and died. He was seventy-six years old.

As he had directed, his body was cremated, though not before his brain had been surgically removed for further study. His ashes were scattered to the wind on the wooded grounds of the Institute for Advanced Study in Princeton.

Days later, the English philosopher Bertrand Russell received in the mail the last communication that Albert Einstein had signed before his death. It was a letter authorizing Russell to append his name to, and make public, a document that came to be known as the Russell-Einstein Manifesto. Published in London on July 9, 1955, the manifesto was a stark declaration of the menace posed by the prospect of thermonuclear war, and at the same time, a dire prophecy of what might occur if the people of all nations did not find some way to live together in peace. In its closing, Einstein appealed to humanity's higher instincts, asking the world to ignore its petty differences and quarrels in quest of wisdom and happiness instead. "If you can do so, the way lies open to a new Paradise," he predicted. "If you cannot, there lies before you the risk of universal death."

Acknowledgements

As always, I am in debt to my indefatigable agent, Cynthia Manson, for her encouragement throughout this long endeavor.

And I would also like to thank my brilliant editor, Caitlin Alexander, and my very supportive publisher, Jason Kirk, for helping me in so many ways to bring the book to its full fruition. For his help as a translator, I wish to express my gratitude, too, to Mr. Christoph Haas-Heye.

Although much of the book is true to the historical record, some of it is speculation, too—most notably, Einstein's involvement in the creation of the atom bomb. His discoveries may have laid the groundwork for the atomic age, and he did indeed alert President Roosevelt to the danger of nuclear weapons, but he was later denied a security clearance to work on the Manhattan Project, and there is no evidence to suggest that he had a practical hand in the actual process of developing the bomb. Nor were the Nazis all that far along; although they'd made a good start, once Hitler was warned by his scientists that a nuclear reaction could conceivably backfire and immolate the Reich itself, he decided to prosecute the war the old-fashioned way—with tanks and planes and battleships.

I have also taken some liberties—chronological and geographical—with the Princeton campus, the progress of the war in Europe, and the creation of the Cultural Recovery Commission; modeled on the Monuments Men, this particular group did not exist.

Overall, and as a way of accounting for all my other sins of both omission and commission, I would simply emphasize that this novel is, of course, a flight of fancy (dark fancy at that), and I am very grateful to you, the reader, for coming along.

About the Author

A native of Evanston, Illinois, Robert Masello is an award-winning journalist, television writer, and the best-selling author of many novels and nonfiction books. His most recent novels, published in over a dozen languages, include *The Romanov Cross*, *The Medusa Amulet*, and *Blood and Ice*. A longstanding member of the Writers Guild of America, he has often taught and lectured at prominent colleges and universities, ranging from the Columbia University Graduate School of Journalism to Claremont McKenna College, where he served as the Visiting Lecturer in Literature for six years. He now lives and works in Santa Monica, California.

Center Point Large Print
600 Brooks Road / PO Box 1
Thorndike, ME 04986-0001 USA

(207) 568-3717

US & Canada:
1 800 929-9108
www.centerpointlargeprint.com